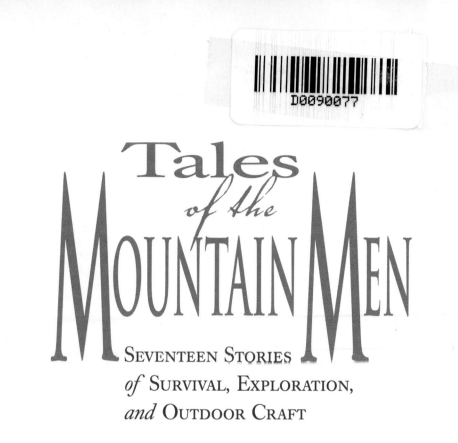

Tales *of the* MOUNTAIN MEN

SEVENTEEN STORIES *of* SURVIVAL, EXPLORATION, *and* OUTDOOR CRAFT

Edited by Lamar Underwood

THE LYONS PRESS
Guilford, Connecticut
An imprint of The Globe Pequot Press

Copyright © 2004 by Lamar Underwood
Cover photograph copyright © James L. Amos/CORBIS

The Lyons Press is an imprint of The Globe Pequot Press.

10 9 8

Printed in the United States of America

Designed by Kirsten Livingston

Library of Congress Cataloging-in-Publication Data

ISBN 13: 978-1-59228-423-8

Tales of the mountain men : seventeen stories of survival, exploration, and outdoor craft / edited by Lamar Underwood.
        p. cm.
  ISBN 978-1-59228-423-8 (trade paper)
  1. Pioneers–West (U.S.)–Biography–Anecdotes. 2. Explorers–West (U.S.)–Biography–Anecdotes. 3. Fur traders–West (U.S.)–Biography–Anecdotes. 4. Trappers–West (U.S.)–Biography–Anecdotes. 5. Adventure and adventurers–West (U.S.)–Biography–Anecdotes. 6. Frontier and pioneer life–West (U.S.)–Anecdotes. 7. West (U.S.)–Description and travel–Anecdotes. 8. West (U.S.)–Discovery and exploration–Anecdotes. 9. West (U.S.)–Biography–Anecdotes. I. Underwood, Lamar.
F596.T355 2004
917.804'2'0922–dc22
                                                                2004013945

Tales
of the
MOUNTAIN MEN

ALSO BY LAMAR UNDERWOOD

Classic Hunting Stories
Classic War Stories
The Greatest Adventure Stories Ever Told
The Greatest Disaster Stories Ever Told
The Greatest Fishing Stories Ever Told
The Greatest Flying Stories Ever Told
The Greatest Hunting Stories Ever Told
The Greatest Survival Stories Ever Told
The Greatest War Stories Ever Told
Into the Backing
Man Eaters
The Quotable Soldier
Theodore Roosevelt on Hunting
Whitetail Hunting Tactics of the Pros

The mountain men were a tough race, as many selective breeds of Americans have had to be; their courage, skill, and mastery of the conditions of their chosen life were absolute or they would not have been here. Nor would they have been here if they had not responded to the loveliness of the country and found in their way of life something precious beyond safety, gain, comfort, and family life.

–Bernard DeVoto
Across the Wide Missouri

Contents

Introduction

UNDER A GROVE OF WALNUTS alongside the Missouri River, his face soft in the glow of the campfire, the hunter-trapper's voice is emphatic, yet serene, heard above the crackling of logs in the flames and the clink of pots and spoons preparing the evening meal.

"I seed most of it. Colter's Hell and the Seeds-kee-dee and the Tetons standin' higher'n clouds, and north and south from Nez Perce to Comanche, but God Almighty, there's nothin' richer'n the upper Missouri. Or purtier. I seen the Great Falls and traveled Marias River, dodgin' the Blackfeet, makin' cold camps and sometimes thinkin' my time was up, and all the time livin' wonderful, loose and free's ary animal. That's some, that is."

"Lord God!"

"A man gets a taste for it."

There you have it: the mantra of the mountain man. The pleasures and dangers, the life lived in the open, in the wilderness of the Rocky Mountains in the 1830s, summed up in one remarkable and skillful paragraph in *The Big Sky*, the book that perhaps more than any other created a new American icon rivaling the cowboy.

Long the dominant symbol embodying the spirit of America's frontier past, the image of the cowboy no longer stands alone as the ultimate icon of self-reliance and independence. The great canvas of the western landscape–in art, books, and film–is today shared by the figure called the mountain man. These men were the trappers of the Rocky Mountain fur trade in the years following the Lewis and Clark Expedition of 1804–'06. With their bold journeys peaking, roughly speaking, during the period 1830–1840, they were the first white men to enter the vast wilderness reaches of the Rockies in search of beaver skins–"plews," in mountain man parlance. They feasted on the abundance of buffalo and elk and other game while living the ultimate free-spirited wilderness life. Often, they paid the ultimate price for their ventures under the arrows, tomahawks, and knives of those native Americans whose lands they had entered.

Today, the words *the big sky* are engraved in the American lexicon. We Americans love nicknames, and what better way to describe the great high country of the west? You can find the *big sky* label on everything from ski resorts to housing developments to magazines. Everybody wants a piece of the big sky these days. Truly, as the mountain man Dick Summers said beside the campfire, "A man gets a taste for it."

Although literature about the mountain man certainly existed before A. B. Guthrie, Jr., published *The Big Sky* in 1947, Guthrie's novel brought the mountain man into the forefront of critically acclaimed American literature. And it brought the words *the big sky* to the esteemed station they hold today. Were they actually uttered in the novel, or were they used only as a title? Indeed, they were taken directly from a single page, the only time in the novel the words appear. Which page was it? I shall not tell you, for that would spoil your own pleasure of fully discovering the many reader rewards in this classic of American literature.

Guthrie's *Big Sky* portrait of mountain man Dick Summers is so vivid and skillfully drawn that since reading the book as a young man, I have carried his constant image as an icon–a mountain man prototype. This personal obsession has no doubt been helped along by Arthur Hunnicutt's memorable portrayal of the Summers character (renamed Zeb Callaway) in Howard Hawks's film version of the book. Hunnicutt's onscreen character seems exactly what Guthrie had in mind. He is the ultimate mountain man: skilled in the ways of wilderness survival, leading the way into the great unknown, wise and reflective on the natural world, its beauty and its dangers.

The Big Sky and its Dick Summers character opened my eyes to the reading pleasures of mountain man literature, both fiction and non-fiction. Over the years I have encountered many, many other characters like Dick Summers, and I have followed them through Indian fights and blizzards, on buffalo hunts and beaver trapping on countless streams lost in the vastness of the mountains.

As an avid movie buff, I have been fascinated by the work of director Sydney Pollack and Robert Redford in creating *Jeremiah Johnson*, which surely, to any mountain man junkie, ranks as a classic film.

Howard Hawks's *The Big Sky* (1952) is marred, in my opinion, by his decision to shoot the film in black and white. The film version of *The Big Sky* you sometimes see today is colorized—an ersatz computerized attempt to juice up the images, but no substitution for what we would have gotten had the film been shot in Technicolor. Despite some superb shots on location on the Snake River beneath the Tetons, Arthur Hunnicutt's performance, and a rousing score by the legendary Dimitri Tiomkin, Hawks's *The Big Sky* lacks a clear, compelling story line, partly because it dwells too long on Part One of the novel, which takes place before the leading characters even get on the Missouri at St. Louis. Note to filmmakers: If you ever remake the movie, throw out Part One of the novel. Begin on the river with Part Two. Note to Kevin Costner: Why don't you try to mount your own remake of *The Big Sky*? You're the only one around who could do it properly. By the way, I fully realize that the black-and-white cinematography in *The Big Sky* was nominated for an Academy Award, but I stand by my call: It was a sin to not shoot this story of the great outdoors in color.

If the mountain men you are going to meet in the pages ahead do not hold your interest as a reader, then this editor should stick to putting commas in the right places and resolve to stop foisting his literary tastes upon an unsuspecting public. My hunch tells me, however, that you are here because the bug has bitten you too—the passion for reading about the mountain men, and through their lives seeing the great unexplored West as it can never be experienced again. Of sharing campfires and stories, of "keeping our ha'r" when confronted by hostile Indians, of hunts that succeeded and those that failed, of high mountain passes and bitter winds and blizzards. Of being on our own, with nothing but our skills and our "possibles" bag.

Included in these selections are excerpts from some of the finest mountain man fiction ever written; actual accounts of the mountain man lifestyle from journals and diaries; and illuminating and engaging pieces from great historical works, such as Bernard DeVoto's enduring *Across the Wide Missouri*.

If you're already an appreciator of mountain man stories, you know that their colorful language often contains an expression best pointed out with a note of explanation and compassion. In most literary texts, mountain men constantly refer to themselves with terms like "this child" and "this nigger" or "that nigger." No literary professor I, but my personal take on the word as used by the mountain men is that they liked the expression to identify themselves with the oppressed, the outcasts—the banished, if you will. The word is always uttered with pride.

In this introduction, I shall not bore you by repeating what you can see on the contents page. The stories in these pages will speak for themselves and become individual reading experiences that make your appreciation of the world of the mountain men seem more real to you than ever.

Wagh…this child's certain! They's fat doin's just ahead.

–Lamar Underwood
Springtime, 2004

Tales
of the
MOUNTAIN MEN

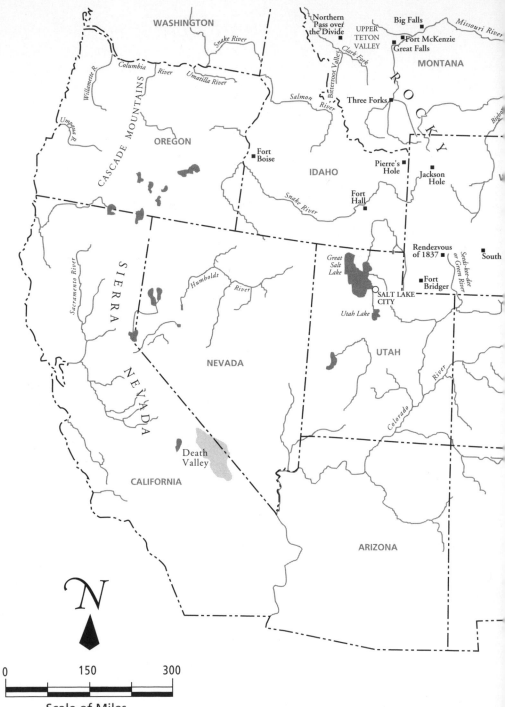

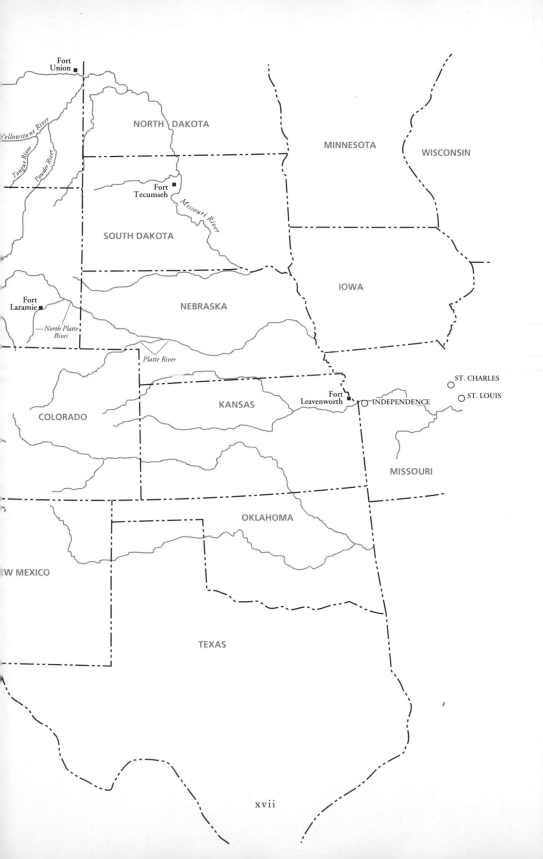

Fort
Union ■

Yellowstone River

Tongue River

Powder River

NORTH DAKOTA

MINNESOTA

WISCONSIN

Fort
Tecumseh ■

Missouri River

SOUTH DAKOTA

IOWA

Fort
Laramie ■

NEBRASKA

— *North Platte River*

Platte River

COLORADO

KANSAS

Fort
Leavenworth ■

○ ST. CHARLES

○ ST. LOUIS

○ INDEPENDENCE

MISSOURI

OKLAHOMA

EW MEXICO

TEXAS

Chapter I

"A MUCH MORE FURIOUS *and* FORMIDABLE ANAMAL"

LEWIS AND CLARK ENCOUNTER THE GRIZZLY BEAR

From *The Journals of Lewis and Clark,*
Edited by Bernard DeVoto

Although it is convenient to think of them as the first mountain men, the members of the Lewis and Clark Expedition of 1804–06 were preceded in some areas of the northern Rockies by intrepid fur trappers and traders from Canada. Still, the chronicles of Meriwether Lewis and William Clark give us the first detailed, personal portrait of the unexplored American wilderness. The journals of the Corps of Discovery, as the expedition was called, have provided historians and naturalists with a treasure trove of events and impressions that allow us to see and feel the unblemished lands.

Writing in an age when freedom from spelling was the norm for the average correspondent, Lewis and Clark filled their diaries and journals with day-by-day happenings and discoveries. Books such as the late Stephen Ambrose's bestselling and critically acclaimed *Undaunted Courage* translate the diaries into modern, mainstream prose. Others, such as the legendary historian Bernard DeVoto, present the accounts of Lewis and Clark as they were actually written, adding footnotes and comments where necessary.

In this selection from DeVoto's *The Journals of Lewis and Clark,* we are with the explorers as they become the first easterners to meet the grizzly. As they were quick to relate in their prose, the grizzly was a "much more furious and formidable anamal" than the black bears they were accustomed to encountering in the forests of home.

•   •   •

[LEWIS]
SUNDAY APRIL 28TH 1805.
Set out this morning at an early hour; the wind was favourable and we employed our sails to advantage. Capt Clark walked on shore this morning, and I proceeded with the party. we saw great quantities of game today; consisting of the common and mule deer, Elk, Buffaloe, and Antelopes; also four brown bear, one of which was fired on and wounded by one of the party but we did not get it;   the beaver have cut great quantities of timber; saw a tree nearly 3 feet in diameter that had been felled by them.

MONDAY APRIL 29TH 1805.

I walked on shore with one man. about 8. A.M. we fell in with two brown or yellow bear;[1] both of which we wounded; one of them made his escape, the other after my firing on him pursued me seventy or eighty yards, but fortunately had been so badly wounded that he was unable to pursue me so closely as to prevent my charging my gun; we again repeated our fir and killed him. it was a male not fully grown, we estimated his weight at 300 lbs. not having the means of ascertaining it precisely. The legs of this bear are somewhat longer than those of the black, as are it's tallons and tusks incomparably larger and longer. the testicles, which in the black bear are placed pretty well back between the thyes and contained in one pouch like those of the dog and most quadrupeds, are in the yellow or brown bear placed much further forward, and are suspended in separate pouches from two to four inches asounder; it's colour is yellowish brown, the eyes small, black, and piercing; the front of the fore legs near the feet is usually black; the fur is finer thicker and deeper than that of the black bear. these are all the particulars in which this anamal appeared to me to differ from the black bear; it is a much more furious and formidable anamal, and will frequently pursue the hunter when wounded. it is astonishing to see the wounds they will bear before they can be put to death. the Indians may well fear this anamal equiped as they generally are with their bows and arrows or indifferent fuzees, but in the hands of skillfull riflemen they are by no means as formidable or dangerous as they have been represented.

---

1   A grizzly, the first one. Lewis presently loses his easy superiority, the result of the ease with which this one was killed. His erroneous statement that the grizzly's testicles are provided separate individual scrota, which he later repeats, is inexplicable. Though far from being the first description of a grizzly as some texts have said, this is the first detailed one. Henry Kelsey, in 1691, was probably the first white man to see a grizzly.

game is still very abundant we can scarcely cast our eyes in any direction without perceiving deer Elk Buffaloe or Antelopes. The quantity of wolves appear to increase in the same proportion; they generally hunt in parties of six eight or ten; they kill a great number of the Antelopes at this season; the Antelopes are yet meagre and the females are big with young; the wolves take them most generally in attempting to swim the river; in this manner my dog caught one drowned it and brought it on shore; they are but clumsey swimers, tho' on land when in good order, they are extreemly fleet and dureable. we have frequently seen the wolves in pursuit of the Antelope in the plains; they appear to decoy a single one from a flock, and then pursue it, alturnately relieving each other untill they take it. on joining Capt Clark he informed me that he had seen a female and faun of the bighorned anamal; that they ran for some distance with great aparent ease along the side of the river bluff where it was almost perpendicular; two of the party fired on them while in motion without effect. we took the flesh of the bear on board and proceeded. Capt. Clark walked on shore this evening, killed a deer, and saw several of the bighorned anamals.[2]

[CLARK]
MAY 2ND THURSDAY 1805

The wind blew verry hard all the last night,   this morning about sunrise began to Snow, (The Thermomtr. at 28. abov 0) and continued untill about 10 oClock, at which time it seased, the wind continued hard untill about 2 P.M.   the Snow which fell today was about 1 In deep, a verry extraodernarey climate, to behold the trees Green & flowers spred on the plain, & Snow an inch deep. we Set out about 3 oClock and proceeded on about five ½ miles and encamped on the Std Side, the evening verry

---

2   The bighorn or Rocky Mountain sheep. Its meat was one of the great delicacies of the West.

cold, Ice freesing to the Ores. I shot a large beaver & Drewyer three in walking on the bank, the flesh of those animals the party is fond of eating &c.

MAY 3RD FRIDAY 1805
we Set out reather later this morning than useal owing to weather being verry cold, a frost last night and the Thermt. stood this morning at 26 above 0. which is 6 degrees blow freeseing. the ice that was on the Kettle left near the fire last night was ¼ of an inch thick. The snow is all or nearly all off the low bottoms, the Hills are entireley covered; three of our party found in the back of a bottom 3 pieces of scarlet [cloth] one brace[3] in each, which had been left as a sacrifice near one of their swet houses, on the L.S. we passed to day a curious collection of bushes tied up in the shape of *faccene* about 10 feet diamuter, which must have been left also by the natives as an offering to their medison which they [are] convinced protected or gave them relief near the place, the wind continued to blow hard from the West, altho' not sufficently so to detain us. Great numbers of Buffalow, Elk, Deer, antilope, beaver, Procupins, & water fowls seen to day, such as, Geese, ducks of dift. kinds, & a fiew Swan.

MAY 4TH SATTURDAY 1805
The rudder Irons of our large Perogue broke off last night, the replaceing of which detained us this morning untill 9 oClock at which time we set out The countrey on each side of the Missouri is a rich high and butifull the bottoms are extencive with a great deal of timber on them all the fore part of this day the woodland bordered the river on both Sides, in the after part of butifull assending plain on the Std Side we encamped

---

3 A rough measurement of length, from fingertip to fingertip with the arms stretched out.

on the Std. Side a little above. Saw great numbers of anamals of different kinds on the banks, we have one man Sick. The river has been falling for several days passed; it now begins to rise a little, the rate of rise & fall is from one to 3 inches in 24 hours

5TH OF MAY SUNDAY 1805

We set out verry early and had not proceeded far before the rudder Irons of one of the Perogus broke which detained us a short time Capt Lewis walked on shore this morning and killed a Deer, after brackfast I walked on shore Saw great numbers of Buffalow & Elk Saw also a Den of young wolves, and a number of Grown Wolves in every direction, The Countrey on both sides is as yesterday handsom & fertile. The river rising & current Strong & in the evening we saw a Brown or Grisley beare on a sand beech, I went out with one man Geo Drewyer & Killed the bear, which was verry large and a turrible looking animal, which we found verry hard to kill we Shot ten Balls into him before we killed him, & 5 of those Balls through his lights This animal is the largest of the carnivorous kind I ever saw

[LEWIS]
SUNDAY MAY 5TH 1805

it was a most tremendious looking anamal, and extreemly hard to kill notwithstanding he had five balls through his lungs and five others in various parts he swam more than half the distance across the river to a sandbar, & it was at least twenty minutes before he died; he did not attempt to attack, but fled and made the most tremendous roaring from the moment he was shot. We had no means of weighing this monster; Capt. Clark thought he would weigh 500 lbs. for my own part I think the estimate too small by 100 lbs. he measured 8. Feet 7½ Inches from the nose to the extremety of the hind feet, 5 F. 10½ Ins. arround the breast, 1 F. 11. I. arround the middle of the arm, & 3.F. 11.I. arround the neck; his tallons which were five in number on each foot were 4⅜ Inches in length. he was in good order, we therefore divided him among the party and made them boil the oil and put it in a cask for future uce; the oil is as hard as hogs lard when cool, much more so than that of the black bear. this bear differs from the common black bear in several respects; it's tallons are much longer and more blont, it's tale shorter, it's hair which is of a redish or bey brown, is longer thicker and finer than that of the black bear; his liver lungs and heart are much larger even in proportion with his size; the heart particularly was as large as that of a large Ox. his maw was also ten times the size of black bear, and was filled with flesh and fish.

The party killed two Elk and a Buffaloe today, and my dog caught a goat, which he overtook by superior fleetness, the goat it must be understood was with young and extreemly poor.

MONDAY MAY 6TH 1805.

saw a brown [grizzly] bear swim the river above us, he disappeared before we can get in reach of him; I find that the curiossity of our party is pretty well satisfyed with rispect to this anamal,   the formidable appearance of the male bear killed on the 5th added to the difficulty with which they die when even shot through the vital parts, has staggered the resolution [of] several of them, others however seem keen for action with the bear;   I expect these gentlemen will give us some amusement shotly as they [the bears] soon begin now to coppolate. saw a great quantity of game of every species common here. Capt Clark walked on shore and killed two Elk, they were not in very good order, we therefore took a part of the meat only;   it is now only amusement for Capt. C. and myself to kill as much meat as the party can consum.

WEDNESDAY MAY 8TH 1805.

we nooned it just above the entrance of a large river which disimbogues on the Lard. [*Starbd*] side; I took the advantage of this leasure moment and examined the river about 3 miles; I have no doubt but it is navigable for boats perogues and canoes, for the latter probably a great distance. from the quantity of water furnished by this river it must water a large extent of country; perhaps this river also might furnish practicable and advantageous communication with the Saskashiwan river; it is sufficiently large to justify a belief that it might reach to that river if it's direction be such. the water of this river posseses a peculiar whiteness, being about the colour of a cup of tea with the admixture of a tablespoonfull of milk. from the colour of it's water we called it Milk river. we think it possible that this may the river called by the Minitares *the river which scoalds at all others*[4] Capt Clark who walked this morning on the Lard. shore ascended a very high point opposite to the mouth of this river; he informed me that he had a perfect view of this river and the country through which it passed for a great distance probably 50 or 60 Miles, that the river from it's mouth bore N.W. for 12 or 15 Miles when it forked, the one taking a direction nearly North, and the other to the West of N. West.

Capt C. could not be certain but thought he saw the smoke and some Indian lodges at a considrable distance up Milk river.

THURSDAY MAY 9TH 1805.

Capt C. killed 2 bucks and 2 buffaloe, I also killed one buffaloe which proved to be the best meat, it was in tolerable order; we saved the best of the meat, and from the cow I killed we saved the necessary materials for making what our wrighthand cook Charbono calls the *boudin*

---

[4] This identification of the stream here named Milk River as the one which the Indians had called the River That Scolds All the Others was to be responsible for considerable anxiety later on. One result which Lewis does not allude to was to make the expedition believe it was nearer the Three Forks than in fact it was.

(poudingue) blanc, and immediately set him about preparing them for supper; this white pudding we all esteem one of the greatest delacies of the forrest, it may not be amiss therefore to give it a place. About 6 feet of the lower extremity of the large gut of the Buffaloe is the first mosel that the cook makes love to,   this he holds fast at one end with the right hand, while with the forefinger and thumb of the left he gently compresses it, and discharges what he says *is not good to eat,* but of which in the s[e]quel we get a moderate portion;   the mustle lying underneath the shoulder blade next to the back, and fillets are next saught, these are needed up very fine with a good portion of kidney suit; to this composition is then added a just proportion of pepper and salt and a small quantity of flour;   thus far advanced, our skilfull opporater C–o seizes his recepticle, which has never once touched the water, for that would intlrely distroy the regular order of the whole procedure; you will not forget that the side you now see is that covered with a good coat of fat provided the anamal be in good order; the operator sceizes the recepticle I say, and tying it fast at one end turns it inward and begins now with repeated evolutions of the hand and arm, and a brisk motion of the finger and thumb to put in what he says is *bon pour manger;*   thus by stuffing and compressing he soon distends the recepticle to the utmost limmits of it's power of expansion, and in the course of it's longtudinal progress it drives from the other end of the recepticle a much larger portion of the [blank space in MS.] than was previously discharged by the finger and thumb of the left hand in a former part of the operation; thus when the sides of the recepticle are skilfully exchanged the outer for the iner, and all is compleatly filled with something good to eat, it is tyed too scant;   it is then baptised in the missouri with two dips and a flirt and bobbed into the kettle; from whence, after it be well boiled it is taken and fryed with bears oil untill it becomes brown, when it is ready to esswage the pangs of a keen appetite or such as travelers in the wilderness are seldom at a loss for.

TUESDAY MAY 14TH 1805.

one of the party wounded a brown [grizzly] bear very badly, but being alone did not think proper to pursue him. In the evening the men in two of the rear canoes discovered a large brown bear lying in the open grounds about 300 paces from the river, and six of them went out to attack him, all good hunter; they took the advantage of a small eminence which concealed them and got within 40 paces of him unperceived, two of them reserved their fires as had been previously conserted, the four others fired nearly at the same time and put each his bullet through him, two of the balls passed through the bulk of both lobes of his lungs, in an instant this monster ran at them with open mouth, the two who had reserved their fir[e]s discharged their pieces at him as he came towards then, boath of them struck him, one only slightly and the other fortunately broke his shoulder, this however only retarded his motion for a moment only,   the men unable to reload their guns took to flight, the bear pursued and had very nearly overtaken them before they reached the river; two of the party betook themselves to a canoe and the others seperated an[d] concealed themselves among the willows, reloaded their pieces, each discharged his piece at him as they had an opportunity   they struck him several times again but the guns served only to direct the bear to them,   in this manner he pursued two of them seperately so close that they were obliged to throw aside their guns and pouches and throw themselves into the river altho' the bank was nearly twenty feet perpendicular; so enraged was this anamal that he plunged into the river only a few feet behind the second man he had compelled [to] take refuge in the water, when one of those who still remained on shore shot him through the head and finally killed him;   they then took him on shore and butch[er]ed him when they found eight balls had passed through him in different directions;   the bear being old the flesh was indifferent, they therefore only took the skin and fleece, the latter made us several gallons of oil.

FRIDAY JUNE 14TH 1805.

[On this day Lewis reconnoiters the remaining four falls and the intervening rapids which compose the Great Falls, going as far as Sun River,
which during the winter they had named Medicine River. He is on the
way to the latter as the entry continues.[5]]

I decended the hill and directed my course to the bend of the Missouri near which there was a herd of at least a thousand buffaloe; here I
thought it would be well to kill a buffaloe and leave him untill my return
from the river and if I then found that I had not time to get back to
camp this evening to remain all night here there being a few sticks of
drift wood lying along shore which would answer for my fire, and a few
s[c]attering cottonwood trees a few hundred yards below which would
afford me at least the semblance of a shelter. under this impression I
scelected a fat buffaloe and shot him very well, through the lungs; while
I was gazeing attentively on the poor anamal discharging blood in
streams from his mouth and nostril, expecting him to fall every instant,
and having entirely forgotten to reload my rifle, a large white, or reather
brown bear, had perceived and crept on me within 20 steps before I
discovered him;   in the first moment I drew up my gun to shoot, but
at the same instant recolected that she was not loaded and that he was
too near for me to hope to perform this opperation before he reached
me, as he was then briskly advancing on me; it was an open level plain,
not a bush within miles nor a tree within less than three hundred yards
of me; the river bank was sloping and not more than three feet above
the level of the water; in short there was no place by means of which I
could conceal myself from this monster untill I could charge my rifle;
in this situation I thought of retreating in a brisk walk as fast as he was

---

5 There are five falls in a ten-mile stretch of the river. The highest one is the farthest upstream
   and is the one which Lewis here calls the Great Falls. Power installations have entirely
   destroyed their beauty and spectacle.

advancing untill I could reach a tree about 300 yards below me, but I had no sooner terned myself about but he pitched at me, open mouthed and full speed,   I ran about 80 yards and found he gained on me fast, I then run into the water   the idea struk me to get into the water to such debth that I could stand and he would be obliged to swim, and that I could in that situation defend myself with my espontoon, accordingly I ran haistily into the water about waist deep, and faced about and presented the point of my espontoon,   at this instant he arrived at the edge of the water within about 20 feet of me; the moment I put myself in this attitude of defence he sudonly wheeled about as if frightened, declined to combat on such unequal grounds, and retreated with quite as great precipitation as he had just before pursued me.

As soon as I saw him run in that manner I returned to the shore and charged my gun, which I had still retained in my hand throughout this curious adventure. I saw him run through the level open plain about three miles, till he disappeared in the woods on medecine river; during the whole of this distance he ran at full speed, sometimes appearing to look behind him as if he expected pursuit. I now began to reflect on this novil occurence and indeavoured to account for this sudden retreat of the bear. I at first thought that perhaps he had not smelt me bofore he arrived at the waters edge so near me, but I then reflected that he had pursued me for about 80 or 90 yards before I took the water and on examination saw the grownd toarn with his tallons immediately on the imp[r]ession of my steps; and the cause of his allarm still remains with me misterious and unaccountable. so it was and I felt myself not a little gratifyed that he had declined the combat. my gun reloaded I felt confidence once more in my strength.

in returning through the level bottom of Medecine river and about 200 yards distant from the Missouri, my direction led me directly to an anamal that I at first supposed was a wolf; but on nearer approach or about sixty paces distant I discovered that it was not,   it's colour was a brownish yellow; it was standing near it's burrow, and when I approached it thus nearly, it couched itself down like a cat looking immediately at me as if it designed to spring on me. I took aim at it and fired,   it instantly disappeared in it's burrow;   I loaded my gun and ex[a]mined the place which was dusty and saw the track from which I am still further convinced that it was of the tiger kind. whether I struck it or not I could not determine, but I am almost confident that I did; my gun is true and I had a steady rest by means of my espontoon, which I have found very serviceable to me in this way in the open plains. It now seemed to me that all the beasts of the neighbourhood had made a league to distroy me, or that some fortune was disposed to amuse herself at my expence, for I had not proceded more than three hundred yards from the burrow of this tyger cat, before three bull buffaloe, which wer feeding with a large herd about half a mile from me on my left, seperated from the herd and ran full speed towards me,   I thought at least to give them some amusement and altered my direction to meet them; when they arrived within a hundred yards they mad[e] a halt, took a good view of me and retreated with precipitation. I then continued my rout homewards passed the buffaloe which I had killed, but did not think it prudent to remain all night at this place which really from the succession of curious adventures wore the impression on my mind of inchantment; at sometimes for a moment I thought it might be a dream, but the prickley pears which pierced my feet very severely once in a while, particularly after it grew dark, convinced me that I was really awake, and that it was necessary to make the best of my way to camp.

Chapter 2

"A MOUNTAIN MAN, WAGH!"

From *Life in the Far West,*
By George Frederick Ruxton
Edited by Leroy R. Hafen

"Seldom do we find in one individual the passion for rugged adventure, the hardihood to survive it, and the literary ability to portray it vividly. But such were the talents of George Frederick Ruxton."

Leroy R. Hafen's words from the introduction of the 1951 edition of Ruxton's *Life in the Far West* define exactly the qualities that make Ruxton and his work a classic in American literature. Ruxton was the first writer to portray the mountain men exactly as he found them. And find them he did, living with the mountain men in their camps and forts, sharing the campfires and buffalo hump meat, and noting with uncanny accuracy the colorful banter and tall tales that made mountain-man talk so special.

Ruxton was born and educated in England. He died in St. Louis at the age of 27, in 1848–the same year his tales were first published in *Blackwood's Edinburgh Magazine*. They were first published in book form in 1849.

Hafen calls *Life in the Far West* "fictionized history." Factual, but not a reliable historical chronicle. Nevertheless, it makes compelling reading, as you will see. And for the first time in this volume, you will hear the mountain man's favorite, oft-used expression, "Wagh!" A deep, guttural grunt and exclamation, saying "Why . . . " Meaning, "Need I say more? It's all as plain as day."

●   ●   ●

AWAY TO THE HEAD WATERS of the Platte, where several small streams run into the south fork of that river, and head in the broken ridges of the "Divide" which separates the valleys of the Platte and Arkansa, were camped a band of trappers on a creek called Bijou.[1] It was the month of October,[2] when the early frosts of the coming winter had crisped and dyed with sober brown the leaves of the cherry and quaking asp, which belted the little brook; and the ridges and peaks of the Rocky Mountains were already covered with a glittering mantle of snow, which sparkled in the still powerful rays of the autumn sun.

---

1   Bijou Creek was named for Joseph Bijeau, guide and interpreter with Major Stephen H. Long's 1820 expedition to the Rocky Mountains. The various branches of this north-flowing stream rise in high, grass-covered Bijou Basin, located some thirty miles northeast of the city of Colorado Springs, Colorado.

2   The year is 1847, according to the references presently to the murder of Bent at Taos (which occurred in January of 1847), and later to Tharp's death (May 28, 1847). At another time Ruxton infers that the meeting was in 1846, since after spending the winter with the Utes, Killbuck and La Bonté meet Ruxton in South Park in the spring of 1847.

The camp had all the appearance of being a permanent one; for not only did one or two unusually comfortable shanties form a very conspicuous object, but the numerous stages on which huge strips of buffalo meat were hanging in process of cure, showed that the party had settled themselves here in order to lay in a store of provisions, or, as it is termed in the language of the mountains, "make meat." Round the camp were feeding some twelve or fifteen mules and horses, having their fore-legs confined by hobbles of raw hide, and, guarding these animals, two men paced backwards and forwards, driving in stragglers; and ever and anon ascending the bluffs which overhung the river, and, leaning on their long rifles, would sweep with their eyes the surrounding prairie. Three or four fires were burning in the encampment, on some of which Indian women were carefully tending sundry steaming pots; whilst round one, which was in the center of it, four or five stalwart hunters, clad in buckskin, sat cross-legged, pipe in mouth.

They were a trapping party from the north fork of Platte, on their way to wintering-ground in the more southern valley of the Arkansa; some, indeed, meditating a more extended trip, even to the distant settlements of New Mexico, the paradise of mountaineers. The elder of the company was a tall gaunt man, with a face browned by a twenty years' exposure to the extreme climate of the mountains; his long black hair, as yet scarcely tinged with gray, hung almost to his shoulders, but his cheeks and chin were cleanly shaved, after the fashion of the mountain men. His dress was the usual hunting-frock of buckskin, with long fringes down the seams, with pantaloons similarly ornamented, and mocassins of Indian make. As his companions puffed their pipes in silence, he was narrating a few of his former experiences of western life; and whilst the buffalo "hump-ribs" and "tender loin" are singing away in the pot, preparing for the hunters' supper, we will note down the yarn as it spins from his lips, giving it in the language spoken in the "far west":

"'Twas about 'calf-time,' maybe a little later, and not a hundred year ago, by a long chalk, that the biggest kind of rendezvous was held 'to' Independence, a mighty handsome little location away up on old Missoura. A pretty smart lot of boys was camp'd thar, about a quarter from the town, and the way the whisky flowed that time was 'some' now, I can tell you. Thar was old Sam Owins—him as got 'rubbed out'[3] by the Spaniards at Sacramenty, or Shihuahuy, this hos doesn't know which, but he 'went under'[4] any how. Well, Sam had his train along, ready to hitch up for the Mexican country—twenty thunderin big Pittsburg waggons;

---

3 Killed, reference adapted from the Indian figurative language. Ruxton's note.

4 Died, reference adapted from the Indian figurative language. Ruxton's note.

5 Samuel Owens, prominent merchant of Independence and trader on the Santa Fé Trail, enlisted in the Mexican War and was killed at the Battle of Sacramento, February 28, 1847.

Here are brief accounts of the figures mentioned in the following paragraph:

William Bent, one of the sons of Judge Silas Bent of St. Louis, was the principal owner and operator of famous Bent's Fort, located on the north bank of the Arkansas River about seven miles northeast of the present La Junta, Colorado.

Bill Williams, one of the most picturesque figures among the Mountain Men and fur trappers, has been portrayed by various writers. See A. H. Favour, *Old Bill Williams* (Chapel Hill, 1936), and Chauncey P. Williams, *Lone Elk, the Life Story of Bill Williams, Trapper and Guide of the Far West* (Denver, 1935). A more definitive biography, by Frederic Voelker of St. Louis, is nearly ready for publication.

William Tharp was killed on the Walnut Creek branch of the Arkansas in May of 1847, while on his way to the States. See *Ruxton of the Rockies,* 270–271, and Lewis Garrard, *Wah-To-Yah and the Taos Trail* (edited by R. P. Bieber [Glendale, California, 1938]), 173.

John Hatcher, prominent on the Santa Fé Trail, is given a lead part in Lewis Garrard's excellent historical narrative, *Wah-To-Yah and the Taos Trail.* R. P. Bieber gives biographical data on Hatcher in his edition of Garrard's book, p. 219.

Bill Garey (William Guerrier) was one of William Bent's traders at Bent's Fort on the Arkansas. Guerrier married a Cheyenne woman. See George B. Grinnell, "Bent's Old Fort and Its Builders," in the Kansas State Historical Society *Collections,* Vol. XV (1919), 37–38; and "The W. M. Boggs Manuscript about Bent's Fort, Kit Carson, the Far West, and Life Among the Indians," in the *Colorado Magazine,* Vol. VII, No. 2 (March, 1930), 49.

Jean Baptiste Charbonneau, son of Sacajawea (Bird Woman) of the Lewis and Clark expedition of 1804–1806, had a colorful career. Adopted and educated by William Clark, he and the way *his* Santa Fé boys took in the liquor beat all—eh, Bill?"[5]

"*Well*, it did."

"Bill Bent—his boys camped the other side the trail, and they was all mountain men, wagh!—and Bill Williams, and Bill Tharpe (the Pawnees took his hair on Pawnee Fork last spring): three Bills, and them three's all 'gone under.' Surely Hatcher went out that time; and wasn't Bill Garey along, too? Didn't him and Chabonard sit in camp for twenty hours at a deck of Euker? Them was Bent's Indian traders up on Arkansa. Poor Bill Bent! them Spaniards made meat of him. He lost his topknot to Taos. A 'clever' man was Bill Bent as *I* ever know'd trade a robe or 'throw' a buffler in his tracks. Old St. Vrain could knock the hind-sight off him though, when it come to shootin, and old silver heels spoke true, she did: 'plum-center' she was, eh?"

"*Well*, she was'nt nothin else."

"The Greasers[6] payed for Bent's scalp, they tell me. Old St Vrain went out of Santa Fé with a company of mountain men, and the way

---

accompanied Prince Paul of Wurttemburg to Europe in 1823 and remained there with the Prince until 1829. Returned to the United States, he joined a trapping expedition to the Rockies and for fifteen years was in the wilds as a Mountain Man. In 1846 he served as hunter and guide to Colonel St. George Cooke on the march of the Mormon Battalion from Santa Fé to San Diego. In his later years Charbonneau returned to his Shoshone relatives on the Wind River Reservation of Wyoming. Here he married into the tribe and remained until his death. See Ann W. Hafen, "Baptiste Charbonneau, Son of Bird Woman," in *The Westerners Brand Book* (Denver, 1950).

William Bent lived until May 19, 1869. It was his brother, Charles Bent, who was killed and scalped at Taos on January 19, 1847, during the uprising against Americans. Charles Bent had been appointed by General S. W. Kearny as the first American governor of New Mexico.

Ceran St. Vrain went to New Mexico in 1824 and was in a trapper band on the Gila River of Arizona as early as 1826. In 1831 he joined Charles Bent to form Bent, St. Vrain and Co., thereafter prominent in the Santa Fé trade. Ceran's younger brother, Marcelline, a trapper and trader with the Indians, was a famous hunter. See T. M. Marshall, "St. Vrain's Expedition to the Gila in 1826," in *The Pacific Ocean History* (edited by H. M. Stephens and H. E. Bolton [New York, 1917], 429–438; and [P. A. St. Vrain], The *de Lassus St. Vrain Family* [1944]).

6 The Mexicans are called "Spaniards" or "Greasers" (from their greasy appearance) by the Western people. Ruxton's note.

they made 'em sing out was 'slick as shootin.' He 'counted a coup' did St Vrain.[7] He throwed a Pueblo as had on poor Bent's shirt. I guess he tickled that niggur's hump-ribs. Fort William[8] aint the lodge it was, an' never will be agin, now he's gone under; but St Vrain's 'pretty much of a gentleman,' too; if he ain't, I'll be dog-gone, eh, Bill?"

"He is *so-o.*"

"Chavez had his waggons along. He was only a Spaniard any how, and some of his teamsters put a ball into him his next trip, and made a raise of *his* dollars, wagh! Uncle Sam hung 'em for it, I heard, but can't b'lieve it, no-how.[9] If them Spaniards wasn't born for shootin', why was beaver made? You was with us that spree, Jemmy?"

"No *sire-e;* I went out when Spiers[10] lost his animals on Cimmaron: a hundred and forty mules and oxen was froze that night, wagh!"

"Surely Black Harris[11] was thar; and the darndest liar was Black Harris—for lies tumbled out of his mouth like boudins out of a buffler's stomach. He was the child as saw the putrefied forest in the Black Hills. Black Harris come in from Laramie; he'd been trapping three year an'

---

7   Captain St. Vrain led a company of volunteers in Colonel Sterling Price's campaign to put down the uprising of January, 1847.

8   Bent's Indian trading fort on the Arkansa. Ruxton's note. Fort William, named for William Bent and generally known as Bent's Fort, was established in 1832 and was the most famous trading post of the Southwest. See Grinnell, "Bent's Old Fort and Its Builders."

9   Don Antonio José Chavez left New Mexico in February of 1843 with two wagons, fifty-five mules, furs, and some $10,000 in gold and silver. He was going to Missouri to purchase trade goods. When nearing his destination he was robbed and murdered by a gang of ruffians led by John McDaniel. The outlaws were later apprehended and tried in St. Louis. John McDaniel and his brother David were hanged, and others of the gang were imprisoned. See R. E. Twitchell, *The Leading Facts of New Mexican History* (5 vols., Cedar Rapids, Iowa, 1911–17), II, 83–84.

10 Albert Speyer and Dr. Henry Connelly lost three hundred mules in a storm on the Cimarron in the early winter of 1844. J. L. Collins' report in Twitchell, *ibid.,* 126.

11 Moses ("Black") Harris divides with Jim Bridger the honor of being the biggest liar among the Mountain Men. Harris, prominent trapper, was later an important emigrant guide.

more on Platte and the 'other side'; and, when he got into Liberty, he fixed himself right off like a Saint Louiy dandy. Well, he sat to dinner one day in the tavern, and a lady says to him:

"'Well, Mister Harris, I hear you're a great travler.'

"'Travler, marm,'" says Black Harris, "'this niggur's no travler; I ar' a trapper, marm, a mountain-man, wagh!'

"'Well, Mister Harris, trappers are great travlers, and you goes over a sight of ground in your perishinations, I'll be bound to say.'

"'A sight, marm, this coon's gone over, if that's the way your 'stick floats.'[12] I've trapped beaver on Platte and Arkansa, and away up on Missoura and Yaller Stone; I've trapped on Columbia, on Lewis Fork, and Green River; I've trapped, marm, on Grand River and the Heely (Gila). I've fout the 'Blackfoot' (and d–d bad Injuns they are); I've 'raised the hair'[13] of more *than one* Apach, and made a Rapaho 'come' afore now; I've trapped in heav'n, in airth, and h–, and scalp my old head, marm, but I've seen a putrefied forest.'

"'La, Mister Harris, a what?'

"'A putrefied forest, marm, as sure as my rifle's got hindsights, and *she* shoots center. I was out on the Black Hills, Bill Sublette[14] knows the time–the year it rained fire–and every body knows when that was.[15] If thar wasn't cold doin's about that time, this child wouldn't say so. The snow was about fifty foot deep, and the buffler lay dead on the ground like bees

---

12 Meaning, if that's what you mean! The "stick" is tied to the beaver trap by a string; and, floating on the water, points out its position, should a beaver have carried it away. Ruxton's note.

13 Scalped. Ruxton's note.

14 William Sublette was the most prominent of five brothers–Milton, Andrew, Solomon, and Pinckney, being the others. He was one of the business successors of W.H. Ashley in the Rocky Mountain fur trade and was founder, with Robert Campbell, of Fort William (later Fort Laramie) on the Laramie Fork of the North Platte. One of his purposes in going into the mountains was to combat tuberculosis; but he succumbed to the disease in 1845.

15 The "Year the Stars Fell"–the meteoric shower of November 12, 1833.

after a beein'; not whar we was tho', for *thar* was no buffler, and no meat, and me and my band had been livin' on our mocassins (leastwise the parflesh),[16] for six weeks; and poor doin's that feedin' is, marm, as you'll never know. One day we crossed a 'canon' and over a 'divide,' and got into a periara, whar was green grass, and green trees, and green leaves on the trees, and birds singing in the green leaves, and this in February, wagh! Our animals was like to die when they see the green grass, and we all sung out, 'hurraw for summer doin's.'

"'Hyar goes for meat,' says I, and I jest ups old Ginger at one of them singing birds, and down come the crittur elegant; its darned head spinning away from the body, but never stops singing, and when I takes up the meat, I finds it stone, wagh!'

"'Hyar's damp powder and no fire to dry it,'" I says quite skeared.

"'Fire be dogged,' says old Rube.[17] 'Hyar's a hos as'll make fire come'; and with that he takes his axe and lets drive at a cottonwood. Schr-u-k– goes the axe agin the tree, and out comes a bit of the blade as big as my hand. We looks as the animals, and thar they stood shaking over the grass, which I'm dog-gone if it wasn't stone, too. Young Sublette comes up, and he'd been clerking down to the fort on Platte, so he know'd something. He looks and looks, and scrapes the tree with his butcher knife, and snaps the grass like pipe stems, and breaks the leaves a-snappin' like Californy shells.

"'What's all this, boy?' I asks.

"'Putrefactions,' says he, looking smart, 'putrefactions, or I'm a niggur.'

"'La, Mister Harris,' says the lady; 'putrefactions, why, did the leaves, and the trees, and the grass smell badly?'

"'Smell badly, marm,' says Black Harris, 'would a skunk stink if he was froze to stone? No, marm, this child didn't know what putrefactions

---

16 Soles made of buffalo hide. Ruxton's note.

17 Rube Herring, whom Ruxton met at the Mormon settlement near Pueblo, Colorado, early in 1847. See *Ruxton of the Rockies,* 255–256. He is to appear subsequently in this story.

was, and young Sublette's varsion wouldn't 'shine' nohow, so I chips a piece out of a tree and puts it in my trap-sack, and carries it in safe to Laramie. Well, old Captain Stewart[18] (a clever man was that, though he was an Englishman), he comes along next spring, and a Dutch doctor chap was along too. I shows him the piece I chipped out of the tree, and he called it a putrefaction too; and so, marm, if that wasn't a putrefied peraira, what was it? For this hos doesn't know, and *he* knows 'fat cow' from 'poor bull,' anyhow.'

"Well, old Black Harris is gone under too, I believe. He went to the 'Parks' trapping with a Vide Pôche Frenchman, who shot him for his bacca and traps.[19] Darn them Frenchmen, they're no account any way you lays your sight. (Any 'bacca in your bag, Bill? this beaver feels like chawing.)

"Well, any how, thar was the camp, and they was goin to put out the next morning; and last as come out of Independence was that ar English-man. He'd a nor-west[20] capôte on, and a two-shoot gun rifled. Well, them English are darned fools; they can't fix a rifle any ways; but that one did shoot 'some'; leastwise *he* made it throw plum-center. He made the buffler 'come,' *he* did, and fout well at Pawnee Fork too.[21] What was his name? All the boys called him Cap'en, and he got his fixings from old Choteau;[22] but

---

18 Captain William Drummond Stewart, famed Scottish traveler and hunter, who first came into the West in 1833.

19 This report is false, as Black Harris died of cholera at Independence on May 6, 1849.

20 The Hudson Bay Company, having amalgamated with the American North West Company, is known by the name "North West" to the southern trappers. Their employes usually wear Canadian *capôtes*. Ruxton's note.

21 The reference is to William Drummond Stewart. Bernard DeVoto calls Killbuck's references to Stewart "embroidery," and thinks the Scotsman never traveled the Santa Fé Trail and fought at Pawnee Fork. However, Stewart's movements in the spring of 1834 may possibly have brought him to Pawnee Fork. See Bernard DeVoto, *Beyond the Wide Missouri* (Boston, 1947), 46, 420.

22 Pierre Choteau and Company were successors to the Western Department of the American Fur Company at St. Louis and did an outfitting business.

what he wanted out thar in the mountains, I never jest rightly know'd. He was no trader, nor a trapper, and flung about his dollars right smart. Thar was an old grit in him, too, and a hair of the black b'ar at that.[23] They say he took the bark off the Shians when he cleared out of the village with old Beaver Tail's squaw. He'd been on Yaller Stone afore that: Leclerc know'd him in the Blackfoot, and up in the Chippeway country; and he had the best powder as ever I flashed through life, and his gun was handsome, that's a fact. Them thar locks was grand; and old Jake Hawken's nephey (him as trapped on Heely [Gila] that time), told me, the other day, as he saw an English gun on Arkansa last winter as beat all off hand.[24]

"Nigh upon two hundred dollars I had in my possibles, when I went to that camp to see the boys afore they put out; and you know, Bill, as I sat to 'Euker' and 'seven up'[25] till every cent was gone.

"'Take back twenty, old coon,' says Big John.

"'H—'s full of such takes back,' says I; and I puts back to town and fetches the rifle and the old mule, puts my traps into the sack, gets credit for a couple of pounds of powder at Owin's store, and hyar I ar on Bijou, with half a pack of beaver, and running meat yet, old hos: so put a log on, let's have a smoke.

"Hurraw, Jake, old coon, bear a hand, and let the squaw put them tails in the pot; for sun's down, and we'll have to put out pretty early to reach 'Black Tail' by this time tomorrow. Who's fust guard, boys: them cussed 'Rapahos' will be after the animals to-night, or I'm no judge of

---

23 A spice of the devil. Ruxton's note.

24 Jake and Samuel Hawken were famous gunsmiths at St. Louis. Samuel went to the new town of Denver in 1859 and set up a gunsmith shop there. Among early trappers the Hawken was the most prized weapon of the West.

  Ruxton calls the person "John Hawkens" who entertained him at Pueblo on the Arkansas in January of 1847, and this is doubtless the person referred to here. The English gun mentioned would be Ruxton's own, which he showed the trappers at Pueblo.

25 "Euker," "poker," and "seven-up," are the fashionable games of cards. Ruxton's note.

Injun sign. How many did you see, Maurice?"

"Enfant de Gârce, me see bout honderd, when I pass Squirrel Creek, one dam war-party, parce-que, they no hosses, and have de lariats for steal des animaux. May be de Yutes in Bayou Salade."[26]

"We'll be having trouble to-night, I'm thinking, if the devils are about. Whose band was it, Maurice?"

"Slim-Face–I see him ver close–is out; mais I think it White Wolf's."

"White Wolf, maybe, will lose his hair if he and his band knock round here too often. That Injun put me afoot when he was out on 'Sandy' that fall. This niggur owes him one, any how."

"H–'s full of White Wolves: go ahead, and roll out some of your doins across the plains that time."

"You seed sights that spree, eh, boy?"

"*Well,* we did. Some of em for their flints fixed this side of Pawnee Fork, and a heap of mule-meat went wolfing. Just by Little Arkansa we saw the first Injun. Me and young Somes was ahead for meat, and I hobbled the old mule and was 'approaching' some goats,[27] when I see the critturs turn back their heads and jump right away for me. 'Hurraw, Dick!' I shouts, 'hyars brown-skin acomin',' and off I makes for the mule. The young greenhorn sees the goats runnin up to him, and not being up to Injun ways, blazes at the first and knocks him over. Jest then seven darned red heads top the bluff, and seven Pawnees come a-screeching upon us. I cuts the hobbles and jumps on the mule, and, when I looks back, there was Dick Somes ramming a ball down his gun like mad, and the Injuns flinging their arrows at him pretty smart, I tell you. 'Hurraw, Dick, mind your hair,' and I ups old Greaser and let one Injun 'have it,' as was going plum into the boy with his lance. *He* turned on his back handsome, and Dick gets the

---

26 Bayou Salade (Salt Valley), now known as South Park (Colorado), was a hunter's paradise. It took its name from the salt spring and marsh at the southern end of this high mountain valley.

27 Antelope are frequently called "goats" by the mountaineers. Ruxton's note.

ball down at last, blazes away, and drops another. When we charged on em, and they clears off like runnin cows; and I takes the hair off the heads of the two we made meat of; and I do b'lieve thar's some of them scalps on my old leggings yet.

"Well, Dick was as full of arrows as a porkypine: one was sticking right through his cheek, one in his meat-bag, and two more 'bout his hump ribs. I tuk 'em all out slick, and away we go to camp (for they was jost a-campin' when we went ahead), and carryin' the goat too. Thar was a hurroo when we rode on with the scalps at the end of our guns. 'Injuns! Injuns!' was the cry from the greenhorns; 'we'll be 'tacked to-night, that's certain.'

"''Tacked be–,' says old Bill; 'ain't we men too, and white at that. Look to your guns, boys; send out a strong hos'-guard with the animals, and keep your eyes skinned.'

"Well, as soon as the animals were unhitched from the waggons, the guvner sends out a strong guard, seven boys, and old hands at that. It was pretty nigh upon sundown, and Bill had just sung out to 'corral.' The boys were drivin' in the animals, and we were all standin' round to get 'em in slick, when, 'howgh-owgh-owgh-owgh,' we hears right behind the bluff, and 'bout a minute and a perfect crowd of Injuns gallops down upon the animals. Wagh! War'nt thor hoopin'! We jump for the guns, but before we get to the fires, the Injuns were among the cavayard. I saw Ned Collyer and his brother, who were in the hos'-guard, let drive at 'em; but twenty Pawnees were round 'em before the smoke cleared from their rifles, and when the crowd broke the two boys were on the ground, and their hair gone. Well, that ar Englishman just saved the cavayard. He had his horse, a regular buffalo-runner, picketed round the fire quite handy, as soon as he sees the fix, he jumps upon her and rides right into the thick of the mules, and passes through 'em, firing his two-shoot gun at the Injuns, and by Gor, he made two come. The mules, which was a snortin' with funk and running before the Injuns, as soon as they see the Englishman's mare (mules'ill go to h– after a horse, you all know), followed her right into the corral, and thar they was safe. Fifty Pawnees come screechin' after 'em, but we was ready that time, and the way we throw'd 'em was something handsome, I tell you. But three of the hos'-guards got skeared—leastwise their mules did, and carried 'em off into the peraira, and the Injuns having enough of *us,* dashed after 'em right away. Them poor devils looked back miserable now, with about a hundred red varmints tearin' after their hair, and whooping like mad. Young Jem Bulcher was the last; and when he seed it was no use, and his time was nigh, he throw'd himself off the mule, and standing as upright as a hickory wiping stick, he waves his hand to us, and blazes away at the first Injun as come up, and dropped him slick; but the moment after, you may guess, *he* died.

"We could do nothin', for, before our guns were loaded all three were dead and their scalps gone. Five of our boys got rubbed out that time, and seven Injuns lay wolf's meat, while a many more went away gun-shot, I'll lay. How'sever, seven of us went under, and the Pawnees made a raise of a dozen mules, wagh!"

Thus far, in his own words, we have accompanied the old hunter in his tale; and probably he would have taken us, by the time that the Squaw Chili-pat had pronounced the beaver tails cooked, safely across the grand prairies—fording Cotton Wood, Turkey Creek, Little Arkansa, Walnut Creek, and Pawnee Fork—passed the fireless route of the Cook Creeks; through a sea of fat buffalo meat, without fuel to cook it; have struck the big river, and, leaving at the "Crossing" the waggons destined for Santa Fé, have trailed us up the Arkansa to Bent's Fort; thence up Boiling Spring, across the divide over to the southern fork of the Platte, away up to the Black Hills, and finally camped us, with hair still preserved, in the beaver-abounding valleys of the Sweet Water, and Câche la Poudre, under the rugged shadow of the Wind River mountains; if it had not so befell, that as this juncture, as all our mountaineers sat crosslegged round the fire, pipe in mouth, and with Indian gravity listened to the yarn of the old trapper, interrupting him only with an occasional wagh! or the assured exclamations of some participator in the events then under narration, who would every now and then put in a corroborative– "This child remembers that fix," or, "hyar's a niggur lifted hair that spree," &c.–that a whizzing noise was heard through the air, followed by a sharp but suppressed cry from one of the hunters,

In an instant the mountaineers had sprung from their seats, and, seizing the ever-ready rifle, each one had thrown himself on the ground a few paces beyond the light of the fire (for it was now nightfall); but not a word escaped them, as, lying close, with their keen eyes directed towards the gloom of the thicket, near which the camp was placed, with rifles cocked, they waited a renewal of the attack. Presently the leader of the band, no other than Killbuck,[28] who had so lately been recounting some of his experiences across the plains, and than whom no more crafty woodsman or more expert trapper ever tracked a deer or grained a beaverskin, raised his tall, leather-clad form, and, placing his hand over his mouth, made the prairie ring with the wild protracted note of an Indian war-whoop. This was instantly repeated from the direction where the animals belonging to the camp were grazing, under the charge of the horse-guard, and three shrill whoops answered the warning of the leader, and showed that the guard was on the alert, and understood the signal. However, with this manifestation of their presence, the Indians appeared to be satisfied; or, what is more probable, the act of aggression had been committed by some daring young warrior, who, being out on his first expedition, desired to strike the first *coup,* and thus signalise himself at the onset of the campaign. After waiting some few minutes, expecting a renewal of the attack, the mountaineers in a body rose from the ground and made towards the animals, with which they presently returned to the camp; and, after carefully hobbling and securing them to pickets firmly

---

28 For a discussion of his identity see Appendix B, at the end of this volume.

driven into the ground, and mounting an additional guard, they once more assembled round the fire, after examining the neighboring thicket, relit their pipes, and puffed away the cheering weed as composedly as if no such being as a Redskin, thirsting for their lives, was within a thousand miles of their perilous encampment.

"If ever thar was bad Injuns on these plains," at last growled Killbuck, biting hard the pipe-stem between his teethe, "it's these Rapahos, and the meanest kind at that."

"Can't beat the Blackfeet anyhow," chimed in on La Bonté,[29] from the Yellow Stone country, and a fine, handsome specimen of a mountaineer.

"However, one of you quit this arrow out of my hump," he continued, bending forwards to the fire, and exhibiting an arrow sticking out under his right shoulder-blade, and a stream of blood trickling down his buckskin coat from the wound.

This his nearest neighbor essayed to do; but finding, after a tug, that it "would not come," expressed his opinion that the offending weapon would have to be "butchered" out. This was accordingly effected with the ready blade of a scalp-knife; and a handful of beaver-fur being placed on the wound, and secured by a strap of buckskin round the body, the wounded man donned his hunting-shirt once more, and coolly set about lighting his pipe, his rifle lying across his lap, cocked and ready for use.

It was now nearing midnight—dark and misty; and the clouds, rolling away to the eastward from the lofty ridges of the Rocky Mountains, were gradually obscuring the little light which was afforded by the dim stars. As the lighter vapours faded from the mountains, a thick black cloud succeeded them, and settled over the loftier peaks of the chain, which were faintly visible through the gloom of night, whilst a mass of fleecy scud soon overspread the whole sky. A hollow moaning sound crept

---

29 The questions of the identity of La Bonté is considered below, in Appendix B.

through the valley, and the upper branches of the cottonwoods, with their withered leaves, began to rustle with the first breath of the coming storm, Huge drops of rain fell at intervals, hissing as they fell on the blazing fires, and pattered on the skins which the hunters were hurriedly laying on their exposed baggage. The mules near the camp cropped the grass with quick and greedy bites round the circuit of their pickets, as if conscious that the storm would soon prevent their feeding, and were already humping their backs as the chilling rain fell upon their flanks. The prairie wolves crept closer to the camp, and in the confusion that ensued from the hurry of the trappers to cover the perishable portions of their equipment, contrived more than once to dart off with a piece of meat, when their peculiar and mournful chiding would be heard as they fought for the possession of the ravished morsel.

As soon as everything was duly protected, the men set to work to spread their beds, those who had not troubled themselves to erect a shelter getting under the lee of the piles of packs and saddles; while Killbuck, disdaining even such care of his carcass, threw his buffalo robe on the bare ground, declaring his intention to "take" what was coming at all hazards, and "any how." Selecting a high spot, he drew his knife and proceeded to cut drains round it, to prevent the water running into him as he lay; then taking a single robe he carefully spread it, placing under the end farthest from the fire a large stone brought from the creek. Having satisfactorily adjusted this pillow, he adds another robe to the one already laid, and places over all a Navajo blanket, supposed to be impervious to rain. Then he divests himself of his pouch and powder-horn, which, with his rifle, he places inside his bed, and quickly covers up lest the wet reach them. Having performed these operations to his satisfaction, he lighted his pipe by the hissing embers of the half-extinguished fire (for by this time the rain was pouring in torrents), and going the rounds of the picketed animals, and cautioning the guard round the camp to keep their "eyes skinned, for there would be 'powder burned' before morning," he returned to the fire, and kicking with his mocassined foot the slumbering ashes, squats down before it, and thus soliloquises:

"Thirty year have I been knocking about these mountains from Missoura's head as far sothe as the starving Gila. I've trapped a 'heap,'[30] and many a hundred pack of beaver I've traded in my time, wagh! What has come of it, and whar's the dollars as ought to be in my possibles? Whar's the ind of this, I say? Is a man to be hunted by Injuns all his days? Many's the time I've said I'd strike for Taos, and trap a squaw, for this child's getting old, and feels like wanting a woman's face about his lodge for the balance of his days; but when it comes to caching of the old traps, I've the smallest kind of heart, I have. Certain, the old state comes across my mind now and again, but who's thar to remember my old body? But them diggings gets too over crowded now-a-days, and its hard to fetch breath amongst them big bands of corncrackers to Missoura. Beside, it goes against natur to leave bufler meat and feed on hog; and them white gals are too much like picturs, and a deal too 'fofarraw' [fanfaron]. No; darn the settlements, I say. It won't shine, and whar's the dollars? However, beaver's 'bound to rise'; human natur can't go on selling beaver a dollar a pound;[31] no, no, that arn't a going to shine much longer, I know. Them was the times when this child first went to the mountains: six dollars a plew—old 'un or kitten. Wagh! but it's bound to rise, I says agin; and hyar's a coon knows whar to lay his hand on a dozen pack right handy, and then he'll take the Taos trail, wagh!"

Thus soliloquising, Killbuck knocked the ashes from his pipe, and

---

30 An Indian is always a "heap" hungry or thirsty—loves a "heap"—is a "heap" brave—in fact, "heap" is tantamount to very much. Ruxton's note.

31 The old trapper was loath to leave his traps. Though the price of beaver was down, he was sure it would rise again. This was a faith often expressed by those who saw their occupation slipping from them.

placed it in the gaily ornamented case which hung round his neck, drew his knife-belt a couple of holes tighter, and once more donned his pouch and powder-horn, took his rifle, which he carefully covered with the folds of his Navajo blanket, and striding into the darkness, cautiously reconnoitred the vicinity of the camp. When he returned to the fire he sat down as before, but this time with his rifle across his lap; and at intervals his keen gray eye glanced piercingly around, particularly towards an old weatherbeaten, and grizzled mule, who now, old stager as she was, having filled her belly, was standing lazily over her picket pin, with head bent down and her long ears flapping over her face, her limbs gathered under her, and with back arched to throw off the rain, tottering from side to side as she rests and sleeps.

"Yap, old gal!" cried Killbuck to the animal, at the same time picking a piece of burnt wood from the fire and throwing it at her, at which the mule gathered itself up and cocked her ears as she recognized her master's voice. "Yep, old gal! and keep your nose open; thar's brown skin about, I'm thinkin', and maybe you'll get 'roped' [lasso'd] by a Rapaho afore mornin."[32] Again the old trapper settled himself before the fire; and soon his head began to nod, as drowsiness stole over him. Already he was in the land of dreams; revelling amongst bands of "fat cow," or hunting along a stream well peopled with beaver; with no Indian "sign" to disturb him, and the merry rendezvous in close perspective, and his peltry selling briskly at six dollars the plew,[33] and galore of alcohol to ratify the trade. Or, perhaps, threading the back trail of his memory, he passed rapidly through the perilous vicissitudes of his hard, hard life–starving one day, revelling in abundance the next; now beset by whooping savages thirsting for his blood, baying his enemies like the hunted deer, but with the

---

[32] The mule was an excellent detector of Indians and the trapper expected warning from his mule of the approach of Indians.

[33] "Plew" (*plus*) in trapper talk signified a prime beaver skin, and was a unit of exchange.

unflinching courage of a man; now, all care thrown aside, secure and forgetful of the past, a welcome guest in the hospitable trading fort; or back, as the trail gets fainter, to his childhood's home in the brown forests of old Kentuck, tended and cared for—no thought his, but to enjoy the homminy and johnny cakes of his thrifty mother. Once more, in warm and well remembered homespun, he sits on the snake fence round the old clearing, and munching his hoe-cake at set of sun, listens to the mournful note of the whip-poor-will, or the harsh cry of the noisy catbird, or watches the agile gambols of the squirrels as they chase each other, chattering the while, from branch to branch of the lofty tameracks, wondering how long it will be before he will be able to lift his father's heavy rifle, and use it against the tempting game.

Chapter 3

THE WINTER LODGE

From *Across the Wide Missouri,* by Bernard DeVoto

If one were to be limited to only two books about the days of the mountain men—one fiction, one non-fiction ("poor doin's" as the mountain man would say)—the obvious choices for this reader would be the novel *The Big Sky* by A. B. Guthrie, Jr., and Bernard DeVoto's historical classic, *Across the Wide Missouri.* From the frontispiece where he presents the lyrics to the melancholy tune that gives the book its title, a tune often called "Shenandoah," DeVoto's book is a spell-binding classic—one of the finest volumes in this legendary historian's works. The chapter "The Winter Lodge," from which this excerpt is taken, is one of the book's most intimate portraits of the daily life of the mountain man.

Here, also, for your enjoyment, is the first stanza of the lovely tune that gave DeVoto his title.

Oh, Shennydore, I long to hear you.
Away, you rolling river!
Oh, Shennydore, I can't get near you.
Away, away, I'm bound away
Across the wide Missouri.

●   ●   ●

IT WAS BAD TO TELL the tales in summer, old Red Water informed Francis Parkman, up in the Laramie Mountains of Wyoming where Whirlwind's village of Oglala Sioux had made their hunting camp. If he should sit down to tell stories before the frost began, the young men going out on war parties would be killed. But one afternoon while the skirt of the lodge was turned up to catch the breeze and the camp slept in still heat, the old man fell to remembering the first time he had ever seen white people.

It was when he was a boy. He and three or four others set out to hunt beaver. But he was by himself when he found a beaver house. He wanted to see what it was like and so he had to dive down to the tunnel entrance under the water and then crawl a long way till he came out under the dome. It was dark and close and little Red Water was tired. He slept or fainted. When he woke in the darkness again he could hear the voices of his companions far away, singing a death song–a death song for him. But also he could dimly see a man and two women sitting at the edge of a forest pool. They were white people and their paleness frightened him. So with great difficulty he made his way out to daylight again. He went straight to the place above that pool of water. He beat a hole in the ground with his war club and sat down to watch it. Soon the nose of an old male beaver appeared in the hole. Red Water dragged him out, and two female beavers came up through the hole and he took them too.

The beaver were the white people he had seen. And Red Water knew that this was right. For, he remarked to Parkman, beavers and the whites were the wisest people on earth: they must be the same species.

In the Indian bestiary all animals were wise and had supernatural powers but the beaver was always among the most sagacious. The religious rituals for taking him were very complicated. The wilderness mind of the white trappers might also call on magic to assist the hunt when it was going badly, and not a few regularly invoked amulets or incantations when they set their traps. They too knew that the beaver was very wise—and their job was to outthink him.

Part of the trapper's skill was to know the habits of beaver, to recognize likely sign, and to decide the right places to set his traps. A brigade making a hunt broke up into small parties which normally worked by themselves for several days at a time, splitting further into twos and threes for the actual trapping. They worked the streams and we must think of them mostly in mountain meadows or similar flats where the streams were slow enough to be dammed. Late in the afternoon, 'between sunset and dark' was the usual time to set traps. In some secrecy. For, says Osborne Russell, one of our best annalists, 'it was not good policy for a trapper to let too many know where he intended to set his traps'—plews were valuable. Normally they worked upstream, because sign of the other trappers or of Indians might come downstream and because the country grew safer as you moved higher. With the incessant cognition of electronics, the trapper's mind was receiving and recording impressions all the time. He hunted beaver, read the country, recorded his route, watched for hostiles, and planned for all eventualities—in a simultaneous sentience.

The beaver had built his house of small branches, with five-inch plastering of mud for roof and outer walls, on the edge of the pool his dam had created. It was perhaps six feet high and twice as broad. In the middle of the earth floor was such a pool as young Red Water had seen.

There were in fact two such pools, sometimes more than two; they were the exits of the tunnels which had been dug down through the earth to the stream bed above the dam. There, weighted down with the mud and waterlogged snags, was the winter hoard of saplings and branches whose bark was the beaver's food. Before the Indians learned to use traps they were accustomed to hunt by blocking these tunnels, chopping through the roof of the house, and then digging out the beaver.

The white man set his traps at the natural runways of the beaver, just inside the water where a path came down from the bank or the dam or where the slide entered the pool. That was when he expected to take the beaver on its lawful occasions. Mostly, however, he baited the traps and set them in places favorable for attracting the beaver and for drowning him when caught. The bait was a musky secretion taken from the beaver's preputial glands. It was used straight or doctored with other odorous substances in whose efficacy the trapper believed. He called it 'medicine,' 'castoreum,' or the like and carried it in a plugged horn bottle at his belt. (It perfumed him, vocationally.) Selecting the proper place for his trap, he set it in the water of the proper depth and drove a stout, dry 'trap pole' through the ring at the end of the five-foot steel chain into the bank or bed of the stream. This was to keep the beaver from dragging the trap (which weighed at least five pounds) out on the ground and into the air, for if he did so he would escape by gnawing off the paw by which he had been caught. He was killed, that is, by drowning. Sometimes his struggles unmoored the trap but too late; in that event the pole or a separate 'float stick' that had been attached would show where the carcass was. When every other preparation had been made, the trapper smeared a little of the pungent castoreum on a twig or willow which he arched just above the surface directly over the trap's trigger. The scent attracted the beaver—a dog owner will think of his pet's behavior when there is a bitch in heat in the same block—and when he approached the bait stick he was caught by the foot.

All this was subject to infinite variations, the adaptation to circumstance that is a large part of skill. It was all conducted in the water too, for the man scent had to be eliminated. The trapper waded into the stream at a sufficient distance from the selected place, carrying the already set trap, and after he had sited and baited it he waded a sufficient distance before leaving the stream. He splashed water over his own trail and took many other precautions.

Normally the traps were raised at sunrise or before, in the dimness that was both most dangerous and most secure. A full-grown beaver weighs thirty to sixty pounds and the pelt a pound and a half or two pounds when finally prepared. The catch was usually skinned on the spot and the trapper, whose line was five or six traps, took the pelt and the medicine glands back to camp. (Camp was never in the same place two nights straight.) He usually took the tail too for it was considered a delicacy when charred in the fire to remove the horny skin and then boiled. At camp the pelt had to be rough-cured. The flesh side was scraped free of tissue and sinew and then the hide was stretched on a frame of willow like an embroidery hoop and given the sun for a day or two. When it was dry it was folded with the fur inside and marked with the trapper's or the company's symbol. When 'packs' were made they were pressed into compact bales of about a hundred pounds at the posts by machines made for the purpose or at rendezvous by rigged-up contraptions of logs and stones.

All this was work for the swampers or the camp-tenders in company brigades. The free trapper had to prepare his plew himself unless he had a wife or there was a village of Indians at hand where he could hire a squaw. Care of the catch from here on was like everything else in mountain life, an individual responsibility. It involved keeping the pelts dry, drying them promptly if they got wet, and perpetually safeguarding them on the trail. At lower altitudes they had to be periodically beaten and aired but there were no moths in the mountains.

Trapping was complicated by high waters during the spring hunt, which produced the best furs. Spring or fall it was conducted in the water of mountain streams, and the mountain man's occupational disease was rheumatism. His joints creaked and he will be seen at dawn limbering his legs and arms at the fire. The water got colder as the days shortened and the blue of canyon shadows deepened. Before the end of September there would be a dust of snow in the basins and mountain meadows. The brigades moved down to the bench lands and on toward the plains. Ice formed along the edges of even the swiftest streams and trapping would seldom last anywhere later than early November. Time to think of wintering.

SKILL DEVELOPS FROM controlled, corrected repetitions of an act for which one has some knack. Skill is a product of experience and criticism and intelligence. Analysis cannot much transcend those truisms. Between the amateur and the professional, between the duffer and the expert, between the novice and the veteran there is a difference not only in degree but in kind. The skillful man is, within the function of his skill, a different integration, a different nervous and muscular and psychological organization. He has specialized responses of great intricacy. His associative faculties have patterns of screening, acceptance and rejection, analysis and sifting, evaluation and selective adjustment much too complex for conscious direction. Yet as patterns of appraisal and adjustment exert their automatic and perhaps metabolic energy, they are accompanied by a conscious process fully as complex. A tennis player or a watchmaker or an airplane pilot is an automatism but he is also criticism and wisdom.

It is hardly too much to say that a mountain man's life was skill. He not only worked in the wilderness, he also lived there and he did so from sun to sun by the exercise of total skill. It was probably as intricate a skill as any ever developed by any way of working or living anywhere.

Certainly it was the most complex of the wilderness crafts practiced on this continent. The mountains, the aridity, the distances, and the climates imposed severities far greater than those laid on forest-runners, rivermen, or any other of our symbolic pioneers. Mountain craft developed out of the crafts which earlier pioneers had acquired and, like its predecessors, incorporated Indian crafts, but it had a unique integration of its own. It had specific crafts, technologies, theorems and rationales and rules of thumb, codes of operating procedure–but it was a pattern of total behavior.

Treatises could be written on the specific details; we lack space even for generalizations. Why do you follow the ridges into or out of unfamiliar country? What do you do for a companion who has collapsed from want of water while crossing a desert? How do you get meat when you find yourself without gunpowder in a country of barren game? What tribe of Indians made this trail, how many were in the band, what errand were they on, were they going to or coming back from it, how far from home were they, were their horses laden, how many horses did they have and why, how many squaws accompanied them, what mood were they in? Also, how old is the trail, where are those Indians now, and what does the product of these answers require of you? Prodigies of such sign-reading are recorded by impressed greenhorns, travelers, and army men, and the exercise of critical reference and deduction which they exhibit would seem prodigious if it were not routine. But reading formal sign, however impressive to Doctor Watson or Captain Frémont, is less impressive than the interpretation of observed circumstances too minute to be called sign. A branch floats down a stream–is this natural, or the work of animals, or of Indians or trappers? Another branch or a bush or even a pebble is out of place–why? On the limits of the plain, blurred by heat mirage, or against the gloom of distant cottonwoods, or across an angle of sky between branches or where hill and mountain meet, there is a tenth of a second of what may have been movement–did men or animal make it, and, if animals, why? Buffalo are moving downwind, an elk is in an unlikely place or posture, too many magpies are hollering, a wolf's howl is off key—what does it mean?

Such minutiae could be extended indefinitely. As the trapper's mind is dealing with them, it is simultaneously performing a still more complex judgment on the countryside, the route across it, and the weather. It is recording the immediate details in relation to the remembered and the forecast. A ten-mile traverse is in relation to a goal a hundred miles, or five hundred miles, away: there are economies of time, effort, comfort, and horseflesh on any of which success or even survival may depend. Modify the reading further, in relation to season, to Indians, to what has happened. Modify it again in relation to stream flow, storms past, storms indicated. Again in relation to the meat supply. To the state of the grass. To the equipment on hand . . . . You are two thousand miles from depots of supply and from help in time of trouble.

All this (with much more) is a continuous reference and checking along the margin or in the background of the trapper's consciousness while he practices his crafts as hunter, wrangler, furrier, freighter, tanner, cordwainer, smith, gunmaker, dowser, merchant. The result is a high-level integration of faculties. The mountain man had mastered his conditions—how well is apparent as soon as soldiers, goldseeker, or emigrants come into his country and suffer where he has lived comfortably and die where he has been in no danger. He had no faculties or intelligence that the soldier or the goldseeker lacked; he had none that you and I lack. He had only skill. A skill so effective that, living in an Indian country, he made a more successful adaptation to it than the Indian—and this without reference to his superior material equipment. There was no craft and no skill at which the mountain man did not come to excel the Indian. He saw, smelled, and heard just as far and no farther. But there is something after all in the laborious accretion that convolutes the forebrain and increases the cultural heritage, for he made more of it.

• • •

AS THE SNOW—and the game—came farther down the mountainsides, the trappers prepared for winter. Free trappers were welcome at the fixed posts, which would receive them up to the limit of accommodations and extend their courtesies to the overflow who had to camp near-by. This had the merits readily available supplies, a basic store of food in bitter weather, co-operation in hunting meat, and variegated companionship. It had disadvantages too; large horse herds were an even harder problem than small ones, large meat hunts required long expeditions, and the winter of the plains where the posts were located was more severe than that of the mountain basins. As the years passed trappers set up winter posts of their own. Jim Beckwourth built one at what is now Pueblo, Colorado, there came to be others in or near the Front Range, and a species of institutional wintering developed at them.

The commoner practice of free trappers and the invariable custom of the company brigades, however, was to winter in the mountains. This necessitated finding a favorable campsite. It must have as mild weather as possible, plenty of wood and forage, and abundant game. The answer was some sheltered valley head in the lee of prevailing winds, with wooded streams, a south slope so that the snow would blow away from the suncured bunch grass, preferably with wintering buffalo and with forested mountainsides where other game would be found. We have seen Bonneville, the RMF Company, and the American Fur Company wintering in such valleys along the Salmon and Bear River and in Cache Valley (Utah). Brown's Hole came to attract small parties and South Park became a kind of winter paradise—both are in Colorado. Jim Bridger eventually built his trading post on Black's Fork, the southwestern corner of Wyoming, in a basin where he had wintered with the RMF Company. Such valleys, which were frequently intervales, had gentler weather than the higher altitudes and the lower plains. Habitués of Sun Valley will understand why.

Cottonwoods or evergreen groves would shelter the stock during storms. The trappers built cabins or lived in tipis, for tipis were admirable winter dwellings. (They were admirable dwellings at any season.) These were sited with regard to sun and wind and water and might have accessory structures for storage. Bands or even villages of friendly Indians–Nez Perces, Flatheads, Snakes–were encouraged to winter with the whites or near-by. They and their horses increased the problems of supply but they were interesting neighbors, they were valuable for defense, and their women could be hired to do most of the winter work.

Much of this had to do with tailoring. We have seen that the mountain man preferred wool clothing when he could get it but probably he had little that was still serviceable when winter came. If he had worn skin breeches, he had staggered them at the knees and sewn on legs of blanketing which would not shrink intolerably when they dried. But now he or his wife or his customs tailor would have to make entire outfits, moccasins, leggings, breeches, shirts, caps, mittens, robes. Many skins, dressed free of hair, were used regularly: doe, buck, antelope, bighorn, elk, even rabbit skin. Each had its specific uses, advantages, and drawbacks. Robes, either with or without the hair, were made from many of the same skins and from such others as beaver (very expensive, of course), wolf, or even rockchuck. Buffalo hides had innumerable uses. The hides obtained in summer and fall hunts were tanned for tipis, bags, the carryalls called parfleches, containers of many kinds, rawhide in all its forms. But the robes used for winter wear, for bedclothes and bed covering, and for winter moccasins, were made of hides taken in the winter, when the hair was thickest. Moccasins were also made of many other skins, for many purposes, in many patterns. For winter they might be fur-lined like those just mentioned, or, if not, might be stuffed with loose hair or even leaves or sagebrush bark. Women's moccasins were more likely than men's to have knee-length leggings sewed to them. For both sexes the elaborately quilted or beaded moccasins displayed by museums were ceremonial or Sunday-best shoes rather than daily wear. The ordinary work shoe was made in quantity, for it was not a durable article. Trappers, who preferred to buy them but frequently had to make their own, did a large traffic in them with the squaws at a few cents per pair. Those of the Plains tribes usually had parfleche soles, for the unsoled ones of the forest tribes would not turn cactus.

For moccasins and the leggings which both Indians and trappers wore, usually to the hip, the best material was last year's tipi. New lodges were made annually—with much ceremony, by squaws who had ritualistic training and collected fees—and the skins of the old ones were saved for clothing. They had had a year's smoking from the daily fire and so dried smooth and without stretching. The squaws kept a stock of rolled skins of all kinds which had been tanned when taken. (Winter was the best time for tanning since cold and lack of sunlight would lengthen the process.)

Stormbound days and long evenings made it the best time for dressmaking too, and your wife and those of your Indian neighbors were forever busy with their rolled skins, awls, and sinews. (The various animal sinews, especially those of the buffalo, were the Indian's thread. Splitting them for size was a task of exquisite skill. Those taken from different parts of the body had different properties which gave them specific uses.) They made your garments, their own, and a surplus for trade. The squaws had been trained in sewing from early childhood and any museum will show the fineness of their work. This was also a time for embroidery and decoration. Beads, porcupine quills, various bird quills, grasses, paints, ermine tails, fringes of other fine furs, small animal and bird bones, bits of metal, bells, braided hair, various fleeces and feathers—such materials filled the squaw's workbasket which she had repacked at every move throughout the year. She worked in traditions of art and craft that were old and very rigid. Religious rituals were part of her task; so were certain social obligations to older women who had either taught her skills or sold her the proprietary right to use them. Some specialized tasks or some steps in ordinary ones might be forbidden her; these she would have to have performed by women who had the right, with accompanying fees and feasts. But she was a skilled artisan and a happy one. She sang, chattered, made jokes, and marriage never looked better to a bachelor than when he saw a pardner's squaw sewing.

Winter was a preserving season for women and to some extent trappers. For example, it was a good time to make pemmican, the best of all concentrated foods. The 'winter pemmican' of the literature, which is sometimes spoken of unfavorably, was made not in winter but following the fall hunt, when the weather was likely to be unsettled and thorough drying difficult, so that the product might turn sour. 'Summer pemmican,' the Grade A stuff, was made in late winter and early spring. The meat, almost but not quite exclusively buffalo meat, was first dried in the way always used by trappers and Indians whenever they had a surplus following a hunt. It was cut into slices and strips an inch or so thick, scored crisscross, and spread out on racks of cottonwood poles high enough to keep it from dogs, wolves, and vermin. Not so much the sun as the wind dried it and the process, which winter cold did not affect, took four or five days. It could be shortened to three days if during the first one a slow, smoky fire was maintained under the frame, and such smoking made the product sweeter and tastier. The result was the universal dried meat, jerky, or *charqui,* of the literature, a first-rate food in itself. It was always carried by trapping parties.

Pemmican, however, was in a class by itself. All the gristles and sinews that might be present in jerky were removed and the residue was pounded in a mortar or on a parfleche till it was pulverized. This powder was loosely packed in a parfleche bag, melted fat was poured over it, and the mouth of the bag was sewed up. Thus packed, pemmican would keep for years. It was a splendid high-energy food, a complete diet in itself.

It was also a great treat (some cynics dissenting), incomparably richer and more flavorsome than jerky. It could be eaten uncooked or fried, roasted, or boiled, by itself or in combination with anything you had on hand. The luxury article was 'berry pemmican,' into which pulverized dried fruits of any available kind had been mixed, most often wild cherries with their stones.

Fats were preserved separately. The boiled and refined 'tallow' that played an important part in the Canadian trade served all the uses of butter. Like pemmican, it was sewn up in bags of standard size and weight. The most abundant buffalo fat was that which lay along the back. When sun-dried it was a gourmet's delicacy. It was also slowly fire-dried, cut up into sticks, and wrapped, or it was dried after being boiled; in these forms it was a staple rather than a treat. Kidney fat, if not eaten raw, was dried in long slices or briefly boiled. Tribes which raised or bought corn used kidney fat in a favorite tidbit, softening it over the fire and then pounding it and the corn together in a mortar.

Squaws were good cooks and the Indian diet, which the wintering trapper took over entire when he had a wife or lived among Indians, was by no means sparse or monotonous as the books say, if the camp was in good country. Its basis was the pot of meat which was always stewing over the fire in the middle of the lodge and a portion of which was set before every visitor as soon as he entered. (Indians had no fixed hours for meals; they and the trappers ate when they were hungry.) This was replenished with whatever fresh-killed meat came in. Roasted and boiled, baked in kettles or the ground, other meat dishes were standard. All were flavored with herbs, roots, leaves, and grasses which the squaws dried and whose properties they knew. The edible roots already mentioned were prepared in various ways. Roots, leaves, and buds that made good salads could be found under the snow. In short, trappers and Indians lived high when food was abundant, and winter camps were pitched in places where it was expected to be abundant.

Protracted storms or the migration of game would produce short-ages. And hunting was a daily job. The boys ranged through the woods, hillsides, and plains, usually on snowshoes. If the snow was too soft or deep for horses, they had to carry their take on their backs. There were problems of keeping the surplus from wolves. If the meat could be hung in trees it was safe from them but not from animals that could climb. Russell tells of burying some under three feet of snow and burning gunpowder on top to add another deterrent to the man-scent, but it did not work. No device worked for very long.

Protecting the meat from large or small vermin was a constant problem, winter or summer, in camp or on the trail. From porcupines to grizzlies the entire fauna liked to have their meals killed for them, as the modern camper knows. The modern camper, however, seldom if ever is troubled by the most skillful of all thieves, the wolverine. This pest is not considered by the modern students to have any extraordinary animal intelligence. But they could not have convinced the mountain men. To them the 'carcajou' was literally demoniac: he had an infernal ancestry. He would even steal beavers from traps and he regularly made a bloody garbage of the winter trap line that was run for fine furs. No cache of meat was safe from him and he did not work on shares. Few ever saw him, so his supposed size varies in the annals. The painter, Alfred Miller, who claims to have seen one, makes him the size of a St. Bernard dog, which is too big, and adds that his body was shaped like a panther. Osborne Russell saw one at work. Russell had killed a couple of bighorns for meat. He took some cuts back to camp and hung the rest in a tree. Next morning he went back for it and found a wolverine at the foot of the tree. 'He had left nothing behind worth stopping for,' Russell says. 'All the traces of the sheep I could find were some tufts of hair scattered about the snow. I hunted around for some time but to no purpose. In the meantime the cautious thief was sitting on the snow at some distance, watching my movements as if he was confident I had no gun and could not find his meat and wished to aggravate me by his antics. He had made roads in every direction from the foot of the tree, dug holes in the snow in a hundred places, apparently to deceive me.'

Russell conceded that 'a wolverine had fooled a Yankee,' but half-breeds and voyageurs had a different explanation: Ruxton reports them as believing that the carcajou was 'a cross between the devil and a bear.' Ruxton's companion in Colorado, a Canadian, said that he had once fought with one for upwards of two hours and had 'fired a pouchful of balls into the animal's body, which spat them out as fast as they were shot in.' Later when Ruxton drew a bead on one the Canuck shouted so loud that he missed; in fact, he missed with both barrels of his rifle, and his companion refused to let him waste more powder. If he had shot fifty balls, 'he not scare a damn.'

SOME YEARS BEFORE Miles Goodyear established a species of ranch on the eventual site of Ogden, Utah, Osborne Russell's small party of trappers wintered there with some halfbreeds and some Snakes for neighbors. A Canadian who had a Flathead wife invited the bachelor Russell to join his lodge and Russell was glad to do so, for the woman was a good house-keeper. He instances their Christmas dinner. They had stewed elk and boiled deer meat (not 'venison,' Russell says, calling that a greenhorn's word). The Flathead had hoarded some sugar, which was rare, and some flour, which if it was wheat flour and not a meal made of roots, was price-less. She made cakes and a pudding, tricking out the latter with a sauce of dried berries. There were six gallons of coffee with the sweetenin' boiled into it and 'tin cups and pans to drink out of, large chips or pieces of bark supplying the places of plates. On being ready, the butcher knives were drawn and the eating commenced at the word given by the land-lady.' (Squaws would not eat till their men had finished.) Whites, breeds, and Snakes gorged themselves and fell to discussing 'the political affairs of the Rocky Mountains.' One Snake chief was losing his constituency and a brother would probably succeed him. This led to a critical discussion—by experts—of the fighting qualities of other Snakes, and on to their rivals among the neighboring Bannocks, Flatheads, Nez Perces, and Crows. This would introduce the stately autobiographies of the warriors here present. It was not only ritual but etiquette to recite your valorous deeds and the degrees and privileges they had earned for you. Dinner finished, the men smoked fraternally, then went out to celebrate the day by shooting at a mark.

The trapper who had a wife was most enviable in winter. A woman kept a lodge as neat as any farm kitchen. With snow banked deep around the skirt of the lodge, heavy skins over the entrance, and curtains running round the entire circumference inside, it was easily heated and free of drafts. The floor had been packed hard. Bed springs were willow frames, mattresses were buffalo robes, and there were robes and blankets for bedclothes. There were backrests of rawhide thongs and screens that could be used against either heat or draft. All one's possessions had their proper places and the orderliness that determined them had the usual overlay of ritual. Any squaw had too many relatives and too many friends and they visited her too often, filling the lodge with gabble till its proprietor protested. When there was no company your wife chattered continuously. She talked while she was cleaning your rifle, cutting and sewing a shirt, rubbing a skin smooth. Some of her talk would have raised blisters on an oak. Much of it rose from the black and steamy ferment of savage fears. It was full of dreams, tribal gossip, legends of prescient animals or demons or heroes who lived before we came out of the earth, the ancients, signs and portents and warnings and ghosts and voices, traditional proverbs and aphorisms supposed to contain the world's wisdom, and wisecracks that had been handed down the ages and may have grown a little thin by now, especially when attributed to magpies or grasshoppers. Nevertheless, it was woman's talk—under the peaks by firelight with the winter wind outside.

The ease of the winter camp might be broken by marauders, by prolonged storms, by the need of moving if forage or game should be exhausted. We have seen various brigades shifting to other valleys in midwinter, and that or any other move that led out of the sheltered places risked disaster in mountain winter. To travel at all in snow was so nearly impossible for horses and mules that only necessity justified the risk. The crust gashed their legs; a few miles of floundering to their bellies broke them down; the storms that swirled out of the peaks killed whole herds. The winter journeys of the annals, from camp to camp or from camp to Indian village, were by snowshoe and long expresses were by snowshoe and dog-sled. It was not uncommon for a brigade wintering 'on the other side' to send a midwinter report or a requisition to St. Louis. Black Harris was one specialist in winter travel. Such a party would consist of no more than two or three (Bill Sublette and Joe Meek in one instance) and a sledge loaded with robes and pemmican. It would travel through December, January, and February, in the awful cold of the peaks and the more awful cold of the plains.

The stories of winter desperation, however, are not of such business trips but of hunters getting lost, snowblinded, blizzard-bound, and eventually without gunpowder. They wandered till they starved or a skulking Blackfoot lifted their hair, when their friends would find their wolf-cleaned bones in the ultimate canyon next spring. Or else the compass needle in their cerebellum steadied to a course, the will that a blizzard could not extinguish kept pulsing, and, feeding every fourth day on winter buds exposed by a gale or on the remnant intestines of a jackrabbit from which they had scared a wolf away, they kept on till at last they crawled to the edge of a grove where the day's work party was stripping cottonwood bark for the horses.

Chapter 4

BROWNSKINS *and* BEAVER

From *Carry the Wind,* by Terry C. Johnston

The sequence of mountain man sagas that Terry Johnston began when he wrote *Carry the Wind* form a reading experience so engaging and illuminating that one feels privileged to have the opportunity to enjoy them all, page by page, volume by volume. Only *The Big Sky* by A. B. Guthrie, Jr., and *Mountain Man,* by Vardis Fisher, can stand with Johnston's trilogy, which focuses on the wannabe mountain man, young Josiah Paddock, and his mentor, Titus Bass, called Ol' Scratch, who is wise in the ways of the mountains. The three books, all in print in paperback, are *Carry the Wind, Borderlords,* and *One-Eyed Dream.* Johnston followed these classics with several other titles set in the mountains he describes with such power and passion.

• • •

"CROW CALL THIS'R TIME A Y'AR 'When the Ponies Grow Lean,'" Bass chattered in the cold, charcoal gray of predawn labors. Little light remained except from the waning bright moon of the night before. "Cold mother it can be, this time. Colder'n later on, it seems to a man, Guessin' it's 'cause by the middle a robe season this here child's got hisse'f use ta the queersome aches in my bones." Again and again he turned the stout limb in his hands as he shaved it clear of dried bark with his knife. Josiah, sitting beside Scratch on the frozen crust of earth within the midst of their baggage, looked up at Scratch now and then as the older man spoke on, watching the words come forth from Bass's lips accompanied by puffs of pale smoke that muffled the words in the bone-splitting cold. The older man raised his eyes from his work as he set the finished limb beside his leg in a pile of some half-dozen others and looked into the sky. "Take you a lookee there." He gestured for Josiah to gaze beyond his shoulder. "See them halo rings round the moon there?" He paused to watch Josiah's head drop and rise in affirmation. "When such get real thicklike, like the fog risin' off a beaver pond jest afore get-up, means a snow's comin' in, Josiah."

"Cold 'nough for it," Paddock replied as he set back to work on the limb across his lap.

"Sometimes, it can jest be too damned cold for it to be snowin'," Scratch responded. "Then a coon knows there won' be new snow for him to be fightin'." He paused while he leaned over to pick up the last of the limbs to be peeled. "All a man's gotta think 'bout then is keepin' 'live whilst he keeps his wits 'bout him." He set his knife to work peeling the thin bark from the aspen limb. In the ensuing silence every sound seemed magnified in the cold, still air, seemed suspended for detailed inspection before disappearing. "Son, grab you your rifle an' these here sticks." Bass rose from the ground as if his joints had become frozen from sitting. "I'll be takin' the traps. Let's be gettin' us these cold doin's outta the way now." The new skin over his wound was as taut as a stretched beaver plew but he was no longer bothered by pain.

The two men moved out from the edge of the trees onto the bottom of a gummy mire of grass that stretched across the small bowl where they had chosen to camp the day before. Josiah turned to look about him at the mountains rising around this tiny bowl. Against the paling gray blue of the predawn sky were dark outlines of the peaks in bold slashes of contrast, as though painted by an artist's brush. His attention was wrenched back to lifting one leg and putting it front of the other. Into the bottom they moved with their loads. Paddock readjusted the bundle of limbs tucked at his side beneath his arm. Scratch tugged at the heavy buffalo-hide sack that contained their combined treasure of steel traps. Through the frozen grass that stood like icy sentries snapped brutally downward with the weight of the sack, Bass struggled on with the load he was dragging. With each step the men took across the grass came a rhythmic staccato that accompanied the constant drone of the sack across the icy bottom. A few more steps and the ground was no longer merely spongy beneath their weight. The mire in this beaver marsh now became deeper and more yearning of sucking a man's moccasins from his feet. Each man planted a foot, then brought the trailing one up as the one in the lead broke through the thin crust of ice and sank into the muck of mud and grass. Occasionally a foot would stumble on a rock hidden beneath the icy cap glazed over the mire and the man would use it as firm footing for a single step before plunging back into the mud and cold of the freezing water that seeped from the ground with every succeeding step.

Josiah looked over at the older man, wondering if he would stop for a few minutes to rest. Looking nowhere but at the mire immediately before his next step, Bass continued on, unaware that Paddock had turned to look at him momentarily. Titus was intent on moving them to their sets quickly this morning before the sun caught them out. Paddock studied the intensity of the old face a moment more and decided to go on without a word. He sighed, glanced ahead where the dark gray of the stream bank stood out in the distance against the lighter gray of the mire, and sighed again, his lungs burning in the frigid air. He would continue with his own agonizing plodding. At least he was getting warmer now from his exertion. Still the air seemed to seep within the flaps of the capote. The chill bit at his ears as the air snaked into the hood of the blanket coat. He held the limbs tighter to his stomach and tried to pull his hand back farther into the long sleeve of the coat. Paddock's other hand brought the rifle up to his head; he attempted to pull the hood farther down over his brow. His toes struck the trap sack and he stumbled over the obstruction before stopping to turn around.

"Where you goin', young'un?" Scratch inquired crisply.

Josiah now pushed the hood back a little and realized the man had dropped the trap sack on the ground and it was over the sack he had stumbled. He turned his head to the side within the hood and saw they were near the stream bank. Cold and fatigued, Josiah had been heedless of direction and destination. Only of movement was he aware.

"Drop you them sticks now," Scratch commanded, and Paddock let them fall from his grasp. They fell with a faint clatter onto the trap sack and tumbled to the frozen ground. "You say you trapped afore?" he inquired of his young partner as he knelt to untie the drawstring at the top of the sack.

"Catched me one . . . some time ago." He brought the rifle across his chest and cradled it against his body while each hand sought a warm haven up the opposite sleeve.

"One?" Bass looked up at the man standing beside him. "What'd you use for bait, son?"

"Didn't have me no bait . . . "

"Sounds to the likes of it, " Scratch interrupted. "If'n you catched only one, you'd have no bait till you catched him. Wagh!" The word was a faint growl in the frozen air and seemed to hang between them for a moment. "This here nigger's been doin' the trappin' for the past moon since't we broke up outta Henry's Lake—time it be for Josiah Paddock to be bringin' beaver to bait. Freeze into it, boy." He brought a trap from the sack and set it on the frozen ground with a sharp clink. Pulling his hand from the metal, Scratch could feel the tug at his skin where flesh had become frozen to the trap.

For the past three weeks or more, since they had been riding north from the small mountain-valley lake where the wolf had been slain, Titus had insisted that only he and Asa go out trapping. Josiah was instructed to remain behind in camp with the plunder, ponies, and McAfferty's squaw. Bass had quietly commented when the younger man had protested being left one morning, "Son, it's a damned sight better to count your ponies' ribs–leavin' 'em in camp–than your ponies' tracks, if'n they get runned off by some red niggers." Their path north from the lake was taking them straight for the Three Forks of the Missouri River. Leaving a man in camp with the worldly possessions seemed a sensible precaution to Scratch. But to Josiah Paddock it was a blow to his young ego. It was as if Bass did not consider him competent to perform the labors of a trapper. He was left behind to perform the duties of a camp keeper and cook.

Day after day the moving camp was filled with the dull-red trophies of the trappers. The beaver hides were stretched on willow hoops until they gave the appearance of large round dollars. Flesh side up to expose the hide to the sun for drying, the beaver currency dotted the small camp each day the group was not moving farther north toward the British holdings. Paddock would watch the men return from their traps carrying the spoils of their labors. The dead animals were then piled unceremoniously for Josiah to skin and flesh before stretching them on the willow hoops he made while the two older men were away from camp. It had increasingly eaten at him not to be included in the hunt, having to sit behind with the squaw, who stayed bundled in her robes by the fire she continually played with during the daylight hours. Every morning when the men left camp she would rise and move into the forest, where he could hear her wretching and gagging as she vomited. He would watch her return and drink a meaty broth she kept warm by the fire before burying herself beneath the buffalo robes once more. It was a ritual painful to watch. Always he wondered why she never vomited those days they moved farther north on the trail of McAfferty's choosing. Only those mornings they set up camp to trap for a few days. Only then.

"Mind you, son," Scratch interrupted Josiah's thoughts, "the leaves ain't dropped yet from the trees. Getting' late, it is, for 'em to be droppin'. This'll l'arn you, so listen up. When them leaves drop early, your fall'll be a short one. But the winter to foller'll be none too bad. Howsomever, Josiah, when them leaves don' drop till late on, it tells a man of one thing: we gonna have us a rough winter ahead. Cold-ass doin's, for sure." Bass pushed one of the aspen limbs toward Josiah. "Go crack you the ice on the stream up next to the bank an' start makin' that lil' shelf I tol't you 'bout, where you'll set your trap."

Paddock scooted to the edge of the water and broke through the thin crust of ice with the broad point of the limb. He broke more and more of the frozen layer from the side of the stream and then set to carving out a shelf from the soil of the bank about a foot below the water line. His hands grew numb as they dipped beneath the icy liquid. He pulled them back out and pushed up the sleeves on both arms. Again the hands went back into the water to continue building the shelf as he heard the older man settle back on the frozen grass.

"'Member that rabbit you snare't up two night ago, son?" Bass continued to whisper, referring to the small animals they had been forced to snare in order to eat when game could not be found and when they feared firing their rifles if elk or deer could be tracked. "I pointed you out one a the critter's hind foots—all that fine heavy fur on the bottom of it— didn't tell you what I wanted you to look at it for, did I?" Scratch did not wait for an answer from the younger man. "Well, I didn'. Snowshoe rabbit like that 'un gets some heavy fur 'long the downside of his foots, 'nother sign for a man that's a cold winter comin' on. Jest 'minded me of that lookin' out to that beaver lodge over there, son." Titus nodded his head in its general direction as Josiah looked up from his numbing work. "Here on the north side a that lodge you can see them beavers' been addin' more an' more wood—more'n you see 'long that east or west sides. Man with his whits 'bout him takes that as sure sign from the beaver there's gonna be cold doin's in the mountains this y'ar. Yessir. Ma Nature takes care of her own, Josiah. It's only man what's gotta catch up an' pay heed to help she's given all other critters 'ceptin' him." Bass snuggled close against his rifle and was silent a few moments. He spoke again. "Lookin' back, Ol' Scratch 'members the dark squirrels taken 'em up lotta nuts early to the fall, too. Even seen 'em taken up green nuts. Ma tellin' 'em lil' critters got 'em a long, hard winter comin' on. Cold doin's for certain. More sign to that than there be sign in a squar's heart."

Paddock leaned away from the stream to straighten his cold back. He began to cough a little and put his hand over his mouth. Feeling as if something were in his chest needing to be brought up, he continued to force the cough until there was the feel of thick phlegm at the back of his throat. He turned his head away from Bass.

"Don' you spit, son!" Scratch snapped quietly, rising to a sitting position. "Don' you ever catch yourself spittin' round where a trap is bein' set." Josiah turned to look at him, feeling the mucous in the back of his throat choking him. "Jest swaller it hard now." He finally leaned back and relaxed the tone in his voice. "Less'n you jest gotta spit, then you can spit into the tail of your coat an' rub it in." Paddock swallowed hard once, then twice, grimacing with revulsion at the thick, syrupy mucous sliding down his throat. "Beaver smell that spit round your trap set, why you might well as taken a shit right here. Spit round a trap set an' you ain't gonna bring 'em to bait."

"Aww right," Josiah said, then choked a little on some remaining phlegm. He cleared his throat and swallowed hard a third time. "Aw right," he repeated, "am I ready to set the trap an' lay her down?"

"Look to be." Scratch said. "Lemme see you set the trap here."

Josiah selected one of the traps and stood over it, placing first one foot, then the other over the springs at either side of the jaws. He rocked back off the balls of his feet so that his weight was transferred from his heels to the two springs, which gradually gave way under pressure. Kneeling slowly, Paddock could now open the jaws with no restriction and set the trigger over one jaw before locking it in a notch on the pan arm. Carefully he brought his hands away from within the jaws, saw that the set was good, and rocked back onto the balls of his feet. He smiled within as he stood up.

"Here." Bass threw him a twig little more than a foot long. "Your bait stick. Put it there in your capote belt, grab you one a them stakes, an' you're ready to get in the water."

Josiah stuffed the small twig into his belt as instructed, then tucked one of the six-foot limbs beneath his arm and knelt to pick the readied trap up carefully in one hand. Stepping into the water around the edge of the carved-out shelf he felt the icy water bite first at his feet, then at his ankles and calves. Carefully he brought the trap below the water where he set it down upon the shelf and seated it firmly, the jaws yawning wide and menacingly. Beneath the water his right hand located the trap chain. Bringing it back up above the water Josiah slipped the ring at the end of the chain around the long dry limb. Now he backed up slowly until most of the five-foot chain had been played out. Here he sank the sharp end of the limb into the rocky bottom of the slow, dammed-up stream. Moving cautiously back toward the bank where the trap was set, Paddock looked up at Bass.

"You're ready for the beaver milk, son," Scratch instructed. "That be what the twig's for."

The young man put his right hand into the front of his capote and located the small vial of castoreum hanging from his belt. He brought it out and pulled the antler stopper from the horn container.

"Dip your twig in it," Bass continued.

Into the vial went the peeled end of the twig. When he brought it out the twig was covered with the smelly, brownish cream donated by a previous unfortunate beaver. After returning the antler stopper to the container, Josiah stuffed the vial back into his pouch hanging at his side over the coat. By now the smell of the castoreum was lifting to his nostrils. It nauseated him at first and he wrinkled up his nose. Then the odor recalled a fleeting memory of smearing the musky essence over his flesh to keep troublesome insects from biting. Finally it dawned upon him—this substance gave the mountain trappers their peculiar smell. These men trapped the beaver and smelled like them too, he thought.

"Stick 'er in the mud . . . there, jest up from your trap, Josiah." Bass interrupted. "That long twig'll mean you should catch the beaver on his back foot. Short one'll get the beaver by a foreleg. Long like that'un'll make the critter stand up to smell your bait. An' when he comes to take a sniff of it, on the end of the twig in the cut of the bank, a hind leg steps on the pan." Paddock sank the bait stick in the edge of the bank so the castoreum-coated end hung a few inches over the top of the water cleared of its thin crust of ice. "Beaver's a critter as gets hisse'f kilt wantin' to know what other beaver's come in on his staked-out country, you see. Smells him a strange critter in the area an' he's jest gotta find out whose settin' up lodge in his neck a the woods. Critter gets squampshus-like, but his wantin' to know gets the best of 'im. So he comes on up to take a sniff of your bait. Snap goes your trap on his leg an' he'll start divin' for the bottom with a big splash. That's when he pulls the chain down your set pole where the ring gets hooked on the notch we carved on the pole."

Josiah stepped out of the water and shook his legs free of the water that had not already turned to ice on his leggings in the cold air.

"Critter ain't got him a prayer's chance of gnawin' through your iron chain," Bass continued, "can't even gnaw through his leg without air for as long as it takes. He cain't come up for air with that ring locked on the bottom of the stream. Yep. Critter drowns then, an' jest waitin' for you is that pelt. Out there in the stream where no critters such as painter cats or coyotes'll get to him. When you come back to pull 'im up, you're hopin' he ain't pulled your set pole an' all, then got hiss'f to some air. Howsomever, he cain't last too long with that trap holdin' him down an' draggin' that pole. Might be you're a child as'll have to trail that beaver downstream for better'n a mile afore you find your stick. An' where you find you stick, you're always prayin' you're gonna find your beaver." Bass paused and pushed one of the traps toward Josiah with his foot. "You don' find your beaver, you don' find your trap. That's the true an' simple of it. An' mind you what them traps cost a nigger up here in the hills. You don't wanna never loose you a trap. Ever' one's worth the trouble it takes you to find it, certain sure that be. Here with these ponds an' lodges all round, you go losin' a trap means we gotta go drain these here critters' dams an' bust into theys lodges to get it back. I don' cotton to them doin's much, I don'. Not sayin' I ain't got the stomach for clubbin' beaver over the head—why, boy, you seen me set to it with that Injun, ain't you? I ain't one to be skeert of killin', Titus Bass ain't." He tapped momentarily on his rifle while he paused. "Jest, jest that them critters we come up here for—the critter ever'body's wantin' for furs back east—they jest like a lil' pet, they can be. Catch you a lil' one like I done afore, back to havin' to break up a beaver lodge, an' rub his lil' head like you would your own puppy dog. Why, that critter'll turn up his lil' head an' cry like a babe for you. Had me one I brung back to my camp once't—put it inside my coat an' carried it 'long with me for a few days whilst I was in that camp. Next to your best huntin' hound, a lil' beaver make you a good pet as any this here child knows of."

Paddock had set the jaws of a second trap and was kneeling to pick up another limb when Bass rose to his feet and tugged his blanket coat more tightly about him, knocking some slivers of ice from where he had lain in the grass.

"I be on the tramp back to camp, Josiah. Want you put down least a dozen of them sets afore you come back in. We'll see what bark you got to you." He began to move off a step, then turned around to whisper once more to the young man. "You got you shot an' powder, don' you, son?" Paddock patted his pouch for the older man to see. "Good," Scratch nodded. "You be quiet settin' your traps now, you hear? String 'em on downstream from here, but do it fast. Don' let the light catch you out. Try your damndest to be back to camp afore the sun creeps up on you. Don' like me the feel of this here country. There'd be brownskins about— no s'prise to me. Mind you we be close to the Three Forks now. Don' know why McAfferty's trappin' up here when he could be a nigger to trap the likes of the Uinty down south. Cold up here—so cold you go to feel your squar's breasties an' they feel like'n you're touchin' the nose on Ol' Man North hisse'f." Bass shook his head while looking at the ground, then raised his eyes to Josiah. "you're on your own, son. We'll be seein' the ha'r of the b'ar in you by sunup—you get through wadin' these'r streams. My bones feelin' rheumy already an' we ain't even halfsome into the season." He moved his hips from side to side. "See you back to camp, son." He left abruptly.

Josiah watched his form slowly disappear into the dim light, hearing the faint crunch and suck of each step through the marsh as he moved out of sight. He sighed with small relief at being alone, then nervously looked over each shoulder before setting off downstream as his partner had instructed. Winding his way around and between the willow hugging the stream bank, Josiah found a place for his second set. As he knelt at the edge of the water to begin chipping ice from the bank he remembered he had left his rifle some fifty yards back at the site of the first set. Paddock straightened up and sucked in a quick gasp of the brutally cold air. His heart racing, the young man began to weigh the odds of going back now to retrieve the weapon or finishing preparing this second trap. The rest of the traps and limbs were back there too, he thought. He would just hurry through this one, get it finished and in place before going back for the rifle, traps, and poles. The dull-gray fear that set his body to trembling slightly was passed off to the cold. Nervously he looked over each shoulder again to reassure himself he was not being watched. The second shelf was prepared and he turned to pick up the trap. There was a soft crunch downstream. Josiah froze with his hand on the trap, feeling himself drawing up inside as if to make himself all the smaller, all the less visible. The faint crunch that had drifted to his ears was not followed by another. His heart began to slow.

He turned slightly to pick the trap up, and placed it underwater. Reaching for the stout limb, he decided he would not enter the water here. Instead, he would cut short his time spent in this set by reaching out to jam the pole into the stream bottom from the bank. After slipping the ring of the trap chain over the pole, Josiah lay down on the bank with his chest suspended over the icy water and drove the pole into the muddy, rocky bottom with both hands. Now he realized he had suspended himself between the bank and the pole. Still gripping the limb, he tried to squirm backward to put more of his body and its weight on the edge of the bank. Firmly gripping the pole with his right hand, Josiah took the left from the limb and put it into the water. His palm found the bottom of the rocky stream and his shoulder muscles tensed. The right hand unwound from the pole and he pushed himself backward toward the shore with the left arm, squirming and wriggling with his lower body to assist him. Finally back on the bank, Josiah rose to his knees and shook the left arm, then tried to wring the wet blanket coat and his leather shirt of the cold water. It was already frozen.

Knocking his right hand against the wet left arm and rubbing the cold hand, he set off upstream. The distance seemed longer than that which he remembered traveling downstream from where he had left the traps and rifle. Against a clump of willow he could make out the dark mass that was the trap sack. There he stopped and looked around the frozen earth.

His rifle was not there. Putting his hand across his mouth to tug at his cheeks in fear and bewilderment, Josiah let out a low moan of despair. He dropped to his knees and nervously looked about him once more. Down on his hands he went to begin crawling along the bank, low sobs catching at the back of his throat.

"My . . . my rifle," he whimpered breathlessly. "Scratch come got it 'cause I didn' take it with me." He kept crawling back and forth along the bank near the trap sack. "My rifle . . . my rifle!" Sobbing, he finally stopped and felt near collapse. Clutching his face in both hands to muffle the despairing groans coming up from his throat, Josiah fell forward against the earth and felt the pain bite into his forearm. He lifted his head, blinking his eyes clear of the cold-bitten tears. Then numb fingers inadvertently touching the cause of his pain, he felt the familiar form of a rifle. Both hands clutched the weapon and brought it to his chest, where he cradled it tightly, passionately. Now he sobbed in relief. "I found you," he cried with muted words, caressing the rifle full-length with his hands. The flesh seemed warmed, at least not as numb now, being filled with his rifle.

He took one hand away and wiped his eyes, then his nostrils, and rose to his feet. Checking the frizzen, he found it still locked over the pan. The warmth of relief flooded him. Securing the weapon in the crook of his right elbow, Josiah knelt to pick up the remaining limbs and place them alongside the rifle. With his left hand around the top of the heavy trap sack, he rose and marched downstream once more.

By the time he had made eight sets, the young man was feeling fairly sure of himself regarding the trapper's craft. He had been running those things Scratch had told him around in his mind. Usually, the older man had instructed, a mountain trapper would place his traps in the darkening light of dusk and travel to them the following dawn, when he could skin his beaver out, flesh the hides, and await the coming of another dusk to reset the traps. But such a schedule, Bass had said, was not really necessary in country like this, "stinkin' thick with beavers." What with all the ponds and signs of immense beaver activity, a man had only to be careful of his sets and he could clear a whole stretch of some stream of its furry fortune. One word of warning Bass had given, however. There was a reason why the country crawled with beaver— Blackfeet. Trappers rarely came into this, the southern reaches of, Blackfoot country to wrest its treasure out from under the noses of the Pieds Noirs. In this neck of the woods, the beaver thrived with secure abandon. A man could make his set in the morning and pull his trophies up at dusk. If he was careful where he made his sets. If he kept his eyes open and his ears on the alert. If he paid attention to what the forest around him told those who would listen.

Chapter 5

WAH-TO-YAH

A MOUNTAIN MAN TALL TALE CLASSIC

From *Wah-to-Yah and the Taos Trail,*
By Lewis H. Garrard

Get ready for a tour de force of mountain man lingo. If you like hearing such talk as the mountain men shared around their campfires, you're in for a feast of tall tales worthy of the mouth-watering buffalo hump that no doubt accompanied their telling.

The mountain man doing the talking is John Hatcher, a hunter on the Santa Fe and Taos Trails who eventually, along with Kit Carson and thirty other men, drove a herd of sheep from New Mexico to California. Hatcher's conversation is recalled by young Lewis H. Garrard (1829–1887), in his incredible book on his 1846–47 western travels, *Wah-to-Yah and the Taos Trail,* first published in 1850.

In his introduction to a republished version of *Wah-to-Yah* by the University of Oklahoma Press in 1955, novelist A. B.

Guthrie, Jr., provides a whimsical translation of typical mountain man talk recorded by Garrard and by Ruxton in *Life in the
Far West* (see chapter 2).

"Well, hos! I'll dock off buffler, and then if thar's any meat
that 'runs' that can take the shine outen 'dog,' you can slide."

Translated by Guthrie: "Well, friend, I'll except buffalo, and
then if there's any meat afoot that surpasses dog, you're crazy!"

Another: "Hatch, old hos! Hyar's the coon as would like
to hear tell of the time you seed the old gentleman. You's the
one as savvys all 'bout them diggin's."

Guthrie's translation: "Hatch, old boy, I'd like to hear of
the time you saw the devil. You understand all about his place."

From time to time in the pages ahead, you may wish Mr.
Guthrie were along to continue translating, but, alas, you're on
your own.

●   ●   ●

NO MULES TO BE SEEN in the morning; Louy had been out an hour for
them; so, partaking of a cup of coffee, Hatcher and I started in search.

"Them Purblos have *câched* our cavyard, I 'spect; howsomever, mules
is mules, an' they *will* stray about–'specially when tired. You know that pass
was rough yesterday, an' we'd better look good–many's the time my
animals have strayed in the timber, and me a lookin' for 'em, a cussin' for
darned niggurs, all the Injuns atween the Heely [Gila] an' Bayou Salade."

By this time we were at a point of the mountain on either side of
which diverged a valley of gradual slope, bare of rocks and cedar and
carpeted with russet-brown grass, with small thickets of the smooth-
barked aspen studding the easy declinations–presenting an inviting

walk in comparison to the rugged, scoria-strewn mountainside up which we had just been laboring. On Hatcher's saying–"You take that pass, an' I'll take this [he started up the left one from our position], the cavyard's maybe gone up one or t'other–guess you'll find the trail of a rope, or some kind of 'sign.' If you do, shoot your rifle–this child's heerd it so often crack 'gainst buffler–an' Camanches too, wagh!–he knows the sound, an' he'll come an' help you."

A fatiguing walk of half an hour brought me to greater aspen groves and almost impenetrable cedar thickets. My close scrutiny for "sign" was, at length, rewarded, while examining a leaf deposit. The foot of a mule, lately sunk in the soft ground and a tiny print, not far distant, convinced me of being on the right trail.

In front, an isolated peak towered two hundred feet above, affording a good view of the contiguous small valleys; a tiresome clamber over stones and encounters with the bristling cactus brought me to the apex, where I fell carelessly down with momentary exhaustion of strength.

I espied the stray *caballada* below, in a sheltered oasis, quietly cropping the sweet grass–a grateful change from the scanty portion of corn at Taos; for it was scarce, and worth nine dollars the fanega. Untying the hobbles, I drove them in a trot down to camp, with shouts, first charging my rifle for Hatcher. Saddling up, we soon were wending our way.

As we left Taos, Bill Garmon went in. He was to stay one night and overtake us, so we expected him all day to clatter at full speed down the mountain behind us. At sundown, crossing a wide valley, we camped amid huge, detached rocks, in a bower of pine branches made by some vagrant *ranchero.*

The spiral smoke, turning in the twilight, rose from the brush fire through Louy's exertions; the *caballada,* in single file, slowly returned from water, followed by Hatcher, with gun on shoulder, whistling abstractedly, and through habit, searching the hills and the plain with his eye for game or foe; and I, by the fire, undid the leathern bag of *biscoche,* filled the little kettle from a bubbling rill, and, with butcher knife in hand, cut thin slices of beef along (not across) the grain, in most approved style, and laid them on a wisp of grass; for we had no plates or other superfluous kitchen furniture–the only articles requisite to a mountaineer's *cuisine* being a long knife and tin cup.

During the convenient disposition of the meat and coffee, Louy detected a horseman approaching at a lope, from the direction of Taos.

"Wagh! Bill Garmon!" ejaculated he.

"How are ye?" shouted Bill at the top of his voice, as far as he could be heard, at the same moment waving his old white-wool hat–"How are ye old fellers? lookee hyar," he spoke in a less audible tone, as he threw his leg off the saddle, and held up a black flask of *aguardiente,* "Hi, hi-i, hi, he-he, he-he-a, hay a hay [rung out a Bacchanal song]. Whooopee! horray for Taos an' arwerdenty, eh, old hos," said he to Hatcher.

"*Well* now, you is *some,* I swan. Do'ee hyar, this beaver went down to Taos without bringin' a pint of 'baldface,' as is only in his meatbag [patting his stomach]; howsomever, you have more'n enough for all; besides it's bad idée to bring *much* of the cussed stuff what a feller *has* to keep his eye skinned an' his ears picked for the Rapahoes, an' other Injun varmint; but, as you *have* it, old hos, this child doesn't refuse, 'specially from a *companyero!*"

"Now, hobble your cavyard," said Louy, relaxing in a smile at the liquor and calling Garmon's one mule a whole cavyard, "an' drink coffee with us–*you* is true grit, an' them' the sort as kin have everything 'on the prairie' as belongs to me."

"Yes!" pulling off the saddle and depositing it beside ours, in its proper place for the night, to serve as pillows and protection for his head–"Yes! I know that, without you telling it to me, Louy; you've been in the mountains too long, old feller, to have the meanness in you yet; it's 'rubbed out' beaver season outen mind"–time whereof the memory runneth not to the contrary.

Notwithstanding Cassio's eloquent soliloquy on "putting that in a man's mouth which stealeth away his brains," the *aguardiente* gurgled out, amid the stifled grunts occasioned by throwing the head too far back when the bottle was applied to the mouths of the jovial, yet quiet, group of mountaineers. Perchance a sweetened dram was wanted, and the pattering of the liquor on the bottom of the tin cup could be heard—a sharp click for the first few drops and in filling more confused and indistinct. With brown sugar fished from the open bag and stirred in with the broad butcher knife, it was tossed off with the hunter's toast of, "Luck, boys!" There was not enough to leave unpleasant effects. It put Hatcher in a story-telling and the rest of the group in a good-natured listening humor.

Hatcher was always full of stories of an amusing, serious, and often of a marvelous cast; and we easily persuaded him to recount a few scenes in his wayward, ever changing life. Though he frequently indulged in rough slang, he did not partake of the Western's unsubdued nature altogether. I have chosen to select the more strange parts of his conversations as being the more strikingly illustrative of mountain character. He, at times, for his own, as well as our, amusement, would yarn in the most approved voyageur's style, or tell the hardest story of sights in his range; in short, Hatcher was *au fait* in everything appertaining to the Far West; whether mimicking a Canadian Frenchman, cowing down a score of Mexicans in *fandango* row, "lifting" the "hair" of a Pawnee, playing poker for beaver at rendezvous, or trading a robe, or sitting, with grave face, in Indian council, to smoke the long pipe and discuss with the aborigines the many grievances to which they consider themselves subject by the innovations of the whites, or the rapaciousness and cruelties of their enemies of their own copper complexion.

"Hatch, old hos! hyar's the coon as would like to hear of the time you seed the old gentleman. You's the one as savvys[1] all 'bout them diggin's."

---

1   *Savvy*—Fr. *savoir*—Sp. *Sabe*—"to know."

"Well, Louy; sence you ask it, and as Garmon's *aguardiente is* good, I don't care ef I *do* tell that yarn; but it's mity long."

"What one is that?" asked Garmon.

"Why, the old beaver says as how he was in hell once–eh, Hatch?"

"Sartain! this old hos wasn't anywhar else–wagh!" replied Hatcher to Louy's doubting remark; "an' I tellee, it's me *kin* tell the yarn."

He kept the pipe in his mouth, the stem hard held between the teeth, using his hands and knife to cut from a solid plug of "Missouri manufactured" a fresh pipe of strong tobacco. His eyes were fast fixed on an imaginary object in the yellow-pine blaze, and his face indicated a concentration of thought to call back important items for the forthcoming incongruous story, attractive by reason of improbability–interesting the manner of delivery.

"Well!" taking a puff at his pipe to keep in fire, "it's me as had been to Fort William [Bent's Fort] to get powder, Galena, an' a few contraptions, one beginning of robe season. I stuck around, waitin' for my possibles, which Holt was fixin' for me. Only a small train was from the States, an' goods were high–two plews[2] a plug for bacca, three fur powder, an' so on. Jim Finch, as went under on the 'Divide,' told me thar was lots of beaver on the Purgatoire. Nobody knowed it; they think the creek's cleared. At the kanyon, three suns from the fort, I sot my traps. I was by myself; fur you know beaver's not to be trapped by two–they're shy as coyote as runs round camp to gnaw a rope, or steal an apishamore. I'll be darned if ten Injuns didn't come screechin' rite onter me. I cached–I *did*– an' the niggurs made for the prairie with my animals. I tellee, this hos was *fawché* [mad], but he kept dark fur an hour. I heerd a trampin' in the bushes, an' in breaks my little gray mule. Thinks I, them Rapahoes ain't smart; so I ties her to grass. But the Injuns had skeered the beaver, an' I

---

2 A *plew* is one beaver skin.

stays in camp, eatin' *par flêche* and lariat. Now I 'gan to feel wolfish and squeamish, an' somethin' was pullin' an' gnawin' at my innards, like a wolf in a trap. Jest then an idee struck me, that I'd been hyar afore, tradin' liquor to the Yutes.

"I looked round fur sign, and hurraw fur the mountains, if I didn't find the cache. An' now, if this hos hasn't kissed the rock as was pecked with his butcher knife to mark the place, he's ongrateful. Maybe the gravel wasn't scratched up from that cache *some!* an' *me,* as would have given my taps fur *'old bull,'* rolled in the awardenty—wagh!

"I was weaker an' a goat in the spring; but when the Touse was opened, I fell back, an' let it run in. In four swaller' 'cluded to pull up stakes fur the headwaters of Purgatoire for meat. I roped old Blue, tied on my traps, an' left.

"It used to be the best place in the mountains fur meat—me an' Bill Williams *has* made it *come*—but nothin' was in sight. Things looked mity strange, an' I wanted to make back track; 'but,' sez I, 'hyar I ar, an' doesn't turn, surely.'

"The bushes was scorched an' curled, an' the cedar was like fire had been put to it. The big brown rocks was covered with black smoke, an' the little drink in the bottom of the kanyon was dried up. We was now most under the old twin peaks of Wah-to-yah; the cold snow on top looked mity cool an' refreshin'.

"Somethin' was wrong; I must be shovin' backards, an' that afore long, or I'll go under; an' I jerked the rein, but I'll be doggone—an' it's true as there's meat a runnin'—Blue kept goin' forrad. I laid back, an' cussed an' kicked till I *saw blood,* sartain; an' I put out my hand fur my knife to kill the beast, but the Green River wouldn't come. I tellee some onvisible sperit had a paw thar, an' it's me as says it—bad 'medicine' it was that trappin' time.

"Loosin' my pistol—the one traded at 'Big Horn,' from Suckeree Tomblow, time I lost my Yute squaw—an' primin' my rifle, I swore to keep rite on; fur, after stayin' ten years that's past in these mountains, to be fooled this way wasn't the game fur me, no how.

"Well, we—I say 'we,' fur Blue *was* some—good as a man any day; I could talk to her, an' she'd turn her head as ef she onderstood me. Mules *are* knowin' critters—next thing to human. At a sharp corner, Blue snorted, an' turned her head, but couldn't go back. Thar, in front, was a level kany-on, with walls of black an' brown an' gray stone, an' stumps of burnt piny-on hung down ready to fall onter us; an', as we passed, the rocks and trees shook an' grated an' creaked. All at oncet Blue tucked tail, backed her ears, bowed her neck, an' hinnied rite out, a raring onto her hind legs, pawin' an' snickerin'. This hos doesn't see the cute of them notions; he's fur examinin', so I goes to jump off, to larn the fool; but I was stuck tight as ef tar was to the saddle. I took my gun—that ar iron [pointing to his rifle, leaning against a tree], an' pops Blue over the head, but she squealed an' dodged, all the time pawin'; but 'twasn't no use, an' I says. 'You didn't cost moren two blankets when you was traded from the Yutes, an' two blankets ain't worth moren six plews at Fort William, which comes to *dos pesos*[3] a pair, you consarned ugly picter—darn you, anyhow!' Jest then I heerd a laffin'. I looks up, an' two black critters—they wasn't human, sure, fur they had tails an' red coats (Injun cloth, like that traded to the Navy-hoes), edged with shiny white stuff, an' brass buttons.

"They kem forrad an' made two low bows. I felt fur my scalp knive (fur I thought they was 'proachin' to take me), but I couldn't use it—they were so *darned* polite.

"One of the devils said, with a grin an' bow, 'Good mornin', Mr. Hatcher?'

"'H——!' sez I, 'How do you know me? I swar *this* hos never saw you afore.'

---

3   *Dos pesos*—"two dollars"—Spanish term.

"'Oh! we've expected you a long time,' said the other, 'and we are quite happy to see you—we've known you ever since your arrival in the mountains.'

"I was gittin' sorter scared. I wanted a drop of arwerdenty mity bad, but the bottle was gone, an' I looked at them in astonishment, an' said—'the devil!'

"'Hush!' screamed one, 'you must not say that here—keep still, you will see him presently.'

"I felt streaked, an' cold sweat broke out all over me. I tried to say my prayers, as I used to at home when they made me turn in at night—

Now I lay me down to sleep—
Lan'lord fill the flowin' bowl.

"P'shaw! I'm off again, I can't say it; but if this child *could* have got off his animal, he'd tuk 'har' and gone the trail fur Purgatoire.

"All this time the long-tailed devils was leadin' my animal (an' me on top of her, the biggest fool dug out) up the same kanyon. The rocks on the sides was pecked as smooth as a beaver plew rubbed with the grain, an' the ground was covered with bits of cedar, like a cavyard of mules had been nippin' an' scatterin' 'em about. Overhead it was roofed; leastwise it was dark in thar, an' only a little light come through holes in the rock. I thought I knew whar we was, an' eeched awfully to talk, but I sot still an' didn't ax questions.

"Presently we were stopped by a dead wall—no opening anywhar. When the devils turned from me, I jerked my head around quick, but thar was no place to get out—the wall had growed up ahind us too. I was mad, an' I wasn't mad nuther; fur expected the time had come fur this child to go under. So I let my head fall onter my breast, an' I pulled the old wool hat over my eyes, an' thought for the last of the beaver I had trapped, an' the buffler as had took my G'lena pills in thar livers, an' the 'poker' an' 'euker' I'd played to rendevoo an' Fort William. I felt cumfortable as eatin' 'fat cow' to think I hadn't cheated anyone.

"All at once the kanyon got bright as day. I looked up, an' thar was a room with lights, an' people talkin' an' laffin', an' fiddles a screechin'. Dad an' the preacher to Wapakonnetta told me the fiddle was the Devil's invention; I believe it now.

"The little feller as has hold of my animal squeaked out—'Get off your mule, Mr. Hatcher!'

"'Get off!' sez I, for I was mad as a bull pecked with Camanche lances fur his disturbin' me, 'Get off? I have been trying to, ever sence I came in this infernal hole.'

"'You can do so now. Be quick, for the company is waitin',' sez he, piert-like.

"They all stopped talking' an' were lookin' rite at me. I felt riled. 'Darn your company. I've got to lose my scalp anyhow, an' no difference to me how soon—but to obleege ye'—so I slid off as easy as ef I'd never been stuck.

"A hunchback boy, with little gray eyes in his head, took old Blue away. I might never see her agin, an' I shouted—'Poor Blue! Good-bye Blue!'

"The young devil snickered; I turned around mity starn—'Stop your laffin' you hellcat—ef I am alone, I can take you,' an' grabs fur my knife to wade into his liver; but it was gone—gun, bullet pouch, an' pistol—like mules in a stampede.

"I stepped forrad with a big feller, with har frizzled out like an old buffler's just afore sheddin' time; an' the people jawin' worse 'an a cavyard of parokeets, stopped, while Frizzly shouted—

"'Mr. Hatcher, formerly of Wapakonnetta, latterly of the Rocky Mountains!'

"*Well,* thar I stood. Things was mity strange, an' every darned niggur on 'em looked so pleased like. To show 'em manners, I said—'How are ye!'

an' I went to bow, but chaw my last 'bacca ef I could, my breeches was so tight—the heat way back in the kanyon had shrunk them. They were too polite to notice it, an' I felt fur my knife to rip the doggone things, but recollecting the scalp taker was stolen, I straightens up an' bows my head. A kind-lookin' smallish old gentleman, with a black coat and briches, an' a bright, cute face, an' gold spectacles, walks up an' pressed my hand softly—

" 'How do you do, my dear friend? I have long expected you. You cannot imagine the pleasure it gives me to meet you at home. I have watched your peregrinations in the busy, tiresome world with much interest. Sit down, sit down; take a chair,' an' he handed me one.

"I squared myself on it, but a ten-pronged buck[4] wasn't done sucking when I last sot on a cheer, an' I squirmed awhile, oneasy as a gut-shot coyote. I jumps up, an' tells the gentleman them sort of 'state fixins,' didn't suit this beaver, an' he prefers the floor. I sets cross-legged like in camp as easy as eatin' *boudin*. I reached for my pipe—a feller's so used to it—but the devils in the kanyon had cached *it* too.

" 'You wish to smoke, Mr. Hatcher?—we will have cigars. Here!' he called to an imp near him, 'some cigars.'

"They was brought on a waiter, size of my bullet bag. I empties 'em in my hat, for good cigars ain't to be picked up on the peraira every day, but lookin' at the old man, I saw somethin' was wrong. To be polite, I ought to have taken but one.

" 'I beg pardon,' says I, scratchin' my old scalp, 'this hos didn't think— he's been so long in the mountains, he forgets civilized doins,' an' I shoves the hat to him.

" 'Never mind,' says he, wavin' his hand an' smilin' faintly, 'get others,' speakin' to the boy aside him.

---

4   A deer adds a prong to each succeeding year of his existence—hence a ten-pronged buck is ten years old.

"The old gentleman took one, and touched his finger to the end of my cigar—it smoked as ef fire had been sot to it.

"'Wagh! the devil!' screams I, drawin' back.

"'The same!' chimed in he, biting off the little end of his'n, an' bowin' an' spittin' it out—'the same, sir.'

"'The same! what?'

"'Why—the Devil.'

"'H——! this ain't the holler tree for this coo—I'll be makin' "medicine"'; so I offers my cigar to the sky, an' to the earth, like Injun.

"'You must not do that *here*—out upon such superstition,' says he, sharp-like.

"'Why?'

"'Don't ask so many questions—come with me,' risin' to his feet, an' walkin' off slow, a blowin' his cigar smoke over his shoulder in a long line, an' I gets alongside of him, 'I want to show you my establishment—did not expect to find this down here, eh?'

"My briches was stiff with the all-fired heat in the kanyon, an' my friend seein' it, said, 'Your breeches are tight; allow me to place my hand on them.'

"He rubbed his fingers up an' down once, an' by beaver they got as soft as when I traded them from the Pi Yutes on the Heely. (You mind, Louy, my Yute squaw; old Cutlips, her bos, came with us far as Sangry Christy gold mine. *She's* the squaw that dressed the skins.)

"I now felt as brave as a buffler in spring. The old man was so clever, an' I walked 'longside like a 'quaintance. We stopped afore a stone door, an' it opened without touchin'.

"'Hyar's damp powder an' no fire to dry it,' shouts I, stoppin'.

"'What's the matter—do you not wish to perambulate through my possessions?'

"'This hos doesn't savvy what the "human" for perambulate is; but I'll walk plum to the hottest fire in your settlement, if that's all you mean.'

"The place was hot, an' smelt bad of brimstone; but the darned screechin' *took* me. I walks up to t'other eend of the 'lodge,' an' steal my mule if thar wasn't Jake Beloo, as trapped with me to Brown's Hole! A lot of hellcats was a pullin' at his ears, an' a jumpin' on his shoulders, a swingin' themselves to the ground by his long hair. Some was runnin' hot irons in him, but when we came up, they went off in a corner laffin' and talkin' like wildcats' gibberish on a cold night.

"Poor Jake! he came to the bar, lookin' like a sick buffler in the eye. The bones stuck through the skin, an' his har was matted an' long–all over jest like a blind bull, an' white blisters spotted him, with water runnin' out of 'em. 'Hatch, old feller! *you* here, too?–how are ye? says he, in a faint-like voice, staggerin' an' catchin' on to the bar fur support–'I'm sorry to see you *here,* what did you–he raised his eyes to the old man standin' ahind me, who gave him *such* a look: he went howlin' an' foamin' at the mouth to the fur eend of the den, an' fell down rollin' over the damp stones. The devils, who was chucklin' by a furnis, whar was irons a heatin', approached easy, an' run one into his back. I jumped at 'em and hollered, 'You owdacious little hellpups, let him alone; ef my skulp taker was hyar, I'd make buzzard feed of your meat, an *par flêche* of your dogskins,' but they squeaked out to 'go to the devil."

" 'Wagh!' says I, 'ef I *ain't* pretty close to his lodge, I'm a niggur!'

"The old gentleman speaks up, 'Take care of yourself, Mr. Hatcher,' in a mity soft, kind voice; an' he smiled so calm an' devilish–it nigh on froze me. I thought ef the ground would open with a yairthquake an' take me in, I'd be much obleeged any how. Thinks I–you saint-forsaken, infernal hell-chief, how I'd like to stick my knife in your withered old breadbasket.

" 'Ah! my dear fellow, no use in tryin'–that is a *decided* impossibility'– I jumped ten feet. I swar, a 'medicine' man couldn't a heerd me, for my lips didn't move; an' how *he* knew is moren this hos *kin* tell.

" 'Evil communications corrupt good manners. But I see your nervous equilibrium is destroyed–come with me.'

"At t'other side, the old gentleman told me to reach down for a brass knob. I thought a trick was goin' to be played on me, an' I dodged.

"'Do not be afraid; turn it when you pull–steady there–that's it'–it came, an' a door, too. He walked in. I followed while the door shut of itself.

"'Mity good hinges!' sez I, 'Don't make a noise, an' go shut without slammin' an' cussen' 'em.'

"'Yes–yes! Some of my own importation; no! they were made here.'

"It was dark at first, but when the other door opened, thar was *too* much light. In another room was a table in the middle, with two bottles an' little glasses like them to the Saint Louy drink houses, only prettier. A soft, thick carpet was on the floor–an' a square glass lamp hung from the ceiling. I sat cross-legged on the floor, an' he on a sofy, his feet cocked on a cheer an' his tail quoiled under him, cumfortable as traders in a lodge. He hollered somethin' I couldn't make out, an' in comes two, black, crooked-shank devils, with a round bench on one leg an' a glass with cigars in it. They *vamoosed*, an' the old coon, inviting me to take a cigar, helps himself, an' rared his head back, while I sorter lays on the floor, an' we smoked an' talked.

"We was speakin' of the size of the apple Eve ate, an' I said thar were none but crabapples until we grafted them, but he replied, thar *was* good fruit until the flood. Then Noah was so hurried to git the yelaphants, pinchin bugs, an' sich varment aboard, he furgot good applesseed, until the water got knee-deep; so he jumps out, gathers a lot of sour crabs, crams 'em in his pockets, an' Shem pulled him with a ropy in the ark agin.

"I got ahead of him several times, an' he sez–'Do you *really* believe the preachers, with their smooth faces, upturned eyes, and whining cant?'

"'Sartainly I do! cause they're mity kind and good to the poor.'

"'Why I had no idea you were so ignorant–I assuredly expected more from so sensible a man as you.'

"'Now, look'ee hyar, this child isn't used to be abused to his own face–I–I tell 'ee it's mity hard to choke down–ef it ain't, skulp me!'

" 'Keep quiet, my young friend, suffer not your temper to gain the mastery; let patience have its perfect work. I beg your pardon sincerely–and so you believe the Bible, and permit the benighted preachers to gull you unsparingly. Come, now! What is the reason you imagine faith in the Bible is the work to take you to Heaven?'

" 'Well, don't *crowd* me an' I'll think a little–why, it's the oldest history anyhow; so they told me at home. I used to read it myself, old hos–this child did. It tells how the first man an' his squaw got hyar, an' the buffler, an' antelope, an' beaver, an' hosses, too. An' when I see it on the table, somethin' ahind my ribs thumps out: "Look, John, thar's a book you must be mighty respectful to," an' *somehow* I believe it's moren human, an I tell 'ee, it's agin natur to believe otherwise, wagh!'

"Another thing the old gentleman mentioned, I thought was pretty much the fact. When he said he fooled Eve an' *walked* about, I said it was a *snake* what deceived the ole 'oman.

" 'Nonsense! snake indeed! I can satisfactorily account for that–but why do think you so?'

" 'Because the big Bibles, with picters, has a snake quoiled in an apple tree, pokin' out his tongue at Adam's squaw.'

" 'P'shaw! the early inhabitants were so angry to think that Satan could deceive their first mother and entail so much misery on them that, at a meeting to which the principal men attended, they agreed to call me a serpent, because a serpent can insinuate himself so easily. When Moses compiled the different narratives of the earlier times in his five books, he wrote it so, too. It is typical, merely, of the wiles of the devil–my humble self'–an' the old coon bowed, 'and an error, it seems, into which the whole world, since Moses, have irretrievably fallen. But have we not been sitting long enough? Take a fresh cigar, an' we will walk. That's Purgatory[5] where

---

5   Hatcher was no Roman Catholic, but if he saw Purgatory, surely I should mention it.

your quondam friend, Jake Beloo, is. He will remain there a while longer, and, if you desire it, can go, though it cost much exertion to entice him here, and then only after he drank hard.'

"'I wish you would, sir. Jake's as good a companyero as ever trapped beaver or gnawed poor bull in spring, an' he treated his squaw as ef she was a white woman.'

"'For your sake, I will; we may see others of your acquaintance before leaving this,' sez he, sorter queer-like, as if to say–'no doubt of it.'

"The door of the room we had been talkin' in shut of its own accord. We stopped, an' he touchin' a spring in the wall, a trapdoor flew open, showin' a flight of steps. He went first, cautioning me not to slip on the dark sta'ars; but I shouted 'not to mind me, but thankee for tellin' it though.'

"We went down, an' down, an' down, till I 'gan to think the old cuss was goin' to get *me* safe, too, so I sung out 'Hello! which way, we must be mity nigh under Wah-to-yah, we've been goin' on so long?'

"'Yes!' sez he, much astonished, 'We're just under the twins. Why, turn and twist you ever so much, you loose not your reckoning.'

"'Not by a long chalk! This child had his bringin' up to Wapakon-netta, an' that's a fact.'

"From the bottom we went on in a dampish, dark sort of a passage, gloomingly lit up with one candle. The grease was runnin' down the block as had an auger hole bored in it for a candlestick, an' the long snuff to the eend was red, an' the blaze clung to it, as ef it hated to part company, an' turned black, an' smoked at the p'int in mournin'. The cold chills shook me, an' the old gentleman kept so still, the echo of my feet rolled back so hollow an' solemn. I wanted liquor mity bad–mity bad.

"Thar was noise smothered-like, an' some poor feller would cry out worse 'an Camanches chargin'. A door opened, and the old gentleman touchin' me on the back, I went in, an' he followed. It flew to, an' though I turned rite round, to look fur 'sign' to 'scape, ef the place got too hot, I couldn't find it.

" 'Wa-agh!' sez I.

" 'What now, are you dissatisfied?'

" 'Oh, no! I was just lookin' to see what sort of a lodge you have.'

" 'I understand perfectly, sir–be not afraid.'

"My eyes were blinded in the light, but rubbin' 'em, I saw two big snakes comin' at me, thar yaller an' blood-shot eyes shinin' awfully, an' thar big red tongues dartin' back an' forad, like a painter's paw when he slaps it on a deer, an' thar wide jaws open, showin' long, slim, white fangs. On my right, four ugly animals jumped at me, an' rattled ther chains–I *swar,* ther heads were bigger an' a buffler's in summer.[6] The snakes hissed an' showed thar teeth, an' lashed thar tails, an' the dogs howled, an' growled, an' charged, an' the light from the furnis flashed out brighter an' brighter; an' above me, an' around me, a hundred devils yelled, an' laffed, an' swore, an' spit, an' snapped ther bony fingers in my face, an' leaped up to the ceiling into the black, long spiderwebs, an' rode on the spiders bigger an' a powderhorn, an' jumped off onter my head. Then they all formed in line, an' marched, an' hooted, an' yelled; an when the snakes jined the percession, the devils leaped on thar backs an' rode. Then some smaller ones rocked up an' down on springin' boards, an' when the snakes kem opposite, darted way up in the room an' dived down in their mouths, screechin' like so many Pawnees for sculps. When the snakes was in front of us, the little devils came to the eend of the snakes' tongues, laffin, an' dancin', an' singin' like eediuts. Then the big dogs jumped clean over us, growlin' louder 'an a cavyard of grisly b'ar, an' the devils holdin' on to thar tails flopped over my head, screamin'–'We've got you–we've got you at last!'

"I couldn't stand it no longer, an' shuttin' my eyes, I yelled rite out, an' groaned.

---

6   A buffalo being divested of hair in the hot season, his head looks larger at that period.

" 'Be not alarmed,' and my friend drew his fingers along my head an' back, an' pulled a little narrow black flask from his pocket with–'Take some of this.'

"I swallered a few drops. It tasted sweetish an' bitterish–I don't exactly *savvy* how, but soon as it *was* down, I jumped up five times an' yelled–'Out of the way, you little ones, an' let me ride'; an' after runnin' longside, and climbin' up his slimy scales, I got straddle of a big snake, who turned his head around, blowin' his hot, sickenin' breath in my face. I waved my old wool hat, an' kickin' him in a fast run, sung out to the little devils to git up behind, an' off we all started, screechin' 'Hooraw fur Hell!' The old gentleman rolled over an' bent himself double with laffin,' till he putty nigh choked. We kept goin' faster an' faster till I got on to my feet (though the scales were mity slippery) an' danced Injun, an' whooped louder than 'em all.

"All at once, the old gentleman stoped laffin', pulled his spectacles down on his nose an' said–'Mr. Hatcher, we had better go now,' an' then he spoke somethin' I couldn't make out, an' the animals all stood still; I slid off, an' the little hellcats a pinchin' my ears, an' pullin' my beard, went off squeakin'. Then they all formed in halfmoon afore us–the snakes on ther tails, with heads way up to the black cobwebby roof; the dogs rared on thar hind feet, an' the little devils hangin' eveywhar. Then they all roared, an' hissed, an' screeched seven times, an' wheelin' off, disappeared, just as the light went out, leaving us in the dark.

" 'Mr. Hatcher,' sez the old gentleman agin, movin' off, 'you will please amuse yourself until I return'; but seein' me look wild, 'You have seen too much of me to feel alarmed for your own safety. Take this imp for a guide, an' if he is impertinent, *put him through;* and, for fear the exhibitions may overcome your nerves, imbibe a portion of this cordial,' which I did, an' everything danced afore my eyes, an' I wasn't a bit scairt.

"I started fur a red light as came through the crack of a door, a stumblin' over a three-legged stool, an' pitchin' my last cigar stump to one of the dogs chained to the wall, who ketched it in his mouth. When the door was opened by my guide, I saw a big blaze like a peraira on fire—red and gloomy; an' big black smoke was curlin', an' twistin', an' shootin', an' spreadin', and the flames a licking the walls, goin' up to a pint, and breakin' into a wide blaze, with white an' green ends. Thar was bells a tollin', an' chains a clinkin', an' mad howls an' screams; but the old gentleman's 'medicine' made me feel as independent as a trapper with his animals feedin' round him, two pack of beaver in camp, with traps sot fur more.

"Close to the hot place was a lot of merry devils laffin' an shoutin' with an' old pack of greasy cards—it minded me of them we played with to rendezvoo—shufflin' 'em to 'Devil's Dream,' an' 'Money Musk'; then they 'ud deal in slow time, with 'Dead March in Saul,' whistlin' as solemn as medicine men. Then they broke out of a sudden with 'Paddy O'Rafferty,' which made this hos move about in his moccasins so lively, one of them as was playin' looked up an' sed—'Mr. Hatcher, won't you take a hand—make way, boys, fur the gentleman.'

"Down I sot amongst 'em, but stepped on the little feller's tail, who had been leadin' the Irish jig. He hollered till I got off it—'Owch! but it's on my tail ye are!'

"'Pardon,' sez I, 'but you're an Irishman!'

"'No, indeed! I'm a hellimp, he! he! who-oop! I'm a hellimp,' an' he laffed an' pulled my beard, an' screeched till the rest threatened to choke him ef he didn't stop.

"'What's trumps?' sez I, 'an' whose deal?'

"'Here is my place,' sez one, 'I'm tired playin'; take a horn,' handing me a black bottle, 'the game's poker, an' it's your deal next—there's a bigger game of poker on hand,' an' pickin' up an iron rod heatin' in the fire, he pinched a miserable burnin' feller ahind the bars, who cussed him an' run way in the blaze outen reach.

"I thought I was *great* at poker by the way I took the plews an' traps from the boys to rendezvoo, but hyar the slick devils beat me without half tryin'. When they slapped sown a bully pair, they 'ud screech an' laff worse 'an fellers on a spree. Sez one–'Mr. Hatcher, I recon you're a hos at poker away to your country, but you can't shine down here–you are nowhar'. That feller lookin' at us through the bars was a preacher up to the world. When we first got him, he was *all-fired* hot and thirsty. We would dip our fingers in water an' let it run in his mouth to get him to teach us the best tricks–he'a trump–he would stand an' stamp the hot coals, and dance up and down, while he told us his experience. Whoopee! how we would laugh! He has delivered two long sermons of a Sunday and played poker at night on fip antes with the deacons for the money bagged that day; and, when he was in debt, he exhorted the congregation to give more fur the poor heathen in a foreign land, a dying and losing their souls for the want of a little money to send 'em a gospel preacher–that the poor heathen 'ud be damned to eternal fire ef they *didn't* make up the dough. The gentleman as showed you around–Old Sate, we call him–had his eye on the preacher for a long time. When we got him, we had a barrel of liquor and carried him around on our shoulders until tired of the fun, and then threw him in the furnace yonder. We call him "Poke," for that was his favorite game. Oh, Poke!' shouted my friend, 'come here; thar's a gentleman wishes you–we'll give you five drops of water, an' that's more than your old skin's worth.'

"He came close, an' though his face was poor an' all scratched, an' his har swinged mity nigh off, 'make meat' of this child if it wasn't old Cormon as used to preach to the Wapakonnetta settlement! Many a time this coon's har's stood on eend when he preached about t'other world. He came close, an' I could see the chains tied on his wrists, whar they had worn to the bone, showin' the raw meat an' dried and runnin' blood. He looked a darn sight worse an' ef Camanches had skulped him.

"'Hello! old coon,' sez I, 'we're both in that awful place you talked so much about, but I ain't so bad off as you, yet. This young gentleman,' pointing to the devil who told me of his doins–'this young gentleman has been tellin' me how you took the money you made us throw in on Sunday.'

"'Yes,' sez he, 'ef I had only acted as I told others to do, I would not have been here scorching for ever and ever—water! water! John, my son, fur my sake, a little water.'

"Just then a little rascal stuck a hot iron in him, an' off he ran in the flames, caching on the cool side of a big chunk of fire, a lookin' at us fur water; but I cared no more fur him than the Pawnee whose topknot was tucked in my belt fur stealin' my cavyard to the Coon Creeks; an' I sez—

"'This hos doesn't give a *cuss* fur you; you're a sneakin' hypercrite; you deserve all you've got an' more too—an', lookee hyar, old boy, it's me as says so.'

"I strayed off a piece, pretendin' to get cool; but this coon 'gan to git *scairt,* an' that's a fact, fur the devils carried Cormon till they got tired of *him;* 'an',' sez I to myself, 'an' *hain't* they been doin' me the same way? I'll *cache*—I will—fur I'm not overly good, specially since I came to the mountains. Wagh! but this beaver must be movin' fur deep water, if that's the way your stick floats' [a floating stick attached to the chain marks the spot of the submerged beaver trap].

"Well now, this child felt sorter queer, so he santers 'long slowly, till he saw an' open place in the rock; not mindin' the imp who was drinkin' away like trappers on a bust. It was so dark thar, I felt my way mity still (fur I was afraid they 'ud be after me); I got almost to a streak of light, when thar was sich a rumpus back in the cave as give me the trimbles. Doors was slammin', dogs growlin' an' rattlin' thar chains, an' the devils screamin'. They come a chargin'. The snakes was hissin' sharp an' wiry; the beasts howled out long an' mournful; an' thunder rolled up overhead, an' the imps was yellin' an' screechin' like mad.

"'It's time to break fur timber, sure,' and I run as ef a wounded buffler was raisin' my shirt with his horns. The place was damp, an' in the narrow rock, lizards an' vipers an' copperheads jumped out at me, an' clum on my legs, but I stompt an' shook 'em off. Owls, too, flopped thar wings in my face, an' hooted at me, an' fire blazed out an' lit the place up, an' brimstone smoke came nigh on chokin' me. Lookin' back, the whole cavyard of hell was comin', an' devils on devils, nothin' but devils, filled the hole.

"I threw down my hat to run faster, an' then jerked off my old blanket, but still they was gainin'. I made one jump clean out of my moccasins. The big snake on front was closer an' closer, with his head drawed back to strike; then a helldog raked up nearly 'long side, pantin' an' blowin' with slobber runnin' outen his mouth, an' a lot of devils hangin' on to him, was cussin' me an' screechin' I strained every jint, but no use, they still gained—not fast—but gainin' they was. I jumped an' swore, an' leaned down, an' flung out my hands, but the dogs was nearer every time, an' the horrid yellin' an' hissin' way back, grew louder an' louder. At last, a prayer mother used to make me say, I hadn't thought of fur twenty year or more, came rite afore me clear as a powderhorn. I kept runnin' an' sayin' it, an' the niggurs held back a little. I gained some on them—Wagh! I stopped repeatin', to get breath, an' the foremost dog made such a lunge at me, I forgot it. Turnin' up my eyes, thar was the old gentleman lookin' at me, an' keepin' alongside without walkin'. His face wasn't more than two feet off, an' his eyes was fixed steady, an' calm an' devilish. I screamed rite out. I shut my eyes, but he was thar, too. I howled an' spit an' hit at it, but couldn't git the darned face away. A dog ketched hold of my shirt with his fangs, an' two devils, jumpin' on me, caught me by the throat, a tryin' to choke me. While I was pullin' 'em off, I fell down, with about thirty-five of the infernal things, an' the dogs an' the slimy snakes a top of me, a mashin' an' taren' me. I bit big pieces out of them, an' bit an' bit again, an' scratched an' gouged. When I was most give out, I heerd the Pawnee skulp yell, an' use my rifle fur a pokin' stick, ef in didn't charge a party of the best boys in the mountains. *They* slayed the devils right an' left, an' sot 'em runnin' like goats, but this hos was so weak fightin', he fainted away. When I come to, we was on the Purgatoire, just whar I found the liquor, an' my companyeros was slappin' thar wet hats in my face to bring me to. Round whar I was layin', the grass was pulled up an' the ground dug with my knife, and the bottle, cached when I traded with the Yutes, was smashed to flinder 'gainst a tree.

"'Why, what on airth, Hatcher, have ye bin doin' hyar? You was a kickin' an' taren' up the grass, an' yellin' as ef yer 'har' was taken. Why, old hos, this coon don't *savvy* them hifelutin' notions, he doesn't!'

"'The devils from hell was after me,' sez I mity gruff, 'This hos has seen moren ever he wants to agin.'

"They tried to git me outen the notion, but I swar, an' I'll stick to it, this child saw a heap more of the all-fired place than he wants to agin; an ef it ain't fact, he doesn't know 'fat cow' from 'poor bull'—Wagh!"

So ended Hatcher's tale of Wah-to-yah, or what the mountaineer saw when he had the *mania potu.*

Chapter 6

CAPTURED *by the* BLACKFEET

From *Mountain Man,* by Vardis Fisher

Vardis Fisher's *Mountain Man* sits on a shelf in my modest library directly alongside A. B. Guthrie Jr.'s *The Big Sky* and Terry Johnston's trilogy (see chapter 4). For my personal taste, these five novels belong at the top of the pyramid in mountain man fiction.

Mountain Man is the story of Sam Minard, a giant of a man in both physical stature and character. His encounters with the dreaded Pied Noir, the Blackfeet, fill the book with dramatic situations of incredible force. Fisher's prose spares no detail in the action, but it also paints the nature and landscape of the region with vivid sensitivity.

Mountain Man was one source of material for the popular film *Jeremiah Johnson,* starring Robert Redford.

In this excerpt from *Mountain Man,* Sam finds himself in a predicament of the sort that "rubbed out" many of his trapper peers. His only chance for survival is to make a seemingly impossible escape and find his way through the frozen wilderness to the cabin of a homesteader named Kate, whom he had befriended earlier.

Good reading about the days of the mountain men and their Rocky Mountain adventures just doesn't get any better than this.

●   ●   ●

AT THE BIG BEND of the Musselshell he took from a cache the keg of rum, the kettle, and a few other things, and then sat on the bay and looked west and south, wondering of he should take the safer way over the Teton Pass or the more dangerous way by Three Forks. Storm determined it. It was snowing this morning, and all the signs said it would be an early and a long hard winter. If he went by the pass it would take twice as long and he might find himself snowbound up against the Tetons or the southern Bitterroots. By far the easier route was by Three Forks, where John Colter had made his incredible run to freedom; where the Indian girl who went west with Lewis and Clark had been captured as a child; and where beaver were thickest in all the Western land. It was there also that more than one trapper had fallen under the arrows or bullets of the Blackfeet.

It was a foolhardy decision but mountain men were foolhardy men.

For a hundred and fifty miles, with snow falling on him most of the way, he went up the river, and then followed a creek through a mountain pass. He was leaving a trail that a blind Indian could follow. Straight ahead now was the Missouri; on coming to it he went up it to the Three Forks, the junction of the Gallatin, Madison, and Jefferson rivers. He knew this area fairly well. Lewis and Clark had gone up the Jefferson River, which came down from the west, but Sam planned to go south-west and cut across to a group of hot springs in dense forest. The snow was almost a foot deep now and still falling, but he had seen no tracks of redmen, only of wild beasts, and he had no sense of danger. Just the same he hastened out of the Three Forks area, eager to lose his path in forest-ed mountains. He might have made it if pity had not overthrown pru-dence. He had gone up the Beaverhead, past a mountainous mass on his left, and hot springs that would be known as the Potosi, and then ridden straight west to a group of hot springs deep in magnificent forest, when suddenly he came in view of a mountain tragedy that stopped him.

Two great bulls of the wapiti or elk family had been fighting and had got their horns locked, and a pack of wolves was circling them, while turkey buzzards sat in treetops, looking down. Sam saw at once that it had been a terrific fight; the earth was torn and the brush trampled over half an acre. The two bulls looked evenly matched, each with a hand-some set of antlers, and beautifully muscled shoulders and neck. Sam had sometimes wondered why the Creator had put such an immense growth of bone on the head of elk and moose; their antlers were about all their necks could carry, much less handle on a run through heavy timber, or in a fight with another bull. It was not an uncommon thing to find bulls dead with horns entangled in dense underbrush, or interlocked, as now. These two had their rumps up in the air to the full length of their hind legs but both were on their knees and unable to move their heads at all. Any moment the wolves would have moved in to hamstring them and bring them down, and feast in their bellies while they still breathed. If Sam had found one bull dead and the other bugling over him he would have thought it all right, but to find two magnificent warriors unable to continue their fight, who deeply wanted to, was such an ironic miscar-riage of the divine plan that he was outraged. He would set them free if he could, so they could resume their fight.

Sam looked round him and listened. Thinking that he was many miles from danger, he secured his horses to a tree, hung his rifle from the saddlehorn, and walked about a hundred feet to the bulls. He went closer to them to study the interlocking of the antlers. The astonishing thing about it was that bulls were able to do it; Sam had heard men say that they had taken two antlered heads and tried for hours to get the horns inextricably locked. These two sets were so firmly and securely prisoners of one another that it looked to Sam as if he would have to cut through two or three bones to set them free. He had no saw but he had a hatchet. While considering the matter he walked around the two beasts, studying them with the practiced eye of one who knew the good points of a fighter. Yes indeed, they were well matched; he thought there was not thirty pounds' difference in their weight; their antlers had the same number of points and in clay banks had been honed to the same sharpness. They had been in a great battle, all right; their eyes were bloodshot, their chin whiskers were clotted with the stuff that fury had blown from their nostrils, and both had been savagely raked along ribs and flank. What a handsome pair they were! Sam patted them on their quivering hams and said, "Old fellers, I kallate I'll have to chop some of your horns off. It'll hurt just enough to make you fight better." He again studied the antlers. So absorbed by the drama that he had been thinking only of the two warriors, he glanced over toward the horses where his hatchet was and turned rigid, his eyes opening wide with amazement.

Seven Blackfeet braves had slipped soundlessly out of the forest and seven rifles were aimed at Sam's chest. Seven hideously painted redmen were holding the rifles, their black eyes glittering and gleaming with triumph and anticipation, for they were thinking of rum and ransom and the acclaim of the Blackfeet nation. Why in God's name, Sam wondered, hadn't he smelled them? It was because the odors of elk and battle had filled his nostrils. In the instant when he saw the seven guns aimed at his heart, at a distance of eighty feet, Sam had also seen a horde of red devils around his horses. He knew that if he moved toward the revolvers at his belt seven guns would explode.

Slowly he raised his hands.

He had turned gray with anger and chagrin. This was the first time in his adult life that he had been taken completely by surprise. A Blackfeet warrior over six feet tall, broad and well-muscled, with the headdress of a subchief, now lowered his gun and came forward. He came up to Sam, and gloating black eyes looked into enraged blue-gray eyes, as red hands took the knife from its sheath and unbuckled the revolver belt. Guns and knife were tossed behind him. The chief then hawked phlegm up his throat, and putting his face no more than twelve inches from Sam's and looking straight into his eyes, he exploded the mouthful into Sam's face. A tremor ran through the whiteman from head to feet. In that moment he could have killed the chief but in the next he would have fallen under the guns. Other warriors now came over from the horses, all painted for battle. They began to dance around their captive, in the writhing snakelike movements of which the red people were masters. Sam thought there were about sixty of them. He stood immobile, the saliva and mucus dripping from his brows and beard, his eyes cold with hate; he was fixing the chief's height and face in his mind, for he was already looking forward to vengeance.

After a few moments the chief put aside his dignity and joined the dance. It seemed that all these warriors had rifles and long knives and tomahawks. In a victorious writhing snake dance they went round and round Sam, their black eyes flashing their contempt at him; and Sam looked at them and considered his plight. Now and then one gave shrieks of delight and redoubled his frenzies; or one, and then a second and a third, would pause and aim their guns at Sam, or raise knife or tomahawk as though to hurl it. Sam stood with arms folded across his chest. In the way he looked at them he tried to express his scorn but these shrieking writhing killers were children, for whom the only contempt was their own. Not one of them had paid the slightest attention to the bulls with locked horns, or cared with what agonies or humiliation they died.

When at last the Indians made preparations to take their prisoner and depart they still paid no attention to the bulls. With loud angry curses and then signs Sam made them conscious of the two beasts; and they spat with contempt and said, with signs, that they had plenty of meat and would leave these to the wolves. Their insolence filled Sam with fresh rage. He was now less concerned for himself than for two helpless fighters who had a right to another chance—who in any case were too brave and too noble to die with wolves chewing into their bellies and with buzzards sitting on their horns. Speaking in tones that rang with anger and with angry signs, Sam told the chief that he should shoot the two bulls or chop a part of their horns off, or he should crawl off like a sick woman and die with the rabbits. After appearing to give the matter some thought the chief went to the beasts and looked at their horns. He shouted then to his warriors and several of them ran over to him; he spoke again, and they put muzzles at the base of the skulls and fired. The two bulls sank to the earth, locked together in death.

Sam had been hoping that the Indians would break open the keg of rum and drink it here but the wily chief had other plans. One plan was to humiliate and degrade the whiteman until he was delivered to the vengeance of the Crows. He would not be delivered with all possible dispatch; he would be taken north to the principal Blackfeet village, where the squaws could shriek round him and hurl dung and urine on him, and with the voices of ravens and magpies caw and gaggle and screech at him; and where the children, emulating their elders in ferocities and obscenities, could smear him with every foul thing they could find and shoot arrows through his hair, as he stood thonged and bound to a tree. Such thoughts were going through Sam's mind. He expected all that red cunning and ingenuity could devise, though he imagined that they would not seriously wound him, or starve him until he could not walk, if they expected to collect a huge ransom. It would be childlike contempts and indignities all day and all night.

These had begun when the chief exploded in his face. As soon as they had him manacled with stout leather ropes the other warriors vied with one another in heaping abuse and insult upon him, With leather thongs soaked in the hot waters of a spring they bound his hands together; and around the leather between his wrists was tied the end of a leather rope thirty feet long. A huge brave took the other end of the rope and made it secure to his saddle. Mounting his horse, he jerked the rope tight, and with pure devilment kept jerking it, after taking his position in the line. About half the warriors went ahead of Sam, about half behind, with the chief at the rear, riding Sam's bay and leading the packhorse. Now and then one of the redmen, eager to torment the captive, would leave his position in the line; and breaking off a green chokecherry branch, he would slash stinging blows across Sam's defenseless face. With blood running from brow or cheek Sam would look hard at the painted face, hoping to fix it in memory and telling himself that these were the fiends who had slaughtered the defenseless family of the mother on the Musselshell. He had the face of the chief in memory; the red varmint had a scar just under the left chin. If with God's help he could ever free himself he would hunt down that face. In some such manner as this, he supposed, they had taken Jesus to the hill; but Jesus had carried a great burden, under which he had fallen again and again; and when he fell they spat on him and kicked him and cursed him. The one who had slashed at Sam's face had been rebuked by the chief, but his boldness had given ideas to other braves; and hour after hour as Sam moved through heavy snowstorm one man after another dropped out of line to hawk and spit on him or hurl snow in his face or make murderous gestures at him. After a while the braves seemed to understand that it was all right to show their contempt if they did not wound him; and so by turns they hawked and spat and shrieked, or hurled snow, mud, and pine cones at his face. In their black eyes was a clear picture of what they wanted to do with him, for they knew not only that he was the Crow-killer but that he was the one who had scalped the four Blackfeet warriors and impaled their skulls on the stakes around the cabin.

It was the snowfall that worried Sam more than the insults. This storm looked like the real thing. If winter was already setting in and there was to be three or four feet of snow in the mountains in the next week or two, as there sometimes was this far north, what good would escape do him, with the snow too deep to wade through? It would be a dim future for him if it kept snowing, and they meanwhile weakened him with starvation and cold.

Why the red people so loved to torture their helpless captives was a riddle to all the mountain men. Sam thought it was because they were children. A lot of white children tortured things. Windy Bill said he could tell stories from childhood that would curdle the blood of a wolf. Sam had never heard of a whiteman who tortured a captive. Once when a wounded redman was singing his death song Sam had seen Tomahawk Jack pick up a stone to knock the helpess Indian on the head, and had heard Mick Boone let off a howl of rage as he struck the stone from Jack's hand. "Shoot him decent like, if you wanta!" Mick had roared. "He ain't no coyote." Sam had once seen a whiteman kick a wounded Indian in the belly and head; he had seen another scalp a redman while he was alive and conscious; but deliberate torture for torture's sake he thought he had never seen. Torture for the redman was as normal as beating their wives. The wolf ate his victim alive but he was not aware of that. The blowfly hatched its eggs in the open wounds of helpless beasts, and maggots swarmed through the guts of an animal before its pain-filled eyes closed in death. The shrike impaled on thorns the live babies of lark and thrush. The weasel and the stoat were ruthless killers. A horde of mosquitoes as thick as fog would suck so much blood from a deer or an elk that it would die of enervation; and sage ticks, bloated with blood until they were as large as a child's thumb, sometimes so completely covered an old beast that it seemed to be only a hair bag of huge gray warts. But the red people tortured for the pure hellish joy of seeing a helpless thing suffer unspeakable agonies. It was chiefly for this reason that mountain men loathed them, and killed them with as little emotion as they killed mosquitoes.

If he could have done it Sam would have struck all these warriors dead and ridden away with never a thought for them. As it was, his mind was on escape and vengeance. These redmen knew, all the red people knew, that if a mountain man was affronted, when helpless, and treated with derision, contempt, mockery, and filth, the mountain men would come together to avenge the wrong, and that the vengeance would be swift, merciless, and devastating. Sam had no doubt that this chief knew it. There could be only one thought in his mind, that this captive would never escape from the Blackfeet or from the Crows, and that mountain men would never know what became of him. The chief would take his captive to his people, so that they could gloat over him and see with their own eyes that he was not invincible after all–that he had been captured by the Bloods, mightiest of warriors, boldest and most fearless and most feared, and most envied of all fighting men on earth. Sam thought that he might be slapped, spat on, kicked, knocked down, but not severely injured; that some of the squaws might squat over him; that children might drag their filthy fingers through his hair and beard and pluck at his eyelids and threaten his privates; and that dogs of the village might howl into the heavens their eagerness to attack him. He would be given, once a day, a quart of foul soup, with ants and beetles and crickets in it, for the red people knew that some of their food made white people gag, and this kind they took delight in forcing on white captives. For as long as he was a prisoner that would be his fate. Then four hundred warriors in full war paint and regalia would march off with him in the direction of the Crow nation. On arriving at the border between the two nations they would encamp and kill a hundred buffalo, and feast and sing and dance, while scouts went forth to tell the old chief that his enemy was bound and helpless. For days the wildest and craftiest old men in the two nations would haggle and dispute over the size of the ransom. The Bloods would demand many kegs of rum, many rifles, a ton of ammunition, at least four hundred of their finest horses, and piles of their beaded buckskin. The Crows would give no more than a tithe of what was demanded. The Bloods knew that. They would ask for a hundred, hoping for fifty, prepared to settle for twenty, even ten, plus the privilege of watching the torture of Sam Minard.

Well, if it kept snowing this way they could not take him to the Crows before late Spring. If he was not able to escape he would have a long winter of starvation and cold and insults. Sam did not for a moment intend to be delivered to the Crows. He did not believe that the Creator would allow a man to be taken and tortured and killed for no reason but that he had sought vengeance for the murder of his wife and child. The holy book said that God claimed vengeance as His own. In Sam's book of life it was a law that man best served the divine plan who made a supreme effort to help himself.

Sam intended his effort to be supreme. Now and then, while trudging along, he looked at the elkskin that bound his wrists. If he got a good chance he could chew it in two but he knew that when he was not marching his hands would be bound behind him. To sever tough leather rope when his hands were behind him would be impossible, unless he could abrade it against something hard and sharp, such as stone, a split bone, or wood. During the nights he would have one guard, or possibly two. He would have to eat what they gave him to eat, no matter what it was, and preserve his strength as well as he could. He would do his best to sleep a good part of each night. He would act as if resigned to his fate. If only they would make camp and open the rum!

The day of his capture they moved without pause until almost midnight. All day long a heavy snow fell. While walking in the deep wide trail made by those ahead of him Sam tried to look through the storm to the mountains roundabout. By branches on trees he knew they were going north. He supposed that this war party would traverse mountain valleys and passes west of the Missouri until they came to the bend, where, he had heard, they had a large village on Sun River, and another over on the Marias. They might take him all the way to Canada but he doubted that they would, for if they did it would be a long journey to the Crows. By the time dusk fell he thought he had been walking about five hours. He was hungry. When his bound hands reached down to get snow for his thirst the savage on the horse ahead of him would jerk at the rope and try to shake the snow out of his hands. He was a mean critter, that one. Sam would clench the snow in his palms to hold it but the moment he moved hands toward his mouth, the watchful redskin would jerk at the rope with all his might. Sam said aloud to him, "I reckon I better fix your face in my mind, for somewhere, someday, we might have a huggin match." When a third or fourth time the Indian jerked the rope Sam in sudden rage swung his arms to the right and far back, hoping to break the Indian's grasp on the other end. But the other end was tied round the saddlehorn. To punish Sam, the Indian kept jerking at the rope, and rage in Sam grew to such violence that it took all his will to restrain a forward rush to seize and strangle his foe. I'd best calm down, he thought; for if he got weak and fell he would be dragged along like a dead coyote. His time would come: he refused to think of alternatives: his time would come, somewhere, and he would hear bones crack in this Indian's neck, and he would see the black eyes pop out of the skull, as though pushed from behind.

When at last at midnight the party made camp Sam was tied to a tree and put under guard. Snow was still falling. The snow where he was to stand, sit, or lie during the remainder of the night was about eighteen inches deep, a third of it new snow. If the storm broke away it would be a bitter night. He did not expect them to give him a blanket or a robe; he would be surprised if they gave him food. They would want to weaken him some. He would sit or lie by the tree all night, with the storm covering him over, and at daylight he would march again. The man assigned to guard him had a large robe (it looked to Sam like one of his own). On a part of which he sat, with the remainder up over his shoulders and head like a great furry cape. He had a rifle across his lap and a long knife at his waist. Under his fur tent he sat, immobile, sheltered, warm, his black eyes never leaving Sam's face, save now and then to glance at his hands. Sam wondered if this would be his only guard. If so, and if the man dozed, Sam could chew at the bonds. He knew that it would take his strong teeth an hour or two to chew through the tough wet leather, and he knew that two or three minutes would likely be all the time he would have. About fifty feet beyond him and the guard the party had pitched camp and built fires, but Sam could see no sign of rum-drinking. Possibly they would not drink until they came to the village.

About an hour after the first fire was built he saw a warrior coming toward him with something in his hands. As the redman drew near Sam saw that it was one of his own cups or one just like it, and that the cup was steaming. The Indian proffered the cup and Sam took it, knowing that this was his supper; and after the Indian had gone away he looked into the cup and sniffed at its steam. He didn't know what was in the cup but his grim humor imagined that it was a stew of coprophagous insects. There was almost a pint of it. All through the soup he could see what looked like hairs and small bugs, but with both hands he put the cup to his mouth and gulped the contents. Two or three small pieces of half-cooked flesh he chewed. Ten feet from him the guard ate his supper, his eyes fixed most of the time on Sam. Sam set the tin cup aside. With snow he washed the beard around his mouth.

Under him he felt the wetness of melting snow; his rump and thighs itched in wet leather. If he had to march day after day in deep snow-paths and eat only this thin slop he would need sleep, but how could a man sleep with melting snow under and over him? Before morning he would be chilled through. One thing was now plain to him: when a man faced torture and death he was forced to do some thinking. Looking up through the lovely swirling flakes, he told himself that if the Creator was all-mighty there would be justice in the world; and if that were so, there would be justice here, for him. He suspected that this was a childish thought but it comforted him. It comforted him to reach emotionally across the wintry desolation to the shack where Kate sat, talking to her children, with the snow falling white on her gray hair. While thinking of her, alone and half frozen and facing a bitter winter, there came a flash of recognition that made him pause in his breathing: in this war party were some of the braves who had slaughtered her family. The brute who had jerked the rope was one of them. They knew they had in their power the man who set the four Blackfeet heads on the stakes. What a struggle must be convulsing their wild savage souls, as they wavered between avarice and blood lust! How they would have loved to drink the whiteman's firewater, while with insane shrieks they hacked his flesh off in little gobbets and filled his wounds with the big red ants!

Having now, it seemed to him, seen his plight in clear terms, Sam faced the question whether greed or blood lust would win. He saw now all the more reason why his escape, if he were to make one, should be as early as possible. It would be fatal for him if they took him to one of the larger villages, because there the squaws would tear the floor out of hell and blood lust would win. He studied the guard before him, praying that the villain would fall asleep. The hope was dashed when about two in the morning two fresh guards came to relieve him. The crafty chief was taking no chances.

Of the two savages who now sat and faced him Sam could have said only that they had black hair. Each had a rifle across his lap, a knife at his waist. Sam knew there could be no escape this night. In two hours other guards would relieve these two, and at first gray of daylight he would march again. He probably would have to walk from daylight till dark, with no more than a cup or two of stinking soup to nourish him. The only thing to do was to try to sleep.

He pushed his legs out and lay back, his face turned to the golden bark of a yellow pine tree. He closed his eyes. Even if he could not sleep with snow melting under and over him he could relax and doze and that would be good. He thought an hour had passed when he felt a presence close to him. He smelled it. He smelled an Indian strong with the Blackfeet odor but he did not open his eyes and stare, as a greenhorn would have done. If a savage had come over, eager to thrust a knife into him, he would need in his black heart only the most trivial excuse. He could say to his chief that the paleface had opened his eyes and leapt at him, and in self-defense he had struck. Telling himself as a warning that the redman was emotional, high-strung, impulsive, Sam allowed nothing in his face and posture to change, as a guard, drawn knife in hand, bent over him and studied his face. In his mind Sam had the picture. He could have leapt with his incredible speed and even with bound hands he could have broken the man's neck, but that would only have brought on slow torture and death. There was nothing to do but pretend to sleep and trust in a Being whose first law was justice . . . .

Sam would have said that the redskin bent over him for at least five minutes. Then the rancid odor went away. But even then Sam did not open his eyes or stir. The snow had been melting on his eyelids and face, and his eyes and face were wet. About four o'clock he actually sank into sleep, and slept until he heard the first movements at daylight. Chilled through and half frozen, he struggled to his feet and tried to shake moisture from his leather clothing. It was plain to him now that if he were to going to make an effort to escape it would have to be in the next twenty-four hours.

He sank to the snow by the tree and waited.

●　●　●

HIS BREAKFAST WAS ANOTHER CUP OF SOUP. He thought the scraps of meat in it were dog or owl or crow. Today, as yesterday, the redmen were all mounted, with the chief on Sam's bay. Again Sam had to walk. This day and this night were like the former day and night. He had no chance to escape. His wily captors put the rope twice around the leather that bound his wrists, and both ends around the tree and over to the guards. His second night was ten miserable chilled hours under storm and guards.

The third day and night repeated the first and second, and Sam knew that after two or three more days like these he would be too weak to escape, or to want to. He would make a move, even if it was desperate and useless. After camp was pitched the chief came to Sam where he was tied to a fir tree and looked into his eyes. The redskin had on fresh war paint and more rancid grease on his hair; nothing about him looked human, not even his eyes, for in his hideous face his eyes could have been those of a beast. There was in them no trace of the human or the civilized—they were the hard glittering eyes of an animal looking at its prey. Sam thought the falcon must look like that when it moved to dive and strike.

He had not expected the Indian to hit him, and when, with startling swiftness, the blow fell across his cheek, Sam's eyes opened wide in astonishment. Then he looked steadily at the creature before him, telling himself that if he escaped he would never rest until he had tracked this coward down. He again made note of the man's shape, height, weight, the length of his hair, the scars, and the exact appearance of his teeth when his lips parted to snarl. Sam had no notion of why the fool had come over to strike him; years ago he had given up trying to understand the Indian male. Some infernal evil was busy in this man's mind and heart.

The chief turned to shout and there hastened over a brave who, like his boss, smelled of rancid grease and redbank war paint. The chief spoke to the brave as he came up, and at once this man stepped so close to Sam that his face was only fourteen inches from Sam's face. He looked into Sam's eyes and made an ugly sound. Sam knew it was an expression of contempt. The warrior then said, "Brave, uggh!" and again hawked the contempt up. Sam was startled; he had not known that any man in this party spoke English. "Yuh brave?" the redskin asked, and turned to spit a part of his contempt. Sam stared at the fellow, wondering if he was a half-breed. With signs and broken English the warrior told Sam that for the chief he was a coward and a sick old dog. He was an old coyote covered over with scabs and wood ticks. When the chief slapped him he had challenged him to a fight, but here the paleface stood, cowering and trembling. Were there any brave men among the palefaces?

Sam was silent. He knew that this was an Indian trick but he didn't know the reason for it. It was a preposterous lie to say that the chief would fight him, with fists, knives, or guns, or with any weapon. It was a trick. Was it some plan to cripple him, so that he could not possibly escape—to hamstring him or blind him? Sam looked up into the storm and waited for what was to come.

In his crippled English the warrior was now telling Sam that they were going to ransom him to the Crows. What the Crows would do to him he tried to suggest by stripping fir needles and pretending that they were gobbets of flesh, and by pretending with a finger to slice his nose, lips, tongue, genitals, until they were all gone. He indicated that the joints of the fingers and toes would be broken, one by one; with a piece of hooked wire each eye would be pulled out of its socket; and with a string tied around each eyeball he would be led through the village, while the squaws sliced off his buttocks and tossed them to the dogs.

What purpose the creature had in mind with his catalogue of horrors Sam did not know. All the while redskin talked and gestured, with glittering of his black eyes and guttural gloatings of joy, Sam's mind was busy. He now suspected that this band of warriors had been begging the chief to turn the prisoner over to them, and their share of the rum, so that they could torture and drink and celebrate. The animal before him had worked himself into such a frenzy of maiming and bloodletting that Sam was afraid the frenzy might prove contagious. He decided to speak. He would not speak as a normal man or in a normal voice. He would speak as The Terror, as the man of all mountain men most feared by the red people, and as a great leader and chief.

His first sound was a thunderous roar from his deep chest, and it came with such a shattering explosion that the astounded and terrified redskin almost fell backwards. The chief retreated with him and there they stood, two braves with their black eyes popped out, as Sam flung his mighty arms toward the sky and trumpeted his disdain in his deepest and most dreadful voice. "Almighty God up there in Your kingdom, look down on Your son, for he will be gone beaver before he will stand such insults! These cowards have about used up my patience! I will stand no more of it!" Now, with a deliberate effort to astound and abash them, he swiftly puffed his cheeks in and out, to make the heavy golden beard dance and quiver over most of his face; he bugged and rolled his eyes, and they shone and gleamed like polished granite; and flinging both arms heavenward, he cried in a voice that could have been heard two miles away, "Almighty Father, I wasn't born to be slapped around and spit on and the first thing I know I'll open up this red niggur and pull his liver out and choke him with it! Look down, and give me the strength of Samson!" He then burst into a crazy-man wild hallooing and exulting that sent the two Indians and guards into further retreat, and brought into view all those in camp.

The redmen, drunk and sober, could raise an infernal racket, but such a trumpet-tongued deafening uproar of bombination and reverberation they had never heard; and while they all stared as though hypnotized the golden-bearded giant began to jump up and down and contort himself like a monster in convulsions, his voice rising to a shrieking caterwauling that set the dogs to howling and the horses to whinnying. His fires fed by enormous anger and contempt for these ill-smelling creatures who had him in their power, Sam simply turned himself loose and bellowed and howled out of him the emotions that had been filling him to bursting. All the while he was thinking of such things as Beethoven's sonatas in C major and F minor, and his own act he put on with such a shattering crescendo that even he felt a little unnerved by it. These unspeakable creatures had even taken from him his tobacco, his harp, and the lock of hair from the head of his wife; and they had fondled his revolvers and pointed them at him, and with his knife had made movements at his throat. They opened his baggage in plain sight of him and with shrieks of delight had held up to view one thing and another–his moccasins, skins, flour, coffee, cloth–until he had got so utterly filled with anger for their insolence and contempt and stinking soup that he could only unleash his whole being to the Almighty in a war song menace and challenge, and get it out of him so that he could again breathe naturally. For a full five minutes he kept it up, his thunderous overture to the infinite; and then, covered with sweat, he stepped back and stood against the tree, arms folded on his chest with his bound hands under his chin, his eyes looking at them. Fifty-eight pairs of black eyes were looking at him. Such a tempest of rage and challenge they had never heard from man or beast and would never hear again.

It was the chief who approached Sam. He came within ten feet of him and stood like a man who thought this bearded giant might explode, as the infernal spirit regions in Colter's hell exploded. After studying Sam a full minute he summoned the brave who spoke English. But Sam had the offensive and he intended to keep it; he could tell that these superstitious children were not sure now whether he was man or some kind of god. So, with prodigious gestures of menace and challenge, and a great roaring into the sky, Sam made them understand that he would fight any five of them in a fight to the death, all of them to come against him as one man, in full view of the Blackfeet people and a hundred mountain men; and after he had slain the five, the hundred mountain men would fight the whole Blackfeet nation, the thousand of them or ten thousand, or as many as the leaves on trees and the berries on bushes. He knew that his challenge would not be accepted, or even considered; but he had in mind a plan. He went on to say that if they were no braver than sick squaws crawling in the sagebrush, or dying coyotes with their heads in holes— if they were no more than rabbits, if they were a nation of magpies with broken wings, they should take him to the Sparrowhawks and get the thing over with. But if big ransom was what they wanted–tobacco and rum and guns and beads and bullets and coffee and sugar–they should ransom him to the mountain men, who would pay much more; and after he was set free they could capture him again and sell him again. But whatever they did, they would all die like puking coyotes in their vomit if they forgot for a moment that he was a great chief and a mighty one, who wore fifty eagle feathers in his headpiece; and he was to be treated with dignity and honors; and if he was not, all the mountain men would march against them and hunt them down to the last crippled dog.

To further confuse and addle their wits he burst into tremendous song. As before, the redmen seemed hypnotized as Sam smote his breast and shot his arms skyward and poured out of his lungs the furious majesties of impatience and anger. As suddenly as he had begun he stopped, and then roared at the pidgin brave, telling him to come forward if he were not a coward hiding under a stinkbush. The man advanced, slowly and with absurd caution, as if expecting Sam to blow him off the scene. Sam told him that he, Samson John Minard, was a chief, and a bigger and more important chief than the contemptible eater of crickets who slapped his face. Sam said to tell him that he would raise his hair and pull his scent bag off if he didn't treat him the way a chief should be treated. "Go, you quivering coyote, and tell him! Tell him Chief Samson is to be put in a tent, as befits a great one, and given his pipe and tobacco." Sam knew he would get no tobacco: once the smokers of kinnikinic and cedar bark and willow got hold of whiteman's tobacco they sucked it into their lungs day and night until it was gone. But he saw that he had aroused some of the warriors to clamorous proposals, and that the chief was talking things over with them. After a few minutes the brave told Sam that a tent would be prepared for him and he would have a robe to lie on.

A half hour later several braves came over, and untying the rope from the tree, led Sam like a beast to the tent. There he exploded in another deliberate tantrum; flinging his bound arms wildly, he said they would take the tether rope off his wrists, for did they think he was a horse to be hobbled and staked out? Hadn't they among their fifty-eight one who was warrior enough to guard an unarmed prisoner? This taunt bore results. The chief had Sam taken into one of the larger tepees, and put as guard over him one, he was told, who had made a coup when only a boy, and had more Flathead and Crow scalps than Sam had fingers and toes. Sam then repeated his proposal, in words and signs, that they should ransom him to the mountain men, and then see if they were brave enough to capture him a second time, for a second ransom.

When first made, this proposal had fired the greed of some of the warriors. Their passions had caught flame like tall dry prairie grass, as they foresaw innumerable kegs of rum and piles of tobacco. As children with little sense of the realities, they had no doubt that they could capture him a second time, or many times; and if there was to be so much firewater in the future why not drink what they had just captured? This was what Sam had hoped for. Once thirst possessed their senses there could be no prevailing against them. The chief knew that, but he was eager as any to unstop the rum and pour the liquid fire down his throat. He gave orders, and men rushed into the forest to find dead wood; other braves made ready three elk, which had been killed that afternoon. As Sam watched the preparations he tried to look sleepy and very hopeless. Five gallons might not lay them all out senseless but it was strong rum; forty pints for fifty-eight would average almost eleven ounces to the man. That ought to be enough.

The rope had been untied from the leather that bound Sam's wrists, and he had been given a small thin robe that had lost most of its hair. On this in the tent he sat and planned and waited. The brave who had been sent to guard him was taller and heavier than most Indians: Sam thought he stood an inch or two above six feet and weighed more than two hundred pounds. He supposed that the chief had chosen one of his boldest and most dependable men, and one of the most savage, for this critter hadn't sat a full minute when with Sam's Bowie he made passes across his throat. He took from his lap a tomahawk and made movements with it to show Sam how he would split his skull. His face expressionless, Sam watched the grim pantomime; inside he was thinking: If my plan works, you dog-eater, you and me will be huggin before this night is over.

Sam was weighing his chances in every way he could conceive of. The tent was about ten feet across and about eight feet high where it was anchored to the center pole. If he were to move fast inside it, Sam told himself, he would have to bend over, for if his head struck the tent the Indians outside might see the movement. The guard sat on a heavy robe. As he faced Sam he was just to the left of the flap, which had been thrown open and back. There were three big fires blazing outside; the voices were shrill. The firelight cast flickering illuminations over the guard's face and gave a horrifying appearance of evil to his war paint. His right hand clasped the handle of the knife, his left the handle of the tomahawk. He had no gun. He was alert but tense; he had to turn his head now and then to peer out. Sam knew the man was burning with infernal thirst and was wondering if he would share the rum or be forgotten. Oh, they would bring him a chunk of roasted elk but would they bring him the water that turned a man into fire? If only he were the one who spoke English, Sam could have talked to him and tried to make a frenzy of his resentment and impatience. As it was, he did nothing and said nothing; it would be best to look sleepy and tired. Sam was sitting straight across from the guard; their faces were only about six feet apart, their moccasined feet only about two. Sam's face was in shadow; he knew that the guard could not see him clearly, but Sam could see the emotions convulsing the guard's face. That Injun's belly was burning for rum. If they forgot him he would be mad enough to grease hell with war paint before this night was over.

The guard made no move that Sam's lidded eyes did not see. During the first hour he had turned to look out at least once every ten minutes; he was then looking out every five minutes; and at the end of an hour and a half he was looking out every minute or less, and the way he moved showed that he was itching with resentment and suspicion and that his thirst was like hell's own. Nothing, Sam told himself, was more likely to make a guard think his prisoner secure than a boiling passion that took his mind off him and returned it and took it off again. Alcohol could do it; a female could do it. Alcohol, it now seemed to Sam, was the redman's curse, and woman the whiteman's . . . .

Just itch all over, Sam thought, his bound hands in plain view on his lap, his head sunk as though he were half gone in fatigue and sleep. Just itch, you bastard, and keep looking. Sam had never felt more brilliantly alert, as though all his senses and mind and emotions shone in the full blaze of noon sunlight. Never had his eyes been sharper. Just git yourself a thirst like that in hell, Sam was saying inside; and over and over calculated the risks and his chances. He figured that he had been sitting with the guard about two hours. For nearly an hour he had smelled the roasting flesh. He knew that tripods of green trees had been set up and that hanging from them were the carcasses, slowly roasting in flames and smoke. Redmen when hungry never waited for flesh to cook but almost at once began to hack off bloody gobbets; and by the time their hunger was appeased there wasn't much left but bone and gristle. Before long now these Indians would be drinking. Sam had hoped they would drink before they ate. Once they started drinking they would have pictures of mountain men bringing them whole rivers and lakes of rum, to ransom the Crow-killer, so that a second time they could capture him, for more lakes and rivers. What dreams children dreamed!

There now came to the door of the tent a face whose war paint had been smeared over with fresh blood. In this brave's hands was a piece of pine bark, on which rested a pound or two of hot elk meat. The guard set the meat by him and began to gesticulate, and to talk in a high shrill voice ill-becoming a bold brave warrior; Sam knew that he was asking why he had not been fetched a cup of spirit water. The two braves gestured and yelled at one another, and the one who had brought the meat then went away. Sam did not move or lift the lids on his eyes, for he knew that his moment was drawing near. Very gently he tried to ease his cramps and relax his muscles.

In only a few moments the Indian returned with a tin cup in his hand. Sam knew that in the cup was rum. The guard eagerly took the cup and sniffed, and he was so enchanted that he laid the knife on his lap, and seizing the cup with both hands, put the rim to his lips. Sam's gaze was on the other Indian; he was praying that the fellow would go away. He had hoped that the guard would be alone with him when he drank and that his first gulp would be so large it would strangle him. Sam was to say later that both his prayers were answered. The Indian in the tepee doorway, eager to get back to the drinking and feasting, did vanish; and the blockhead with the cup of rum did take such a huge mouthful that the fiery spirits choked him. He suddenly tightened all over and was fumbling to set the cup down when Sam moved with swiftness that had become legendary. In an instant his powerful hands were on the redman's throat. Everything that he did now had been thought through, over and over, so that there would be no false move or wasted moment. As hands seized the throat a knee came with terrific force into the man's diaphragm, paralyzing his whole torso. In the next instant Sam released the throat and his right hand seized the knife. He twisted his right hand around until he could put the blade to the leather and sever it, and the moment that was done, the left hand was back to the throat to be sure it made no sounds, and the right hand was gathering the robe, tomahawk, and piece of elk meat. He then slipped under the back of the tent into the gray-white night.

In a flash he was gone across the pale snow and into the trees.

IT WAS SNOWING HARD. During the hours when he sat waiting for his chance Sam had known that he would need Almighty's help if he were to outrun the pursuit of fifty-eight hell-fiends, and the bitter cold and deep snows of winter. His instincts told him that he was going east but he was not sure of it. During this day's march he had seen a range of mountains west of him, another north, and another east, and he had thought the range on the east was the Continental Divide. If it was, the Missouri River was only forty or fifty miles east of it, and from there across the desolation to Kate was a hundred and fifty or two hundred miles.

During his many hours of thinking and planning he had recognized that it would be folly to go south, over the trail up which they had come, or west to the Flatheads. His captors would expect him to take one of these routes. They would not expect him to go north into Blood and Piegan land, or to be fool enough to try to cross the Divide after heavy snows had come. Earlier in the day the war party had crossed a river but he did not know what river it was. He had never been through this country. He had heard that there were several rivers in this area, all of which came down from the Divide and flowed west. Up one of these rivers looked to him like the only possible way to freedom.

After he had trotted swiftly for four or five miles he stopped to listen. He could hear no sounds. He put the piece of meat to his nostrils, for he was as famished as a wolf. While sitting and waiting he had wondered if he ought to take one of the guard's thighs, but he was a sentimental man and he thought he would rather starve than eat human flesh. He had calculated all the risks and had decided that in starvation lay his greatest danger. He could hope to get his hands on little except roots along streams, berries still clinging to bushes, a fool hen possibly, a fish now and then in a shallow pool, rose hips, marrow in old bones; or, if very lucky, a deer or antelope stuck in deep snow.

He was glad that it was snowing hard. He was singing inside at the thought of being free. He thanked God for both and he thanked Him for rum. He hoped that rum and rage would make fifty-seven warriors so drunk that they would fall down and freeze to death. He thought he had heard bones snap in the guard's neck. If they found him dead all hell would break loose; they would run round and round and the dogs would be baying at their heels. But Sam doubted that they would take his trail before morning. They would think he had gone back down the path to the Three Forks and that they could catch him in a day or two; or they would think he had headed for his in-laws and would get stuck in deep snow. If it were to snow all night they might not be able to tell by morning which way he had taken. But the dogs would know.

There was a cold wind down from the mountains. He listened again and thought he heard faint shrieks, and dogs barking, but he could not be sure. His direction now was due north and two hours before daylight he came to a river. Taking off his moccasins and leather leggins he waded into the shallow stream and turned up it, to the east, walking rapidly as he could, in water only ankle-deep or sometimes to his crotch. It was cold but for a while it did not seem cold; his blood was hot from exertion, his soul singing, his hopes high. He had yanked off the guard's medicine bag and was amazed to find in it his mouth harp. It was as if a brother had joined him, or Beethoven's ugly face in the sky had smiled. When first captured he would not have given a buckskin whang for his life; but now, with God's help, he was a free man again, and he would remain free and alive, even if he had to live on tree bark. The redmen might follow his path to the river but there they would lose it, and two or three of them might go upriver but most of them would go downriver. He could not, like John Colter, find an acre of driftwood and lie under it for half a day and most of the night; he could only hoard his strength and keep going. Some of the river stones cut his feet but he remembered that John's feet had been filled with cactus thorns; he was starved but he told himself that Colter had lived on hips and roots; Hugh Glass with maggots swarming in his wounds had crawled for a hundred miles; and a man named Scott, starved and sick unto death, had dragged himself forward for sixty miles. And yonder Kate sat in the cold and sang. A man could do it if he had to. He recalled other tales of heroism and fortitude, to warm and cheer him as he struggled up the river.

Sam was not feeling sorry for himself. He was not that kind. He was not telling himself that he would perish. He was only warming himself with the feats of brave free men, his kind of men. Afraid that he was moving only about three miles in an hour in his tortuous journey up the river, he looked round him but there was no other way. Until daylight he would keep moving and perhaps for an hour after daylight, for he thought it would take the redmen half the morning to find his path and follow it to the river. He would find some snuggery back under the bank—an old beaver house or a wash under an overhanging earth ledge or a pile of driftwood; and he would hole up until night came again. He could catch a few hours' sleep, if he lay on his belly, for in that position his snoring, Lotus had told him, was light. He would eat half the elk meat and all the rose hips he could find; and when darkness came he would be gone again.

What he found was a high-water eddy underwash, under a grove of large aspen; the spring torrents had raised the river four or five feet above its present level, and the high waters swirling round and round in the eddy had cut away the earth back under the trees. Sam crawled for thirty feet and after putting on his leggins and moccasins and wrapping the robe around him he cut off morsels of flesh and chewed them thoroughly. Never had elk tasted so good. Looking out the way he had come, he could see only a hint of daylight. If the Indians were to wade up the river, as he had done, it was possible that they would spot his hideaway and crouch low to look back under. But they would never wade far in a river. They would think he made a raft and gone downriver, toward his in-laws, and by the time they discovered their error he would be over the Divide.

All day until dusk he rested and slept a little and heard no Indians and saw nothing alive but one hawk. All day the snow fell. All night he took his slow way up the river. By midnight he had reached the foothills; by morning he was fighting white water. An hour after daylight he had found no hiding place, but in shallow pools he had caught a few small trout, a part of which he ate for breakfast, with a handful of rose pods. He was still struggling upward on bruised and bleeding feet when about noon he saw a cavern back in a ledge of stone. Its mouth was close to the river, with a wide shelf of spilled stone at the entrance. Leaving the river, he climbed up across talus to look in. The cavern was far deeper than he had expected, so deep in fact that his gaze went blind back in the gloom. He smelled wild-beast odors, and the odors of dove, bat, and swallow. After entering the cave he stood under a ceiling thirty feet high and looked round him. At one side he saw a smaller cave that also ran back into gloom; this he explored to find a spot where he could lie down.

The animal smells in the smaller cave were overpowering. They were so heavy and so saturated with mustiness and dusts that he could feel them in his nostrils.

Returning to the mouth of the cavern, he stood by a brown stone wall to give him protective coloring and looked back down the river. The falling snow was only a thin mist now, the kind that makes way for freezing cold; he could see far down the river's meandering course and across the valley. There was no smoke from Indian fires anywhere. He went down to the river for a water-washed stone on which to lay his meat and fish. Then, sitting in the cavern mouth, he cut off about three ounces of meat and ate it, and two fish no larger than his finger. Along the riverbanks he had gathered about a quart of rose hips. How a man could live and walk for a week on nothing but these, as some men were said to have done, he could not imagine.

While looking round him he sneezed. The echoes of it startled him, for they were remarkably loud and clear. Impressed by the cavern's acoustics, he spoke, saying, "Hot biscuits," and sang a few bars of an old ballad. The echoing astonished him and then alarmed him. It was somewhat like music from a great organ, rolling through vaulted chambers, with ceilings high and low. He burst into a Mozart theme, and the echoes rolling away from him into the far dark recesses sounded to him like an orchestra playing. He wondered if he was losing his mind. After he had found a spot where he could lie and try to sleep he thought of the Rocky Mountains caverns he had explored, and of the strange sculpturing that water, wind, and time had made underground. "Almighty God–" he said, and liked so well the amplified and golden-toned echo that he uttered other words. "Dear Lotus, dear son–Lotus!" he said more loudly, and from all around him back in the stone mountains the word came back to him like an organ tone.

Sam was not a man who usually felt gooseflesh in moments of danger but he had been enfeebled by hunger and want of sleep. Gooseflesh spread over him in the moment when he smelled the danger; turning swiftly to a sitting position, tomahawk in one hand and knife in the other, he saw ambling toward him not more than fifty feet away a grizzly so large that it seemed almost to fill the cavern. In a flash Sam knew the reverberating echoes had disturbed the monster's slumber, somewhere back in the gloom, and it had come to give battle to its enemy. That it intended to give battle Sam knew the instant he saw it. The next moment he was on his feet, advancing, the hatchet ready to strike and the knife to plunge. He marched right up to the beast and smote the prow of the nose a crushing blow with the head of the axe. In an instant his arm came back and he struck again, and this time the blow fell across the sensitive nostrils. The big furry fellow said *woof-woof* and began to back off, with Sam after him, hoping for grizzly steaks; but almost at once the beast vanished, and there was only the whimpering plaintive sound of a frightened child, as the shuffling fur ball hastened back to its winter bed.

Pale from fright and weakness and breathing hard, Sam watched it disappear. He felt for a moment that he was being tested with more than he could bear. Hungry, weary to the depths of his marrow, and numbed through with cold, he would now have to leave the cavern and go. There might be a whole pack of grizzlies back in the dark; and even if there were not, the whimpering one would nurse his injuries and come forth again. Over by the entrance Sam stood a few moments, looking out. He knew by the nimbus around the winter sun that the weather was going to change. After seven days of deep storm the temperature would fall; sometimes in this area it went thirty, forty, or even to fifty below. Sometimes there were blizzards that not even the wolves and hawks could endure. There was cold that split trees open with the sound of gunfire; that froze broad rivers from bank to bank and almost to their bottoms; and the snow so hard that even the giant moose with its sharp hoofs could walk on it. It was cold that welded a man's hand to the steel of gun or knife, if he was fool enough to touch it.

After searching the valley for sign of Indians and seeing none Sam looked up the river gorge to the continental backbone. After he had crossed the Divide the rivers would be flowing east instead of west, and he would be going down instead of climbing. With robe flung across his left shoulder the food enfolded by a piece of it and tucked up under an armpit, the hatchet in his left hand and the knife in his right, he scrambled down the water's edge; sat and took off moccasins and leggins and trousers; and thrust wounded feet into the icy waters. Then he waded upstream. He guessed he might as well eat the remainder of the elk and the three small fish, and keep going and keep going. After he had gone a mile or two he peeled the outer bark off a spruce and licked the juice of the cambium. It was resinous and bitter. Hank Cady had said that lessen a man has something better he kin live on it if he hafta. The cambium itself Sam found unchewable, and so peeled off strips of it and licked the juice, as he had licked fruit juices off his hands as a child. While licking the juice he looked round him, wondering if there was anything else on this mountain that a man could eat. During the long miles up this river he had seen no birds, except a hawk or two and one duck; no sign of grouse or sage hen, no sign of deer or elk trail. On the mountain slopes above him he could see no snowpaths. The untramped, unmarked snow on either side of the river was about three feet deep. He wondered if it would be less exhausting to plow through it than to fight his way up over slippery boulders, in water from a foot to three feet deep. Wading in river waters up a mountain canyon was the most fatiguing toil he had ever known; he was sure he was not covering more than two miles an hour but kept at it, doggedly, all day long, pausing only when night closed round him.

He then searched both banks, hoping to find a shelter in which he could sleep. But he found only an arbor, under a dense tangle of berry vines and mountain laurel, over which the snow had formed a roof; he crawled back under it, out of sight. After putting on his clothes he wrapped the robe round him, and lying on his left side facing the river, he put two fish on leaves a few inches from his face, hatchet and knife within reach, and in a few minutes was sound asleep. His first dream was of his wife; they were somewhere in buffalo land, and while she gathered berries and mushrooms he cooked steaks and made hot biscuits. It was a cold night and he slept cold, but for eight hours he did not awaken. It was the first solid rest he had had in a week.

When at daylight he stirred it took him a few moments to understand where he was. Then, like Jedediah Smith, he gave thanks to God; dwelt for a few minutes on the bones of his wife and child, yonder in the winter, and on a mother sitting in a pile of bedding looking out an empty white world; and then ate the two fish. Yes, it had turned colder. On the eastern side of the Divide would be the wild storm-winds down from Canada; there he would need more than a mouthful of frozen fish to keep him going. But he felt cheerful this morning and he told himself that he was as strong as a bull moose. He thought he was safe from the Blackfeet now. Ahead of him lay an ordeal that might be the most difficult he would ever endure, but he would struggle through it, day after day, all the way across the white winter loneliness, until he came at last to Kate's door.

"Keep a fire for me, and a light," he said, and faced into the sharp winds from the north.

Chapter 7

BIGHORNS *and* WIND RIVER RANGE

From *The Adventures of Captain Bonneville U.S.A.
In the Rocky Mountains of the Far West,*
by Washington Irving

In what certainly ranks as one of American literature's most successful "rewrite jobs," the talents of Washington Irving (1783–1859) lifted an unpublishable manuscript into the ranks of the classics of western history. Born in Paris but educated at West Point and a professional soldier, Captain Benjamin Louis Eulalie de Bonneville (1796–1878) took leave from the Army in 1831 to seek travel and adventure in the Rocky Mountain West. This was the peak of fur trade exploration and competition, and Bonneville personally knew and recorded the exploits of famous mountain men such as Joe Walker, Thomas Fitzpatrick, Milton Sublette, and many others.

Irving shared Bonneville's passion for western adventure, and when he met with Bonneville in 1835, he had already produced the work *A Tour on the Prairies* and was working on his

book *Astoria*. The journal over which Bonneville had been agonizing (apparently his skills in the outdoors were not matched
by his skills with the pen) was thought to be unpublishable by
the professionals of that time. Irving purchased the manuscript
for $1,000 and set to work making it a highly readable book,
using his own experiences and observations and studies from
other sources with Bonneville's original material. The Irving
book was published in 1837.

In this excerpt, Captain Bonneville and nine trappers are
headed to Bighorn Mountain, with the Green River and the
Wind River Range on beyond.

●　　●　　●

THE ADVENTURES of the detachment of ten are the first in order. These
trappers, when they separated from Captain Bonneville at the place where
the furs were embarked, proceeded to the foot of the Bighorn Mountain,
and having encamped, one of them mounted his mule and went out to set
his trap in a neighboring stream. He had not proceeded far when his steed
came to a full stop. The trapper kicked and cudgelled, but to every blow
and kick the mule snorted and kicked up, but still refused to budge an inch.
The rider now cast his eyes warily around in search of some cause for this
demur, when, to his dismay, he discovered an Indian fort within gunshot
distance, lowering through the twilight. In a twinkling he wheeled about;
his mule now seemed as eager to get on as himself, and in a few moments
brought him, clattering with his traps, among his comrades. He was jeered
at for his alacrity in retreating; his report was treated as a false alarm; his
brother trappers contented themselves with reconnoitering the fort at a
distance, and pronounced that it was deserted.

As night set in, the usual precaution, enjoined by Captain Bonneville on his men, was observed. The horses were brought in and tied, and a guard stationed over them. This done, the men wrapped themselves in their blankets, stretched themselves before the fire, and being fatigued with a long day's march, and gorged with a hearty supper, were soon in a profound sleep.

The camp fires gradually died away; all was dark and silent; the sentinel stationed to watch the horses had marched as far, and supped as heartily as any of his companions, and while they snored, he began to nod at his post. After a time, a low trampling noise reached his ear. He half opened his closing eyes, and beheld two or three elks moving about the lodges, picking, and smelling, and grazing here and there. The sight of elk within the purlieus of the camp caused some little surprise; but having had his supper, he cared not for elk meat, and, suffering them to graze about unmolested, soon relapsed into a doze.

Suddenly, before daybreak, a discharge of firearms, and a struggle and tramp of horses, made every one start to his feet. The first move was to secure the horses. Some were gone; others were struggling, and kicking, and trembling, for there was a horrible uproar of whoops, and yells, and firearms. Several trappers stole quietly from the camp, and succeeded in driving in the horses which had broken away; the rest were tethered still more strongly. A breastwork was thrown up of saddles, baggage, and camp furniture, and all hands waited anxiously for daylight. The Indians, in the meantime, collected on a neighboring height, kept up the most horrible clamor, in hope of striking a panic into the camp, or frightening off the horses. When the day dawned, the trappers attacked them briskly and drove them to some distance. A desultory fire was kept up for an hour, when the Indians, seeing nothing was to be gained, gave up the contest and retired. They proved to be a war party of Blackfeet, who, while in search of the Crow tribe, had fallen upon the trail of Captain Bonneville on the Popo Agie, and dogged him to the

Bighorn; but had been completely baffled by his vigilance. They had then waylaid the present detachment, and were actually housed in perfect silence within their fort, when the mule of the trapper made such a dead point.

The savages went off uttering the wildest denunciation of hostility, mingled with opprobrious terms in broken English, and gesticulations of the most insulting kind.

In this melée, one white man was wounded, and two horses were killed. On preparing the morning's meal, however, a number of cups, knives, and other articles were missing, which had, doubtless, been carried off by the fictitous elk, during the slumber of the very sagacious sentinel.

As the Indians had gone off in the direction which the trappers had intended to travel, the latter changed their route, and pushed forward rapidly through the "Bad Pass," nor halted until night; when, supposing themselves out of the reach of the enemy, they contented themselves with tying up their horses and posting a guard. They had scarce laid down to sleep, when a dog strayed into the camp with a small pack of moccasons tied upon his back; for dogs are made to carry burdens among the Indians. The sentinel, more knowing than he of the preceeding night, awoke his companions and reported the circumstance. It was evident that Indians were at hand. All were instantly at work; a strong pen was soon constructed for the horses, after completing which, they resumed their slumbers with the composure of men long inured to dangers.

In the next night, the prowling of dogs about the camp, and various suspicious noises, showed that Indians were still hovering about them. Hurrying on by long marches, they at length fell upon a trail, which, with the experienced eye of veteran woodmen, they soon discovered to be that of the party of trappers detached by Captain Bonneville when on his march, and which they were sent to join. They likewise ascertained from various signs, that this party had suffered some maltreatment from the Indians. They now pursued the trail with intense anxiety;

it carried them to the banks of the stream called the Gray Bull, and down along its course, until they came to where it empties into the Horn River. Here, to their great joy, they discovered the comrades of whom they were in search, all strong fortified, and in a state of great watchfulness and anxiety.

We now take up the adventures of this first detachment of trappers. These men, after parting with the main body under Captain Bonneville, had proceeded slowly for several days up the course of the river, trapping beaver as they went. One morning, as they were about to visit their traps, one of the camp-keepers pointed to a fine elk, grazing at a distance, and requested them to shoot it. Three of the trappers started off for the purpose. In passing a thicket, they were fired upon by savages in ambush, and at the same time the pretended elk, throwing off his hide and his horn, started forth an Indian warrior.

One of the three trappers had been brought down by the volley; the others fled to the camp, and all hands, seizing up whatever they could carry off, retreated to a small island in the river, and took refuge among the willows. Here they were soon joined by their comrade who had fallen, but who had merely been wounded in the neck.

In the meantime the Indians took possession of the deserted camp, with all the traps, accoutrements, and horses. While they were busy among the spoils, a solitary trapper, who had been absent at his work, came sauntering to the camp with his traps on his back. He had approached near by, when an Indian came forward and motioned him to keep away; at the same moment, he was perceived by his comrades on the island, and warned of his danger with loud cries. The poor fellow stood for a moment, bewildered and aghast, then dropping his traps, wheeled and made off at full speed, quickened by a sportive volley which the Indians rattled after him.

In high good humor with their easy triumph, the savages now formed a circle round the fire and performed a war dance, with the unlucky trappers for rueful spectators. This done, emboldened by what they considered cowardice on the part of the white men, they neglected their usual mode of bush-fighting, and advanced openly within twenty paces of the willows. A sharp volley from the trappers brought them to a sudden halt, and laid three of them breathless. The chief, who had stationed himself on an eminence to direct all the movements of his people, seeing three of his warriors laid low, ordered the rest to retire. They immediately did so, and the whole band soon disappeared behind a point of woods, carrying off with them the horses, traps, and the greater part of the baggage.

It was just after this misfortune that the party of ten discovered this forlorn band of trappers in a fortress, which they had thrown up after their disaster. They were so perfectly dismayed, that they could not be induced even to go in quest of their traps, which they had set in a neighboring stream. The two parties now joined their forces, and made their way, without further misfortune, to the rendezvous.

Captain Bonneville perceived from the reports of these parties, as well as from what he had observed himself in his recent march, that he was in a neighborhood teeming with danger. Two wandering Snake Indians, also, who visited the camp, assured him that there were two large bands of Crows marching rapidly upon him. He broke up his encampment, therefore, on the 1st of September, made his way to the south, across the Littlehorn Mountain, until he reached Wind River, and then turning westward, moved slowly up the banks of that stream, giving time for his men to trap as he proceeded. As it was not in the plan of the present hunting campaigns to go near the caches on the Green River, and as the trappers were in want of traps to replace those they had lost, Captain Bonneville undertook to visit the caches, and procure a supply. To accompany him in this hazardous expedition, which would take him through the defiles of the Wind River Mountains, and up the Green River valley, he took but three men; the main party were to continue on trapping up toward the head of Wind River, near which he was to rejoin them, just about the place where that stream issues from the mountains. We shall accompany the captain on his adventurous errand.

HAVING FORDED wind river a little above its mouth, Captain Bonneville and his three companions proceeded across a gravelly plain, until they fell upon the Popo Agie,[1] up the left bank of which they held their course, nearly in a southerly direction. Here they came upon numerous droves of buffalo, and halted for the purpose of procuring a supply of beef. As the hunters were stealing cautiously to get within shot of the game, two small white bears suddenly presented themselves in their path, and, rising upon their hind legs, contemplated them for some time with a whimsically solemn gaze. The hunters remained motionless; whereupon the bears, having apparently satisfied their curiosity, lowered themselves upon all fours, and began to withdraw. The hunters now advanced, upon which the bears turned, rose again upon their haunches, and repeated their serio-comic examination. This was repeated several times, until the hunters, piqued at their unmannerly staring, rebuked it with a discharge of their rifles. The bears made an awkward bound or two, as if wounded, and then walked off with great gravity, seeming to commune together, and every now and then turning to take another look at the hunters. It was well for the latter that the bears were but half grown, and had not yet acquired the ferocity of their kind.

The buffalo were somewhat startled at the report of firearms; but the hunters succeeded in killing a couple of fine cows, and, having secured the best of the meat, continued forward until some time after dark, when, encamping in a large thicket of willows, they made a great fire, roasted buffalo beef enough for half a score, disposed of the whole of it with keen

---

1   A short distance south of modern Riverton, Wyoming.

relish and high glee, and then "turned in" for the night and slept sound-ly, like weary and well fed hunters.

At daylight they were in the saddle again, and skirted along the river, passing through fresh grassy meadows, and a succession of beautiful groves of willows and cotton-wood. Toward evening, Captain Bonneville observed a smoke at a distance rising from among hills, directly in the route he was pursuing. Apprehensive of some hostile band, he concealed the horses in a thicket, and, accompanied by one of his men, crawled cau-tiously up a height, from which he could overlook the scene of danger. Here, with a spy-glass, he reconnoitered the surrounding country, but not a lodge nor fire, not a man, horse, nor dog, was to be discovered; in short, the smoke which had caused such alarm proved to be the vapor from several warm, or rather hot springs of considerable magnitude, pouring forth streams in every direction over a bottom of white clay. One of the springs was about twenty-five yards in diameter, and so deep that the water was of a bright green color.

They were now advancing diagonally upon the chain of Wind River Mountains, which lay between them and the Green River valley. To coast round their southern points would be a wide circuit; whereas, could they force their way through them, they might proceed in a straight line. The mountains were lofty, with snowy peaks and cragged sides; it was hoped, however, that some practicable defile might be found. They attempted, accordingly, to penetrate the mountains by following up one of the branches of the Popo Agie, but soon found themselves in the midst of stupendous crags and precipices that barred all progress. Retracting their steps, and falling back upon the river, they consulted where to make another attempt. They were too close beneath the mountains to scan them generally, but they now recollected having noticed, from the plain, a beautiful slope rising, at an angle of about thirty degrees, and apparently without any break, until it reached the snowy region. Seeking this gentle acclivity, they began to ascend it with alacrity, trusting to find at the top one of those elevated plains which prevail among the Rocky Mountains. The slope was covered with coarse gravel, interspersed with plates of freestone. They attained the summit with some toil, but found, instead of a level, or rather undulating plain, that they were on the brink of a deep and precipitous ravine, from the bottom of which rose a second slope, similar to the one they had just ascended. Down into this profound ravine they made their way by a rugged path, or rather fissure of the rocks, and then labored up the second slope. They gained the summit only to find themselves on another ravine, and now perceived that this vast mountain, which had presented such a sloping and even side to the distant beholder on the plain, was shagged by frightful precipices, and seamed with longitudinal chasms, deep and dangerous.

In one of these wild dells they passed the night, and slept soundly and sweetly after their fatigues. Two days more of arduous climbing and scrambling only served to admit them into the heart of this mountainous and awful solitude; where difficulties increased as they proceeded. Sometimes they scrambled from rock to rock, up the bed of some mountain stream, dashing its bright way down to the plains; sometimes they availed themselves of the paths made by the deer and the mountain sheep, which, however, often took to the brinks of fearful precipices, or led to rugged defiles, impassable for their horses. At one place, they were obliged to slide their horses down the face of a rock, in which attempt some of the poor animals lost their footing and rolled to the bottom, and came near being dashed to pieces.

In the afternoon of the second day, the travellers attained one of the elevated valleys locked up in this singular bed of mountains. Here were two bright and beautiful little lakes, set like mirrors in the midst of stern and rocky heights, and surrounded by grassy meadows, inexpressibly refreshing to the eye. These probably were among the sources of those mighty streams which take their rise among these mountains, and wander hundreds of miles through the plains.

In the green pastures bordering upon these lakes, the travellers halted to repose, and to give their weary horses time to crop the sweet and tender herbage. They had now ascended to a great height above the level of the plains, yet they beheld huge crags of granite piled one upon another, and beetling like battlements far above them. While two of the men remained in the camp with the horses, Captain Bonneville, accompanied by the other men [man], set out to climb a neighboring height, hoping to gain a commanding prospect, and discern some practicable route through this stupendous labyrinth. After much toil, he reached the summit of a lofty cliff, but it was only to behold gigantic peaks rising all around, and towering far into the snowy regions of the atmosphere. Selecting one which appeared to be the highest, he crossed a narrow intervening valley, and began to scale it. He soon found that he had undertaken a tremendous task; but the pride of man is never more obstinate than when climbing mountains. The ascent was so steep and rugged that he and his companion were frequently obliged to clamber on hands and knees, with their guns slung upon their backs. Frequently, exhausted with fatigue, and dripping with perspiration, they threw themselves upon the snow, and took handfuls of it to allay their parching thirst. At one place, they even stripped off their coats and hung them upon the bushes, and thus lightly clad, proceeded to scramble over these eternal snows. As they ascended still higher, there were cool breezes that refreshed and braced them, and springing with new ardor to their task, they at length attained the summit.

Here a scene burst upon the view of Captain Bonneville, that for a time astonished and overwhelmed him with its immensity. He stood, in fact, upon that dividing ridge which Indians regard as the crest of the world; and on each side of which, the landscape may be said to decline to the two cardinal oceans of the globe. Whichever way he turned his eye, it was confounded by the vastness and variety of objects. Beneath him, the Rocky Mountains seemed to open all their secret recesses: deep, solemn valleys; treasured lakes; dreary passes; rugged defiles, and foaming torrents; while beyond their savage precincts, the eye was lost in an almost immeasurable landscape; stretching on every side into dim and hazy distance, like the expanse of a summer's sea. Whichever way he looked, he beheld vast plains glimmering with reflected sunshine; mighty streams wandering on their shining course toward either ocean, and snowy mountains, chain beyond chain, and peak beyond peak, till they melted like clouds into the horizon. For a time, the Indian fable seemed realized: he had attained that height from which the Blackfoot warrior, after death, first catches a view of the land of souls, and beholds the happy hunting ground spread out below him, brightening with the abodes of the free and generous spirits. The captain stood for a long while gazing upon this scene, lost in a crowd of vague and indefinite ideas and sensations. A long-drawn inspiration at length relieved him from this entertainment of the mind, and he began to analyze the parts of this vast panorama. A simple enumeration of a few of its features may give some idea of its collective grandeur and magnificence.

The peak on which the captain had taken his stand commanded the whole Wind River chain; which, in fact, may rather be considered one immense mountain, broken into snowy peaks and lateral spurs, and seamed with narrow valleys. Some of these valleys glittered with silver lakes and gushing streams; the fountain heads, as of it were, of the mighty tributaries to the Atlantic and Pacific Oceans. Beyond the snowy peaks, to the south, and far, far below the mountain range, the gentle river, called the Sweet Water, was seen pursuing its tranquil way through the rugged regions of the Black Hills. In the east, the head waters of Wind River wandered through a plain, until, mingling in one powerful current, they forced their way through the range of Horn Mountains, and were lost to view. To the north were caught glimpses of the upper streams of the Yellowstone, that great tributary of the Missouri. In another direction were to be seen some of the sources of the Oregon, or Columbia, flowing to the northwest, past those towering landmarks the Three Tetons, and pouring down into the great lava plain; while, almost at the captain's feet, the Green River, or Colorado of the West, set forth on its wandering pilgrimage to the Gulf of California; at first a mere mountain torrent, dashing northward over a crag and precipice, in a succession of cascades, and tumbling into the plain where, expanding into an ample river, it circled away to the south, and after alternately shining out and disappearing in the mazes of the vast landscape, was finally lost in a horizon of mountains. The day was calm and cloudless, and the atmosphere so pure that objects were discernible at an astonishing distance. The whole of this immense area was inclosed by an outer range of shadowy peaks, some of them faintly marked on the horizon, which seemed to wall it in from the rest of the earth.

It is to be regretted that Captain Bonneville had no instruments with him with which to ascertain the altitude of this peak. He gives it as his opinion that it is the loftiest point of the North American continent; but of this we have no satisfactory proof. It is certain that the Rocky Mountains are of an altitude vastly superior to what was formerly supposed. We rather incline to the opinion that the highest peak is further to the northward, and is the same measured by Mr. Thompson, surveyor to the Northwest Company; who, by the joint means of the barometer and trigonometric measurement, ascertained it to be twenty-five thousand feet above the level of the sea; an elevation only inferior to that of the Himalayas. [Editor's note: Irving got the elevation wrong. Mt. McKinley in Alaska is the highest mountain on the North American continent at 20,320 feet. Gannett Peak, the highest in the Wind River Range, tops out at 13,785.]

For a long time, Captain Bonneville remained gazing around him with wonder and enthusiasm; at length the chill and wintry winds, whirling about the snow-clad height, admonished him to descend. He soon regained the spot where he and his companions [companion] had thrown off their coats, which were now gladly resumed, and, retracing their course down the peak, they safely rejoined their companions on the border of the lake.

Notwithstanding the savage and almost inaccessible nature of these mountains, they have their inhabitants. As one of the party was out hunting, he came upon the solitary track of a man in a lonely valley. Following it up, he reached the brow of a cliff, whence he beheld three savages running across the valley below him. He fired his gun to call their attention, hoping to induce them to turn back. They only fled the faster, and disappeared among the rocks. The hunter returned and reported what he had seen. Captain Bonneville at once concluded that these belonged to a kind of hermit race, scanty in number, that inhabit the highest and most inaccessible fastnesses. They speak the Shoshonie language, and probably are offsets from that tribe, though they have peculiarities of their own, which distinguish them from all other Indians. They are miserably poor; own no horses, and are destitute of every convenience to be derived from an intercourse with the whites. Their weapons are bows and stone-pointed arrows, with which they hunt the deer, the elk, and the mountain sheep. They are to be found scattered about the countries of the Shoshonie, Flathead, Crow, and Blackfeet tribes; but their residences are always in lonely places, and the clefts of the rocks.

Their footsteps are often seen by the trappers in the high and solitary valleys among the mountains, and the smokes of their fires descried among the precipices, but they themselves are rarely met with, and still more rarely brought to a parley, so great is their shyness, and their dread of strangers.

As their poverty offers no temptation to the marauder, and as they are inoffensive in their habits, they are never the objects of warfare: should one of them, however, fall into the hands of a war party, he is sure to be made a sacrifice, for the sake of that savage trophy, a scalp, and that barbarous ceremony, a scalp dance. These forlorn beings, forming a mere link between human nature and the brute, have been looked down upon with pity and contempt by the creole trappers, who have given them the appellation of "les dignes de pitie," or "the objects of pity." They appear more worthy to be called the wild men of the mountains.

Chapter 8

"BUFFLER!"

From *The Big Sky,* by A. B. Guthrie, Jr.

As I have not-so-subtly suggested in my introduction to this book, A. B. Guthrie, Jr.'s, *The Big Sky* stands atop the realm of mountain man literature like a colossus. The book is an irresistible, unforgettable achievement of storytelling and descriptive powers. In the tale, Dick Summers is the veteran mountain man leading a French expedition of fur traders into the northernmost reaches of the Missouri River.

Many weeks of hard pulling from St. Louis now, the expedition's boat, called the *Mandan,* has finally reached buffalo country. For Summer's student, young Boone Caudill, an aspiring mountain man of the first rank, the beginning of the greatest hunting of all is at hand.

●　●　●

BOONE PICKED HIS WAY among the sleeping men. Jourdonais' face, faintly horned with the spikes of his mustache, was a dark circle against his darker robe. He was snoring the long deep snore of a man worn out.

"I got you a Hawken," Summers said from the keelboat, keeping his voice low. He handed a gun and horn and pouch over the side to Boone. "It's the real beaver, for buffler or anything."

Boone hefted the rifle and tried it at his shoulder. It was heavier than Old Sure Shot, and it was a flintlock, not a cap and ball, but it felt good to him—well-balanced and stout, like a piece a man could depend on.

A kind of flush was coming into the sky, not light yet but not dark, either. The men lying in their blankets looked big, like horses or buffalo lying down. The mast of the keelboat, dripping with dew, glistened a little. Boone could hear the water lapping against the sides of the *Mandan*. Farther out, the river made a quiet, busy murmur, as if it were talking to itself of things seen upcountry. Once in a while one of the men groaned and moved, easing his muscles on the earth.

"It's winter ground mostly," said Summers, coming down from the boat, "but might be we can get our sights on one."

They started up the river, moving out from the fringe of trees to the open country at the base of the hills, hearing a sudden snort and the sound of flight from a thicket. "Elk," said Summers. "Poor doin's, to my way of thinking, if there's aught else about. We'll git one, if need be. They're plenty now."

"Poor? I was thinkin' they're tasty, the ones we shot so far."

"Nigh anything's better. Dog, for a case. Ever set your teeth in fat pup?" Summers made a noise with his lips. "Or horse? A man gets a taste for it. And beaver tail! I'm half-froze for beaver tail. And buffler, of course, fat fleece and hump rib and marrow bones too good to think of."

"That's best, I reckon."

"You reckon wrong. Painter meat, now, that's some. Painter meat, that's top, now." Summers' moccasined feet seemed to make no noise at all. "But meat's meat, snake meat or man meat or what."

Boone turned to study the hunter's lined and weathered face, wondering if he had eaten man meat, seeing an arm or leg browning and dripping over the fire.

"Injuns like dead meat. You'll see 'em, towin' drowned buffler to shore, buffler that would stink a man out of a skunk's nest. This nigger's et skunk, too. It ain't so bad, if he ain't squirted. The Canadians, now, they set a heap of store by it. It's painter meat to them."

The stars had gone out, and the sky was turning a dull white, like scraped horn. A low cloud was on fire to the east, where the sun would come up. Boone could make out the trees, separate from each other now and standing against the dark hills–short, squatty trees, big at the base, which could hold against the wind. They walked slow, just dragging along, while Summers' eyes kept poking ahead and the light came on and Boone could follow the Missouri with his eye, on and on until it got lost in a far tumble of hills. The ground was spotted in front of them with disks of old buffalo manure under which the grass and weeds grew white, as in a root house. When he turned one over with his toe, little black beetles scurried out into the grass.

"Ain't any fresh," he said. His eyes searched the hills and the gullies that wormed up through them from the river bottom. "Reckon we won't find any?"

Summers didn't answer right away. He would look east, up on the slope of the hills and west to the woods and river and beyond them to where other hills rose up, making a cradle for the Missouri, and sometimes his eyes would stop and fix on something as if it might be game or Indians, and go on after a while and stop again. Boone tried to see what he was seeing, but there was only the river winding ahead and the slopes of the hills and the gullies cutting into them and here and there a low tree, flattened at the top, where birds were chirping.

Half the sun was showing, shining in the grass where the dew was beaded. There wasn't a cloud in all the sky, not even a piece of one now that the one to the east had burned out, and the air was still and waiting-like, as if it were worn out and resting up for a blow.

"Sight easier to kill game along the river, where a man don't have to tote it," Summers said, following the valley with his eyes. "Let's point our stick up, anyway." He turned and started uphill.

From the top Boone could see forever and ever, nearly any way he looked. It was open country, bald and open, without an end. It spread away, flat now and then rolling, going on clear to the sky. A man wouldn't think the whole world was so much. It made the heart come up. It made a man little and still big, like a king looking out. It occurred to Boone that this was the way a bird must feel, free and loose, with the world to choose from. Nothing moved from sky line to sky line. Only down on the river he could see the keelboat showing between the trees, nosing up river like a slow fish. He marked how she poked ahead. He looked on to the tumble of hills that closed in on the river and wondered if she could ever get that far.

Summers had halted, his nose stuck out, like a hound feeling for a scent. "Air's movin' west, if it's movin' at all, I'm thinkin'. All right." He stepped out again, walking with a loose, swift ease.

The sun got up, hot and bright as steel. Off a distance the air began to shimmer in it. Summers kept along the crest of the hills, going slow when they came in sight of a gully or a swale.

It was in one of them that they saw the buffalo, standing quiet with its head down, as if its thoughts were away off. Summers' hand touched Boone's arm. "Old bull," he said, "but meat's meat." The bull lifted his great head and turned it toward them, looking, his beard hanging low.

"He seen us," Boone whispered. "He'll make off."

"Shoo!" said Summers, putting his hand on the lifted barrel of Boone's rifle. "They can't see for nothin', and hearin' don't mean a thing to 'em. It's all right, long as he don't get wind of us." He started forward, walking slow. "You kin shoot him."

"Now?"

"Wait a spell."

The bull didn't move. He stood with his head turned and down, as if for all his blindness he knew they were there. Boone's mind went back to his blind Aunt Minnie who could always tell when someone was around. Her head would pivot and her face would wait, while she looked out of eyes that didn't see.

"Take your wipin' stick. Make a rest. Like this." Summers put the stick out at arm's length and had Boone hold it with his left hand and let the rifle lie across his wrist. "Let 'im have it."

The rifle bucked against Boone's shoulder, cracking the silence. The ball made a gun-shot sound, and a little puff of dust came from the buffalo, as if he had been hit with a pebble. For an instant he stood there looking dull and sad, as if nothing had happened, and then he broke into a clumsy gallop, heading out of the gully. Boone watched him, and heard another crack by his side and saw the bull break down at the knees and fall ahead on his nose. He lay on his side, his legs waving, his breath making a snore in his nose.

Summers was reloading, grinning as he did so. "Too high." Boone felt naked in the bright blue gaze of his eyes, as if what he felt in his mind was standing out for the hunter to see. Summers' face changed. "Don't think nothin' of it. Nigh everybody shoots high, first time. Just a hand and a half above the brisket, that's the spot. It's a lesson for you. Best load up again, afore anything."

Quicker than Boone could believe, Summers charged his gun. He hitched his pouch and powder horn around, drew the stopper from the horn with his teeth, put the mouth of it in his left hand, and with his right turned the horn up. He was ramming down his load before Boone got his powder measured out.

The buffalo's eyes were fading. They looked soft now, deep and soft with the light going out of them. His legs still waved a little. Summers put his knife in his throat. "We'll roll him over, and this child'll show you how to get at good feedin'." He planted the four legs out at the sides, so that the buffalo seemed to have been squashed down from above. The hunter's knife flashed in the sun. It made a cut crosswise on the neck, and Summers grabbed the hair of the boss with his other hand and separated the skin from the shoulder. He laid the skin open to the tail and peeled it down the sides, spreading it out. "Can't take much," he said, chopping with his hatchet. "Tongue and liver and fleece fat and such. Or maybe one of us best go and git some help from the boat. Wisht we had a pack mule."

"There's a wolf."

Summers looked around at the grinning face that watched them from behind a little rise. "Buffler wolf. White wolf." He spoke in jerks while his knife worked. "I seen fifteen-twenty of 'em circled around sometimes."

"Don't you never shoot 'em?"

"Have to be nigh gone for meat. Ain't enough powder and ball on the Missouri to shoot 'em all."

Boone found a rock and pitched it at the wolf. The head disappeared behind the rise and came into sight again a jump or two away.

Summers kept looking up from his butchering, turning to study every direction, and then going back to the bull again. "See them cayutes?" Boone watched them slink up, their feet moving as if they ran a twisting line, their eyes yellow and hungry. They came closer than the wolf and sat down. Their tongues came out and dripped on the grass. "Watch!" Summers threw a handful of gut toward them. The bigger one darted in, seized the gut, and made off, but he hadn't got far before the wolf jumped on him and took it away. The coyote came back and sat down again. "Happens every time," said Summers. He had the liver out, and the gall bladder. He cut a slice of liver and dipped it in the bladder and poked it in his mouth, chewing and gulping while he worked. "For poor bull, it ain't so bad. Want some?"

Boone took a slice. While he was making himself chew on it, he saw the cloud of dust. It came from behind a little pitch of land maybe two miles to the north, and it wasn't a cloud so much as a vapor, a wisp that he expected to disappear like a fleck in the eye. He wondered whether to point it out to Summers. The wisp came on to the top of the pitch. There was a movement under it. He said then, "Reckon you catched sight of that?"

Summers looked along, the knife idle in his hand. "I be dogged! Hold still now! It's brown skin, sure as I be, but maybe just Puncas." After what seemed to Boone a long time, he added, "Let's back up toward cover. We can cache, maybe. Here's a hoss as don't like it."

He peeled off his shirt and spread it on the ground and put on it the parts of the carcass he had cut out to save, folding the shirt over afterward. Boone narrowed his eye against the glare. Those were horses under the dust cloud, with riders on them.

"Might be we can git back with this here," said Summers. "They seen us all right." He lifted his parcel. "Poor doin's, anyhow, to let Injuns think you're runnin'. Even the squaws get braved up then, and full of hell. Ease away, now." His voice was sure and quiet.

Boone scanned the river, looking for the *Mandan*. "Ain't hardly had time to pull this fur," said Summers, "with no breeze to help."

They dropped down behind the crest of the hills, out of sight of the Indians. "Hump it! Hump it some!" They broke for the thin timber two hundred yards and more away, with Summers holding his bundle out from him so as not to hinder his leg.

"I'll take 'er," Boone panted, but Summers only shook his head.

"All right." Summers slowed to an unhurried walk. The Indians came to the top of the hill and halted, outlined against the sky.

"We'll make peace sign." Summers put his parcel down and fired his rifle at the sky. Afterwards, he took his pipe out and held it high for the Indians to see.

The Indians looked and talked among themselves, until one of them yelled and all joined in, kind of high, quavering yell. They sent their horses down the bluff, the hoofs making a clatter in a patch of stones.

"Gimme your Hawken and load this 'un." They were still a throw away from the fringe of woods along the river. Summers took the wiping stick from its slot while he watched. "Sioux, by beaver, or this nigger don't know Injun. They can't circle us here, anyways. Git ready, old hoss, but hold fire till I give the sign." He planted his wiping stick out before him and laid the rifle on its rest. "That's it, hoss, and line your sights on the belly, not the head."

A hundred and fifty yards away the Indians pulled up. Boone counted them. Twelve men. They were naked from the waist up, unless a man counted the feathers stuck in their hair. Their skin looked smooth and soft, like good used leather. It would make a better strop than the one he'd left in Louisville. Three or four had guns in their hands, and the others bows. Their horses minced around as they waited.

"It ain't a war party, anyhow," Summers said, as if he was making talk at night around the fire.

"How can a body tell?"

"No paint. No shields. They're huntin', I'm thinkin'."

Summers stood up. His voice went out, rough and steady and strong, in language Boone didn't understand, and his hands made movements in front of him.

The Indians listened, sitting their horses as if they were grown on them. Sometimes as the horses moved Boone could see the Indians' hair, hanging far down in plaits. The foremost of them, though, the one who seemed to be the leader, had chopped it off short.

Summers' voice came to a halt. To Boone he said, "A man never knows about Sioux."

The Indians sat their milling horses. Their heads moved, and their hands, as they talked to one another. The Indian with the short hair rode out. The tail of some animal hung from his moccasin. His voice was stronger than Summers' and came more from his chest.

"Asks if we're squaws, to run," Summers translated. "And what have we got for presents? His tongue is short but his arm is long, and he feels blood in his eye."

The Indian halted, waiting for Summers' reply. "I'm thinkin' they just met up with an enemy and got the worst of the tussle. That makes 'em mean as all hell. I'll tell 'em our tongues ain't so long either, but our guns is a heap longer'n them crazy fusees." His voice went out again.

Suddenly, while the rest watched, the Indian with the short hair let out a yell and put his horse to a gallop, coming straight at them. He was low on his horse, just the top of him showing and the legs at the sides.

Summers dropped to one knee again and leveled his gun, and nothing seemed to move about him except the end of the barrel bearing on the rider. Boone was down, too, with his rifle up, seeing the out-flung hoofs of the horse and the flaring nostrils. He would be on them in a shake. The horse bore out a little, and the cropped head moved, and the black of a barrel came over the horse's neck. Summers' rifle spoke, and in a wink the horse was running free, shying out in a circle and going back. The Indian lay on his belly. He didn't move. "That's one for the wolves," Summers said. His hand came over and gave Boone the empty rifle and took the loaded one and drew away with it. "Load up!"

The Indians had sat, watching the one and yelling for him. They hushed when he fell and then all began to yell again, the voices rising shrill and falling. They set their horses to a run streaking to one side and then the other, not coming directly at Boone and Summers, but working closer as the line went back and forth. Sometimes one, bolder than the rest, would charge out of the line and come nearer, waving his gun or bow while he shouted, and then go back to the line again. "Hold your sights on one," Summers said, "the one with the speckled pony. Hold fire till I tell you. Then plumb center with it." He had taken his pistols from his belt and had them out before him, ready to his hand.

The Indians made themselves small on the horses, swinging to the off side as they turned. "Shoo!" Summers said. "They can't ride for nothin'. Can't shine with Comanches, or even Crows."

"Why'n't they charge, all of 'em?"

Summers' eye ran along the barrel of his gun. "They got no stummick for that kind of doin's, save once in a while ones like to shine alone, like that nigger out there."

A rifle cracked, and in front of them the ground exploded in a little blast of dust. "Steady. Time to go ag'in." Out of the corner of his eye Boone saw smoke puff from the gun. A running horse stumbled and fell. The Indians shouted, higher and wilder. The fallen horse lay on its rider. Boone saw the rider, just the head and jerking hands of him beyond the horse, trying to pull his leg free. Summers handed over the empty rifle. Two Indians flew to the one who was down, slipped from the off sides of their horses, and, stopping behind the downed horse, rolled the withers up. The fallen rider tried to arise and went off crawling, dragging one leg.

The others, driven back a little by the shot, began to come in again, working to and fro. One of them bobbed up and swung his rifle over. The ball sang past Boone. He had the rifle primed again, and the Indian on the speckled pony on his sights. "Kin I shoot one?" He didn't wait. The sights seemed to steady of themselves and fix just above the pony's neck. His fingers bore on the trigger, like it had a mind of its own. The rifle jumped.

"I be dogged."

The speckled pony shied off. Behind him a man squirmed on the ground, squirmed and got up and went back, bent at the middle.

"Slicker'n ice, Caudill."

The Indians bunched up, talking and gesturing. "They had nigh enough, I'm thinkin'," said Summers, raising his cheek from his rifle. He added, "For now."

"That's the boat."

The trumpet had sounded, cutting through the still air, rolling up the river and out to the hills and coming back on itself. Boone saw the *Mandan*. The oars made little even flashes as the men laid them back.

Someone was busy in the bow. It looked like Jourdonais. It was him, working at the swivel gun, which was a bar of light in the bow. The Indians looked, holding their horses tight, easing them backward away from the river. The swivel belched smoke, and the sound of it came to them, a rolling boom like thunder. Jourdonais got busy with it again.

"First shot was just to skeer'em. Second'll be business."

But the Sioux drew off, turning back and shouting and shaking their arms as they went. Boone watched them long enough to see that they picked up the two crippled warriors.

Summers put his pistols back in his belt and fitted his wiping stick to his rifle. He and Boone walked ahead, to the Indian who lay in the grass. Summers stooped over. His knife cut into the scalp and made a rough circle, from which the blood beaded. He got hold of the Indian's short hair and tore the circle loose, leaving the piece of skull naked and raw. "Take his gun. This Injun's had a grief lately. Some of his kin's gone under—a brother, maybe. That's why he chopped his tails off. Looks recent, don't it? Like as not it just happened. That's why they was so froze for our scalps, so's they wouldn't have to go home beaten and with nary thing to shine with." He went back and picked up his bundle of meat, carrying scalp and bundle in one hand.

The *Mandan* pulled in, so close they could hop aboard. Jourdonais' bold, dark face questioned Summers. The Creoles looked at him, too, their eyes big and watchful like the eyes of a frog ready to jump if a man took another step.

Summers said, "We put one under and winged two." The barrel of his rifle swung toward Boone. "There's a hoss as'll shoot plumb center." In tones that Boone barely overheard he went on, "We ain't seen the last of 'em, I'm thinkin'."

NARRATIVE *of a* MOUNTAIN MAN

From *Narrative of the Adventures of Zenas Leonard Written by Himself*

Zenas Leonard (1809-1857) was a young Pennsylvanian whose mountain man adventures began in 1831, when he left St. Louis in a fur trading company of seventy men. Leonard later was in the employ of Captain Bonneville and was with Joseph Walker's party exploring the Great Salt Lake area. Leonard's journal, while certainly no prose masterpiece, still stands as an interesting, highly readable perspective on the mountain man life. Some historians have pointed out some important discrepancies between Leonard's accounts of certain events and those of Washington Irving's "rewrites" of Bonneville's journals. Readers with a scholarly interest in mountain man literature are strongly urged to read both the Leonard and Bonneville narratives and their accompanying introductions.

• • •

OCT. 22ND. The nights getting somewhat cold, and snow falling more or less every day, we began to make preparations to return to our winter quarters, at the mouth of Laramies river; and on the 25th commenced our tour down the river. On the 28th we arrived at the mountain, that we crossed going up, but found it impossible, owing to the enormous depth of the snow to pass over it. On the morning of the 30th we started a number of men up and down the valley, on search of a place to cross the mountain, who returned the next day and reported that they had found no passing place over the mountain; when under these circumstances a majority of the company decided in favor of encamping in this valley for the winter, and when the ice melted out of the river, in the spring, commence trapping until such times as the snow melted off the mountain; when we would return to the mouth of the river, where we had secreted our goods.

On the 1st day of November we commenced travelling up the valley, on search of a suitable place to pass the winter, and on the evening of the 4th, we arrived at a large grove of Cottonwood timber, which we deemed suitable for encamping in.–Several weeks were spent in building houses, stables, &c. necessary for ourselves, and horses during the winter season.– This being done, we commenced killing buffaloe, and hanging up the choice pieces to dry, so that if they should leave the valley we would have a sufficient quantity of meat to last us until spring. We also killed Deer, Bighorn Sheep, Elk, Antelope, &c., and dressed the hides to make moccasins.

About the 1st of December finding our horses getting very poor, we thought it necessary to commence feeding them on Cottonwood bark; for which purpose each man turned out and peeled and collected a quantity of this bark, from the grove in which we were encamped for his horses; but to our utter surprise and discomfiture, on presenting it to them they would not eat it, and upon examining it by tasting, we found it to be the bitter, instead of the sweet Cottonwood. Immediately, upon finding we were deceived, men were dispatched up and down the valley, on search of Sweet Cottonwood, but returned without success. Several weeks were spent in fruitless exertion to obtain feed for our horses; finally we were compelled to give it up, and agreed that our horses must all starve to death. The great depth of the snow, and the extreme coldness of the weather, soon prevented our horses from getting any thing to subsist upon, & they commenced dying. It seldom happened during all our difficulties, that my sympathies were more sensibly touched, than on viewing these starving creatures. I would willingly have divided my provision with my horses, if they would have eat it.

On new-years day, notwithstanding our horses were nearly all dead, as being fully satisfied that the few that were yet living must die soon, we concluded to have a feast in our best style; for which purpose we made preparation by sending out four of our best hunters, to get a choice piece of meat for the occasion. These men killed ten Buffaloe, from which they selected one of the fattest humps they could find and brought in, and after roasting it handsomely before the fire, we all seated ourselves upon the ground, encircling, what we there called a splendid repast to dine upon. Feasting sumptuously, cracking a few jokes, taking a few rounds with our rifles, and wishing heartily for some liquor, having none at that place we spent the day.

The glorious 8th arrived, the recollection of the achievements of which, are calculated to gladden the hearts of the American people; but it was not so glorious to us. We found our horses on that day, like Pakenham's forces, well nigh defunct. Here we were in this valley, surrounded on either side by insurmountable barriers of snow, with all our merchandize and nothing to pack it upon, but two mules–all the rest of our horses being dead. For ourselves we had plenty to eat, and were growing fat and uneasy;–but how we were to extricate ourselves from this perilous situation, was a question of deep and absorbing interest to each individual. About the 10th we held a consultation, to decide what measures should be taken for our relief. Mr. Stephens, our pilot, having been at Santafee, in New Mexico, some 8 or 10 years previous, informed the company that horses in that place, were very cheap; and that he was of the opinion he could take them to it, if they saw proper to follow him. It was finally agreed upon by the company, that a part of them should start for Santafee; but not, however, without a good deal of confusion; as many were of the opinion that the snow on the mountain in the direction of Santafee, would be found to be as insurmountable, as in the direction of their merchandize, and also that the distance was too great to attempt to travel on foot, at that season of the year. It appearing from the maps to be little short of 800 miles.

On the morning of the 14th, finding every thing in readiness for our Santafee trip, we set out, each man with his bedding, rifle and nine Beaver skins, packed upon his back; leaving four men only to take care of our merchandize, and the two mules. The beaver skins we took for the purpose of trading to the inhabitants of Santafee for horses, mules, &c. We appointed from the middle of April till the middle of may, as our time for returning; and if we did not return within that time, our four men were to wait no longer, but return to the mouth of the Laramies river, to meet the rest of the company. We continued in the direction of Santafee, without any extraordinary occurrence, for several days—found game plenty and but little snow, until we arrived at the foot of a great mountain, which appeared to be totally covered with snow. Here we thought it advisable to kill and jirk some buffaloe meat, to eat while crossing this mountain, after which we continued our course; finding much difficulty in travelling, owing to the stormy weather & deep snow—so much so indeed, that had it not been for a path made by the buffaloe bulls it would have been impossible to travel.

The channel of the river where it passes through these mountains is quite narrow in places and the banks very steep. In such places the beaver build their dams from bank to bank; and when they become old the beaver leave them, and they break and overflow the ground, which then produces a kind of flag grass. In the fall of the year, the Buffaloe collect in such places to eat this grass, and when the snow falls too deep they retreat to the plains; and it was in these trails that we ascended the mountain.

We still continued our course along this buffaloe path, which led us to the top of the mountain; nothing occurring more than it continued to snow day and night. On the 25th we arrived on the top of the mountain, and wishing to take a view of the country, if it should cease snowing. In the morning it still continued to snow so rapidly that we were obliged to remain in the camp all day, and about the middle of the day, we eat the last of our jirk, and that evening we were obliged to go to bed supperless.

On the 29th it still continued to snow, and having nothing to eat, we thought it high time to be making some move, for our preservation, or we must perish in this lonely wilderness. The question then arose, shall we return to the valley from whence we came, or continue in the direction of Santafee. This question caused considerable disturbance. Those who were in favor of going ahead, argued that it was too far back to game—that it would be impossible to return before starving to death; while those who were for returning contented that it was the heighth of imprudence, to proceed in the direction of Santafee. Accordingly we made preparations, and started. We travelled across the summit of the mountain, where we found a plain about a mile wide, which with great difficulty, owing to the fierceness of the wind, we succeeded in crossing; but when we attempted to go into the timber, on the opposite side from the mountain, we found it impossible, in consequence of the depth of the snow, and were obliged to turn back and recross the plain. As we returned by the fire we had made going over the plain the first time, we halted for the purpose of mutually deciding what to do; when it was determined by the company, that we would, if possible, return to our four men & two mules. We then started on search of the buffaloe path which we had followed to the top of the mountain; but owing to the strong wind, that had blown for several days, and the increased depth of the snow, it was invisible. We then attempted to travel in the snow without the path, but we found this equally as impossible, as in the direction of Santafee.

Here we were, in a desolate wilderness, uninhabited (at that season of the year) by even the hardy savage or wild beast—surrounded on either side by huge mountains of snow, without one mouthful to eat, save a few beaver skins—our eyes almost destroyed by the piercing wind, and our bodies at times almost buried by the flakes of snow which were driven before it. Oh! how heartily I wished myself at home; but wishing, in such a case appeared useless—action alone could save us. We had not even leather to make snow shoes, but as good fortune would have it, some of the men had the front part of their pantaloons lined with deer skin, and others had great coats of different kinds of skin, which we collected together to make snow shoes of. This appeared to present to us the only means of escape from starvation and death. After gathering up every thing of leather kind that could be found, we got to making snow shoes, and by morning each man was furnished with a pair. But what were we to subsist upon while crossing the mountain, was a painful question that agitated every bosom, and employed every tongue in company. Provision, we had none, of any description; having eaten every thing we had that could be eat with the exception of a few beaver skins, and, after having fasted several days, to attempt to travel the distance of the valley, without any thing to eat, appeared almost worse than useless. Thinking, however, that we might as well perish one place as another, and that it was the best to make an exertion to save ourselves; and after each man had selected two of the best beaver skins to eat as he travelled along, we hung the remainder upon a tree, and started to try our fortune with the snow shoes. Owing to the softness of the snow, and the poor construction of our snow shoes, we soon found this to be a difficult and laborious mode of travelling. The first day after we started with our snow shoes we travelled but three or four miles and encamped for the night, which, for want of a good fire, we passed in the most distressing manner. Wood was plenty but we were unable to get it, and it kept one or two of the men busy to keep what little fire we had from going out as it melted the snow and sunk down. On the morning (30th Jan.) after roasting and eating some of our beaver skins, we continued our journey through the snow. In this way we continued to travel until the first day of February, in the afternoon, when we came to where the crust on the snow was sufficiently strong to carry us. Here we could travel somewhat faster, but at the best not much faster than a man could crawl on his hands and feet, as some of the men from hunger and cold were almost insensible of their situation, and so weak that they could scarcely stand on their feet, much less walk at speed. As we approached the foot of the mountain the snow became softer and would not carry us. This caused the most resolute despair, as it was obviously impossible, owing to extreme weakness, for us to wade much further through the snow. As we moved down the mountain plunging and falling through the snow, we approached a large spruce or cedar tree, the drooping branches of which had prevented the snow from falling to the ground about its trunk–here we halted to rest. While collected under the sheltering boughs of this tree, viewing, with horrified feelings, the way-worn, and despairing countenances of each other, a Mr. Carter, a Virginian, who was probably the nighest exhausted of any of the company, burst into tears and said, "here I must die." This made a great impression upon the remainder of the company, and they all, with the exception of a Mr. Hockday and myself, despaired of going any further. Mr. Hockday, however, after some persuasion, telling them that if they had the strength to follow us we would break the road as far as possible, if not out to the valley, succeeded in getting them started once more.–Mr. Hockday was a large muscular man, as hardy as a mule and as resolute as a lion; yet kind and affectionate. He was then decidedly the stoutest man in the company, and myself, probably, the next stoutest.

As for our Captain, Mr. Stephens, he was amongst the weakest of the company.

We resumed our journey, and continued to crawl along through the deep snow slowly till the evening of the fourth, when we arrived in the plain at the foot of the mountain. Here we found the snow so shallow that we could dispense with the use of our snow shoes; and while in the act of taking them off some of the men discovered, at the distance of 70 or 80 yards; two animals feeding in the brush, which they supposed to be buffaloe, but from blindness, caused by weakness and pine smoke, could not be positive. Mr. Hockday and I were selected to approach and kill one of the animals without regard to what they might prove to be, while the remainder of the company were to go to a neighboring grove of timber and kindle a fire. Having used our guns as walking canes in the snow, we found them much out of order, and were obliged to draw out the old loads and put in new ones, before attempting to shoot. After taking every precaution we deemed necessary to insure success, we started and crawled along on our hands and knees, until we approached within ten or fifteen steps of the animals, when Mr. Hockday prepared to shoot; but upon finding that he could not see the sight of the gun or hold it at arms length, forbore, and proposed to me to shoot. I accordingly fixed myself and pulled trigger. My gun missed fire! I never was so wrecked with agitation as at that moment. "There," said I, "our game is gone, and we are not able to follow it much further;" but as good fortune had it, the Buffaloe, (for such we had discovered them to be), did not see nor smell us, and after raising their heads out of the snow, and looking around for a few moments for the cause of the noise, again commenced feeding. I then picked the flint of my gun, fired and broke the back of one of the Buffaloe, my ball not taking effect within 18 inches of where I thought I aimed.–The men in the grove of timber, on hearing the report of my rifle came staggering forth to learn the result, and when they received the heart-cheering intelligence of success they raised a shout of joy. It was amusing to witness the conduct of some of the men on this occasion. Before we had caught the buffaloe they appeared scarcely able to speak—but a moment after that, were able to hollow like Indians at war. I will not describe the scene that followed here—the reader may imagine it—an account of it would be repulsive and offensive rather than agreeable. This was the ninth day since we had eaten anything but dried beaver skins. We remained at this place for four days feasting upon the carcass of this Buffaloe, during which time we recruited considerably in strength and spirits, and on the 8th we resumed our journey down the river in search of our four men and two mules, and soon landed in the valley where game was plenty, and but little snow to obstruct our march. We continued our journey, killing plenty of game and living well, without any strange occurrence until the 14th, when we halted within a short distance of our old camp, and sent two or three of our worst looking men ahead to see whether they would be recognized by the four men. They were not known immediately on arriving at the camp, but no sooner engaged in conversation that they were recognized by the four men, and heartily welcomed back.

Here we remained at our old station until the 14th of March, during which period, having plenty of good buffaloe meat to eat, we regained our usual health and appearance. Anxious to be doing something, eight of us made preparations to start again to Santafee for horses. We were to travel south, along the foot of the mountain till we came to a certain river which heads in the mountain near where we had hung the beaver skins on the pine tree; after finding this river we were to commence trapping, and also to endeavor to get the beaver fur off the mountain into the valley. The balance of the company, 13 in number, were to remain at the camp and secrete the merchandize, and then follow us to this river, where we were to meet; and if we had succeeded in getting the beaver skins off the mountain, we were to join together and proceed in the direction of Santafee. With this understanding we started, and pursued our course slowly along the base of the mountain–found game plenty–met with no obstacle to impede our march, and on the 20th we arrived on the bank of the river. After remaining here a few days the ice melted out of the creeks and we commenced and continued to trap for beaver until the 28th during which time we caught a fine quantity of fur, and built ourselves a wigwam after the Indian fashion. The weather continuing warm and pleasant, and having a large quantity of dried meat on hand we concluded to hide our traps, beaver skins, baggage, &c., in our wigwam and pack a portion of the jirked meat on our backs and make an effort to get the beaver skins off the pine tree where we had left them in January. We started, and after travelling up the river along the side of the mountain for two or three days, we came in contact with huge mountains of snow and insurmountable icebergs, and were compelled to abandon our course & return back again to the plain. When we had arrived within a short distance of our wigwam, on our return, we discovered several trails of moccasin tracks in the snow. Some of the company became somewhat alarmed at these signs, supposing them to be the trails of hostile Indians–others appeared rejoiced, and said it was the remainder of our company.–The dispute was soon decided, for on arriving at our wigwam, we found it completely robbed of everything we had left in it–traps, blankets, beaver skins and other utensils were all gone–nothing remained but the naked frame of the little hut.–We had now nothing left to sleep on save one old blanket for each man which we had with us on the mountain, and had nearly lost all our traps. Under these highly aggravating circumstances some of the men became desperate, declared they would retake their property or die in the attempt. For my part, I viewed the matter calmly and seriously and determined to abide the dictates of prudence only. Seeing from the trail of the Indians that they were not very numerous, and had a number of horses with them, we determined, after some controversy, to rob them of their horses, or other property commensurate to our loss. Accordingly we made preparations for our perilous adventure—we eat supper, prepared our fire arms, and a little after dark set out on search of the enemy—the night was calm and clear. We traversed the valley up and down for several hours without making any discoveries; we then ascended an adjacent hill, from the summit of which we discovered at a considerable distance a number of dim fires. A controversy here arose amongst the men as to the expediency of attacking the Indians. It was finally decided, however, by a majority of the company, that we should attack them at all hazards. We started in the direction of the fires, and after travelling some distance, and having lost sight of the fires, some of the men again became discouraged, and strongly urged the propriety of abandoning the project; but on calling a vote a majority again decided in favor of attacking the Indians and in a few minutes after we arrived on the top of a hill, within 50 or 60 yards of the enemy's camp. Here we halted for the purpose of reconnoitering. At this time the moon was just rising above the summit of the mountain, and casting its glimmering rays o'er the valley beneath, but did not shine on the Indian camp.—There were five fires, and the Indians appearing more numerous than we had expected to find them, we thought it advisable to be as careful and judicious about attacking them as possible. At the foot of this hill, near a large rock, we left our hats, coats and every thing that was unnecessary in action—we also designated this as a point of meeting, in case we should get separated in the skirmish; and had an understanding that but two should fire at a time, and that Capt. Stephens was to command. Mr. Hockday and I were selected to shoot first. We then started & crawled silently along on our hands and knees until we got within eight or ten steps of one of the fires, where we laid down in the brush, with our heads close together to consult as to the most proper mode of surprising the savages, whose dusky forms were then extended in sleep around the dying embers. While in this position, some eager for the conflict, others trembling with fear, a large dog rose from one of the fires and commenced growling and barking in the most terrifying manner. The spell of silence was now broken, and an immediate and final skirmish with our enemy rendered unavoidable. Thinking ourselves rather too much exposed to the fire of the Indians we retreated fifteen or twenty steps down the bank. Some of the Indians then came to the top of the bank and commenced shooting arrows at us, and yelling at the extent of their lungs. At this moment Mr. Stephens was heard to say in a firm tone "now is the time my boys, we must fight or die;" upon this Mr. Hockday and I fired; one of the Indians on the bank was seen to fall, and the remainder ran back to the camp. On hearing the report of our rifles the Indians, to the number of two or three hundred, rose out of the bushes and literally covered the plain, while their terrific war whoop—mingled with an occasional crack of a rifle, rendered the aspect of things more threatening than the most timid had before anticipated. We ran to our appointed place to meet, but before we had time to gather our baggage, we found ourselves completely surrounded and hemmed in on every side by the savages. Finding that we could not escape by flight, but must fight, we ran to the top of the hill, and having sheltered ourselves as well as we could amongst the rocks, commenced yelling and firing in turn, (yelling is a very essential point in Indian warfare.) This scene was kept up for near an hour without any damage to our company, and as we supposed, but little injury to the Indians. The savages seeing we were determined to defend ourselves to the last gave way on the opposite side of the hill from their camp, and we made our escape out of their circle, and were glad to get away with our lives, without any of our property or that of the Indians. The scenes of this night will ever be indelibly impressed upon my memory.

After travelling five or six miles we came to a deep ravine or hollow—we carefully descended the precipice to the flat below, where we encamped for the night; but from fright, fatigue, cold and hunger, I could not sleep, and lay contemplating on the striking contrast between a night in the villages of Pennsylvania and one on the Rocky Mountains.

In the latter, the plough-boy's whistle, the gambols of the children on the green, the lowing of the herds, and the deep tones of the evening bell, are unheard; not a sound strikes upon the ear, except perchance the distant howling of some wild beast, or war-whoop of the uncultivated savage–all was silent on this occasion save the muttering of a small brook as it wound its way through the deep cavities of the gulph down the mountain, and the gentle whispering of the breeze, as it crept through the dark pine or cedar forest, and sighed in melancholy accents; nor is it the retiring of the "god of day" to his couch in the western horizon that brings on this desolate scene–his rising in the east does not change the gloomy aspect–night and day are nearly the same in this respect.

About midnight we were alarmed by a shrill whistle on the rocks above, & supposing it to be the Indians on pursuit of us we seized our guns and ran a few rods from our fires. After waiting for some time, without hearing any more noise, one of the men ascended the precipice, and discovered that the object of our fears was a large drove of Elk. In the morning we continued to travel down this ravine,–and I was struck with the rough and picturesque appearance of the adjacent hills. On our right and left, arose like two perpendicular ramparts, to the heighth of near two hundred feet, two chains of mountains. Not a blade of grass, bush or plant was to be seen on these hard slopes,–huge rocks, detached from the main body, supported by the recumbent weight of other unseen rocks, appeared in the act of falling, and presented a frightful appearance–nothing met the eye but an inexhaustible avalanch of rocks–sombre, gray or black rocks. If Dante had designed to picture in one of his circles, the Hell of Stones, he might have taken this scene for his model.–This is one scenery in the vicinity of the Rocky Mountains; and perhaps an hour's travel would present another of a very different character–one that the artist who designed to depict a beautiful and enchanting landscape would select for a model.

After travelling some fifteen or twenty miles, we came to the trail where the main body of the Indians with whom we had the skirmish the evening before, had passed along. It was near half a mile wide, and the snow was literally trodden into the earth. I have since understood from whites who had been in the habit of trading with this nation, prior to their declaration of hostilities against the whites, that they numbered from seven to eight hundred warriors. Alarmed at this formidable appearance of the hostile Indians, we mutually declined the idea of going to Santa Fee, and turned and travelled in the direction of the main body of our company.

We continued to travel day after day, with all possible speed—occasionally killing a buffaloe, a goat, or a bighorn, as we passed over the plains and prairies which were literally covered with these animals; and on the morning of the 9th of April, we arrived safe at our old camp, & were gratified to find our thirteen men and two mules in the enjoyment of good health, with plenty to eat and drink. After exchanging civilities all around, by a hearty shake of the hand, and taking some refreshment, which was immediately prepared for us, I related to the company the dismal tidings of the near approach of the hostile Indians, and the circumstances of being robbed by them, and being defeated in the attempt to retake our property.—All were now satisfied of the imprudence of attempting to go to Santa Fee by this route, as well as of the necessity of devising some other method of saving our merchandize. We finally concluded to conceal our merchandize, baggage, fur, and every thing that we could not pack on our backs or on the two mules, and return to our appointed winter quarters, at the mouth of the Laramies River, with the expectation of meeting Capt. Gant, and obtaining some assistance from him. On the morning of the 20th of April, having made every necessary preparation, we set out on our journey for the mouth of the Laramies river. After two days travel, we came to the foot of the mountain which we had endeavored in vain to cross in November. The snow was still deep on the top of it; but by aid of the buffaloe trails, we were enabled to scale it without much difficulty, except that our mules suffered with hunger, having had nothing to eat but pine brush. At the foot of the mountain we found an abundance of sweet cottonwood, and our mules being very fond of it, we detained two or three days to let them recruit from their suffering in crosing the mountains. This mountain and the one we left our fur on, are covered with the most splendid timber of different kinds such as fir, cedar, white pine, &c. On the margin of the rivers and creeks in the plains, the only timber is cottonwood, undergrowth, willow and rose bushes; out in the middle of the plains there is none of any description. In the month of June, a person by taking a view of the country east of this mountain with a spy glass, could see nothing but a level plain extending from the foot of the mountain as far as the eye can penetrate, covered with green grass, and beautiful flowers of various descriptions; and by turning to the northwest, the eye meets nothing but a rough and dismal looking mountain, covered with snow, and presenting all the appearance of dreary winter. These plains extend to the state of Missouri, with scarce a hill or a grove of timber to interrupt the sight, and literally covered with game of almost every kind.

On the 25th we again resumed our journey down the river, and continued ahead without any difficulty–passing over nearly the same ground that we had travelled over going up the fall before; killing plenty of game–buffaloe, deer, bear, bighorn, antelope, &c. and on the 20th May we landed at the mouth of the Laramies; but to our utter astonishment and discomfiture we discovered that not one of the parties had returned according to the agreement.

Chapter 10

THE LEGEND *of* BROKEN HAND

From *The Mountain Men,* by George Laycock

Published by The Lyons Press in 1988 and republished in 1996, George Laycock's *The Mountain Men,* with illustrations by Tom Beecham, is one of the best books you can get your hands on for portraits of the most famous mountain men and their exploits. In addition, the book is packed with illustrations and text on gear and skills. Laycock's subject here is the legendary Tom Fitzpatrick.

• • •

TRAPPER TOM FITZPATRICK was known to the Indians by two strange names, both of them earned the hard way. Sometimes they called him "Broken Hand," but after his miraculous escape in the summer of 1832, during which his hair was said to have lost its normal dark-brown color, the Indians named him "White Hair."

Fitzpatrick was born in Ireland, in 1799, and was still a teenager when he found his way to this land of promise. Stories coming from the frontier excited his imagination, and like many another young man of his time, he made his way westward over the mountains and along the rivers until he landed in St. Louis. There, he heard the excited talk of beaver and riches to be earned trapping them, and he joined William Ashley's crew in the spring of 1823, to go up the Missouri.

Although he was of medium height and slender build, he was strong for his size, and possessed natural traits essential to a leader among the trappers: self-assurance, decisiveness, and everyday horse sense.

These qualities soon brought him to the attention of Ashley, who needed dependable men. Fitz, in company with his good friend Jed Smith, was traveling westward with a small trapping party in the harsh winter of 1823–1824. Historians believe that Smith was in charge and Fitzpatrick was second in command. One of their party was Edward Rose, who had friends among the Crows. Rose had heard that across the Continental Divide, in the Green River country, there was an abundance of beaver still untouched by white trappers. Smith and Fitzpatrick, always searching for virgin trapping country, headed for the Green River.

On this trip, nature put them to the test. Game was scarce; the men were hungry much of the time. Bitter, howling winds sapped their strength. Their horses grew weak. That March, they made their way along a broad, flat region that led upward so gradually that it scarcely seemed to be a climb at all. They noticed that the streams were now flowing toward the West instead of the East. The trappers had crossed the Continental Divide and found the South Pass over the Rockies. They had come down into the headwaters of the Green or, as the trappers knew it from the Indians, the Seedskeedee. Their route would become a thoroughfare for trappers and explorers, missionaries, and wagon trains of farmers.

In the Green River country, the beaver turned out to be as plentiful as the Indians predicted. The party split into two parts and began acquiring fat packs of fur. Then, Fitzpatrick's fortunes took a bad turn.

His group had been joined by a band of Shoshones who ate abundantly on the leftover beaver meat the trappers could not use. The Indians seemed friendly, but one night they slipped away and took with them all the trappers' horses. This put Fitzpatrick and his crew in an extremely hazardous situation, and they were hundreds of miles from help.

They had no way to transport their furs to the first summer rendezvous in 1825, so they cached their furs, traps, saddles, and other property, and set off in a somber mood, traveling on foot and hoping to avoid other troublesome Indians. Some days later the little file of white trappers rounded a bend in the mountain trail and came face to face with half a dozen Indians. Shoshones. The horses they rode looked mighty familiar.

Faster than the Indians could make the peace sign, Fitzpatrick's crew had the muzzles of their flintlocks covering them at point-blank range. They took back their mounts, then they forced their captives to guide them to the Indian village, where they reclaimed, at gunpoint, the rest of their horses. After the scowling Shoshones turned over all the horses the trappers could identify, there still remained one horse unaccounted for.

This wasn't going to wash with Fitz. He was plain damn angry and he instantly ordered his men to tie one of the Indians to a nearby tree. While the bound Indian stood looking down the open end of a trapper's gun, Fitzpatrick explained to the Shoshones that unless the last horse was brought in promptly, they would have a funeral ceremony to conduct. The horse appeared.

The trappers now backtracked to their cache, exhumed their furs and traps, saddled and packed their horses, and set off at last for rendezvous. Fitzpatrick led his men across the South Pass and down again where the waters flowed to the east. He had made his name as a leader of men and an explorer who could always find his way through the mountains. These were skills that would put him at the head of many expeditions in the years ahead.

Fitzpatrick, along with Milton Sublette, Jim Bridger, Henry Fraeb, and Jean Baptiste Gervais, bought out the fur company of Smith, Jackson, and Sublette in 1830 and renamed it the Rocky Mountain Fur Company. The real leader of the Rocky Mountain Fur Company was Fitzpatrick.

Later, as time for the 1832 rendezvous in Pierre's Hole approached, Fitzpatrick returned to St. Louis to bring back supplies for the trappers. His big problem was money, but Fitzpatrick arranged with Bill Sublette, older brother of his partner Milt Sublette, to supply The Rocky Mountain Fur Company. It was on this trip, as Fitzpatrick was returning to the mountains with the supply train, that he had his most famous brush with death.

There were other fur companies assembling in Pierre's Hole, and everyone knew that the first supply train to arrive would surely skim off the cream of the furs and beat the competition in the race for high profits. Fitzpatrick decided to hurry on ahead of his supply train with the news that it was coming. He took two swift horses, planning to ride them alternately, and set off at a gallop. He was traveling alone and he was traveling light.

When Bill Sublette arrived at Pierre's Hole with his train of supplies, including the coveted casks of corn whiskey, he figured that Fitzpatrick would already be there waiting. But Sublette was wrong. Old Fitz hadn't shown and this fact alone put a damper on the rendezvous hilarity. Seasoned trappers looked at each other and shook their heads. Old Fitz knew his way sure enough. Couldn't lose him blindfolded in these here mountains. Something must have gone amiss and about the only thing it could have been was Indians, more than likely the danged Blackfeet again. This conclusion wasn't far wrong, but the Indians had to get in line because first Fitzpatrick tangled with a giant grizzly bear.

After leaving the supply train, he rode hard for four days or so and all went well. In the cool mountain air he and his horses made excellent time.

Then, he stopped one day to rest his horses. While his horses grazed, Fitzpatrick sat on a rock gnawing on the last of his little store of jerky.

Suddenly, he heard a bear scrambling across the rocks toward him at what he called "double quick time." Fitz sprang to his feet. He stood his ground as the bear skidded to a halt six feet from him and rose up on its hind feet to investigate. For what seemed a mighty long time, the grizzled mountain man and the towering bear stared each other in the eye. Fitzpatrick understood grizzlies well enough to know that trying to run would bring the animal down on him in an instant. "After discovering that I was in no ways bashful," Fitzpatrick is quoted as saying, "he bowed, turned and ran—and I did the same, and made for my horse."

He should have given the grizzly a little more time. The bear glanced back, saw the man running, and wheeled about. Fitzpatrick calculated that he had enough of an edge to mount and race off ahead of the bear, but his horse, seeing a giant grizzly approaching at full speed, ignored the man grabbing for the saddle, bolted, and threw Fitz flat on his back in front of the chuffing bear.

A less experienced person might have scrambled away trying to escape the bear, but Fitzpatrick kept his senses. Leaping to his feet, he confronted the grizzly. Once more the bear turned and ran off. But it made a mistake: it stopped to eat what was left of Fitzpatrick's lunch, which probably attracted it in the first place. "I crept to my gun," said Fitzpatrick, "keeping the rock between him and me, having reached it, took deliberate aim and killed him on the spot." The trapper feasted on bear steaks, then moved on and covered another three miles or so before making camp for the night.

The next morning he followed a small mountain stream into a beautiful little valley and had the bad luck to be spotted by a band of Gros Ventre trophy hunters who coveted his scalp. The best description of what happened next comes from the writings of Zenas Leonard, a trapper who heard it in Fitz's own words at rendezvous.

Fitz began slipping away, thinking that the Indians might not have seen him. He was wrong. The young braves swung in behind him, bottling him up in the canyon where he was surrounded on three sides by precipitous walls and towering peaks. A man could deal with bears, and maybe even enjoy the excitement of it, but this latest problem was more serious business. Fitzpatrick figured he still had a good chance because his spirited horse could outrun anything the Indians rode. He turned one horse free and set spurs to the other one. It bounded up the steep rocky slope lunging over rocks and slipping in the loose soil. But the horse was soon winded and the Indians, who had left their horses behind to pursue the trapper on foot, were closing the distance rapidly. Fitzpatrick leaped from his saddle and, carrying minimum equipment, began climbing the mountainside on foot.

He soon realized that he would lose this race. There were too many warriors after him, and they were too fast on their feet. They had slowed temporarily while securing his horse, probably reasoning that now the white man was theirs anyhow.

The white man, meanwhile, was racing through a field of boulders and along rock ledges. He momentarily passed from the Indians' sight, and in that instant, found a crevice between the rocks, slid into it, and began stuffing leaves and grass into the opening to hide himself.

The job was barely finished when the first of the Indians came screaming up in mad pursuit. The band passed within a few feet of the silent Fitzpatrick. As Zenas Leonard quoted him, Fitzpatrick is supposed to have said, "What a moment of intense anxiety was this! All chance of escape was cut off. No prospect of mercy if taken! Hope began to die—and death inevitable seemed to be the very next incident that would occur."

The Indians, apparently unable to believe that the white man had escaped, continued to search. They clambered over the slope the rest of that day. Finally, they began retreating back down the mountain. But little bands would suddenly stop and begin talking loudly and motioning until, deciding that they might not have looked hard enough in a certain spot, would scramble back up the slope to search some more. Night came. The Indians, accompanied by their newly acquired horse, went back down the valley.

Fitzpatrick began to breathe easier. Long after darkness filled the valley he crept from his cramped refuge to inspect the scene. He thought he saw a way out of his dilemma. In the blackness, he began a long sneak play down the mountainside, believing that he was slipping around the Indians by a wide margin. He had miscalculated. He suddenly appeared on the edge of the Indian camp. But the weary Indians, and even their dog, slept on, while Fitzpatrick crept back up the mountainside and settled into his hiding place again.

He awakened early the next morning. So did the Indians. Refreshed by their sleep and driven by their lust for scalps, they attacked the hill again, sending blood-curdling war calls up the slopes as they came. The warriors eventually grew weary of this sport and began amusing themselves by racing their new horse against their own ponies. Fitzpatrick, peering down on them from behind the bushes, was pleased to see that his horse acquitted itself nobly.

By the second night Fitzpatrick thoroughly understood the lay of the land. Once more he slipped down the mountain and this time made it around the Gros Ventre camp. He followed the creek for the rest of that night, then hid and stayed out of sight throughout the day. Occasionally, a few Indians passed his hiding place, studying the ground for the slightest sign of the white man.

The next night Fitzpatrick followed the creek to its confluence with Pierre's River. Now he was sure where he was. There were still too many hostiles around so he decided to cross the river. He built a raft of logs, loaded it with his remaining possessions, gun, powder, possibles bag, and shot pouch, climbed aboard, and shoved off into the current. He moved steadily toward the far shore.

Then the current swept the little raft into fast water and carried Fitzpatrick downstream farther than he expected to go. He bounced into a field of rocks. The raft was picked up by the turbulent whitewater and slammed against a boulder that tore it apart, dumping man, gun, and everything else into the rushing stream. When the trapper reached shore, after a tiring fight against the current, he was far poorer than when he started. All he had left now to protect himself against man or bear was the knife on his belt. Weary, wet, and hungry, he " . . . stood on the bank in the midst of despair."

During the days that followed, Fitzpatrick, like a wounded animal, moved with extreme caution, staying hidden as much as possible. For two more days he followed the river, living on roots and plants.

As the days dragged on, Fitzpatrick grew steadily weaker. He wasted time wandering from place to place, searching for food. Finally, he grew so weak he could scarcely walk, and he saw little hope that either trappers or friendly Indians would rescue him.

Meanwhile, Bill Sublette's supply train had arrived at the rendezvous site without Fitzpatrick. The anxious partners sent out a small party to search for Old Fitz. One story says they found him and gently brought him into camp. Another account holds that he was rescued by two Iroquois hunters. It may be that he came into camp on his own. Whatever the truth, he arrived in a dazed condition, nearly starved, clothes mostly ripped off, his feet bare, his body bleeding and bruised, his cheeks hollow.

It was also said that during the ordeal his hair turned white. From this he gained his new name among the Indians–"White Hair."

Precisely how Old Fitz acquired the hand injury that gave him his other Indian name is still debated among historians. One explanation may be found in the archives of the Missouri Historical Society in St. Louis. In a small room at one end of the archives stand files of drawers containing microfilmed editions of Missouri newspapers of long ago.

One of these newspapers, *The Jefferson Inquirer* for December 25, 1847, tells what really happened to Fitzpatrick's left hand.

Again Fitzpatrick, according to this story, was scouting alone when discovered by Blackfeet. Fitzpatrick, as usual, was on a strong, young horse and soon gaining distance on the Indians.

The Indians headed him directly toward a cliff below which the Yellowstone River flowed. There was no time to hesitate, no way to turn back or change course. Fitzpatrick put spurs to his mount and off the cliff they went to splash into the river below. There, while trying to remove his rifle from its cover, Fitzpatrick shot himself in the hand. The accidental shot mutilated his hand, but even then he managed to reload and shoot again, killing two of his pursuers and giving himself time to hide in the woods. During the following days he eluded the Indians and came, eventually, back to his friends. Now the Indians called him "Broken Hand."

Through those years when the fur business flourished, then faded, Fitzpatrick was at the heart of the trapping industry. As a partner in the Rocky Mountain Fur Company he continued to explore and trap. But he saw new trapping companies crowd into the already heavily worked valleys. The wildness of the mountains was feeling the pressure of the growing human presence. Soon there would be lines of covered wagons heading west.

The first of these was ready to move in 1840, and out in front leading the way was the rawboned Fitzpatrick. The following year he led others westward, and his presence probably spelled the difference between success and disaster for the newcomers moving through that vast open land.

When the nationally known John C. Frémont set off on his second western mapping expedition in 1843, his guide was Tom Fitzpatrick. Later Fitzpatrick served as a scout for the army.

These experiences brought the respected Fitzpatrick to the attention of government officials. They appointed him agent to the Indian tribes of the upper Platte and Arkansas, and in this role he dealt successfully with

Arapahoes, Cheyennes, Kiowas, Shoshones, and Sioux, conducting treaty negotiations and dealing with land claims.

The Irish boy who made good in the western mountains was married to a woman whose father was white and whose mother was a member of the Snake tribe. They had two children.

He was off to Washington on official government business in 1854, when pneumonia took him at the age of fifty-five. He had lived well beyond the life expectancy of Rocky Mountain beaver trappers.

Chapter 11

ACROSS *the* SHINING MOUNTAINS

From *The Long Rifle,* by Stewart Edward White

They are mellow now, but like fine wine, Stewart Edward White's Andy Burnett sagas have a way of retaining shelf life in libraries and book collections where frontier literature is of interest. In other words, they are still published and read and appreciated.

As Winfred Blevins points out in his introduction to the edition of *The Long Rifle* republished in 1990, White (1873-1946) was nearly sixty years old when the book was first published, and he was already an author of considerable fame and success. To me, despite his other books and countless magazine articles, White will always be the man who gave us Andy Burnett and the adventures of the mountain life as seen through young eyes.

In this excerpt, our tale begins as Andy and two older mountain man companions set out for the Pierre's Hole area (Jackson's Hole today), where they figure trapping small and quiet is way to get beaver and keep their "ha'r."

● ● ●

A WEEK LATER without very much ceremony the little band split up. Each pair or trio had its picked country for the fall hunt. It was agreed to meet at the beginning of the next summer at Henry's Fork. If Sublette kept his promise, and the goods he brought in were not overpriced, they would deal with him. If not, they could float down to St. Louis on bull boats, for a change. Nobody expressed any desire for the Blackfoot country.

"You kin hev the whole of it," said one. "Me, I choose to keep my ha'r."

Shortly thereafter travel for our three turned almost exaggeratedly slow and cautious. To their left the country flung to the skies in high and glittering mountains through which shortly they must find a pass. In the meantime, they held to the wooded ridges and heights of the foothills and lower mountains. The going was often steep, rocky, obstructed. The worst was through the thicket of quaking asp or popples or lodge-pole pines. The small trees grew close together. Even the horsemen were often put to it to squirm a way through; the pack horses were continually getting stuck. Where high winds had wrought, the trunks lay crisscrossed like jackstraws, and so close together that the horses had to buck jump as from one pen to another. It took hours to win through a mile or so of this sort of thing. The ridiculous part of it was that a few hundred feet below, perhaps, lay the open river valley, or a plain, or a park across which they could have ridden with ease, but in full sight. Andy would have been tempted, especially when exhausted by hours of bitter struggle. Apparently neither of his companions even considered the possibility.

Below the summit of each ridge they halted. The animals rested or grazed while either Kelly or Joe Crane went ahead on foot. Kelly, some time since, had shot a wolf and had taken its skin. He used it now as a blind, drawing the mask over the top of his head which he eased slowly above the skyline. On occasion he lay on his belly for a full half-hour, squinting through the Governor's telescope, before signaling the others to come on.

They stopped in the middle of the afternoon, built a fire, grazed the horses. The fire, when possible, was made in the dry bed of a ravine sheltered on the side toward the lowland by bushes. If they intended to spend the night there, the camp must be overhung by low boughs to prevent reflection on trees overhead. But ordinarily, after both horses and men had fed, they repacked, traveled as rapidly as possible for an hour or so more, and lay down without fire. This was sometimes uncomfortable, for after sundown a fierce chill swept from the snowclad heights.

Even as to the small cooking fires they permitted themselves, they took pains to burn only the odorless and comparatively smokeless wood of the quaking asp, making often considerable excursions afoot for it, collecting and carrying a supply on one of the pack animals when the indications were they would run out of the growth. In his first offer of replenishment Andy learned something.

"Hold on!" admonished Joe, removing from the fire the billet Andy had placed thereon. "Not thataway! Thisaway!"

He explained that a white man ordinarily made his fire so that the logs burned in two at the middle; but that an Indian pointed his logs toward a center and burned the ends. Why advertise the presence of white men?

It was all a queer combination of the most thrilling excitement and an impatience that must be mastered and a vigilance that must never be permitted to relax, not for one instant, even in the face of repeated evidence that these vast and awesome wilds harbored no other human beings but themselves. To his companions this was a second nature; but close of day found Andy's capacity for attention worn thin almost to the point of exhaustion. He had to resist a temptation to leave it all to his competent comrades. But he did resist; and so found that daily his perceptions gained in keenness, tended more and more to become automatic. His eyes, sweeping the prospect, were training themselves to pass over the usual, to stop only on what was unusual or abnormal to such a landscape.

The point of greatest anxiety was the matter of subsistence. It was necessary to kill from time to time; and killing meant shooting. Andy learned to judge country, to estimate the configuration of the hills, above all the nature of the blanketing growth—practical acoustics. It was astonishing how properly selected surroundings would smother the sharp crack of the rifle, and how a slightly different circumstance would re-echo it in seemingly unending reverberation. There must be but one shot. If the marksman was not absolutely certain, he should withhold his fire until he was. Andy was proud that, as a matter of course, his companions permitted him this duty in his turn. That was gratifying. His life seemed full of bitter mortifications and compensations like this.

For the first time he learned the resources of the wilderness. The meat supply was eked out by wild fruits. Joe dug camas root which, when boiled, proved to be not unlike a potato. Another root was dried atop the packs, pulverized between stones, mixed with water and sunbaked. Then there were wild onions; and biter root; and Indian turnips.[1] Andy considered them a pleasing variation: but Joe did not think much of them.

"They're eatin'," he admitted, "but give me good meat."

---

1 Not the botanical Indian turnip; but a root known as such by the trappers.

They tried for a pass across the shining mountains. It was bitter, incredible toil. The horses managed to scramble where Andy would have sworn a goat would have found no foothold. Sometimes it was necessary to explore for hours afoot, working out inch by inch the sketch of a possible route for a few hundred yards. The canyons pinched out, filled with great boulders and slabs among which rushed white water torrents, finally stood on end so that they were forced to the hogbacks, hoping for a grade that might lead to the summit. Mountain sheep stood on bold elevations and looked down on them. Marmots whistled from the rocks. White goats stepped astonishingly across the face of sheer precipices. Andy shot one of them, but it fell from the tiny ledge, whirling over and over, and he could not get down to where it struck. An eagle closed its wings and dropped like a plummet after the falling body. Andy, looking down into the blue abyss, turned giddy. So they worked their way until sheer cliff interposed, or a precipitous gorge. Then they must return. The nights were bitter cold and comfortless.

The third attempt encouraged them. They emerged above timber line to wide boulder-strewn slopes of grass and flowers. Summer dropped below their feet like a garment. It was still early spring. Willows were budding. Snow water trickled busily in tiny rivulets. The grass was short and new and tender. An icily cold wind sucked downward like a draught.

"Bet we're hittin' her!" panted Joe.

The horses' flanks were heaving painfully. They could flounder but a few steps before resting. The slope was gentle but seemed interminable. To right and left the great peaks lifted jagged to unbelievable blue, thrusting skyward through the snows.

Andy was afoot, as were the others. He led his horse, and brought up the rear, behind the pack animals. The elevation caught his wind; his heart was pounding painfully; his eyes were strangely blurred. When the horses stopped, he gulped thankfully at the rarefied air to ease his burning chest. When they moved he gave all his forces just to placing one foot in front of the other, each step a single and separate exertion, his eyes fixed on the ground immediately before him.

"Yere's the *puerto suelo!*" Joe's cry startled him.

Andy looked up. It was unbelievable. The slope had ended. The little group huddled on a narrow level beyond which plunged the blue of descent. He joined his companions.

He saw spread out far below him a tremendous prospect of rolling tumbling hills, like a chop in a tideway, culminating in remote ranges that rose insubstantial to the height of the eye. The mountains on whose backbone they stood curved grandly to meet them in blue distance. Viewed from this height, the lower hills, held like water in this enormous cup, looked mottled in various shades, as the darkness of forests yielded to the olive of brushland or the paler green of grass. Immediately below the pass, almost under their feet as it were, stretched a long lozenge-shaped valley, apparently flat. The most of its floor seemed to be grass-land, but the meander of a stream was plainly marked by a winding strip of trees. It was what the men of that day called a "hole."

"Thar's our kentry!" cried Joe with satisfaction. "Ought to be beaver aplenty in every fold of them hills. And I reckon nary white man ever set moccasin thar!"

For a thousand feet or so the descent was ridiculously easy. The westward slope proved to be more abrupt than that to the east. The horses half slid in the loose shale. The eye could follow a feasible route apparently all the way down. It was most encouraging.

Then of a sudden their way was checked by a sheer drop. It was of not over ten feet; but there seemed to be no way around—except perhaps by a back track too long to undertake to-day. For the first time Joe lost his temper completely, announcing in no uncertain terms what could happen before he'd climb back one foot. His tirade was accompanied by vigorous action. The next half-hour gave Andy a new conception of what could be done with horses in the mountains. Each animal was blindfolded. A rawhide rope was knotted about its middle and turned twice about a handy juniper as a snub. Then with Andy on the other end of the rope to pay it out, Joe led the beast to the edge and shoved it off. Andy had never before heard a horse scream. The animal kicked wildly, turned like a teetotum, bumped the rocky wall, lost a little skin—but landed safely on the lower level where Kelly waited.

"Do you have to do this sort of thing often!" panted Andy, straightening his back after the ninth horse had been landed.

"You do all sorts of things often, ef'n yo' travel in the mountains," said Joe.

But when they came to take stock it was discovered that there had been one irreparable accident. In some manner the brass telescope, presented to Kelly by the Spanish governor, had been crushed against the rocky walls. The eye lense was cracked; the brass tube smashed. Only the object lense remained intact. Andy rescued this from the wreck and slipped it into his "possible" sack.

THE HOLE, from the level of the valley, offered a different impression than when viewed from above. What had seemed to be merely a tumble of hills now proved to be themselves quite respectable mountains, so that the place became a long narrow park, fenced in by apparently unbroken ranges which differed only in that those to eastward were higher and soared upward even beyond the snows. They stood aloof and severe like majestic sentinels: the others closed ranks in guardianship, like friends.

The plain between them was here a full three miles wide. It was a grass-grown, flower-decked prairie, broken by small groves of trees or patches of high brush where tributaries from the flanking hills came forth to join the river.

They angled to the north, riding boldly in the open.

"Yere's where we camp," Joe explained. "Either they's Injuns, or there ain't. We got to find out sometime."

The grasses stood knee high. Game trails crisscrossed in all directions, but dim and overgrown. There was much sign of elk and buffalo, but all old.

"They've followed the snow," said Joe.

At a point where a tongue of the prairie opened through the trees to the river's edge they unpacked. The river proved to be both wide and deep. Its clear waters ran swift. Andy caught the gleam of trout behind the boulders of a riffle, weaving slowly as they held place against the current.

"Now," Kelly told him, "we will leave you in charge for awhile. Keep your eyes open. We will go look for sign."

The two trappers galloped off at full speed, Joe to the north, Kelly to the south.

Andy settled himself, his back against the piled-up packs, the long rifle across his knees. The sun was warm and caressing. The light air was cool, and tingled in his nostrils. Liquid notes of meadow larks and robins seemed to float in suspension, and behind them a steady undertone of cascades falling and the ceaseless busy murmur of the stream. Andy, closing his eyes, could almost imagine himself back in the slumberous summer peace of the old quiet country. He opened them again to the austre majesty of the ranges.

Close under the frowning walls, on the distant green steep slopes of talus, his attention was caught by tiny movements which he at last made out to be that of animals feeding—the black solidity of buffalo, the more scattered lighter brown of elk. Slow-moving creamcolored spots against the black precipices must be goats. A single tiny perfect model of a bighorn stood motionless against the sky. Ravens croaked from the nearby forest. A mother duck, quacking conversationally under her breath, drifted past him down the current, her downy babies bobbing atop the water, light as chips. A long slim, furtive shining animal—it was an otter—slipped from the opposite bank like a shadow into the water, leaving no ripple where it submerged. Small hawks held themselves suspended on vibrating wings. Two eagles crossed circles in leisurely soaring far above them. Black and white magpies chattered raucously, without decorum. His spirit lifted in a great anticipation and a great thankfulness that he was here and not back in the little sun-baked Mexican town. It had become as remote as a dream. And the girl. He shuddered as at the chill of a recalled escape. Surely he had kind gods!

He had no realization of the flight of hours. The shadow of the hills fell across the valley, began a slow relentless march up the eastward slopes. First Kelly, then Joe rode in. They were jubilant. No Indian sign whatever, old or new. Plenty of beaver cuttings. Bear sign; deer in the bottoms;–Joe carried a fat young doe across his saddle;–antelope on the plains to the south; a lake with ducks and geese. The fulfillment of the dream that made bearable the harshness of every trapper's life. Virgin hunting ground! Unknown! Unexplored! All theirs! A new Hole!

"Burnett's Hole: that's her name!" cried Joe. "Shut your trap!" he countered Andy's modesty. "Not for you; for your granddad. Wish I had some likker. I shore like to get drunk and disorderly."

IN SPITE OF THE FACT that all Indian sign in the newly discovered Hole was of last year at latest, the experienced trappers did not therefore abandon all caution. They made hasty and temporary camp in the middle of a willow thicket, and then spent all their time from dark until dark exploring, not only the valley itself, but the neighboring mountains; so that, when they had finished, they knew all the possible entrances and exits. Incidentally they thus obtained knowledge of the fur prospects. Into the Hole flowed a number of tributary streams, all of which supported a teeming beaver population. Kelly and Joe Crane passed on after a gratified glance; but Andy, to whom these animals were strange, would have lingered. The beautiful precision of the treefelling, the uncanny engineering skill evidenced in the placing and construction of the dams, the very appearance of the swimming animals fascinated him. But his companions pushed on. They rode with a haste almost feverish; using all the horses, turn about.

"Time 'nuff for beaver when we get set and aimed," said Joe.

But by the end of the fourth day they knew all about the place.

The Hole was a paradise. Protected by the backbone of high mountains to the east, its feasible entrances from the west were but three. Each showed marks of an Indian trace, but unused of late years. The river foamed out of a gorge to the north. It flowed into a lake at the southerly end of the valley; a lake cliff-bound on the two sides. They rode along the flat shore until their way was barred by the black precipice. Kelly dismounted; took off his clothes; waded out into the water. He cast a comical look back at Joe.

"I wish I knew if you were lying, you old Kaw!'"

"I kain't nuther swim!" asservated Joe vehemently.

Kelly struck out in the long easy stroke of the practiced swimmer. Andy watched him, skirting the base of the cliffs, until his head was small in the distance. Finally he rounded a point and was gone.

Though by now the boy had learned to economize on questions, his curiosity bested him.

"Gone to scout where the lake empties out," Joe replied. "Then we'll know *every* way in—and out. Mout save our ha'r."

At the end of a half-hour Kelly returned. He was shivering like a leaf. His body was blue. His hands were shaking so he could hardly buckle on his equipment. He eyed Joe malevolently. Joe refused to meet his eye; but he could not sustain the pressure.

"I kain't nuther swim!" he repeated, quite gratuitously, for Kelly had said nothing.

"Well, some day when you ain't looking I'm going to push you in where it's deep and find out!" and Kelly vindictively. "That is plain ice water."

He leaped astride his horse and rode off at full speed, but returned at the end of five minutes warmer and better-natured.

"It runs out over a waterfall around a bend," he told them. "Mighty near sucked me in."

This finished the exploration. The Hole had everything. The broken country that looked down upon it swarmed with hundreds of bighorn. On the talus or across the hanging meadows grazed herds and bands of buffalo and elk.

"They'll foller the snow down," said Joe. "Come winter the bottom will be full of them. Fat meat! Wagh!"

Blacktail deer in every clump of clover. Of an evening they grazed out in the grass openings, does and fawns; one could see them in any direction he looked.

"Bucks on the open ridges a-hardenin' their horns," Andy was told.

The abundance of game filled Andy with a hunter's eagerness to be up and at them. But his companions had no time for mere sport. Grizzly tracks were numerous and large. Thrice they saw the great creatures; once, on a sandbar, within a few yards. But the trappers sheered off and rode around them.

"B'ar meat is poor eating'," said Joe. "And b'ar fights git you nowhar!"

Andy looked back longingly at the monster nose raised, sniffing after them as a dog sniffs at something that arouses its curiosity.

"Leave them be, and they'll leave you be," said Joe.

There were even a few small bands of antelope on the open plains at the head of the valley; and a village of comical prairie dogs with their attendant small owls.

These were the outstanding creatures; the most remarkable; possessed of the most interest to a hunter, barring of course the fur bearers. There were plenty of the latter—otter, mink, marten, raccoons, wolves, and their little cousins the coyotes, lynxes, foxes, all sorts of lesser creatures—but, save for the otter perhaps, Kelly and Crane passed them over.

It was twenty years before their time. Still, they were interesting to Andy; as were the grouse, the geese and ducks, the loons, magpies, the meadow larks, robins, the ravens and crows, and the hundreds of unnamed sweet-voiced littler people awaiting their Audubon. The valley was abrim with life, calling to Andy's joyous youth. It was hard to wait upon these maddeningly deliberate preparations.

Kelly and Joe decided to locate the camp in the concealment of aspens near the shore of the lake. For several days all three labored, hacking down slim straight logs, building a crude hut. Until it was finished they slept in the open. At the end of the day's labor Joe and Kelly lay flat on their robes, smoking. But Andy liked better the lake shore. There he sat, his back against a boulder.

The prospect before him was noble and full of voices; the blue still lake, the towering snow range to the right, the carved and castellated buttes of stratified red, green, yellow, and purple sandstone to the left, the bottomland of grass, the brilliant stars of single flowers, the spread blue of flax, the spaced groves of cottonwood and willows, the dark pines of the middle slopes with here and there on a projection a single tall fir like a sentinel.

The night drew on. Across the floor of the valley crept long peaked shadows. Level shafts of sunlight touched the upfling of the ranges, gold against the forests, red against the snow. With it came the cold. Bird voices stilled. The chill subdued the voices of the torrents. Slowly fell the imposition of the night silences.

The golden shafts lifted and were gone. The moon gained strength. It touched the high peaks, and they turned insubstantial against the darkening sky.

Andy was young; he was a hardy pioneer; and instinctively he resented anything that savored of a softening influence. But he could not abstain. Harden his surface as he might, abundance poured into his spirit and lifted it into expansion. He could not realize the irresistible transmutation taking place within him, a transmutation that, unrecognized for what it was, had already taken place in these very men he so admired and desired to emulate, so that thus, and only thus, rough or gentle, they became of one kin with one another and with the mountains, truly the mountain men.

Joe Crane's voice at his elbow startled him.

"Kind of purty, ain't she?" Joe was saying. "Sort of gits you. No matter how fur away you go, somehow yo' got to come back! Makes up for a lot of hard doin's somehow."

The following morning they were up early. This was to be an exciting day. For the first time Andy was to set out the traps he had so long carried in the buffalo-skin bag.

The evening before Joe and Kelly had made some curious preparations. From his "possible" sack Joe had produced a vial made from the tip of an antelope horn scraped thin until it was transparent. This proved to be filled with a queer-smelling mixture which Joe called "castrum."

"Made out of beaver glands," said he. "Use it for bait. Beaver kain't seem to keep away from it nohow. We'll make a plenty more first beaver we catch."

In the meantime he divided the supply carefully in three. He and Kelly cut off their buckskin leg gear at the knee and, with their awls and deer sinew, pieced it out with cloth.

"Got to wade to ketch beaver," Joe told Andy. "Kain't go trompin' around on the banks leavin' a scent. Buckskin's all right when she's dry, But when she's wet yo' got enough to make britches for two men and a boy. And when she dries agin yo' ain't got even enough for the boy, and air so tight yo' kain't make a bow for ordinary politeness."

The traps were all examined for rust; the springs tested. Andy turned in aquiver with eagerness for the morning. For a long time he was too excited to sleep. Then, immediately it seemed to him, Kelly was kicking the coals together in the early dawn.

The promise was of a gorgeous day. It was bitter cold. In the first light the meadows were seen to glitter with white frost. The horses stood about humped up, their hind feet drawn in. Their shaggy hair stood up with the appearance of fur. Andy's fingers were blue and stiff. He shivered in the chill breeze.

But as they ate, over the great ranges, the light poured in a cascade of gold. A woodpecker drummed vigorously. The horses shook themselves and moved slowly atop a little rise, awaiting the sun.

Kelly rode off by himself. Joe took Andy with him.

Arrived at the beaver stream of his choice, Joe spent a few moments clipping a long stake for each trap. Then they left the horses and, their traps slung over their backs by means of the long chains, the two set themselves to wade upstream against the current. At various strategic points—"slides," paths into cuttings, underwater entrances to dens and the like—Joe set the traps. He placed them near shore, in just a certain depth of water. Over the pan he planted long switches, the tips of which he dipped in the little antelope-horn vial of castrum. But the stake to which he attached the end of the five-foot chain he drove as far out toward the middle of the stream as it would extend.

"When a beaver is first ketched he strikes for deep water," said Joe. "Ef'n yo' kin keep him thar, he'll drowned shore. But ef'n he kin git out on the dry bank he'll git away."

In spite of himself Andy felt a queer pang of pity. He stifled it promptly, but from time to time it returned.

In a few spots the water was too deep for this expedient. Joe ran the chain out toward the middle just the same; but attached to it a float stick to mark its position. For the first time Andy understood the significance of the figure of speech he had so often heard—"my stick floats w'th yours"; "there floats my stick."

"That's all there is to this trappin' business," said Joe. "Simple as all git out—once you larn the habits of the critters."

The fur came fast; faster than ever before in all their experience, both Kelly and Joe admitted. This was obviously a virgin field. Even the Indians had not trapped here; at least for a great many years. The tributaries to the main river were numerous; and all contained beaver. For a while fully eighty percent of the traps did business each day.

The first week Andy found the job wholly and engrossingly fascinating. The second week, although his enthusiasm was still keen, he began to see that it came partly under the category of work. For there was no leisure for anything else. It was a whole-time job. Up at daylight and off to make the rounds of the traps which must be emptied and reset, generally at a new place. The catch must be skinned, tied to a hoop stretcher, fleshed with minute care, placed to dry. The pelts caught some days before must be examined and given whatever attention they needed. Those fully dried must be taken from the frames, folded properly, laid or hung in a safe dry place. When enough of them had been accumulated, they must be squeezed together, by a most ingenious scissors-press of logs and rawhide, into a pack. There were sixty skins to each pack, which weighed about a hundred pounds. Joe surveyed the first one with satisfaction.

"Fifteen or sixteen *plew*," he estimated. "We're gittin' rich fast."

Andy had long since learned that a *plew* was six dollars, but that single fact had never satisfied him. His youth made him reluctant to ask questions that would reveal basic ignorance, as it were, but now his curiosity got the better of it.

"I don't know," confessed Joe. "Allus been thataway when you talk of fur. Mout jist as well say dollars, I reckon, but that's the way it is."

But Kelly was better informed.

"In the early days," said he, "a beaver skin traded for four dollars, but a very fine skin brought six, and that came to be the standard of value. The trade was largely French. A fine skin was know as *'plus,'* which is a French word meaning 'more'—that is, more than a common skin."

As is always the case in established routine, the days flashed by rap-idly. Andy seemed, to himself, to be always rolling himself in his robe; another day finished. The work was absorbingly interesting; but it was work, in the sense that it insisted on itself, and would not release him to the enjoyment of any of the thousand fascinations the Hole seemed dan-gling just outside of possibility. The game animals were moving into the bottoms. As he waded the beaver streams, the bright trout darted before him. In spite of Joe's pronouncement that there was nothing in bear fights for a sensible man, Andy's combative spirit leaped to the challenge of the great lumbering grizzlies–white bear, Joe called them. They did very lit-tle hunting. A deer lasted them over a week, and could be shot almost from before the cabin door. The Boone gun seemed to be out of a job. And there were other minor drawbacks. Discomforts of the business which Andy had not, in his first enthusiasm, noticed now forced them-selves upon him–the biting snap of the early mornings, the icy water of the streams. After wading awhile his feet turned numb, and he was con-scious only of a cold ring around his legs; but when he emerged he had for a time to endure a minor torture as circulation re-established itself. He was more or less wet all over, and all of the time. In general the weather held fair, but occasionally violent storms swept down from the peaks. Left to his inclination Andy would have stayed under shelter in the fire's comfort; but since his companions went forth as a matter of course, he had from very shame to follow. And as anybody who has experienced one can testify, a mountain storm in the fall of the year can be a miser-able business.

It must not be understood that Andy was sorry for himself, or that the adventure was becoming in any way distasteful. Quite to the contrary. But it had ceased being entirely a picnic and had turned into a job; which was perfectly proper, and as it should be.

The season advanced with incredible swiftness. The wildflowers were gone; the grasses had ripened. The elk and buffalo and buck deer were working down to the bottomlands. The clear bugling of the former echoed from the cliffs. The aspens had turned a clear pure yellow in striking contrast to the dark pines. Cottonwood leaves, shriveled brown, whirled down the gusts of wind. Suddenly the whole valley was alive with swarms of small busy migratory birds. It was necessary to build a pole corral in which at night to confine the horses, for the buffalo had drawn close about. After dark the bulls came close to the house and the corral, pawed the earth in challenge. Long flights of crows appeared high in the air over the mountains to the north, specks in the sky, dipped toward the valley in ragged whirling flight like windblown leaves, only to rise again and disappear over the mountains to the south. The locusts left the grasses to seek food on the shrubs, where they clung torpid.

"Winter's drawin' in," said Joe. "The Cold Maker's comin', as the Injuns say."

He and Kelly discussed the matter seriously and at length. Shortly, with the next storm, the high passes to the east would be filled with snow. If they were to get out of the Hole, it must be soon. The alternative was to winter in the valley. It was an important decision.

If they went out, they lost the month or so that remained of this superlative trapping before the beaver retired to their winter lodges and were frozen in. They already had caught more than their horses could carry over the rough country. It would be necessary to cache part of the take and return for it in the spring. Here were plenty of game, plenty of firewood, all the essentials of existence. On the other hand, it would be very lonesome and monotonous as compared with the rendezvous, where undoubtedly would be gathered a goodly number of the mountain men, not to speak of a few score of the friendly Indians of that region. Furthermore the wisdom of tempting Providence by too long a sojourn in a hostile country was worth debating. It might be wiser to take what they had and get out.

"Still," Joe pointed out, "we ain't seen ary Injun sign yit. And Blackfeet is no great hands to go projecting' around in dead of winter. Assiniboins, yes; they's plumb fools and likely will start out anywhar in ary weather. I'd shore like to swap yarns with the boys; but I reckon we can git along here without chawin' each other's ears. As long as we got to come back in the spring anyways to git our fur, we mout as well stay and be right on the ground for a spring hunt. We ain't trapped the main river at all. Come spring one of us kin cross the range and git more hosses from the Crows."

The debate was, after all, a matter of form. No true mountain men would ever decide against such hunting as this.

The decision made, Joe at once began preparations to trap the main river. As the volume of water was too great to permit wading, and as it was absolutely essential that the trapper leave no scent on the banks, it became necessary to construct what Joe called a bull boat. Andy found it interesting.

For one thing it gave him a day or so of respite in routine. Joe wanted a number of buffalo skins; and these Andy was permitted to kill, a pleasant hunting interlude in itself. The pelts collected, Joe stuck upright in the ground a circle of light willow poles, bent the ends over toward a common center, and tied them together to form a great inverted basket twelve or fourteen feet long. This he covered with the buffalo skins sewed together. Underneath he built a slow fire. As the skins warmed he assiduously rubbed a mixture of buffalo tallow and resin into the seams, which cooled as hard as the dried hide itself. Then he and Andy, working on opposite sides, carefully pulled up the willows from the earth, turned the thing over, cut off the projecting ends, bound on a rough gunwale of willow.

"Thar she be!" said Joe. "That's a bull boat!"

It floated high and light on the water; carried them both easily and to spare; but Andy had the greatest difficulty in making the thing go any way but around and around. Joe laughed at his efforts until the tears came. The harder he paddled the farther out in the lake he drifted.

"Ef'n yo' don't git ashore by supper time, I'll git Jack to swim out and give yo' a tow!" he shouted.

But, when the time came to use it, even Joe made no attempt to force it against the current.

"She's a downstream boat," said he. "When she has to go upstream she's got to use legs."

So they built a travoy for the gentlest pack horse, and took the bull boat overland to the river's inlet.

As two were required for this sort of thing, Kelly continued work on the smaller streams while Joe and Andy teamed together. They worked the river methodically, dropping down the current, holding their craft by a grasp of the overhanging willows or by a rude stone anchor while they set their traps. Next morning it was necessary to travoy the boat back again in order to pick up the catch; after which the reset was made, another stage downstream. It took them ten days to traverse the length of the river to the lake.

"*And* repeat in the spring!" said Joe, viewing the piled-up packs with satisfaction.

Chapter 12

JOURNAL *of a* TRAPPER

From *Journal Of a Trapper,* by Osborne Russell
Edited by Aubrey L. Haines

For an authentic, highly readable account of what being a mountain man was like in the Rockies during the halcyon fur-trade years, 1834-1843, you need look no further than this amazing book. In a manuscript now skillfully edited by Aubrey Haines, Osborne Russell describes the life of the mountain man with great clarity and detail. The terrain, the wildlife, and the Indians are superbly pictured, just as Russell and the first white men to enter the High Rockies saw them.

Russell, born in 1814 in Maine, passed away in 1892 while living in California. Most mountain men did not fare nearly so well and "went under" while living the life they loved. In this excerpt you'll see one of the reasons why, as Russell and his companions explore the area that is Yellowstone Park today.

● ● ●

WE LEFT THE VALLEY and ascended the mountain S.W. and travelled about 15 Mls to a branch of Henry's fork. Here we staid until the 7th of Septr. and then started down Henry's fork SW. After travelling about 12 Mls we left the pines and travelled parralelle with the stream over rolling ridges among scattered groves of quaking asps when we arrived at the edge of the plains in traveling about 8 Mls. Here we discovered a trail made by a war party of Blackfeet evidently the night previous. We then took a South course and travelled our horses in a trot all day and encamped an hour after dark on Lewis fork about 15 miles above the junction. The next day we Travelled to Blackfoot creek and the day following to Fort Hall we remained at the Fort until the 20th and then started down Snake River trapping with a party of 10 men besides ourselves 22d We arrived at a stream called Cozzu (or Raft River)[1] This we ascended and hunted until the 5th of Octr. when finding the country had been recently hunted we returned to Fort Hall. From thence we started on the 18th with the Fort hunter and six men to kill and dry Buffaloe meat for winter We cruised about on Snake river and its waters until the 23d of Novr. when the weather becoming very cold and the snow about 15 inches deep we returned with our horses loaded with meat to Fort Hall where we stopped until the 1st of Jany 1839 when we began to be tired of dried meat and concluded to move up the river to where Lewis fork leaves the Mountain and there spend the remainder of the winter killing and eating Mountain Sheep We were Six in company and started on the 2d travelling slowly as the snow was deep and the weather cold and arrived at the destined place on the 20th Jany. We were followed by 7

---

1   Raft River was called the "Cassia" by Ferris, and "Casu" by Wyeth. Jason Lee says it "received its name from the circumstances that some of the traders were obliged to make a raft to cross it in high water." Certainly the name must have been given early for Peter Skene Ogden notes in his journal (p. 356): "Monday, March 20th [1825]. I sent two men with traps to examine Raft River."

lodges of Snake Indians. We found the snow shallow about the foot of the Mountain with a plenty of Sheep Elk and some few Bulls among the rocks and low Spurs 26th I started with two white men and several Indians thro the kanyon to hunt Elk after travelling about 4 Mls I left the party and took up the river on the north side whilst the remainder crossed the river on the Ice to follow the trail of some Bulls. I ascended the river travelling on the ice and land alternately about 4 Ms further and encamped for the night. This was a severe cold night but I was comfortably situated with one Blanket and Two Epishemores and plenty of dry wood to make a fire, when I arose in the morning I discovered a band of Elk about half a mile up the mountain. I took my rifle and went to approach them thro the snow 3 ft deep and when within about 250 paces of them they took the wind of me and ran off leaving me to return to my encampment with the consolation that this was not the first time the wind had blown away my breakfast. When I arrived at my camp I found plenty of fresh Buffaloe meat hanging on the bushes near where I had slept. I immediately began to roast and eat as 24 hour's fasting would naturally dictate. Presently a Snake Indian arrived to whom the meat belonged. Near where I was encamped was a small stream which ran from a spring about 100 paces distant and emptied into the river the water was a little more than blood warm. The Beaver had taken the advantage of the situation Damed it up at the Mouth and built a large lodge on the bank at sunrise I discovered three of them swimming and playing in the water.

The next day I killed a Bull and returned thro. the kanyon to our Camp On the 30th I started with my old comrade (Elbridge) back with our traps to try the Beaver the snow was about 2 ft deep on the level plain and it took us till near night to reach the place we encamped in a cave at the foot of the Mountain nearby and I set 4 traps The weather was extremely cold but I felt very comfortable whilst walking about in the warm water but on coming out and running as fast as I could to the Camp 40 rods distant my feet were both frozen. I soon drew out the frost however by stripping them and holding them in the cold snow— next morning I found 4 large fat Beaver in my traps and on the 2d of Feby. we returned to Camp with 12 Beaver. Feby 10th Moved with the camp up the river to where we had caught the Beaver and encamped. Lewis fork comes thro. this kanyon for about 12 Mls. where the rock rises 2 or 300 feet forms a bench and ascends gradually to the Mountain which approaches very close on the Nth side and on the South is about 3 or 4 Mls distant and an occasional ravine running from the mountain to the river thro the rocks on the Nth side forms convenient places for encamping as the bench and low Spurs are well clothed with bunch grass. Here we found imense numbers of Mountain Sheep which the deep snows drive down to the low points of rocks facing the South near the river We could see them nearly every morning from our lodges standing on the points of rock jutting out so high in the air that they appeared no larger than Weasels. It is in this position that hunter delights to approach them from behind and shoot whilst their eyes are fixed on some object below. It is an exercise which gives vigor health and appetite to a hunter to shoulder his rifle at day break on a clear cold morning and wind his way up a rugged mountain over rocks and crags at length killing a fat old Ewe and taking the meat to Camp on his back: this kind of exercise gives him an appetite for his breakfast. But hunt- ing sheep is attended with great danger in many places especially when the rocks are covered with sleet and ice. I have often passed over places where I have had to cut steps in the ice with my butcher Knife to place my feet in directly over the most frightful precipices, but being excited in the pursuit of game I would think but little of danger until I had laid down to sleep at night, then it would make my blood run cold to meditate upon the scenes I had passed thro. during the day and often have I resolved never to risk myself again in such places and as often broken the resolution. The sight of danger is less hidious than the thought of it. On the 18th of March the winter commenced breaking up with a heavy rain and 4 of us started up the river to commence the spring hunt whilst the remainder of the party returned to the Fort. After travelling thro. the kanyon we found the ground bare in many places whilst it still continued to rain. On the 30th of Mch we travelled to the mouth of 'Muddy' this we ascended and crossed the mountain with some difficulty as the snow was very deep on to the head waters of "Gray's Creek." There two of our party (who were Canadians) left us and struck off for themselves. Our Camp then consisted of myself and my old comrade Elbridge,[2] I say old comrade because we had been sometime together but he was a young man, from Beverly Mass and being bred a sailor he was not much of a landsman, woodsman or hunter but a great easy good natured fellow standing 5 feet 10–and weighing 200 lbs On the 2d of april we crossed a high ridge in a Nth direction and encamped on a stream that sinks in the plain soon after leaving the Mountain here we set our traps for Beaver but their dams were nearly all covered with ice excepting some few holes which they had made for the purpose of obtaining fresh provisions we stopped on this stream until the 25th of April and then travelled out by the same way which we came 26th we travelled in a South direction about 25 Mls Crossing several of the head branches of 'Grays Creek' On the 1st of May we travelled about 10 Mls East course and the next day went to the head of Grays Marsh about 20 Mls South course There we deposited the Furs we had taken and the next day [started] for Salt river to get a supply of salt we took an east direction about 6 Mls and fell on to Gardners fork which we descended to the Valley and on the 6th arrived at the Salt Springs on Scotts fork of Salt River Here we found 12 of our old Comrades who had come like our selves to gather salt We staid two nights together at this place when

---

2   The account books of Fort Hall show that Trask entered the service of the Columbia River Fishing and Trading Company September 30, 1835, as a crewman on the supply ship *May Dacre*. His monthly wage was sixteen dollars.

myself and Elbridge took leave of them and returned to Grays Marsh from there we started towards fort Hall travelling one day and laying by 5 or 6 to fatten our horses and arrived at the Fort on the 5th of June. This Post now belongs to the British Hudsons Bay Company who obtained it by purchase from Mr Wyeth in the year 1837 We stopped at the Fort until the 26th of June then made up a party of 4 for the purpose of trapping in the YellowStone and Wind river mountains and arrived at Salt river valley on the 28th 29 we crossed the Valley NE then left it ascending Grays river in an E. direction about 4 Mls into a narrow rugged pass encamped and killed a Sheep 30th We travelled up this stream 30 Mls East and encamped in a small Valley and Killed a bull and the next day we encamped in the South end of Jacksons big hole July 3d we travelled thro. the valley Nth. until night and the next day arrived at Jacksons Lake where we concluded to spend the 4th of July, at the outlet. July 4th I caught about 20 very fine salmon trout which together with fat mutton buffaloe beef and coffee and the manner in which it was served up constituted a dinner that ought to be considered independent even by Britons.[3] July 5 we travelled north paralell with the Lake on the East side and the next day arrived at the inlet or northern extremity 7th We left the lake and followed up Lewis fork about 8 Mls in a NE direction and encamped. On the day following we travelled about 5 Mls when we came to the junction of two equal forks[4] we took up the left hand, on the west sid thro the thick pines and in many places so much fallen timber that we frequently had to make circles of a quarter of a mile to gain a few rods ahead, but our general course was north and I suppose we travelled about 16 Mls in that direction at night we encamped at a lake[5] about 15 Mls in circumference formed by the stream we had ascended July 9th we travelled round this lake to the inlet on the west Side and

---

3 Compare this Fourth of July with the dismal one recorded on pp. 18–19 of *Journal Of a Trapper.*

4 The junction of Lewis River with Snake River in Yellowstone National Park.

5 This is Lewis Lake in Yellowstone National Park.

came to another lake[6] about the same size This has a small prarie on the west side whilst the other is completely surrounded by thick pines. The next day we travelled along the border of the lake till we came to the NW. extremity and where we found about 50 springs of boiling hot water[7] We stopped here some hours as one of my comrades had visited this spot the year previous he wished to show us some curiosities The first Spring we visited was about 10 feet in diameter which threw up mud with a noise similar to boiling soap close about this were numerous [others] similar to it throwing up the hot mud and water 5 or 6 feet high about 30 or 40 paces from these along the side of a small ridge the hot steam rushed forth from holes in the ground with a hissing noise which could be heard a mile distant. On a near approach we could hear the water bubbling under ground some distance from the surface. The sound of our footsteps over this place we like thumping over a hollow vessel of immense size in many places were peaks from 2 to 6 feet high formed of lime Stone, deposited by the boiling water, which appeared of snowy whiteness. The water when cold is perfectly sweet except having a fresh limestone taste. After surveying these natural wonders for sometime my comrade conducted me to what he called the "hour Spring"[8] at this spring the first thing that attracts the attention is a hole about 15 inches in diameter in which the water is boiling slowly about

---

6   Shoshone Lake. This beautiful lake, which is the second largest in Yellowstone National Park, was first mapped by Captain W. W. Delacy, who visited it with a party of prospectors in 1863. Many early maps gave the lake his name, but the United States Geological Survey supplanted it with the name of the linguistic group of Indians which includes the Snake tribe.

7   The Shoshone Geyser Basin. This thermal area contained thirteen active geysers in 1930, three of them erupting to heights of 50 feet or more, and Russell's estimate of 50 hot springs is certainly no exaggeration. A very good description of the area and its features is given by E. T. Allen and Arthur L. Day, in *Hot Springs of the Yellowstone National Park* (Carnegie Institute of Washington, Publication No. 466, 1935) pp. 307-19.

8   None of the geysers presently active in the Shoshone Basin resemble the "Hour Spring" in the interval between eruptions. However, the variability of geyser activity is so well established that a difference is to be expected after such a long span of time.

4 inches below the surface at length it begins to boil and bubble violently and the water commences raising and shooting upwards until the column arises to the hight of sixty feet from whence it falls to the ground in drops on a circle of about 30 feet in diameter being perfectly cold when it strikes the ground It continues shooting up in this manner five or 6 minutes and then sinks back to its former state of Slowly boiling for an hour and then shoots forth as before My Comrade Said he had watched the motions of this Spring for one whole day and part of the night the year previous and found no irregularity whatever in its movements After Surveying these wonders for a few hours we left the place and travelled north about 3 Mls over ascending ground then desended a steep and rugged mountain 4 mile in the same direction and fell on to the head branch of the Jefferson branch of the Missouri[9] The whole country still thickly covered with pines except here and there a small prarie. We encamped and set some traps for Beaver and staid 4 days. At this place there is also large numbers of hot Springs some of which have formed cones of limestone 20 feet high of a Snowy whiteness which make a splendid appearance standing among the ever green pines Some of the lower peaks are very serviceable to the hunter in preparing his dinner when hungry for here his kettle is always ready and boiling his meat being suspended in the water by a string is soon prepared for his meal without further trouble Some of these spiral cones are 20 ft in diameter at the base and not more than 12 inches at the top the whole being covered with small irregular semi-circular ridges about the size of a mans finger having the appearance of carving in bass relieve formed I suppose by the waters running over it for ages unknown. I should think this place to be at least 3,00 ft lower than the Springs we left on the mountain[10] Vast numbers of Black Tailed

---

9   This is the Firehole River, a tributary of the Madison, not the Jefferson. Here Russell was
     among the great geysers of the Upper Geyser basin—the area dominated by Old Faithful.
10   The geyser basins of Shoshone Lake and the Firehole River lie at nearly the same elevation.

Deer are found in the vicinity of these springs and seem to be very familiar with hot waters and steam. The noise of which seems not to disturb their slumbers for a Buck may be found carelessly sleeping where the noise will exceed that of 3 or 4 engines in operation. Standing upon an eminence and superficially viewing these natural monuments one is half inclined to believe himself in the neighborhood of the ruins of some ancients City whose temples had been constructed of the whitest marble. July 15 we travelled down the stream NW. about 12 Mls passing on our route large numbers of hot Springs with their snow white monuments scattered among the groves of pines. At length we came to a boiling Lake about 300 ft in diameter forming nearly a complete circle as we approached on the South side The stream which arose from it was of three distinct Colors from the west side for one third of the diamcter it was white, in the middle it was pale red, and the remaining third on the east light sky blue Whether it was something peculiar in the state of the atmosphere the day being cloudy or whether it was some Chemical properties contained in the water which produced this phenomenon I am unable to say and shall leave the explanation to some scientific tourist who may have the Curiosity to visit this place at some future period–The water was of deep indigo blue boiling like an immense cauldron running over the white rock which had formed [round] the edges to the height of 4 or 5 feet from the surface of the earth sloping gradually for 60 or 70 feet.[11] What a field of speculation this presents for chemist and geologist. The next morning we crossed the stream travelled down the east side about 5 Mls then ascended another fork in an east direction about 10 mls. and encamped. From where we left the Main fork it runs in a NW direction about 40 Mls

---

[11] This is an excellent description of the Grand Prismatic Spring, the largest hot spring in the Midway Geyser Basin. The guidebook to Yellowstone National Park gives a remarkably similar description.

before reaching the Burnt hole[12] July 17 we travelled to the head of this branch about 20 Mls East direction 18th After travelling in the same direction about 7 mls. over a low spur of mountain we came into a large plain[13] on the Yellow Stone river about 8 Mls below the Lake we followed up the Yellow Stone to the outlet of the Lake and encamped and set our traps for beaver. We stopped here trapping until the 28th and from thence we travelled to the "Secluded Valley" where we staid one day. From thence we travelled East to the head of Clarks fork where we stopped and hunted the small branches until the 4th of Aug. and then returned to the Valley On the 9th we left the Valley and travelled two days ovr the mountain NW and fell on to a stream running South into the YellowStone where we staid until the 16th[14] and then crossed the mountain in a NW direction over the snow and fell on to a stream running into the YellowStone plains and entering that river about 40 Mls above the mouth of 25 yard river. 18th We descended this stream within about a mile of the plains and set our traps. The next day my comrades started for the plains to Kill some Bufaloe Cows I remonstrated very hard against their going into the plains and disturbing the buffaloe in such a dangerous part of the country when we had a plenty of fat deer and mutton but to no purpose off they Started and returned at night with their animals loaded with cow meat. They told me they had seen where a village of 3 or 400 lodges of Blackfeet had left the Yellowstone in a NW direction but 3 or 4 days previous. Aug 22 we left this Stream and travelled along the foot of the mountain at the edge of the plain

---

12 The route followed was down the Firehole River to the point where it joins the Gibbon to form the Madison River; then up the Gibbon River. Here the location of "Burnt Hole" is shown in relation to the Firehole geyser basins (cf. Note 60 in *Journal of a Trapper* by Osborne Russell).

13 Hayden Valley, named for Dr. Ferdinand V. Hayden of the United States Geological Survey.

14 Probably on Hell Roaring Creek; from there a northwest course would take them to Mill Creek.

about 20 Mls west cours and encamped at a spring. The next day we crossed the Yellowstone river and travelled up it on the west side to the mouth of Gardnes fork where we staid the next day 25th We travelled to "Gardners hole" then altered our course SE crossing the eastern point of the valley and encamping on a small branch among the pines 26 We encamped on the Yellowstone in the big plain below the lake The next day we went to the lake and set our traps on a branch running into it near the outlet on the NE side[15] 28th after visiting my traps I returned to the Camp where after stopping about an hour or two I took my rifle and sauntered down the shore of the Lake among the [scattered] groves of tall pines until tired of walking about (the day being very warm) I took a bath in the lake for probably half an hour and returned to camp about 4 ockk PM Two of my comrades observed let us take a walk among the pines and kill and Elk" and started off whilst the other was laying asleep—Sometime after they were gone I went to a bale of dried meat which had been spread in the Sun 30 or 40 feet from the place where we slept here I pulled off my powder horn and bullet pouch laid them on a log drew my butcher knife and began to cut We were encamped about a half a mile from the Lake on a stream running into it in a S.W. direction thro. a prairie bottom about a quarter of a mile wide On each side of this valley arose a bench of land about 20 ft high running paralell with the stream and covered with pines On this bench we were encamped on the SE side of the stream The pines immediately behind us was thickly intermingled with logs and fallen trees—After eating a few [minutes] I arose and kindled a fire filled my tobacco pipe and sat down to smoke My comrade whose name was White was still sleeping. Presently I cast my eyes towards the horses which were feeding in the

---

15 The encampment was on the bank of Pelican Creek just north of the point where the high-way now crosses it east of Fishing Bridge settlement. Where the stream enters Lake Yellowstone its course is only a few degrees west of south, however, the general course is southwest.

Valley and discovered the heads of some Indians who were gliding round under the bench within 30 steps of me I jumped to my rifle and aroused White and looking towards my powder horn and bullet pouch it was already in the hands of an Indian and we were completely surrounded We cocked our rifles and started thro. their ranks into the woods which seemed to be completely filled with Blackfeet who rent the air with their horrid yells. on presenting our rifles they opened a space about 20 ft. wide thro. which we plunged about the fourth jump an arrow struck White on the right hip joint I hastily told him to pull it out and I spoke another arrow struck me in the same place but they did not retard our progress At length another arrow striking thro. my right leg above the knee benumbed the flesh so that I fell with my breast accross a log. The Indian who shot me was within 8 ft and made a Spring towards me with his uplifted battle axe: I made a leap and avoided the blow and kept hopping from log to log thro. a shower of arrows which flew around us like hail, lodging in the pines and logs. After we had passed them about 10 paces we wheeled about and took [aim] at them They then began to dodge behind the trees and shoot their guns we then ran and hopped about 50 yards further in the logs and bushes and made a stand— I was very faint from the loss of blood and we set down among the logs determined to kill the two foremost when they came up and then die like men we rested our rifles accross a log White aiming at the foremost and Myself at the second I whispered to him that when they turned their eyes toward us to pull trigger. About 20 of them passed by us within 15 feet without casting a glance towards us another file came round on the [opposite] side within 20 or 30 paces closing with the first a few rods beyond us and all turning to the right the next minute were out of our sight among the bushes They were all well armed with fusees, bows & battle axes We sat still until the rustling among the bushes had died away then arose and after looking carefully around us White asked in a whisper how far it was to the lake I replied pointing to the SE about a quarter of a mile. I was nearly fainting from the loss of blood and the want of water We hobbled along 40 or 50 rods and I was obliged to sit down a few minutes then go a little further and rest again. we managed in this way until we reached the bank of the lake Our next object was to obtain some of the water as the bank was very steep and high. White had been perfectly calm and deliberate until now his conversation became wild hurried and despairing he observed "I cannot go down to that water for I am wounded all over I shall die" I told him to sit down while I crawled down and brought some in my hat. This I effected with a great deal of difficulty. We then hobbled along the border of the Lake for a mile and a half when it grew dark and we stopped. We could still hear the shouting of the Savages over their booty. We stopped under a large pine near the lake and I told White I could go no further "Oh said he let us go up into the pines and find a spring" I replied there was no spring within a Mile of us which I knew to be a fact. Well said he if you stop here I shall make a fire" Make as much as you please I replied angrily This is a poor time now to undertake to frighten me into measurs. I then started to the water crawling on my hands and one knee and returned in about an hour with some in my hat. While I was at this he had kindled a small fire and taking a draught of water from the hat he exclaimed Oh dear we shall die here, we shall never get out of these mountains, Well said I if you presist in thinking so you will die but I can crawl from this place upon my hands and one knee and kill 2 or 3 Elk and make a shelter of the skins dry the meat until we get able to travel. In this manner I persuaded him that we were not in half so bad a Situation as we might be altho. he was not in half so bad a situation as I expected for on examining I found only a slight wound from an arrow on his hip bone but he was not so much to blame as he was a young man who had been brot up in Missouri the pet of the family and had never done or learned much of anything but horseracing and gambling whilst under the care of his parents (if care it can be called). I pulled off a old piece of a coat made of Blanket (as he was entirely without clothing except his hat and shirt) Set myself in a leaning position against a tree ever and anon gathering such leaves and rubbish as I could reach without altering the position of My body to keep up a little fire in this manner miserably spent the night. The next morning Aug 29th I could not arise without assistance When White procured me a couple of sticks for crutches by the help of which I hobbled to a small grove of pines about 60 yds distant. We had scarcely entered the grove when we heard a dog barking and Indians singing and talking. The sound seemed to be approaching us. They at length came near to where we were to the number of 60 Then commenced shooting at a large band of elk that was swimming in the lake killed 4 of them dragged them to shore and butchered them which occupied about 3 hours. They then packed the meat in small bundles on their backs and travelled up along the rocky shore about a mile and encamped. We then left our hiding place crept into the thick pines about 50 yds distant and started in the direction of our encampment in the hope of finding our comrades My leg was very much swelled and painful but I managed to get along slowly on my crutches by Whites carrying my rifle when we were within about 60 rods of the encampment we discovered the Canadian hunting round among the trees as tho he was looking for a trail we approached him within 30 ft before he saw us and he was so much agitated by fear that he knew not whether to run or stand still. On being asked where Elbridge was he said they came to the Camp the night before at sunset the Indians pursued them into the woods where they separated and he saw him no more. At the encampment I found a sack of salt—everything else the Indians had carried away or cut to pieces they had built 7 large Conical forts near the spot from which we supposed their number to have been 70 or 80 part of whom had returned to their Village with the horses and plunder. We left the place heaping curses on the head of the Blackfoot nation which neither injured them or alleviated our distress We followed down the shores of the lake and stopped for the night My companions threw some logs and rubbish together forming a kind of shelter from the night breeze but in the night it took fire (the logs being pitch pine) the blaze ran to the tops of the trees we removed a short distance built another fire and laid by it until Morning We then made a raft of dry poles and crossed the outlet upon it. We then went to a small grove of pines nearby and made a fire where we stopped the remainder of the day in hopes that Elbridge would see our signals and come to us for we left directions on a tree at the encampment which route we would take. In the meantime the Cannadian went to hunt something to eat but without success. I had bathed my wounds in Salt water and made a salve of Beavers Oil and Castoreum which I applied to them This had eased the pain and drawn out the swelling in a great measure. The next morning I felt very stiff and sore but we were obliged to travel or starve as we had eaten nothing since our defeat and game was very scarce on the West side of the Lake and morover the Cannadian had got such a fright we could not prevail on him to go out of our sight to hunt So on we truged slowly and after getting warm I could bear half my weight on my lame leg but it was bent considerably and swelled so much that my Knee joint was stiff. About 10 oclk the Cannadian killed a couple of small ducks which served us for breakfast. After eating them we pursued our journey. At 12 oclk it began to rain but we still kept on until the Sun was 2 hours high in the evening when the weather clearing away we encamped at some hot springs[16] and killed a couple of geese. Whilst we were eating them a Deer came swimming along in the lake within about 100 yards of the shore we fired several shots at him but the water glancing the balls he remained unhurt and apparently unalarmed but still Kept swimming to and fro in the Lake in front of us for an hour and then started along

---

16 The hot springs at West Thumb.

up close to the shore. The hunter went to watch it in order to kill it when it should come ashore but as he was lying in wait for the Deer a Doe Elk came to the water to Drink and he killed her but the Deer was still out in the lake swimming to and fro till dark. Now we had a plenty of meat and drink but [were] almost destitute of clothing I had on a par of trowsers and a cotton shirt which were completely drenched with the rain. We made a sort of shelter from the wind of pine branches and built a large fire of pitch Knots in front of it, so that we were burning on one side and freezing on the other alternately all night. The next morning we cut some of the Elk meat in thin slices and cooked it slowly over a fire then packed it in bundles strung them on our backs and started by this time I could carry my own rifle and limp along half as fast as a man could walk but when my foot touched against the logs or brush the pain in my leg was very severe We left the lake at the hot springs and travelled thro. the thick pines over a low ridge of land thro. the snow and rain together but we travelled by the wind about 8 Mls in a SW direction when we came to a Lake about 12 Mls in circumference[17] which is the head spring of the right branch of Lewis fork. Here we found a dry spot near a number of hot springs under some thick pines our hunter had Killed a Deer on the way and I took the skin wrapped it around me and felt prouder of my Mantle than a Monarch with his imperial robes. This night I slept more than 4 hours which was more than I had slept at any one time since I was wounded and arose the next morning much refreshed These Springs are similar to those on the Madison and among these as well as those Sulphur is found in its purity in large quantities on the surface of the ground. We travelled along the Shore on the south side about 5 Mls in an East direction fell in with a large band of Elk killed two fat Does and took some of the meat. We then left the lake and travelled

---

17   This is Heart Lake. Following the wind for a guide led Russell southeast instead of southwest, bringing him out in the Heart Lake Geyser Basin.

due South over a rough broken country covered with thick pines for about 12 Mls when we came to the fork again which ran thro. a narrow prarie bottom followed down it about six miles and encamped at the forks We had passed up the left hand fork on the 9th of July on horse back in good health and spirits and came down on the right[18] on the 31st of Aug. on foot with weary limbs and sorrowful countenances. We built a fire and laid down to rest, but I could not sleep more than 15 or 20 minutes at a time the night was so very cold. We had plenty of Meat however and made Mocasins of raw Elk hide The next day we crossed the stream and travelled down near to Jacksons Lake on the West side then took up a small branch in a West direction to the head.[19] We then had the Teton mountain to cross which looked like a laborious under-taking as it was steep and the top covered with snow. We arrived at the summit however with a great deal of difficulty before sunset and after resting a few moments travelled down about a mile on the other side and stopped for the night. After appending another cold and tedious night we were descending the Mountain thro. the pines at day light and the next night reached the forks of Henrys fork of Snake river.[20] this day was very warm but the wind blew cold at night we made a fire and gath-ered some dry grass to sleep on and then sat down and eat the remain-der of our provisions. It was now 90 Mls to Fort Hall and we expected to

---

18 Russell's references to "right" or "left" hand of a stream are always made as though looking upstream; just the opposite of the accepted practice today. The date here does not agree with that carried forward from previous entries; it should be September 2.

19 Probably Owl Creek in what is now Grand Teton National Park. Allyn Hanks, formerly chief Ranger there, pointed the route out to me in 1945 as one commonly used by the "mountain men" in crossing the Teton Range. However, the route could have been the *one* later followed by the Marysville freight road which roughly paralleled the south boundary of Yellowstone National Park. While the distances the party covered—twenty miles the first day and thirty the second—seem long marches for wounded men, desperation undoubtedly spurred their exertions.

20 The junction of Henry's Fork and Falls River, or the "Falling Fork," as it was called by the trappers.

see little or no game on the route but we determined to travel it in 3 days we lay down and shivered with the cold till daylight then arose and again pursued our journey towards the fork of Snake river where we arrived sun about an hour high forded the river which was nearly swimming and encamped The weather being very cold and fording the river so late at night caused me much suffering during the night Septr 4th we were on our way at day break and travelled all day thro. the high Sage and sand down Snake river We stopped at dark nearly worn out with fatigue hunger and want of sleep as we had now travelled 65 Mls in two days without eating. We sat and hovered over a small fire until another day appeared then set out as usual and travelled to within about 10 ms of the Fort when I was seized with a cramp in my wounded leg which compelled me to stop and sit down ever 30 or 40 rods at length we discovered a half breed encamped in the Valley who furnished us with horses and went with us to the fort where we arrived about sun an hour high being naked hungry wounded sleepy and fatigued. Here again I entered a trading post after being defeated by the Indians but the treatment was quite different from that which I had received at Larameys fork in 1837[21] when I had been defeated by the Crows

The Fort was in charge of Mr. Courtney M. Walker[22] who had been lately employed by the Hudsons Bay Company for that purpose He invited us into a room and ordered supper to be prepared immediately. Likewise such articles of clothing and Blankets as we called for. After dressin ourselves and giving a brief history of our defeat and sufferings supper was brot. in consisting of tea Cakes butter milk dried meat etc I eat very

---

21 See pp. 101-106 of *Journal Of a Trapper* by Osborne Russell. Correcting the error in dating would make this September 6, 1839.

22 He was one of the "lay assistants" who accompanied the Rev. Jason Lee to Oregon. Walker stayed in the Oregon country, and Wyeth put him in charge of the properties on Sauvies Island at the time Fort Hall was sold. Apparently he took service with the Hudson's Bay Company when they leased the Island from Wyeth.

sparingly as I had been three days fasting but drank so much strong tea that it kept me awake till after midnight. I continued to bathe my leg in warm water and applied a salve which healed it in a very short time so that in 10 days I was again setting traps for Beaver On the 13th of Septr. Elbridge arrived safe at the Fort he had wandered about among the Mountains several days without having any correct knowledge, but at length accidentally falling onto the trail which he had made in the Summer it enabled him to reach the plains and from thence he had travelled to the Fort by his own Knowledge 20th of Octr. We started to hunt Buffaloe and make meat for the winter. The party consisted of 15 men. We travelled to the head of the Jefferson fork of the Missouri where we Killed and dried our meat from there we proceeded over the mountain thro. "Cammas prarie" [23] to the forks of Snake river where most of the party concluded to spend the winter 4 of us however (who were the only Americans in the party) returned to Fort Hall on the 10th of Decr. We encamped near the Fort and turned our horses among the springs and timber to hunt their living during the winter whilst ourselves were snugly arranged in our Skin lodge which was pitched among the large Cotton wood trees and in it provisions to serve us till the Month of April There were 4 of us in the mess One was from Missouri one from Mass. one from Vermont and myself from Maine We passed an agreeable winter We had nothing to do but to eat attend to the horses and procure fire wood We had some few Books to read such as Byrons Shakespeares and Scotts works the Bible and Clarks Commentary on it and other small works on Geology Chemistry and Philosophy—The winter was very mild and the ground was bare in the Valley until the 15 of Jany. when the snow fell about 8 inches deep but disappeared again in a few days. This was the deepest snow and of the longest duration of any we had during the winter.

---

23 This area is still called the "Camas Meadow."

TRAIL BLAZER

CAPTAIN JEDEDIAH STRONG SMITH

From *The Mountain Men,*
By George Laycock

Introduced in Chapter 10, George Laycock's *The Mountain Men* surely deserves an encore, and it receives a proper one here with this chapter on the larger-than-life Captain Jedediah Strong Smith.

• • •

CAPTAIN JEDEDIAH STRONG SMITH earned his high standing among the beaver trappers by an unusual combination of cool-headed leadership, attention to business, and a string of close calls that astounded his fellow trappers. There was frequent speculation on just when the Captain's luck would run out and leave Old Jed "lying wolf meat," his hair dangling from some Blackfoot warrior's lodge.

Smith was tall, over six feet, slender in build, and powerful. He had brown hair and blue eyes. His store of energy seemed boundless, and unlike many mountain men, he was quiet and serious by nature. His companions always figured they could count on Captain Smith in a crisis. He was long on courage and clear thinking in a tight spot.

He had another characteristic setting him apart from most of the beaver trappers: he was so serious about his religion that he always carried a Bible in his possibles bag. This might have labeled a lesser man as a mite queer out in country where it was said that God was always careful to stay east of the Missouri. Smith did not swear, smoke, get drunk, or chase women. His mind was on his work and his eye was on the horizon. For him, life was serious, exciting, and filled with challenges. There is often an element of luck in the background of the successful person, and Jed Smith had that going for him too–some of the time.

After his family moved west from his birthplace in south-central New York, first to Pennsylvania, then Ohio, Jed moved on to arrive in St. Louis in the spring of 1822 when he was twenty-three years old. He had the farm boy's knowledge of the outdoors but knew nothing of the western wilderness, except that it promised a fortune to anyone who could capture the animals and sell their skins.

In St. Louis that spring, Jed responded to General Ashley's call for young men to go to the mountains. He joined the party under the leadership of Ashley's partner, Andrew Henry. The boats made their way up the Missouri as far as the mouth of the Yellowstone, and there Henry and his party spent the winter. Jed Smith, however, journeyed on up the Missouri to the mouth of the Musselshell and hunkered down to wait out the winter. Here he began living in the fashion of the free trappers, subsisting on the meat he shot, and probably protected from the winter blasts by a shelter made of buffalo skins stretched over a framework of tent poles with both ends stuck in the ground.

By spring he was back down at the mouth of the Yellowstone where Henry needed a messenger to travel down the Missouri and meet General Ashley. The restless Jed Smith said quietly that he would carry the message to Ashley, and he was soon headed downriver again. This was how he volunteered himself right into that famous battle where the Arikaras waylaid Ashley.

Following the battle with the Arikara, Ashley and Henry sent Jed Smith out at the head of a dozen or so trappers to explore the untouched beaver country south of the Yellowstone River. It was during this trip that the trappers began addressing Jed Smith, their brigade leader, as Captain.

INDIANS WERE a constant danger. Nobody knew when a band of them would come racing down out of a rocky mountainside or across the plains, clinging to the sides of their ponies, arrows nocked, ready for the full draw. Scouts were kept out to give early warning in case the Indians appeared. From this trip, however, Smith would remember the grizzly bear more vividly than the hostile Indians.

His group traveled for days across a dry land of short grass and prickly pear. There were patches of timber in the draws, and along the streams grew bands of cottonwood and bushes bearing wild fruits. There were buffalo, prairie dogs, elk, antelope, and waterfowl. And there were grizzlies. Even if you didn't see the huge bears, you knew they were there.

One evening the trappers were pushing their way through a thicket toward a river to make camp for the night. They were leading their tired horses. Smith was out at the head of the line. Suddenly a huge grizzly rushed, chuffing and growling, out of the bushes near the middle of the line of men. She wheeled and ran along the line until she met Jed Smith face to face.

Trapper Jim Clyman, a member of Smith's party, later wrote down the events as he recalled them. "Grizzly did not hesitate a moment but sprang on the captain . . . " The huge bear took Smith's head in its mouth and tossed him to the ground. This ripped Smith's scalp open, leaving a flap of hair and bloody skin hanging down and exposing the white skull. The beast then grabbed the young captain by the middle, breaking, not only the blade off Smith's butcher knife, but also several of his ribs. Lead balls began thumping into the old bear's sides until the beast finally dropped, releasing Smith only in its moment of death.

The trappers stood around wondering what to do. Their captain lay bleeding on the ground. These wilderness travelers could treat simple cuts or bruises, boils, and snakebites, but they often depended on luck to see them through serious medical emergencies. None among them had any experience treating wounds of the magnitude the grizzly had rendered on the torn body of Jed Smith. The trappers kept passing the buck, each one suggesting that the next one do something for the captain. Finally, they did the usual and put the question directly to him.

Smith, with his head laid open, ribs shattered, and abdominal lacerations bleeding profusely, was still thinking clearly. He dispatched two men to the river a mile or so away to bring water. Then he told Clyman to get a needle and thread and begin sewing up his head wounds. Clyman found a pair of scissors and cut off as much of the captain's blood-matted hair as he could. Now he could see the tremendous task he faced; he began sewing the flap of scalp back in place.

With this done, he looked at Smith's dangling ear which he said was " . . . torn from his head out to the outer rim." The ear was hanging by a flap of skin and Clyman explained to the captain that there was no way he could save it. This was not what Jed Smith wanted to hear. He instructed the first-time surgeon to take his needle and do his best, and Clyman began putting the ear back on, after a fashion. "I put in my needle stitching it through and through and over and over."

Once he had been patched up, Smith got to his feet, mounted his horse, and rode a mile to the campsite. There his crew installed him in the party's only tent and tried to make him comfortable. He needed recovery time and while he rested in camp, his trappers scouted the surrounding hills. Within ten days Smith's raw wounds had healed sufficiently for him to travel. He rode off with his party, heading west once more toward the high beaver country.

As long as he lived, Smith carried the vivid red scars of his encounter with the grizzly. The missing eyebrow, the gash across his weathered face, the ear somewhat out of place, all marked him as a member of that tough breed of respected men who had tangled with a grizzly bear and survived. The story of Captain Smith and the grizz spread throughout the mountains. The captain wore his hair long to help hide his terrible new scars.

EVENTUALLY, AFTER PROVING HIMSELF as trapper and brigade leader, Smith had the opportunity to become part owner of a fur company. General Ashley, for whom he had worked, was willing to sell out, and the men who purchased the outfit were three of the most capable of all the mountain men, Jedediah Smith, William L. Sublette, and David Jackson. As Ashley headed downriver toward St. Louis and civilization with his profits, the three new partners made their plans for the coming year. Sublette and Jackson would head back into the high country around the headwaters of the Missouri and its tributaries. But Smith had his eyes on an entirely new frontier.

Legend had it that a major river had its beginning somewhere south of Great Salt Lake and flowed on all the way to the Pacific. Here could be new beaver country, waiting for someone to open it, and Jedediah Smith wanted a chance at it. If all went well, he would bring his party back to the summer rendezvous of 1827, on the southern end of Bear Lake which today straddles the Utah-Idaho border.

To the southwest lay a vast expanse of mysterious country unknown to the white man. The map beyond Great Salt Lake was a blank. The Indians were unable to answer Smith's questions about his unmapped region. Jedediah Smith was dreaming of wild streams where the beaver had not yet met the trappers, but the lure of unexplored country was as strong in him as the promise of beaver pelts. He was driven by the knowledge that no one had yet blazed a trail across this strange land all the way to California where the great Pacific rolled in against the shores.

How much of this had been in Smith's mind as he and his partners made their plans during the rendezvous at Willow Valley in northern Utah, in the summer of 1826, we cannot know. But we do know that by the middle of August, seventeen men, led by Smith, set off toward the Southwest. Once more, Jed Smith's eyes were on the horizon. This time his longing to travel where no others of his kind had walked was going to lead him into one of the more incredible of all the mountain men's journeys.

The adventure started with Smith's trappers in high spirits. The line of buckskin-clad men moved south along the east shore of Great Salt Lake, then rode on down the west side of the Wasatch Mountains, a north-south range, stretching for two hundred and fifty miles across the heart of Utah. Then the trail rises sharply from its basins, through coniferous forests, to twelve thousand feet. As long as there was fresh "buffer cow to make meat of," there were good times around the campfires, and uncounted buffalo grazed in the grasslands where these trappers rode.

But as they moved south and westward, the buffalo gradually gave out and the party began munching on the seven hundred pounds of jerky that Smith had directed his crew to pack on the horses. There were still antelope, "black tailed hares," and now and then a bighorn for the pot.

They came to the Sevier River and followed that colorful valley deeper and deeper into the desert. The land offered spectacular colors and memorable sunsets, but one doubts that the beautiful desert landscapes were now much admired by hungry, thirsty mountain men. These were men who had trapped hundreds of beaver from cool mountain streams, then feasted in the evenings on buffalo. The scene had changed. The sweeping mountain views were gone. Now they moved deeper and deeper into the wasteland of the broad, barren Mohave Desert.

In this bone-dry land of sand and rocks, stretching out between the Sierra Nevada and the Colorado river, they traveled beneath the searing sun, buffeted by strong winds, plagued by hunger and thirst. Smith was searching for the great river that he felt must drain Great Salt Lake into the Pacific. But there was no such stream.

After two weeks in the Mohave Desert, the party topped the San Bernardino Mountains. A shining new green land was spread out before them. To the west stood San Gabriel, a prosperous Spanish Mission, its occupants protected from the east by the broad desert fortress no American had yet crossed. San Gabriel was then grazing thousands of head of stock, and producing a wide variety of fruit, including fine grapes that yielded hundreds of barrels of wine each year.

The surprised friars in charge of this wealthy mission treated the newly arrived mountain men well. Smith had his blacksmith fashion a bear trap and gave it to the mission because bears had been raiding the orchards. The friars gave Smith enough cotton cloth for all his men to make themselves new, and badly needed, shirts.

Meanwhile, Smith wrote to the Mexican governor in San Diego, explaining that they had come to California in peace simply to find beaver. They had, he added, run out of provisions and this had made it imperative that they come on into the California country. Now they asked permission to leave.

The Spanish interests extended mainly to agriculture and convincing Indians to abandon their ancient beliefs and embrace the white man's religion. Trapping was of minor interest to them. The governor knew so little about beaver, or trapping them, that he referred to the American hunters as fishermen, perhaps because they knew about trapping sea otters and the otters lived in the edge of the ocean. Furthermore, he thought the story being handed to him by the gangly young captain of the "fishermen" had the sure ring of falsehood. Perhaps these men from the East were soldiers and spies with a clever cover story. The governor eventually sent word to Smith that he and his men could leave California– providing they backtracked along the same trail they followed to get there.

This was not precisely what Jedediah Smith wanted to hear. He always preferred exploring new trails in his search for beaver to retraveling ones he already knew. He led his little party out toward the mountains over which the trappers had come and, some distance from the mission, changed course and headed north toward the San Joaquin Valley. This brought the trappers to green and beautiful valleys lined with trees among which wandered all the deer and elk they needed. Best of all, there were beaver.

But Jed Smith was thinking about the need to return to American territory in time for the summer rendezvous. North of San Francisco he came to the American River and turned his party toward the towering mountains to the east. He was again traveling where no white man had gone before him.

The higher Smith and his trappers climbed, the more difficult the trail became. In the Sierra Nevada they fought bitter weather and howling winds. They floundered in belly-deep snow. The horses were dying and Smith feared for his men. Reluctantly, he turned his party around and headed back down toward the valley. There they turned south again and backtracked to the Stanislaus river.

Smith still had to cross the mountains and the desert to reach the rendezvous site. His partners would be there waiting for a report on his explorations into the Southwest. He decided to try it with a smaller party. He set off again, this time with seven horses and mules and two men,

Robert Evans and the blacksmith Silas Gobel. Historian Dale Morgan, who wrote *Jedediah Smith and the Opening of the West,* concluded that, this time, Smith went by way of Ebbetts Pass, altitude 8,731 feet.

They struggled toward the pass through snow that drifted to eight feet deep. They ran out of food and survived on the flesh of their remaining horses. Finally, they were over the divide and starting down out of the high country. The days grew gradually warmer. The trappers came into the desert again. Now their real enemies were heat and the lack of water. As the days dragged on they knew that they might die in this desert. On rest stops they tried to bury themselves up to their chins in the sand to conserve moisture.

Eventually, from that barren desert south of Great Salt Lake, they could see the Wasatch Mountains ahead. But the distance was too great for Evans. He fell to the ground unable to go farther. Smith and Gobel stumbled on, and after a few more miles came to a spring. They fell on their bellies and buried their faces in the shimmering water. Smith had no sooner slaked his thirst then he started back carrying a kettle with more than a gallon of water for his dying companion.

Evans drank the entire offering and wanted more. This revived him, however, and now the ragged little group moved on toward the shore of Great Salt Lake. They traveled around the lake's south end until they came to the Jordan River and found it flooded out of its banks.

Neither Gobel nor Evans was a strong swimmer so the three trappers began cutting reeds and tying them into bundles which they bound together into a raft. Smith tied a rope to the raft, took the end of it between his teeth, and set off swimming for the far shore. Behind him Gobel and Evans clung to the raft and kicked to help propel it across the sweeping current.

AT BEAR LAKE, the 1827 rendezvous was getting underway. Free trappers, traders, and Indians arrived from the mountains, and there was drinking, bartering, yarning, horseplay, and bargaining with the Indian maidens. Many of the stories being told were of the now-famous Captain Smith who had been chawed so fierce by the grizz, and now hadn't been heard from for nigh onto a year. Speculation was that Old Jed had by now sure enough gone under.

Then, in the middle of the afternoon of July 3, there came into the rendezvous a large party of Snake Indians up from the South, and traveling with them were three Americans, as ragged and beaten a trio as you would find anywhere. They were soon recognized, especially the tall, thin form of Jedediah Smith. Word raced through the community. Trappers already celebrating were given new cause. The small cannon brought out from St. Louis was fired in a special salute.

While the other trappers made the most of the carnival-like atmosphere of the rendezvous, the businesslike Jedediah Smith solemnly spent his time putting together another crew of men and assembling horses for his next trip. After spending only ten days in rendezvous, and laying new plans with his partners, he set off again. Eighteen men were lined out behind him. Jed Smith was going back to see more of California and to pick up the crew of trappers he had left there.

He knew something of the route now. By staying closer to the rivers he reduced somewhat the terrible hardships suffered on his first trip to California. By the middle of August the party reached the Mohave villages on the Colorado. This had been a haven for Smith on his first trip to the coast. The Mohaves had been friendly. They had allowed the trappers to camp with them, to rest and regain their strength. The chief had even assigned two young guides to show the trappers the best way to San Gabriel where some of the Mohave Indians had once lived for a while before deserting the mission and rejoining their people.

What Smith didn't know was that, following the trappers' first visit the year before, the governor of California had been in touch with the Mohaves. He had warned the Indians that the white men coming down the Virgin and Colorado rivers into California were a bunch of rascals and up to no good. As a consequence, the Mohaves' "hearts were bad."

These Indians were capable warriors known for their fierce and unyielding conduct of battle. They were famous as swift runners who could run all night while now and then taking a little water form the ring of animal intestine slung over their shoulders. They were also known for their poison arrows, treated with a lethal mixture of human blood and rattlesnake venom.

While Smith's party spent a few days building rafts to ferry their supplies across the Colorado, the Indians waited, giving the white men no hint of what lay in store for them. The Indians waited until the party was split. Smith, with eight of his men, had moved onto a sandbar that reached out into the water. This was when the Mohaves attacked, killing the ten remaining trappers within minutes. Then they moved in on Smith and the other eight.

Smith took a tally of the weapons they had—five rifles and their knives. They quickly hacked down some of the poles in the nearby thicket, clearing space from which to fight, and used the poles to throw up a flimsy breastwork. "We then fastened our Butcher knives with cords to the end of light poles so as to form a tolerable lance," Smith wrote, "and thus poorly prepared, we waited . . . ."

A few of the Indians were beginning to venture within range of the sharpshooters. Smith gave his trappers orders to fire, two at a time, and they killed two Indians at remarkable distances and wounded one more. This awesome display of marksmanship made the Mohave hesitate and reconsider. As the Indians fell back, the Americans disappeared into the bush, then into the desert. Once more Jed Smith escaped, and in due time his little group reached California.

Here they faced new troubles. The governor held them for several weeks while Smith argued his case. Letters even passed back and forth between the Mexican secretary of state and the United States minister in Mexico City, because the travels of this man Smith were becoming increasingly disturbing to the Mexicans. They must have been well aware that Americans wanted to extend the boundaries of the United States from the Atlantic all the way to the Pacific. Jed Smith was the vanguard.

Smith found the California atmosphere unfriendly, and only when a group of sea captains, anchored offshore, interceded for him was he allowed to depart. He rejoined his trappers left here from his first trip, and the combined group eventually headed north toward the Columbia on a trip certain to be as difficult as any Smith ever made. In the tangled, rocky wilderness of northern California, horses slipped and fell into turbulent mountain streams. Rain fell for days at a time. Men clambered over rocks where there was no trail. " . . . the Mountain over which I was obliged to pass," wrote Smith in his journal, "was so exceedingly Rocky and rough that I was four hours in moving one mile." There were also frequent skirmishes with the Indians, as well as attacks by grizzly bears.

Two of these bear attacks were aimed at Jedediah Smith, who still bore the terrible scars dealt him by the grizzly five years earlier. Smith escaped the first bear by making a high dive into a stream. The next bear charged Smith's horse. The captain wheeled his horse sharply, but the bear grabbed the panicked animal's tail and hung on. The bear tried for fifty yards or so to drag the horse to a halt before giving up and watching horse and rider race away.

But the greatest trouble came to the party in Oregon in July 1828, after Smith and two of his crews set off to scout a route for the main party to follow. Before the party could leave its camp, a large group of Kelawatset Indians attacked and almost wiped the trappers out. One trapper escaped into the forest. He eventually made his way across one hundred and fifty miles of wilderness to the Hudson's Bay outpost, Fort Vancouver, on the Columbia River. When Smith and the two trappers with him also arrived at this fort, they knew that the four of them were all that remained of the two parties of trappers Smith had led into the wilds of California. For the third time in his brief career, Jed Smith had survived an Indian massacre—the Arikara in 1823, the Mohaves in 1827, and how, a year later, the Kelawatset. The Hudson's Bay Company factor at Fort Vancouver quickly sent out a party to punish the Indians responsible for the massacre. Among the items recovered was Smith's journal, which is now safe in the archives of the Missouri Historical Society in St. Louis.

But Jed Smith's travels in the mountains were winding down. The following year he was back with his partners in Montana and spent a year trapping on the upper Missouri and its tributaries.

In October 1830, he returned to St. Louis. He had made money as a partner in his fur company and acquired fame on the frontier. He had come to know the West as well as any man. No other explorer, including Lewis and Clark, had seen as much of western America as Jed Smith had visited.

He wanted to take time out and complete his journals and maps for publication. However, he first agreed to help organize a large trading party to Santa Fe and the Mexican provinces.

This long line of wagons and horsemen moved out of St. Louis in April 1831. After crossing the Arkansas River, the Santa Fe Trail led them into a harsh, dry region. Furthermore, when the party arrived, the Southwest was suffering a severe drought. There were long days without water for man or beast. Hope of finding water was dim late in May, and one morning several little groups of men were sent off in various directions in a last-ditch effort to find a spring or stream.

Smith and one companion struck out southward. They came to a water hole but the hole was dust, so Smith told his companion to stay and try digging while he went on to check out a patch of green trees in the distance. His hunch was right. A few miles ahead he found the only water hole for miles around—and a dozen or more Comanche warriors hid beside the waterhole, waiting for thirsty animals to come.

As nearly as the story could be pieced together, Jed Smith happened onto the group suddenly. There was no hope of escape. As the Comanches rushed him, he had only time enough to get off one shot, which killed the chief. Jedediah Smith was immediately overwhelmed, and on these desert sands, his long string of remarkable escapes came to an end.

The unforgettable Jedediah Smith, who had come west as a kid, had blazed the trial soon to be tramped by thousands of westbound families headed for Oregon and California, had been the first white man to go overland to California, the first to travel the California coast north to the Columbia, the earliest to cross the rugged Sierra Nevada, and the first to explore the Great Basin. When he died that day beside the desert water-hole, Jedediah Smith was thirty-two. In eight years of trapping and exploring, fighting Indians and grizzlies, he had written his name indelibly into the legends of the American West.

Chapter 14

LORD GRIZZLY

THE HUGH GLASS ORDEAL

From *Lord Grizzly,* by Frederick Manfred

Wherever there is talk of mountain men, in print or in conversations at rendezvous reenactments, the name Hugh Glass will eventually become a subject of keen interest. The legend of Hugh Glass, as the story is affectionately known, has been told in just about every form possible, from novel to non-fiction to poetry. The base elements of the tale are true: Hugh Glass was a trapper with a band of thirteen men on a fork of the Grand River in South Dakota. Off on his own, Glass was attacked by a grizzly and so badly mauled that his death seemed certain. Two men were left to care for him while the rest of the band moved on. At some point, the two "caretakers" decided Glass was dead and abandoned him. Glass's survival, on his own, crawling through the wilderness on his hands and knees, was no doubt heroic stuff, though the tales of revenge and other conclusions evident in some accounts of his ultimate journey are unsubstantiated.

In *Lord Grizzly,* a superb novel, Frederick Manfred mines the Hugh Glass material to create a survival adventure treasure, truly one of the best of the West. This excerpt can hardly do justice to the full saga, but it stands on its own as a powerful piece of prose.

●   ●   ●

IT WAS SPORT TO BE OUT on one's own again, alone. The new, the old new, just around the turn ahead, was the only remedy for hot blood. Ahead was always either gold or the grave. The gamble of it freshened the blood at the same time that it cleared the eye. What could beat galloping up alone over the brow of a new bluff for that first look beyond?

The wind from the west began to push a little. It dried his damp buckskins, dried Old Blue too.

The valley slowly widened. Shelving slopes on the right mounted into noble skin-smooth tan bluffs, rose toward Wolf Butte. The country on the left, however, suddenly humped up into abrupt enormous bluffs, three of them almost mountains.

After a time Hugh understood why the valley widened. The Grand River forked up ahead, with one branch angling off to the northwest under Wolf Butte, with the other branch wriggling sharply off to the southwest under the three mountainlike tan bluffs.

There was no game. He didn't see a bird. It was siesta time. The eyes and ears of Old Earth were closed in sleep.

A wide gully swept down out of the hollow between the last two bluffs. A spring drained it and its sides were shaggy with brush. Most of the growth was chokecherry, with here and there a prickly plum tree.

Hugh felt hungry. Looking down into the draw he thought he spotted some plums, ripe red ones at that, hanging in the green leaves. Ripe black fruit also peppered the chokecherry trees. Chokecherries, he decided, chokecherries would only raise the thirst and hardly still the hunger. Plums were better. They were filling.

Before dropping down into the draw, Hugh had a last look around. A man alone always had to make sure no red devils were skulking about, behind some cliff or down in the brush. From under old gray brows, eyes narrowed against the pushing wind, Old Hugh studied the rims of the horizon all around. He inspected the riverbed from one end to the other, including each of the forks. He examined all the brushy draws running down from the bald hills on both sides.

He gave Old Blue the eye too. Horses often spotted danger before humans did.

But if there was danger Old Blue was blissfully unaware of it. Old Blue made a few passes at the dry rusty bunch grass underfoot. Old Blue blew out his nostrils at a patch of prickly-pear cactus. Old Blue snorted lightly at a mound of dirt crumbles heaved up by big red ants.

No sign of alarm in Old Blue. It looked safe all right.

Vaguely behind him, a quarter of a mile back, Hugh could hear the party coming along the river, breaking through brush. Allen and his two men were nowhere in sight ahead.

A turtledove mourned nearby: ooah–koooo–kooo–koo.

With a prodding toe and a soft, "Hep-ah," Hugh started Old Blue down the incline into the brush. Grayblue back arched, legs set like stilts, Old Blue worked his way down slowly. The saddle cinches creaked. Stones rattled down ahead of them. Dust rose. Old Blue lashed his blue tail back and forth.

The first few plum trees proved disappointing. The fruit was small; it puckered the mouth and made a ball of Hugh's tongue. Sirupy rosin drops showed where worms had punctured through.

Holding prickly branches away, sometimes ducking, waving at mosquitoes, Hugh preyed through the thicket slowly, testing, spitting. They were all sour. Bah!

The draw leveled. They broke through the shadowy prickly thicket out onto an open creekbed. Spring water ran cool and swift over clean knobs of pink and brown rock.

Old Blue had the same thought Hugh had. A drink. Hugh got off even as Old Blue began sipping.

Holding onto a rein, laying Old Bullthrower on a big dry pink stone, Hugh got down on his knees. He put a hand out to either side on wet cool sand; leaned down until his grizzled beard dipped into the water; began drinking.

Suddenly Old Blue snorted; started up; jerked the rein free and was off in a gallop lickety-split down the creek, heading for the forks of the Grand.

Hugh humped up; grabbed Old Bullthrower; started running after Old Blue. But Hugh couldn't run much on his wounded game leg, and Old Blue rapidly outdistanced him and disappeared around a turn.

Hugh gave up, cursing. "By the bull barley, what got into him?" Puffing, Hugh took off his wolfskin cap. "Now that does put me in a curious fix. With the major already riled enough to hamshoot me." Hugh waggled his old hoar head. "Wonder what did skeer him off, the old cuss."

Hugh cocked an ear; listened awhile; couldn't make out a thing.

There was an odd smell in the air, a smell of mashed chokecherries mixed in with musky dog. But after sniffing the air a few times, nostrils twitching, he decided it was probably some coyote he'd flushed.

Hugh stood pondering, scratching his head. "Wal, one thing, Ol' Blue won't run far. In strange country, a horse always comes back to a party. Gets lonesome like the rest of us humans."

Hugh put Old Bullthrower to one side; got down on his knees for another drink. The shadow of a hawk flitted over swiftly, touching the trickling water, touching him. Finished drinking Hugh picked up Old Bull-thrower; automatically checked the priming; cocked an eye at the brush.

Hugh worked down toward the Grand River to meet the line of march of the party. Halfway down toward the Grand River another creek came angling out of a second draw, the water joining with the first creek and tumbling on toward the river. Hugh looked up the second draw; saw another cluster of plum trees. Ho-ah. Good plums at last. Smaller but blood ripe. Hugh couldn't resist them. He'd give himself a quick treat and then go to meet the party along the river.

The tiny trickling stream curved away from him, to his left. He broke through low whipping willow branches; came upon a sandy opening.

"Whaugh!" A great belly grunt burped up from the white sands directly in front of him. And with a tremendous tumbler's heave of body, a silvertipped gray she-grizzly, *Ursus horribilis,* rose up before him on two legs. "Whaugh!" Two little brown grizzly cubs ducked cowering and whimpering behind the old lady.

The massive silvertipped beast came toward him, straddling, huge head dipped down at him from a humped neck, humped to strike him. Her big doglike mouth and piglike snout were bloody with chokecherry juice. Her long gray claws were bloody with fruit juice too. Her musky smell filled the air. And smelling the musk, Hugh knew then why Old Blue had bolted and run.

Hugh backed in terror, his heart suddenly burning hot and bounding around in his chest. The little arteries down his big Scotch nose wriggled red. His breath caught. The sense of things suddenly unraveling, or the end coming on, of being no longer in control of either things or his life, possessed him.

She was as big as a great bull standing on two legs. She was so huge on her two legs that her incredible speed coming toward him actually seemed slow. Time stiffened, poured like cold molasses.

She roared. She straddled toward him on her two rear legs. She loomed over him, silver neck ruffed and humped, silver head pointed down at him. Her pink dugs stuck out at him. She stunk of dogmusk.

She hung over him, huge furry arms ready to cuff and strike. Her red-stained ivorygray claws, each a lickfinger long, each curved a little like a cripple's iron hook, closed and unclosed.

Hugh's eyes set; stiffened; yet he saw it all clearly. Time poured slow—yet was fast.

Hugh jerked up his rifle.

But the Old Lady's mammoth slowness was faster. She was upon him before he got his gun halfway up. She poured slow—yet was fast. "Whaugh!" She cuffed at the gun in his hands as if she knew what it was for. The gun sprang from his hands. As it whirled into the bushes, it went off in the air, the ball whacking harmlessly into the white sand at their feet.

Hugh next clawed for his horse pistol.

Again she seemed to know what it was for. She cuffed the pistol out of his hand too.

Hugh stumbled over a rock; fell back on his hands and rump; like a tumbler bounded up again.

The cubs whimpered behind her.

The whimpering finally set her off. She struck. "Whaugh!" Her right paw cuffed him on the side of the head, across the ear and along the jaw, sending his wolfskin cap sailing, the claws ripping open his scalp. The blow knocked him completely off his feet, half-somersaulted him in the air before he hit ground.

Again, like a tumbler, Hugh bounded to his feet, ready for more. He felt very puny. The silvertip became a silver blur in his eyes. She became twice, thrice, magnified.

It couldn't be true, he thought. He, Old Hugh Glass, he about to be killed by a monster varmint? Never.

Hugh crouched over. He backed and filled downstream as best he could.

The she-grizzly, still on two legs, both paws ready to cuff, came after him, closed once more. She roared.

Hugh scratched for his skinning knife. There was nothing for it but to close with her. Even as her great claw swiped at him, stiff but swift, he leaped and got inside her reach. Her clubbing paw swung around him instead of catching him. He hugged her for dear life. He pushed his nose deep into her thick dugmusky whitegray fur. He pressed her so hard one of her dugs squired milk over his leathers.

She roared above him. She cuffed around him like a heavyweight trying to give a lightweight a going-over in a clinch. She poured slow— yet was fast. She snarled; roared. His ear was tight on the huge barrel of her chest, and the roars reverberated inside her chest like mountain avalanches. He hugged her tight and stayed inside her reach. She clawed at him clumsily. Her ivorygray claws brought up scraps of buckskin shirt and strips of skin from his back.

He hugged her. And hugging her, at last got his knife around and set. He punched. His knife plunged through the tough hide and slipped into her belly just below the ribs with an easy slishing motion. He stabbed again. Again and again. The knife plunged through the tough furred hide each time and then slid in easy.

Blood spurted over his hands, over his belly, over his legs and her legs both, came in gouts of sparkling scarlet.

He wrested her; stabbed her.

The great furred she-grizzly roared in an agony of pain and rage. He was still inside her reach and she couldn't get a good swipe at him. She clawed clumsily up and down his back. She brought up strips of leather and skin and red muscle. She pawed and clawed, until at last Hugh's ribs began to show white and clean.

Hugh screamed. He stabbed wildly, frantically, skinning knife sinking in again and again.

Her massive ruffed neck humped up in a striking curve. Then her head dug down at him. She seized his whole head in her red jaws and lifted him off his feet.

Hugh got in one more lunging thrust. His knife sank in all the way up to the haft directly over the heart.

He felt her dogteeth crunch into his skull. She shook him by the head like a dog might shake a doll. His body dangled. His neck cracked.

He screamed. His scream rose into a shrill squeak.

He sank away, half-conscious.

She dropped him.

Raging, blood spouting from a score of wounds, she picked him up again, this time by his game leg, and shook him violently, shook him until his leg popped in its hip socket. She roared while she gnawed. She was a great cat chewing and subduing a struggling mouse. His game leg cracked.

She dropped him.

Snarling, still spouting blood on all sides, coughing blood, she picked him up again, this time by the rump. She tore out a hunk the size of a buffalo boss and tossed it over her shoulder toward the brown cubs.

Hugh lay limp, sinking away. He thought of the boy Jim, of Bending Reed, of a picture-purty she-rip back in Lancaster, of two boy babies.

Time poured slow—yet space was quick.

The next thing he knew she had fallen on him and lay deadheavy over his hips and legs.

He heard a scrambling in the brush. He heard the voices of men. He heard the grizzly cubs whimpering. He heard two shots.

Dark silence.

A COLD NOSE WOKE HIM.

He tried opening his eyes; couldn't found his eyelids crusted shut.

He blinked hard a few times; still couldn't open them; gave up.

The back of his head ached like a stone cracking in heat. His entire back, from high in his neck and across his shoulder blades and through the small of his back and deep into his buttocks, was a slate of tight pain.

The cracking ache and the tight pain was too much. He drifted off into gray sleep.

The cold nose woke him again.

And again he rose up out of gray into wimmering pink consciousness. He blinked hard, once, twice; still couldn't quite uncrack his crusted eyelids.

A dog licking his face? Dogs never licked bearded faces that he remembered.

The cold nose touched him once more, on the brow. And then he knew he wasn't being licked in love. He was being sniffed over.

Hugh concentrated on his crusted eyes, forced all he had into opening them. And after a supreme effort, the stuck lashes parted with little crust-breaking sounds. Blue instantly flooded into his old gray eyes. There was an unusually clear sky overhead. Yellow light was striking up into blue. That meant it was morning. If rust and pink had been sinking away under blueblack it would have been late afternoon. Also a few birds were chirping a little. That proved it was morning. Birds never chirped in the late afternoon in August. At least not that he knew of.

August? Where in tarnation . . . ?

With a jerk Hugh tried to sit up.

The jerk like to killed him. His whole back and his rump and his right leg all three became raging red monsters. He groaned. "Gawd!" His whole chest rumbled with it.

Out of the corner of his eye he saw a bristling whitegray shape jump back. Sight of the jumping whitegray shape kept him from fainting. That whitegray bristling shape had a cold black nose. It was a wolf.

Then it all came back to him. What had happened and where he was. Major Henry had ordered him to shave off his beard. He had refused.

Major Henry had then given the hunting detail to Allen and two other men. He'd got mad and gone off hunting by himself–only to run smack into a she-grizzly.

Miraculously he was still alive then.

Holding himself tight rigid, Hugh opened his eyes as far as he could to size things up. He saw green bottleflies buzzing around him, thousands of them, millions of them. They were like darting spots before the eyes. Every time he rolled his eyes they buzzed up from his beard and wounds and swirled and resettled. Just above him hung a bush heavy with ripe buffalo berries.

He heard water trickling over stones. He heard the wolf padding on the sand, circling him warily. The song of a mourning dove echoed through the brush-choked draw: ooah–koooo–kooo–koo.

He had hands. He moved them. The green bottleflies buzzed up; swarmed; resettled. He moved his hands again, first his right, then his left. The right hand seemed slightly bruised; the left felt whole.

He studied the small blue marks over the back of his right hand. That was where the silvertip she-grizzly had struck him when she'd clubbed first his flintlock and then his horse pistol away from him.

Thinking of his gun, he instinctively reached for it. He couldn't find it. He pawed the sand, the dirt, the edge of a fur, over his belly. Not there. Green flies buzzed up; resettled.

He sighed. Of course. The guns were still in the bushes where the she-grizzly had popped them.

He felt his body. The green death flies rose; swirled; swarmed around him. He found his head bandaged with a narrow strip of cloth. A huge welt ran from his grizzly cheek back past his swollen red ear and up into his scalp. The welt was a ridged seam. Someone had carefully sewn up his long terrible wound with deer sinews. The ridged welt ran up around his entire head. A few small stitched ridges ran off it. The clotted seam also felt fuzzy. Someone had also carefully webbed the bleeding wound with the fuzz plucked from a beaver pelt. Beaver fuzz was the thing for quick crust building. Many and many was the time he'd put it on cuts himself.

He ran his hand over his chest; over his gaunt belly; found everything in order. The front of him was still all in one piece. Even the leathers, his buckskin hunting shirt and leggings, were whole. Flies buzzed up angry; resettled.

He felt of his right leg; reached down too far; stirred up the red monsters in his back and game leg and rump again. "Gawd!!"

The flies began to bite him, on the backs of his hands and the exposed parts of his face and ears and the exposed parts of his shoulders.

He wondered what he was lying on. He felt around with his good left hand; found a bearskin beneath. Lifting his head, brushing away the swirling buzzing flies, looking past a crusted lid and swollen blue nose and clotted beard, he saw it was the skin of the silvertip she-grizzly he'd fought. He let his head fall back.

He felt of it again to make sure. How in tarnation . . . ? Who had skinned the she-grizzly? He couldn't have done it himself. That was impossible. The last thing he remembered was the she-grizzly lying dead-heavy across his belly and legs. So he couldn't have.

He remembered hearing voices. He remembered hearing the little grizzly cubs whimpering. He remembered two shots. Ho-ah! The party had spotted runaway Old Blue and had probably heard him screaming. They had come up to help; had shot the cubs. They had pulled the Old Lady off him and had skinned her and had made a bed out of her fur for him. And they had dressed his wounds. Ae, that was it.

He smiled. Ae, real mountain men, they were, to come to a comrade's relief. He smiled. Real mountain men. They had a code; they had.

"Ae, lads, this child was almost gone under that time, he was."

No answer. Only the trickling of the brook, the buzzing of the green death flies, the padding of the circling hungry wolf.

Flies? Wolf? Silence? What in tarnation? Quickly he perked up again—and the raging red monsters tore into him.

Somehow he managed to roll over on his side, the grizzly fur sticking to his crusted-over back and lifting up off the sand. The weight of the hide tore away some of the flesh from his ribs. He screamed. Eyes closed, he caught his breath and screamed again.

When he opened his eyes once more, he saw it. His grave. Beside him, not a yard away, someone had dug a shallow grave for him, a grave some three feet deep and seven feet long.

Old gray eyes almost blinded with tears, with extreme pain, green bottleflies buzzing all around, he stared at it.

His grave.

He shook his head; blinked.

His grave.

So that was it. He was done for. His time was up.

His grave. He lay on his right side looking at it, bewildered in a wilderness.

"Ae, I see it now, lads. It's this old coon's turn at last."

Or maybe it was the other way around. Maybe he was the only one alive, with all the others ambushed, killed, and scalped.

Cautiously he rolled his eyes around. He looked at the mound of yellow sifting sand beside the yawning grave. He looked at the bullberries hanging ripe overhead. He looked at the silvertip she-grizzly hide under him. He watched the green death flies hovering and buzzing around him. He looked up at the blue sky.

Not a soul or a dead body in sight on that side.

He looked all around again as far as his eye could see; then, despite terrible blinding pain, he rolled over on his left side.

Cautiously he rolled his eyes around. Nothing there either. No horses. No men. There'd been no ambush on that side either, so far as he could see.

What in tarnation had happened? He'd been sewed up and placed on the she-grizzly's hide. Also someone had dug a grave for him. Yet no one was about.

He studied the open grave some more. To dig that the men must have thought him dead.

But if they thought him dead, why in tarnation hadn't they finished burying him?

It was too much for him to understand. His head cracked with it.

"This child feels mighty queersome," he murmured.

He felt of his skull again. Yes, his topknot was still in place, though it was ridged and seamed all over like an old patched moccasin.

He blinked; fainted. He fell back, body flopping with a thud on the fur-covered sand. Green flies resettled on him.

The wolf approached him a couple of steps; sat down on its haunches. It watched him warily with narrowed yellow eyes. The wolf sniffed, brush-tail whirling nervously. Presently the wolf got up; approached a few steps closer; sat down on its haunches again. It waited.

Chapter 15

A FUR TRADER'S NARRATIVE

From *Forty Years a Fur Trader On the
Upper Missouri: The Personal Narrative
of Charles Larpenteur 1833-1872*

First published in 1898, Larpenteur's journal of his experiences
from 1833-1872 is considered one of the most important
sources of information about the life of the fur traders and trappers in the Upper Missouri region. Born in France, Larpenteur
(1807-1872) passed away before seeing his work published. His
manuscript survived him, however, and today it is still one of
the most interesting accounts of what it was like to be a mountain man. This excerpt focuses on Larpenteur's thoughts on
Indian customs, a subject every mountain man confronted in
one way or another.

•   •   •

AMONG THE BLACKFEET the law in regard to adultery is death for the adulteress, and forfeiture of all the property of the adulterer. His lodge is cut into pieces, his horses are either killed or taken from him, and the woman must suffer death.

While I was at Benton an instance of this occurred in a very respectable family—for there are such among Indians. I should have said in two families. The woman was very young and handsome. Contrary to custom they had made it up, and the Indian could be seen with his wife as usual; but, being sensible that he had broken the law, he thought that he was looked upon as a weak-hearted man, and could not resist this tormenting idea. She was handsome; he loved her; he must either keep her or kill her. Tortured by reflections, which he could endure no longer, he took her out to walk, as he had been accustomed to do. They were sitting together, when he took her on his lap, combed her hair neatly—which is a mark of love with all Indians—vermilioned her face beautifully, and told her to sit by his side again. He then said, "My good wife, you have done wrong. I thought at one time I could overlook it, but I am scorned by my people. I cannot suffer you to be the wife of another. I love you too much for that. You must die." So saying, he buried his tomahawk in her skull.

When an Indian sees that his wife makes too free with young men, the penalty for such an offense is a piece of the nose. I have seen several who have undergone that punishment, and awful did they look. After cutting off her nose the husband says, "Go now and see how fond the young men will be of talking to you."

Among the Assiniboines there is no particular law in regard to adultery. This is left at the disposition of the injured individual, who sometimes revenges himself; but, if the relatives of the adulterer are strong, he may be content with a payment. Some give the woman a flogging, and then either drive her away or keep her. Nothing will be said about it, but the woman then bears a bad name—in their language Wittico Weeon,

which means a prostitute, but not one of the first degree. A regular prostitute has no husband, and goes about to "lend herself," as they term it,
for pay. Such a woman is gone beyond redemption. There are three different degrees of prostitution, one of which is looked upon as legal. This
is when she is loaned with the consent of her parents, and then the larger
the payment the more honor it is for the woman. When little quarrels
arise among mothers in regard to the characters of their daughters, they
will say, "What have you to say against my daughter? What did yours get
when you lent her? Look at mine—what she got! You are making a Wittico Weeon of your daughter."

The young man who is courting dresses himself in the best style he
can afford. His hair, which is the main point of attraction, is generally
well combed in front, taking care that his stiff topknot stands straight up,
while a long braid of false hair hangs down to his heels. With large pieces
of California shells [abalone—*Haliotis*] in his ears, his neck and breast covered with an immense necklace of beads, his face vermilioned, and a fine
pair of moccasins on his feet, his dress is complete. His over garment is
either a blanket or a robe. Attired in this style, he commences his
courtship by standing quite still in a place where he thinks that she will
be likely to see him. This may last for many days without saying a word
to her. He then makes friends with her brothers, particularly the elder
one, who has a great deal to say in regard to the marrying of his sister.
Then he watches for her when she goes for wood or water, saying a few
words to her, and giving her a finger ring. When he makes small presents
to the mother, father, and brothers they discover what he is after; but he
never enters the lodge of his sweetheart. At this stage of the proceedings,
if the young couple get very much in love with each other, and the young
man cannot obtain the means to buy her, they elope to another band of
the same tribe. But if he be a young man of means, and has obtained the
consent of the woman, he ties a horse at her lodge; if the horse is accepted,
the girl goes that night to his lodge; if not, the horse remains tied at the

lodge, and the young man sends for it in the morning. If he has other horses, and loves the girl enough, the following day he ties two; and sometimes four or five horses are thus tied–the more horses, the greater honor for all parties. An elopement may also take place when the old folks will not consent, after the girl has been given the refusal of a horse. She is never forced to marry. Sometimes the individual who wants to buy a girl has never asked her whether she would have him or not, but has made very inducing offers to her parents, who then do all they can to persuade her, saying, "Take pity on us, daughter! This man likes us. He has given us a great many things. We are poor; we stand much in need of horses. He is a good hunter; he will make you live well; you need not remain poor." Yet, if they girl does not consent, they will not force her.

After marriage the woman belongs to the man. No one else has any right to her; and if she be the eldest, and have two or three sisters, they are also considered his wives, and cannot be disposed of without his consent. It frequently happens that he will take them all. The son-in-law never speaks to or looks at either of his parents-in-law. When invited to a feast or council where his father-in-law is to be he is duly apprised of it, and he covers himself with his robe and turns his back upon the old gentleman. An Indian who has but one wife will always be poor; but one that has three to four wives may become rich–one of the leading men, if not a chief. The reason of this is that the more wives the more children, and children are a source of wealth, resulting in a large family connection, which gives him power; for "might makes right" with them. An Indian marries also in this light: When his family has increased with one wife till they find it impossible to get along without help, he buys a servant, as there is no such thing as hiring one; but she also becomes his wife, and is not looked upon as a servant. In all cases the old wife is always looked up to as the mistress of the whole. The son-in-law never keeps anything to himself until he gets a family; everything goes to his wife's relations, and this may continue even after he has a considerable family. From such customs it is plainly to be seen that the more wives an Indian has the richer he is–contrary to what the case may be with the whites. Notwithstanding customs so strange to us, these Indians live as peaceably and contentedly as civilized people do. It is a fine sight to see one of those big men among the Blackfeet, who has two or three lodges, five or six wives, twenty or thirty children, and fifty to a hundred head of horses; for his trade amounts to upward of $2000 a year, and I assure you such a man has a great deal of dignity about him.

The medicine lodge, which takes place once a year, in June, is conducted with the view to show how strong are Indians' hearts, and to beg the Great Spirit to have mercy upon the tribe. This lodge is erected of a size suitable to hold whatever number of spectators may be in attendance. A very large pole is planted in the ground, and many smaller ones are set up against it, in the manner of an ordinary lodge. One half of the space inside is reserved for those who are to undergo the torture, of which there are three kinds. In this half of the lodge pews are made with green bushes about four feet high; those for the women being separated from the others. When all is ready for the services to commence, the supposed strong-hearted persons come in and take their stands. They are painted in all colors, looking like so many devils–men and women alike; the former are naked down to their waists, but the latter are dressed. Holding in their mouths a small whistle made of the bone of a crow or pelican, and looking straight up to the center post of the lodge, they keep whistling and jumping up and down for three days and three nights, without drinking or eating; during which time eight or ten musicians, all blackened over, beat drums the whole night and day.

The second torture is done by piercing a hole through the skin of each breast, just above the nipple, and tying to each a lariat, which is then fastened by the other end to the top of the lodge-pole. Bearing all the weight they can upon the lariat, they trot back and forth outside the lodge, the space allowed each being according to the number of performers. This kind of torture goes on with a piteous groaning and lamentation, and these devotees are also painted in all sorts of colors, like the dancers. The third medicine or torture is performed by piercing a hole in each shoulder, to which lariats are fastened as before, but the other ends are tied to three or four dry buffalo skulls, which the communicant drags over the prairie, sometimes even up high ridges, weeping and wailing. Such performances are a great sight to behold.

An Indian chief is looked upon by most civilized people as a powerful and almost absolute ruler of his tribe; but he is not. Every tribe, no matter how small, is divided into bands, each of which has its chief and roams in a different part of the territory belonging to the tribe. As everything must have a head, a chief is appointed to represent the band in councils with the whites, and be consulted in the way of governing. He is a man who has power to do a great deal of harm, but as a general thing does little good. The soldier is the one who governs the band, and rules the chief, too, with a kind of government which the civilians do not like; for when the soldier is established, they are under martial law. His lodge, pitched in the center of the camp, is organized with the view to keep order and regulate the camp; mostly to prevent anyone from going out alone on a hunt, so as not to raise the buffalo, but also for mutual protection against enemies. When anyone is caught outside his dogs are shot, his lodge is cut to pieces, and if he rebels he gets a pounding–the chief not excepted. Those soldiers have their head soldier, to whom each one applies to have his rights respected or enforced. If anything be stolen, the head soldier is apprised of the theft; he takes some of the soldiers to examine the lodges, and if the property is found it is given back to the owner, but nothing is done with the thief. This lodge is supported by the people, who have to find wood, water, and meat. Buffalo tongues go mostly to the soldiers' lodge, and, if there be more than can be eaten, they are sent to be traded for sugar, coffee, and flour to make a big feast. But the regular soldiers' feast is dog, and when they feel like having such, no poor old squaw's fine, fat, young dogs are spared. Take it on the whole, Indians are very glad when the lodge breaks up, and each one can go where he pleases. After that the chief will be left with eight or ten lodges, as they then go by those family connections which make leading men, some of whom actually have more influence than the chief himself–I mean with the people of the band.

All things considered, an educated man will see that their whole system of government amounts to nothing; that they are incapable of enforcing any laws like those of a civilized nation, and consequently not able to comply with treaties made with the United States. But such laws as they have answer their own purposes. As a nation they are kind and good to one another, and live in about as much peace and comfort as civilized people–that is, in their own way. One hears less complaint about hard times among them than among ourselves, except when they make a speech to a white man; then they are all very poor and pitiful, on the begging order. As a general thing the men are not quarrelsome. A fight will take place almost without a word. The women quarrel a good deal, and frequently fight with knives or clubs.

There are men and women doctors among them. They use some kinds of herbs and roots, but their greatest medical reliance is the magic of superstition. When the doctor is sent for, he comes with his drum, and a rattle, made of a gourd or dry hide filled with gravel. He sits beside the patient, and commences to beat the drum and shake the rattle at a great rate, singing a kind of song, or rather mumbling some awful noise. He always find out what ails the patient. Sometimes it is a spell which has been thrown on him by some medicine man in camp, who had a spite against him. Such spells vary. Sometimes they are cords which have been passed through the limbs; at other times wolf hairs have been put between the skin and flesh, or bird claws of different kinds. But all of these he extracts by his magic, and shows the patient the hairs, claws, cords, or whatever may have been the spell. But some maladies are due to the devil, who has got into the sick person. In a case of that kind the doctor stations three or four boys with loaded guns outside the lodge at night; then he beats his drum at an awful rate, and at a certain sound, which is understood by the boys, they fire off their guns at the ground, as though they were shooting at rats running out of the lodge. These are supposed to be the devils whom the doctor has driven out of his patient. Should he continue sick, the treatment is repeated until he is cured or given up. Indians spare nothing to have their families or themselves doctored; they will give their guns, lodges, horses—everything they posses—to a doctor who will cure them. I have seen some completely stripped of all they had to pay the doctor. When a child dies the parents give everything away to mourners; and if the family is rich there will be a great many mourners, particularly among the women, who come to shed a few tears for the sake of plunder. It is thought, "She cries; she loved my child; she must have something." The mourning lasts for a year, unless some relation kills one of their enemies; then the family blacken their faces, which does away with the period of mourning. After this, someone will give a gun, another a horse, some other a lodge, and thus the Indian will get a start again.

Medicine men who are thought able to lay spells are much in danger, and sometimes lose their lives at the hands of the relations of one who dies by such magic. I myself saw a young man kill a fine-looking Indian for having, as he said, laid a spell on his father, who died of consumption. The young man shot him at night, about twenty steps from the fort. We went to see him in the morning; he was lying dead, the ball having penetrated his heart. The young man was there, laughing and whirling his tomahawk over him, saying "That doctor will lay no more spells."

Indians have no words for swearing or cursing, like whites, but they have a way to express wrath a great deal more scornfully than a white man can in words. This is done by gathering the four fingers against the thumb and letting them spring open, at the same time throwing out the arm, straight in one's face, with the body and face half turned away, saying "Warchteshnee," which means, as nearly as I can interpret it, "You villain!"

The Indian idea of futurity and immortality of the soul is something about which I never could find out much. All Indians believe in a Great Spirit, the ruler of all they see and know, but of any future existence, in which the wicked are punished and the good rewarded, they know nothing. They believe in ghosts, who live again in a invisible form, thinking that their dead relations come to see them; and that the only way ghosts make themselves known is by whistling, mostly at night, but sometimes by day, in very lonesome places. In consequence of this belief, they make feasts for the ghosts, consisting principally of dried berries, which they would not for anything omit to gather. They boil these berries with meat, or pound a quantity of buffalo meat with marrow fat, with either of which they go to the place where the dead is deposited, say a few words to the departed, hold the eatables up for him or her to partake of, and then divide the feast among the living who are in attendance. Anyone is allowed to attend this ceremony. But whether the ghosts are in a state of happiness or not, they do not pretend to say, nor do they know what distinction may be made between the good and the wicked. To themselves it makes no difference; they feed both good and bad alike.

On being very hard pressed for a statement expressing their ideas regarding resurrection, most Indians would finally say that they thought once dead was the last of a person. In conversation with them I found much pleasure in hearing their stories, which they relate with great eloquence, using a great many figurative expressions. I had some books printed in their language, which I brought with me from St. Paul. These were religious books, gotten up by missionaries of Minnesota, containing Noah's Ark, Jonah swallowed by the whale, and other miracles; at which they would laugh heartily when I read to them, and then say, "Do the whites believe all this rubbish, or are they stories such as we make up to amuse ourselves on long winter nights?" They were very fond of having me read them such stories; that big boat tickled them, and how could Noah get all those animals into it was the question. Then they would say, "The white man can beat us in making up stories." Telling stories is a great pastime with Indians. There are many among them who are good at it; they are always glad to see such come into a company, saying, "Here is such a one; now we'll have some stories told."

The Indian is born, bred, and taught to be a warrior and a hunter; he aspires to nothing else. There is no regular habit of husbandry among them; they always live from hand to mouth. During the 40 years I was in their country I saw no disposition on their part to ameliorate their condition. They are still in the same state. They have no intellectual invention. In regard to their "medicine," one performance which has attracted my attention I do not attribute to magic but to skill. This is the way in which they bring a band of buffalo into their pens. Such a pen is constructed of poles, and bushes, and any other combustibles they can obtain to make a kind of fence, which is by no means sufficient to keep in the buffalo. This inclosure is made of different sizes, but is generally capable of containing 200 or 300 buffaloes. It is made round, and a pole is stuck up in the middle, with scarlet cloth, kettles, pans, and a great many other articles tied to the top. Those are sacrifices to the Great Spirit, made by the individual who is to go after the buffalo. When this pen is finished two wings are made extending a great distance from the entrance, like an immense quail net. These wings are made either of snow or of buffalo chips, gathered at intervals into small heaps sufficiently large to conceal a person. As the pen must be made where there is little wood, it frequently happens that the buffalo are discovered two or three days' march from the spot. When all is ready, the medicine man starts after the buffalo. When the people of the camp see him coming, they all surround the pen, except those who are stationed at intervals along the wings, each hidden behind a pile of snow or chips. The buffalo follow him, and when the last one has passed, the herd being completely within the wings, the people all rise from their places of concealment. The buffalo then rush into the pen. Then the people who surround the pen also rise up, and are joined by those who were behind the wings. The buffalo, being frightened, keep away from the sides of the pen, running around the pole in the middle; though it sometimes happens that, the pen being too small or too weak, they break through in spite of all the Indians can do. With their bows and arrows the Indians begin the work of destruction, and go on till all the buffalo are killed. It is a good sight to see that one Indian bring in a large band of buffalo, which has followed him for two or three days. He is considered a great medicine man.

Chapter 16

ON THE OREGON TRAIL

From *The Oregon Trail,* by Francis Parkman

If any mellow old classic deserves a second look, this one certainly lives up to that distinction. Perhaps you first encountered *The Oregon Trail* as required reading in school. That's fine, but you're really cheating yourself if you don't give it another go. Parkman (1823-1893) showed us the way west as few prose writers have, and he will continue to deserve readers for generations to come.

●   ●   ●

THE COUNTRY BEFORE US was now thronged with buffalo, and a sketch of the manner of hunting them will not be out of place. There are two methods commonly practised, "running" and "approaching." The chase on horseback, which goes by the name of "running," is the more violent and dashing mode of the two, that is to say, when the buffalo are in one of their wild moods; for otherwise it is tame enough. A practised and skilful hunter, well mounted, will sometimes kill five or six cows in a single chase, loading his gun again and again as his horse rushes through the tumult. In attacking a small band of buffalo, or in separating a single animal from the herd and assailing it apart from the rest, there is less excitement and less danger. In fact, the animals are at times so stupid and lethargic that there is little sport in killing them. With a bold and well-trained horse the hunter may ride so close to the buffalo that as they gallop side by side he may touch him with his hand; nor is there much danger in this as long as the buffalo's strength and breath continue unabated; but when he becomes tired and can no longer run with ease, when his tongue lolls out and the foam flies from his jaws, then the hunter had better keep a more respectful distance; the distressed brute may turn upon him at any instant; and especially at the moment when he fires his gun. The horse then leaps aside, and the hunter has need of a tenacious seat in the saddle, for if he is thrown to the ground there is no hope for him. When he sees his attack defeated, the buffalo resumes his flight, but if the shot is well directed he soon stops; for a few moments he stands still, then totters and falls heavily upon the prairie.

The chief difficulty in running buffalo, as it seems to me, is that of loading the gun or pistol at full gallop. Many hunters for convenience's sake carry three or four bullets in the mouth; the powder is poured down the muzzle of the piece, the bullet dropped in after it, the stock struck hard upon the pommel of the saddle, and the work is done. The danger of this is obvious. Should the blow on the pommel fail to send the bullet home, or should the bullet, in the act of aiming, start from its place and roll towards the muzzle, the gun would probably burst in discharging. Many a shattered hand and worse casualties besides have been the result of such an accident. To obviate it, some hunters make use of a ramrod, usually hung by a string from the neck, but this materially increases the difficulty of loading. The bows and arrows which the Indians use in running buffalo have many advantages over firearms, and even white men occasionally employ them.

The danger of the chase arises not so much from the onset of the wounded animal as from the nature of the ground which the hunter must ride over. The prairie does not always present a smooth, level, and uniform surface; very often it is broken with hills and hollows, intersected by ravines, and in the remoter parts studded by the stiff wild-sage bushes. The most formidable obstructions, however, are the burrows of wild animals, wolves, badgers, and particularly prairie-dogs, with whose holes the ground for a very great extent is frequently honeycombed. In the blindness of the chase the hunter rushes over it unconscious of danger; his horse, at full career, thrusts his leg deep into one of the burrows; the bone snaps, the rider is hurled forward to the ground and probably killed. Yet accidents in buffalo running happen less frequently than one would suppose; in the recklessness of the chase, the hunter enjoys all the impunity of a drunken man, and may ride in safety over gullies and declivities, where, should he attempt to pass in his sober senses, he would infallibly break his neck.

The method of "approaching," being practised on foot, has many advantages over that of "running"; in the former, one neither breaks down his horse nor endangers his own life; he must be cool, collected, and watchful; must understand the buffalo, observe the features of the country and the course of the wind, and be well skilled in using the rifle. The buffalo are strange animals; sometimes they are so stupid and infatuated that a man may walk up to them in full sight on the open prairie, and even shoot several of their number before the rest will think it necessary to retreat. At another moment they will be so shy and wary that in order to approach them the utmost skill, experience, and judgment are necessary. Kit Carson, I believe, stands preeminent in running buffalo; in approaching, no man living can bear away the palm from Henry Chatillon.

After Tête Rouge had alarmed the camp, no further disturbance occurred during the night. The Arapahoes did not attempt mischief, or if they did the wakefulness of the party deterred them from effecting their purpose. The next day was one of activity and excitement, for about ten o'clock the men in advance shouted the gladdening cry of *buffalo, buffalo!* and in the hollow of the prairie just below us, a band of bulls was grazing. The temptation was irresistible, and Shaw and I rode down upon them. We were badly mounted on our travelling horses, but by hard lashing we overtook them, and Shaw, running alongside a bull, shot into him both balls of his double-barreled gun. Looking round as I galloped by, I saw the bull in his mortal fury rushing again and again upon his antagonist, whose horse constantly leaped aside, and avoided the onset. My chase was more protracted, but at length I ran close to the bull and killed him with my pistols. Cutting off the tails of our victims by way of trophy, we rejoined the party in about a quarter of an hour after we had left it. Again and again that morning rang out the same welcome cry of *buffalo, buffalo!* Every few moments, in the broad meadows along the river, we saw bands of bulls, who, raising their shaggy heads, would gaze in stupid amazement at the approaching horsemen, and then breaking into a clumsy gallop, file off in a long line across the trail in front, towards the rising prairie on the left. At noon, the plain before us was alive with thousands of buffalo,–bulls, cows, and calves,–all moving rapidly as we drew near; and far off beyond the river the swelling prairie was darkened with them to the very horizon. The party was in gayer spirits than ever. We stopped for a nooning near a grove of trees by the river.

"Tongues and hump-ribs tomorrow," said Shaw, looking with contempt at the venison steaks which Deslauriers placed before us. Our meal finished, we lay down to sleep. A shout from Henry Chatillon aroused us, and we saw him standing on the cart-wheel, stretching his tall figure to its full height, while he looked towards the prairie beyond the river. Following the direction of his eyes, we could clearly distinguish a large, dark object, like the black shadow of a cloud, passing rapidly over swell after swell of the distant plain; behind it followed another of similar appearance, though smaller, moving more rapidly, and drawing closer and closer to the first. It was the hunters of the Arapahoe camp chasing a band of buffalo. Shaw and I caught and saddled our best horses, and went plunging through sand and water to the farther bank. We were too late. The hunters had already mingled with the herd, and the work of slaughter was nearly over. When we reached the ground we found it strewn far and near with numberless carcasses, while the remnants of the herd, scattered in all directions, were flying away in terror, and the Indians still rushing in pursuit. Many of the hunters, however, remained upon the spot, and among the rest was our yesterday's acquaintance, the chief of the village. He had alighted by the side of a cow, into which he had shot five or six arrows, and his squaw, who had followed him on horseback to the hunt, was giving him a draught of water from a canteen, purchased or plundered from some volunteer soldier. Recrossing the river, we overtook the party, who were already on their way.

We had gone scarcely a mile when we saw an imposing spectacle. From the river-bank on the right, away over the swelling prairie on the left, and in front as far as the eye could reach, was one vast host of buffalo. The outskirts of the herd were within a quarter of a mile. In many parts they were crowded so densely together that in the distance their rounded backs presented a surface of uniform blackness; but elsewhere they were more scattered, and from amid the multitude rose little columns of dust where some of them were rolling on the ground. Here and there a battle was going forward among the bulls. We could distinctly see them rushing against each other, and hear the clattering of their horns and their hoarse bellowing. Shaw was riding at some distance in advance, with Henry Chatillon; I saw him stop and draw the leather covering from his gun. With such a sight before us, but one thing could be thought of. That morning I had used pistols in the chase. I had now a mind to try the virtue of a gun. Deslauriers had one, and I rode up to the side of the cart; there he sat under the white covering, biting his pipe between his teeth and grinning with excitement.

"Lend me your gun, Deslauriers."

"*Oui, Monsieur, oui,*" said Deslauriers, tugging with might and main to stop the mule, which seemed obstinately bent on going forward. Then everything but his moccasins disappeared as he crawled into the cart and pulled at the gun to extricate it.

"Is it loaded?" I asked.

"*Oui, bien chargé;* you'll kill, *mon bourgeois;* yes, you'll kill—*c'est um bon fusil.*"

I handed him my rifle and rode forward to Shaw.

"Are you ready?" he asked.

"Come on," said I.

"Keep down that hollow," said Henry, "and then they won't see you till you get close to them."

The hollow was a kind of wide ravine; it ran obliquely towards the buffalo, and we rode at a canter along the bottom until it became too shallow; then we bent close to our horses' necks, and, at last, finding that it could no longer conceal us, came out of it and rode directly towards the herd. It was within gunshot; before its outskirts, numerous grizzly old bulls were scattered, holding guard over their females. They glared at us in anger and astonishment, walked towards us a few yards, and then turning slowly round, retreated at a trot which afterwards broke into a clumsy gallop. In an instant the main body caught the alarm. The buffalo began to crowd away from the point towards which we were approaching, and a gap was opened in the side of the herd. We entered it, still restraining our excited horses. Every instant the tumult was thickening. The buffalo, pressing together in large bodies, crowded away from us on every hand. In front and on either side we could see dark columns and masses, half hidden by clouds of dust, rushing along in terror and confusion, and hear the tramp and clattering of ten thousand hoofs. That countless multitude of powerful brutes, ignorant of their own strength, were flying in a panic from the approach of two feeble horsemen. To remain quiet longer was impossible.

"Take that band on the left," said Shaw; "I'll take these in front."

He sprang off, and I saw no more of him. A heavy Indian whip was fastened by a band to my wrist; I swung it into the air and lashed my horse's flank with all the strength of my arm. Away she darted, stretching close to the ground. I could see nothing but a cloud of dust before me, but I knew that it concealed a band of many hundreds of buffalo. In a moment I was in the midst of the cloud, half suffocated by the dust and stunned by the trampling of the flying herd; but I was drunk with the chase and cared for nothing but the buffalo. Very soon a long dark mass became visible, looming through the dust; then I could distinguish each bulky carcass, the hoofs flying out beneath, the short tails held rigidly erect. In a moment I was so close that I could have touched them with my gun. Suddenly, to my amazement, the hoofs were jerked upwards, the tails flourished in the air, and amid a cloud of dust the buffalo seemed to sink into the earth before me. One vivid impression of that instant remains upon my mind. I remember looking down upon the backs of several buffalo dimly visible through the dust. We had run unawares upon a ravine. At that moment I was not the most accurate judge of depth and width, but when I passed it on my return, I found it about twelve feet deep and not quite twice as wide at the bottom. It was impossible to stop; I would have done so gladly if I could; so, half sliding, half plunging, down went the little mare. She came down on her knees in the loose sand at the bottom; I was pitched forward against her neck and nearly thrown over her head among the buffalo, who amid dust and confusion came tumbling in all around. The mare was on her feet in an instant and scrambling like a cat up the opposite side. I thought for a moment that she would have fallen back and crushed me, but with a violent effort she clambered out and gained the hard prairie above. Glancing back, I saw the huge head of a bull clinging as it were by the forefeet at the edge of the dusty gulf. At length I was fairly among the buffalo. They were less densely crowded than before, and I could see nothing but bulls, who always run at the rear of a herd to protect their females. As I passed among them they would lower their heads, and turning as they ran, try to gore my horse; but as they were already at full speed there was no force in their onset, and as Pauline ran faster than they, they were always thrown behind her in the effort. I soon began to distinguish cows amid the throng. One just in front of me seemed to my liking, and I pushed close to her side. Dropping the reins, I fired, holding the muzzle of the gun within a foot of her shoulder. Quick as lightning she sprang at Pauline; the little mare dodged the attack, and I lost sight of the wounded animal amid the tumult. Immediately after, I selected another, and urging forward Pauline, shot into her both pistols in succession. For a while I kept her in view, but in attempting to load my gun, lost sight of her also in the confusion. Believing her to be mortally wounded and unable to keep up with the herd, I checked my horse. The crowd rushed onwards. The dust and tumult passed away, and on the prairie, far behind the rest, I saw a solitary buffalo galloping heavily. In a moment I and my victim were running side by side. My firearms were all empty, and I had in my pouch nothing but rifle bullets, too large for the pistols and too small for the gun. I loaded the gun, however, but as often as I levelled it to fire, the bullets would roll out of the muzzle and the gun returned only a report like a squib, as the powder harmlessly exploded. I rode in front of the buffalo and tried to turn her back; but her eyes glared, her mane bristled, and lowering her head, she rushed at me with the utmost fierceness and activity. Again and again I rode before her, and again and again she repeated her furious charge. But little Pauline was in her element. She dodged her enemy at every rush, until at length the buffalo stood still, exhausted with her own efforts, her tongue lolling from her jaws.

Riding to a little distance, I dismounted, thinking to gather a handful of dry grass to serve the purpose of wadding, and load the gun at my leisure. No sooner were my feet on the ground than the buffalo came bounding in such a rage towards me that I jumped back again into the saddle and with all possible dispatch. After waiting a few minutes more, I made an attempt to ride up and stab her with my knife; but Pauline was near being gored in the attempt. At length, bethinking me of the fringes at the seams of my buckskin trousers, I jerked off a few of them, and, reloading the gun, forced them down the barrel to keep the bullet in its place; then approaching, I shot the wounded buffalo through the heart. Sinking to her knees, she rolled over lifeless on the prairie. To my astonishment, I found that, instead of a cow, I had been slaughtering a stout yearling bull. No longer wondering at his fierceness, I opened his throat, and cutting out his tongue, tied it at the back of my saddle. My mistake was one which a more experienced eye than mine might easily make in the dust and confusion of such a chase.

Then for the first time I had leisure to look at the scene around me. The prairie in front was darkened with the retreating multitude, and on either hand the buffalo came filing up in endless columns from the low plains upon the river. The Arkansas was three or four miles distant. I turned and moved slowly towards it. A long time passed before, far in the distance, I distinguished the white covering of the cart and the little black specks of horsemen before and behind it. Drawing near, I recognized Shaw's elegant tunic, the red flannel shirt, conspicuous far off. I overtook the party, and asked him what success he had had. He had assailed a fat cow, shot her with two bullets, and mortally wounded her. But neither of us was prepared for the chase that afternoon, and Shaw, like myself, had no spare bullets in his pouch; so he abandoned the disabled animal to Henry Chatillon, who followed, dispatched her with his rifle, and loaded his horse with the meat.

We encamped close to the river. The night was dark, and as we lay down we could hear, mingled with the howling of wolves, the hoarse bellowing of the buffalo, like the ocean beating upon a distant coast.

NO ONE IN THE CAMP was more active than Jim Gurney, and no one half so lazy as Ellis. Between these two there was a great antipathy. Ellis never stirred in the morning until he was compelled, but Jim was always on his feet before daybreak; and this morning as usual the sound of his voice awakened the party.

"Get up, you booby! up with you now, you're fit for nothing but eating and sleeping. Stop your grumbling and come out of that buffalo-robe, or I'll pull it off for you."

Jim's words were interspersed with numerous expletives, which gave them great additional effect. Ellis drawled out something in a nasal tone from among the folds of his buffalo-robe; then slowly disengaged himself, rose into a sitting posture, stretching his long arms, yawned hideously, and, finally raising his tall person erect, stood staring about him to all the four quarters of the horizon. Deslauriers' fire was soon blazing, and the horses and mules, loosened from their pickets, were feeding on the neighboring meadow. When we sat down to breakfast the prairie was still in the dusky light of morning; and as the sun rose we were mounted and on our way again.

"A white buffalo!" exclaimed Munroe.

"I'll have that fellow," said Shaw, "if I run my horse to death after him."

He threw the cover of his gun to Deslauriers and galloped out upon the prairie.

"Stop, Mr. Shaw, stop!" called out Henry Chatillon, "you'll run down your horse for nothing; it's only a white ox."

But Shaw was already out of hearing. The ox, which had no doubt strayed away from some of the government wagon trains, was standing beneath some low hills which bounded the plain in the distance. Not far from him a band of veritable buffalo bulls were grazing; and startled at Shaw's approach, they all broke into a run, and went scrambling up the hillsides to gain the high prairie above. One of them in his haste and terror involved himself in a fatal catastrophe. Along the foot of the hills was a narrow strip of deep marshy soil, into which the bull plunged and hopelessly entangled himself. We all rode to the spot. The huge carcass was half sunk in the mud, which flowed to his very chin, and his shaggy mane was outspread upon the surface. As we came near, the bull began to struggle with convulsive strength; he writhed to and fro, and in the energy of his fright and desperation would lift himself for a moment half out of the slough, while the reluctant mire returned a sucking sound as he strained to drag his limbs from its tenacious depths. We stimulated his exertions by getting behind him and twisting his tail; nothing would do. There was clearly no hope for him. After every effort his heaving sides were more deeply embedded, and the mire almost overflowed his nostrils; he lay still at length, and looking round at us with a furious eye, seemed to resign himself to fate. Ellis slowly dismounted, and, levelling his boasted yager, shot the old bull through the heart; then lazily climbed back again to his seat. Pluming himself no doubt on having actually killed a buffalo. That day the invincible yager drew blood for the first and last time during the whole journey.

The morning was a bright and gay one, and the air so clear that on the farthest horizon the outline of the pale blue prairie was sharply drawn against the sky. Shaw was in the mood for hunting; he rode in advance of the party, and before long we saw a file of bulls galloping at full speed upon a green swell of the prairie at some distance in front. Shaw came scouring along behind them, arrayed in his red shirt, which looked very well in the distance; he gained fast on the fugitives, and as the foremost bull was disappearing behind the summit of the swell, we saw him in the act of assailing the hindmost; a smoke sprang from the muzzle of his gun and floated away before the wind like a little white cloud; the bull turned upon him, and just then the rising ground concealed them both from view.

We were moving forward until about noon, when we stopped by the side of the Arkansas. At that moment Shaw appeared riding slowly down the side of a distant hill; his horse was tired and jaded, and when he threw his saddle upon the ground, I observed that the tails of two bulls were dangling behind it. No sooner were the horses turned loose to feed than Henry, asking Munroe to go with him, took his rifle and walked quietly away. Shaw, Tête Rouge, and I sat down by the side of the cart to discuss the dinner which Deslauriers placed before us, and we had scarcely finished when we saw Munroe walking towards us along the river-bank. Henry, he said, had filled four fat cows, and had sent him back for horses to bring in the meat. Shaw took a horse for himself and another for Henry, and he and Munroe left the camp together. After a short absence all three of them came back, their horses loaded with the choicest parts of the meat. We kept two of the cows for ourselves, and gave the others to Munroe and his companions. Deslauriers seated himself on the grass before the pile of meat, and worked industriously for some time to cut it into thin broad sheets for drying, an art in which he had all the skill of an Indian squaw. Long before night, cords of raw hide were stretched around the camp, and the meat was hung upon them to dry in the sunshine and pure air of the prairie. Our California companions were less successful at the work but they accomplished it after their own fashion, and their side of the camp was soon garnished in the same manner as our own.

We meant to remain at this place long enough to prepare provisions for our journey to the frontier, which, as we supposed, might occupy about a month. Had the distance been twice as great and the party ten times as large, the rifle of Henry Chatillon would have supplied meat enough for the whole within two days; we were obliged to remain, however, until it should be dry enough for transportation; so we pitched our tent and made other arrangements for a permanent camp. The California men, who had no such shelter, contented themselves with arranging their packs on the grass around their fire. In the mean time we had nothing to do but amuse ourselves. Our tent was within a rod of the river, if the broad sand-beds, with a scanty stream of water coursing here and there along their surface, deserve to be dignified with the name of river. The vast flat plains on either side were almost on a level with the sand-beds, and they were bounded in the distance by low, monotonous hills, parallel to the course of the stream. All was one expanse of grass; there was no wood in view, except some trees and stunted bushes upon two islands which rose from the wet sands of the river. Yet far from being dull and tame, the scene was often a wild and animated one; for twice a day, at sunrise and at noon, the buffalo came issuing form the hills, slowly advancing in their grave processions to drink at the river. All our amusements were to be at their expense. An old buffalo bull is a brute of unparalleled ugliness. At first sight of him every feeling of pity vanishes. The cows are much smaller and of a gentler appearance, as becomes their sex. While in this camp we forbore to attack them, leaving to Henry Chatillon, who could better judge their quality, the task of killing such as we wanted for use; but against the bulls we waged an unrelenting war. Thousands of them might be slaughtered without causing any detriment to the species, for their numbers greatly exceed those of the cows; it is the hides of the latter alone which are used for the purposes of commerce and for making the lodges of the Indians; and the destruction among them is therefore greatly disproportionate.

Our horses were tired, and we now usually hunted on foot. While we were lying on the grass after dinner, smoking, talking, or laughing at Tête Rouge, one of us would look up and observe, far out on the plains beyond the river, certain black objects slowly approaching. He would inhale a parting whiff from the pipe, then rising lazily, take his rifle, which leaned against the cart, throw over his shoulder the strap of his pouch and powder-horn, and with his moccasins in his hand, walk across the sand towards the opposite side of the river. This was very easy; for though the sands were about a quarter of a mile wide, the water was nowhere more than two feet deep. The farther bank was about four or five feet high, and quite perpendicular, being cut away by the water in spring. Tall grass grew along its edge. Putting it aside with his hand, and cautiously looking through it, the hunter can discern the huge shaggy back of the bull slowly swaying to and fro, as, with his clumsy, swinging gait, he advances towards the river. The buffalo have regular paths by which they come down to drink. Seeing at a glance along which of these his intended victim is moving, the hunter crouches under the bank within fifteen or twenty yards, it may be, of the point where the path enters the river. Here he sits down quietly on the sand. Listening intently, he hears the heavy, monotonous tread of the approaching bull. The moment after, he sees a motion among the long weeds and grass just at the spot where the path is channeled through the bank. An enormous black head is thrust out, the horns just visible amid the mass of tangled mane. Half sliding, half plunging, down comes the buffalo upon the river-bed below. He steps out in full sight upon the sands. Just before him a runnel of water is gliding, and he bends his head to drink. You may hear the water as it gurgles down his capacious throat. He raises his head, and the drops trickle from his wet beard. He stands with an air of stupid abstraction, unconscious of the lurking danger. Noiselessly the hunter cocks his rifle. As he sits upon the sand, his knee is raised, and his elbow rests upon it, that he may level his heavy weapon with a steadier aim. The stock is at his shoulder; his eye ranges along the barrel. Still he is in no haste to fire. The bull, with slow deliberation, begins his march over the sands to the other side. He advances his foreleg, and exposes to view a small spot, denuded of hair, just behind the point of his shoulder; upon this the hunter brings the sight of his rifle to bear; lightly and delicately his finger presses the hair-trigger. The spiteful crack of the rifle responds to his touch, and instantly in the middle of the bare spot appears a small red dot. The buffalo shivers; death has overtaken him, he cannot tell from whence; still he does not fall, but walks heavily forward, as if nothing had happened. Yet before he has gone far out upon the sand, you see him stop; he totters; his knees bend under him, and his head sinks forward to the ground. Then his whole vast bulk sways to one side; he rolls over on the sand, and dies with a scarcely perceptible struggle.

Waylaying the buffalo in this manner, and shooting them as they come to water, is the easiest method of hunting them. They may also be approached by crawling up ravines or behind hills, or even over the open prairie. This is often surprisingly easy; but at other times it requires the utmost skill of the most experienced hunter. Henry Chatillon was a man of extraordinary strength and hardihood; but I have seen him return to camp quite exhausted with his efforts, his limbs scratched and wounded, and his buckskin dress stuck full of the thorns of the prickly-pear, among which he had been crawling. Sometimes he would lie flat upon his face, and drag himself along in this position for many rods together.

On the second day of our stay at this place, Henry went out for an afternoon hunt. Shaw and I remained in camp, until, observing some bulls approaching the water upon the other side of the river, we crossed over to attack them. They were so near, however, that before we could get under cover of the bank our appearance as we walked over the sands alarmed them. Turning round before coming within gun-shot, they began to move off to the right in a direction parallel to the river. I climbed up the bank and ran after them. They were walking swiftly, and before I could come within gun-shot distance they slowly wheeled about and faced me. Before they had turned far enough to see me I had fallen flat on my face. For a moment they stood and stared at the strange object upon the grass; then turning away, again they walked on as before; and I, rising immediately, ran once more in pursuit. Again they wheeled about, and again I fell prostrate. Repeating this three or four times, I came at length within a hundred yards of the fugitives, and as I saw them turning again, I sat down and levelled my rifle. The one in the centre was the largest I had ever seen. I shot him behind the shoulder. His two companions ran off. He attempted to follow, but soon came to a stand, and at length lay down as quietly as an ox chewing the cud. Cautiously approaching him, I saw by his dull and jelly-like eye that he was dead.

When I began the chase, the prairie was almost tenantless; but a great multitude of buffalo had suddenly thronged upon it, and looking up I saw within fifty rods a heavy, dark column stretching to the right and left as far as I could see. I walked towards them. My approach did not alarm them in the least. The column itself consisted almost entirely of cows and calves, but a great many old bulls were ranging about the prairie on its flank, and as I drew near they faced towards me with such a grim and ferocious look that I thought it best to proceed no farther. Indeed, I was already within close rifle-shot of the column, and I sat down on the ground to watch their movements. Sometimes the whole would stand still, their heads all one way; then they would trot forward, as if by a common impulse, their hoofs and horns clattering together as they moved. I soon began to hear at a distance on the left the sharp reports of a rifle, again and again repeated; and not long after, dull and heavy sounds succeeded, which I recognized as the familiar voice of Shaw's double-barreled gun. When Henry's rifle was at work there was always meat to be brought in. I went back across the river for a horse, and, returning, reached the spot where the hunters were standing. The buffalo were visible on the distant prairie. The living had retreated from the ground, but ten or twelve carcasses were scattered in various directions. Henry, knife in hand, was stooping over a dead cow, cutting away the best and fattest of the meat.

When Shaw left me he had walked down for some distance under the river-bank to find another bull. At length he saw the plains covered with the host of buffalo, and soon after heard the crack of Henry's rifle.

Ascending the bank, he crawled through the grass, which for a rod or two from the river was very high and rank. He had not crawled far before to his astonishment he saw Henry standing erect upon the prairie, almost surrounded by the buffalo. Henry was in his element. Quite unconscious that any one was looking at him, he stood at the full height of his tall figure, one hand resting upon his side, and the other arm leaning carelessly on the muzzle of his rifle. His eye was ranging over the singular assemblage around him. Now and then he would select such a cow as suited him, level his rifle, and shoot her dead; then quietly reloading, he would resume his former position. The buffalo seemed no more to regard his presence than if he were one of themselves; the bulls were bellowing and butting at each other, or rolling about in the dust. A group of buffalo would gather about the carcass of a dead cow, snuffing at her wounds; and sometimes they would come behind those that had not yet fallen, and endeavor to push them from the spot. Now and then some old bull would face towards Henry with an air of stupid amazement, but none seemed inclined to attack or fly from him. For some time Shaw lay among the grass, looking in surprise at this extraordinary sight; at length he crawled cautiously forward, and spoke in a low voice to Henry, who told him to rise and come on. Still the buffalo showed no sign of fear; they remained gathered about their dead companions. Henry had already killed as many cows as he wanted for use, and Shaw, kneeling behind one of the carcasses, shot five bulls before the rest thought it necessary to disperse.

The frequent stupidity and infatuation of the buffalo seems the more remarkable from the contrast it offers to their wildness and wariness at other times. Henry knew all their peculiarities; he had studied them as a scholar studies his books, and derived quite as much pleasure from the occupation. The buffalo were in a sense companions to him, and, as he said, he never felt alone when they were about him. He took great pride in his skill in hunting. He was one of the most modest of men; yet in the simplicity and frankness of his character, it was clear that he looked upon his pre-eminence in this respect as a thing too palpable and well established to be disputed. But whatever may have been his estimate of his own skill, it was rather below than above that which others placed upon it. The only time that I ever saw a shade of scorn darken his face was when two volunteer soldiers, who had just killed a buffalo for the first time, undertook to instruct him as to the best method of "approaching." Henry always seemed to think that he had a sort of prescriptive right to the buffalo, and to look upon them as something belonging to himself. Nothing excited his indignation so much as any wanton destruction committed among the cows, and in his view shooting a calf was a cardinal sin.

Henry Chatillon and Tête Rouge were of the same age; that is, about thirty. Henry was twice as large, and about six times as strong as Tête Rouge. Henry's face was roughened by winds and storms; Tête Rouge's was bloated by sherry-cobblers and brandy-toddy. Henry talked of Indians and buffalo; Tête Rouge of theatres and oyster-cellars. Henry had led a life of hardship and privation; Tête Rouge never had a whim which he would not gratify at the first moment he was able. Henry moreover was the most disinterested man I ever saw; while Tête Rouge, though equally good natured in his way, cared for nobody but himself. Yet we would not have lost him on any account; he served the purpose of a jester in a feudal castle; our camp would have been lifeless without him. For the past week he had fattened in a most amazing manner; and, indeed, this was not at all surprising, since his appetite was inordinate. He was eating from morning till night; half the time he would be at work cooking some private repast for himself, and he paid a visit to the coffee-pot eight or ten times a day. His rueful and disconsolate face became jovial and rubicund, his eyes stood out like a lobster's, and his spirits, which before were sunk to the depths of despondency, were now elated in proportion; all day he was singing, whistling, laughing, and telling stories. Being mortally afraid of Jim Gurney, he kept close in the neigh-borhood of our tent. As he had seen an abundance of low fast life, and had a considerable fund of humor, his anecdotes were extremely amus-ing, especially since he never hesitated to place himself in a ludicrous point of view, provided he could raise a laugh by doing so. Tête Rouge, however, was sometimes rather troublesome; he had an inveterate habit of pilfering provisions at all times of the day. He set ridicule at defiance, and would never have given over his tricks, even if they had drawn upon him the scorn of the whole party. Now and then, indeed, something worse than laughter fell to his share; on these occasions he would exhibit much contrition, but half an hour after we would generally observe him stealing round to the box at the back of the cart, and slyly making off with the provisions which Deslauriers had laid by for supper. He was fond of smoking; but having no tobacco of his own, we used to provide him with as much as he wanted, a small piece at a time. At first we gave him half a pound together, but this experiment proved an entire failure, for he invariably lost not only the tobacco, but the knife entrusted to him for cutting it, and a few minutes after he would come to us with many apolo-gies and beg for more.

We had been two days at this camp, and some of the meat was nearly fit for transportation, when a storm came suddenly upon us. About sunset the whole sky grew as black as ink, and the long grass at the edge of the river bent and rose mournfully with the first gusts of the approaching hurricane. Munroe and his two companions brought their guns and placed them under cover of our tent. Having no shelter for them-selves, they built a fire of driftwood that might have defied a cataract, and, wrapped in their buffalo-robes, sat on the ground around it to bide the fury of the storm. Deslauriers ensconced himself under the cover of the cart. Shaw and I, together with Henry and Tête Rouge, crowded into the little tent; but first of all the dried meat was piled together, and well protected by buffalo-robes pinned firmly to the ground. About nine

o'clock the storm broke amid absolute darkness; it blew a gale, and torrents of rain roared over the boundless expanse of open prairie. Our tent
was filled with mist and spray beating through the canvas, and saturating
everything within. We could only distinguish each other at short intervals
by the dazzling flashes of lightning, which displayed the whole waste
around us with its momentary glare. We had our fears for the tent; but for
an hour or two it stood fast, until at length the cap gave way before a
furious blast; the pole tore through the top, and in an instant we were
half suffocated by the cold and dripping folds of the canvas, which fell
down upon us. Seizing upon our guns, we placed them erect, in order to lift
the saturated cloth above our heads. In this agreeable situation, involved
among wet blankets and buffalo-robes, we spent several hours of the
night, during which the storm would not abate for a moment, but pelted
down with merciless fury. Before long the water gathered beneath us in
a pool two or three inches deep; so that for a considerable part of the
night we were partially immersed in a cold bath. In spite of all this, Tête
Rouge's flow of spirits did not fail him; he laughed, whistled, and sang
in defiance of the storm, and that night paid off the long arrears of
ridicule which he owed us. While we lay in silence, enduring the infliction
with what philosophy we could muster, Tête Rouge, who was intoxicated
with animal spirits, cracked jokes at our expense by the hour together. At
about three o'clock in the morning, preferring "the tyranny of the open
night" to such a wretched shelter, we crawled out from beneath the fallen
canvas. The wind had abated, but the rain fell steadily. The fire of the
California men still blazed amid the darkness, and we joined them as they
sat around it. We made ready some hot coffee by way of refreshment; but
when some of the party sought to replenish their cups, it was found that
Tête Rouge, having disposed of his own share, had privately abstracted
the coffee-pot and drunk the rest of the contents out of the spout.

In the morning, to our great joy, an unclouded sun rose upon the
prairie. We presented a rather laughable appearance, for the cold and

clammy buck-skin, saturated with water, clung fast to our limbs. The light wind and warm sunshine soon dried it again, and then we were all encased in armor of intolerable stiffness. Roaming all day over the prairie and shooting two or three bulls, were scarcely enough to restore the stiffened leather to its usual pliancy.

Besides Henry Chatillon, Shaw and I were the only hunters in the party. Munroe this morning made an attempt to run a buffalo, but his horse could not come up to the game. Shaw went out with him, and being better mounted, soon found himself in the midst of the herd. Seeing nothing but cows and calves around him, he checked his horse. An old bull came galloping on the open prairie at some distance behind, and turning, Shaw rode across his path, levelling his gun as he passed, and shooting him through the shoulder into the heart.

A great flock of buzzards was usually soaring about a few trees that stood on the island just below our camp. Throughout the whole of yesterday we had noticed an eagle among them; today he was still there; and Tête Rouge, declaring that he would kill the bird of America, borrowed Deslauriers's gun and set out on his unpatriotic mission. As might have been expected, the eagle suffered no harm at his hands. He soon returned, saying that he could not find him, but had shot a buzzard instead. Being required to produce the bird in proof of his assertion, he said he believed that he was not quite dead, but he must be hurt, from the swiftness with which he flew off.

"If you want," said Tête Rouge, "I'll go and get one of his feathers; I knocked off plenty of them when I shot him."

Just opposite our camp, was another island covered with bushes, and behind it was a deep pool of water, while two or three considerable streams coursed over the sand not far off. I was bathing at this place in the afternoon when a white wolf, larger than the largest Newfoundland dog, ran out from behind the point of the island, and galloped leisurely over the sand not half a stone's-throw distant. I could plainly see his red eyes and the bristles about his snout; he was an ugly scoundrel, with a bushy tail, a large head, and a most repulsive countenance. Having neither rifle to shoot nor stone to pelt him with, I was looking after some missile for his benefit, when the report of a gun came from the camp, and the ball threw up the sand just beyond him; at this he gave a slight jump, and stretched away so swiftly that he soon dwindled into a mere speck on the distant sand-beds. The number of carcasses that by this time were lying about the neighboring prairie summoned the wolves from every quarter; the spot where Shaw and Henry had hunted together soon became their favorite resort, for here about a dozen dead buffalo were fermenting under the hot sun. I used often to go over the river and watch them at their meal. By lying under the bank it was easy to get a full view of them. There were three different kinds: the white wolves and the gray wolves, both very large, and besides these the small prairie wolves, not much bigger than spaniels. They would howl and fight in a crowd around a single carcass, yet they were so watchful, and their senses so acute, that I never was able to crawl within a fair shooting distance; whenever I attempted it, they would all scatter at once and glide silently away through the tall grass. The air above this spot was always full of turkey-buzzards or black vultures; whenever the wolves left a carcass they would descend upon it, and cover it so densely that a rifle bullet shot at random among the gormandizing crowd would generally strike down two or three of them. These birds would often sail by scores just above our camp, their broad black wings seeming half transparent as they expanded them against the bright sky. The wolves and the buzzards thickened about us every hour, and two or three eagles also came to the feast. I killed a bull within rifle-shot of the camp; that night the wolves made a fearful howling close at hand, and in the morning the carcass was completely hollowed out by these voracious feeders.

After remaining four days at this camp we prepared to leave it. We had for our own part about five hundred pounds of dried meat, and the

California men had prepared some three hundred more; this consisted of the fattest and choicest parts of eight or nine cows, a small quantity only being taken from each, and the rest abandoned to the wolves. The pack animals were laden, the horses saddled, and the mules harnessed to the cart. Even Tête Rouge was ready at last, and slowly moving from the ground, we resumed our journey eastward. When we had advanced about a mile, Shaw missed a valuable hunting-knife, and turned back in search of it, thinking that he had left it at the camp. The day was dark and gloomy. The ashes of the fires were still smoking by the river-side; the grass around them was trampled down by men and horses, and strewn with all the litter of a camp. Our departure had been a gathering signal to the birds and beasts of prey. Scores of wolves were prowling about the smouldering fires, while multitudes were roaming over the neighboring prairie; they all fled as Shaw approached, some running over the sandbeds and some over the grassy plains. The vultures in great clouds were soaring overhead, and the dead bull near the camp was completely blackened by the flock that had alighted upon it; they flapped their broad wings, and stretched upwards their crested heads and long skinny necks, fearing to remain, yet reluctant to leave their disgusting feast. As he searched about the fires he saw the wolves seated on the hills waiting for his departure. Having looked in vain for his knife, he mounted again, and left the wolves and the vultures to banquet undisturbed.

Chapter 17

RENDEZVOUS
and FAREWELL

From *The Big Sky,* by A. B. Guthrie, Jr.

The Green River Rendezvous of 1837 is the setting chosen by
novelist A. B. Guthrie, Jr., for this pivotal section of *The Big Sky.*
Guthrie paints a vivid portrait of rendezvous time in the trapping community. He also dramatizes with deep compassion
the mountain man Dick Summers's decision to leave the
mountains and return to his old Missouri farm. We are left with
a powerful sense of Summers's loss. His companions, young
mountain man aspirants Boone Caudill and Jim Deakins, and
their outcast Blackfoot Indian "sidekick," Poordevil, will go on
to new adventures as the novel goes forward. But for Summers,
this rendezvous is the end of the trail.

As the story opens, Summers, Caudill, Deakins, and Poordevil are crossing the Teton Pass, with the Green and the rendezvous beckoning ahead. Their thoughts are on selling their

furs and the whisky, women, and new goods they expect to enjoy. A confrontation with a mountain man named Streak lurks in their thoughts, however. In a previous meeting on the trail, Streak has expressed his intense hatred of all Blackfeet, a hatred spawned by seeing many of his companions killed while he himself was almost scalped. A big scar and white plume of hair cover the spot where the Indian's knife had done its vicious work. Streak has indicated a strong desire to "rub that bastard out," meaning Poordevil—a threat to which Boone quickly answered, "You'll get kilt yourself . . . It wasn't Poordevil done it." The ugly trailside encounter seems likely to be settled at the rendezvous days ahead.

●　　●　　●

DICK SUMMERS pulled the hood over his head and brought his capote closer about him. There was no place in God's world where the wind blew as it did on the pass going over to Jackson's Hole. It came keen off the great high snow fields, wave on wave of it, tearing at a man, knocking him around, driving at his mouth and nose so that he couldn't breathe in or out and had to turn his head and gasp to ease the ache in his lungs. A bitter, stubborn wind that stung the face and watered the eye and bent the horses' heads and whipped their tails straight out behind them. A fierce, sad wind, crying in a crazy tumble of mountains that the Indians told many a tale about, tales of queer doings and spirit people and medicines strong and strange. The feel of it got into a man sometimes as he pushed deep into these dark hills, making him wonder, putting him on guard against things he couldn't lay his tongue to, making him anxious, in a way, for all that he didn't believe the Indians' stories. It flung itself on the traveler where the going was risky. It hit him in the face when he rounded a shoulder. It pushed against him like a wall on the reaches. Sometimes on a rise it seemed to come from everywhere at once, slamming at back and front and sides, so there wasn't a way a man could turn his head to shelter his face. But a body kept climbing, driving higher and farther into the wild heights of rock, until finally on the other side he would see the Grand Teton, rising slim and straight like a lodgepole pine, standing purple against the blue sky, standing higher than he could believe; and he would feel better for seeing it, knowing Jackson's Hole was there and Jackson's Lake and the dams he had trapped and the headwaters of the Seeds-kee-dee not so far away.

Summers bent his head into the wind, letting his horse make its own pace. Behind him plodded his pack horse, led by the lariat in his hand, and behind the pack horse came Boone and Jim and Poordevil and their animals.

It was known country to Summers, the Wind Range was, and the everlasting snow fields and the Grand Teton that could come into sight soon, known country and old country to him now. He could remember when it was new, and a man setting foot on it could believe he was the first one, and a man seeing it could give names to it. That was back in the days of General Ashley and Provot and Jed Smith, the cool half-parson whom the Comanches had killed down on the Cimarron. It was as if everything was just made then, laid out fresh and good and waiting for a man to come along and find it.

It was all in the way a man thought, though, the way a young man thought. When the blood was strong and the heat high a body felt the earth was newborn like himself; but when he got some years on him he knew different; down deep in his bones he understood that everything was old, old as time, maybe—so old he wondered what folks had been on it before the Indians themselves, following up the waters and pitching their lodges on spots that he had thought were his alone and not shared by people who had gone before. It made a man feel old himself to know that younger ones coming along would believe the world was new, just as he had done, just as Boone and Jim were doing, though not so strong any more.

There rose the Grand Teton at last, so thin, seen from here, it didn't seem real. Summers pulled up to let the horses blow and felt the wind driving through to his skin and clear to his secret guts, with the keen touch of the snow fields in it. Boone yelled something to him, and Summers shook his head, and Boone cupped his hands around his mouth and yelled again, but sound wouldn't come against the wind; it blew backward down the pass, and Summers found himself wondering how far it would blow until it died out and was just one with the rush of air. He shook his head again, and Boone grinned and made a signal with his hand to show it didn't matter, and afterward tucked his chin around to the side to catch his breath. High to his left Summers could see a mountain sheep standing braced and looking, its head held high under the great load of horn. The trees grew twisted from cracks in the rock, grew leaning away from the wind, bowed and old-looking from the weight of it.

He let his gaze go to the back trail, to Boone and Jim and the horses standing hunched and sorry, their hair making patterns under the push of the wind. They were good boys, both, though different, brave and willing and wise to mountain ways. They were hivernans—winterers—who could smell an Indian as far as anybody and keep calm and shoot plumb center when the time came. Summers wondered, feeling a little foolish inside, that he still wanted to protect them, like an uncle or a pappy or somebody. It was Boone he felt most like protecting, because Boone thought simple and acted straight and quick. He didn't know how to get around a thing, how to talk his way out or to laugh trouble off, the way Jim did. Not that Jim was scared; he just had a slick way with him. Come finally to a fight, he didn't shy off. Boone, now, was dead certain to get himself into a battle at rendezvous with the man called Streak, and not in a play battle, either. It would be one or t'other, Summers was sure, and shook his head to get shut of the small black cloud at the back of it.

When they were going again his thoughts went back. As a man got older he felt different about things in other ways. He liked rendezvous still and to see the hills and travel the streams and all, but half the pleasure was in the remembering mind. A place didn't stand alone after a man had been there once. It stood along with the times he had had, with the thoughts he had thought, with the men he had played and fought and drunk with, so when he got there again he was always asking whatever became of so-an-so, asking if the others minded a certain time. It stood with the young him and the former feelings. A river wasn't the same once a man had camped by it. The tree he saw again wasn't the same tree if he had only so much as pissed against it. There was the first time and the place alone, and afterwards there was the place and the time and the man he used to be, all mixed up, one with the other.

Summers could go back in his mind and see the gentler country in Missouri State, and it was rich, too, if different—rich in remembered nests and squirrels and redbirds in the bush and fish caught and fowl shot, rich in soil turned and the corn rising higher than a boy's head, making a hidey-hole for him. He could go back there and live and be happy, he reckoned, as happy as a hoss could be with the fire going out of him and remembered things coming stronger and stronger into the mind.

Anyhow, he had seen the best of the mountains when the time was best. Beaver was poor doings now, and rendezvous was pinching out, and there was talk about farms over on the Columbia. Had a mountain man best close out, too? Had he best go back to his patch of land and get himself and mule and eat bread and hogmeat and, when he felt like it, just send his mind back to the mountains?

Would he say goodbye to it all, excepting his head? To rendezvous and hunting and set-tos with Indians and lonesome streams and high mountains and the great empty places that made a man feel like he was alone and cozy in the unspoiled beginnings of things? Could he fit himself back among people where he dassn't break wind without looking about first?

A man looking at things for the last time wanted to fix them in his head. He wanted to look separately at every tree and rock and run of water and to say goodbye to each and to tuck the pictures of them away so's they wouldn't ever be quite lost to him.

Jackson Lake and the wind down to a breath, the Three Tetons rising, the Hoary-Headed Fathers of the Snakes, and night and sleep and roundabout to rendezvous, trapping a little as they went, adding to their packs, going on over the divide from the Snake to the headwaters of the Seeds-kee-dee, and then seeing from a distance the slow smoke of campfires rising, the men and motion, the lodges pitched around, the color that the blankets made and the horse grazing, and hearing Boone and Jim yelling and shooting off their rifles while they galloped ahead, drumming at the bellies of their horses. They made a sight, with feathers flying on them and ribbons and the horses' manes and tails woven and stuck with eagle plumes. A greenhorn would take them for sure-enough Indians.

Rendezvous again, 1837 rendezvous but rendezvous of other times, too, rendezvous of 'thirty-two and 'twenty-six and before, rendezvous of all times, of men dead now, of squaws bedded with and left and forgotten, of whisky drunk and enjoyed and drained away, of plews that had become hats and the hats worn out.

Summers' horse began to lope, wanting to keep up with the others, but Summers held his rifle in front of him undischarged. A man got so he didn't care so much about putting on a show.

•   •   •

Boone felt Summers' gaze on him and, when he looked, saw it sink and fasten on the ground, as if Summers didn't want the thoughts he was thinking to be found in his eyes.

Summers said, "This nigger couldn't hit a bull's hind end with a lodgepole after five-six drinks."

"I ain't had too much," Boone answered after a silence. "I can walk a line or spit through a knothole." He drank from the can of whisky by his side. "It ain't true, anyways. You was some, now, yesterday, firin' offhand. You come off best."

"Didn't have more'n a swallow."

Summers and Jim were rumped down on either side of Boone. Poordevil lay on the ground in front of them, snoring, the whites of his eyes glimmering through the parted lids and the spit running from one corner of his mouth and making a dark spot in the dirt.

"Reckon Poordevil thought he could drink the bar'l dry," Summers said.

"I ain't fixin' to drink no bar'l dry."

It was getting along in the afternoon, and over a ways from them a game of hand was starting up, now that the horse racing was about over for the day, and the shooting at a mark. The players sat in a line on either side of the fire. While Boone watched they began to sing out and to beat with sticks on the dry poles they had put in front of them. Every man had his stake close to him. It was skins they were betting, mostly, and credit with the company, and some trade goods and Indian makings and powder and ball, and sometimes maybe a rifle. They weren't worked up to the game yet. Come night, and they would be yelling and sweating and betting high, they and others sided across from other fires. A man could make out Streak easy, with his head bare and the sun catching at the white tuft of hair.

Up and down river Boone could catch sight of Indian lodges, moved in closer than usual to the white camp, maybe because the rendezvous was smaller. Nearer, horses were grazing, and still nearer the mountain men moved, talking and laughing and drinking and crowding up with some Indians at the log counter that Fitzpatrick had set the company goods behind, under cover of skins. The tents of the company men clustered around the store. In back of them, pack saddles and ropes and such were piled. The lodges of the free trappers, from where Boone looked on, were west of the others, away from the river. Behind the counter two clerks kept busy with their account books. In front of it a couple of white hunters showed they had a bellyful. They were dancing, Indian style, and by and by began to sing, patting their bellies with their open hands to make their voices shake, and ending with a big whoop.

Hi–hi–hi–hi,
Hi-i–hi-i–hi-i–hi-i,
Hi-ya–hi-ya–hi-ya–hi-ya,
Hi-ya–hi-ya–hi-ya–hi-ya,
Hi-ya–hi-ya–hi–hi.

The white men were Americans and French from Canada, mostly, but some were Spanish and some Dutch and Scotch and Irish and British. Everybody had arrived by now—the free trappers and the company men and Indians from all over, coming by the Sweetwater and the Wind and over from the Snake and from Cache Valley to the south near the Great Lake, from Brown's Hole and New and Old Parks and the Bayou Salade, coming to wait for Tom Fitzpatrick and trade goods from the States. Just yesterday Fitzpatrick had pulled in, with only forty-five men and twenty carts drawn by mules, but bringing alcohol and tobacco and sugar and coffee and blankets and shirts and such, all the same. At the side of the counter two half-breeds were working a wedge press, already packing the furs for the trip back to St. Louis, making steady knocking noises as they drove the wedges in.

It wasn't any great shakes of a rendezvous—not like they used to have, with companies trying to outdo each other and maybe giving three pints for a good plew. Now there were just the American Fur Company and Bridger and the rest of his old outfit working for it, and whisky cost four dollars and beaver went for four to five a pound, for all there wasn't much of it.

The Crows hadn't brought in more than a mite. They and the other tribes were restless and cranky; they talked about the white man hunting their grounds and about the Blackfeet warring on them and the traders putting low prices on fur and high ones on vermilion and blankets and strouding. They were crying—that's what they said—because the white brother took much and left little. The mountain men grumbled, too, trading pelts for half what they used to bring and hearing talk that maybe this was the last rendezvous.

It wasn't any great shakes of a rendezvous, but still it was all right; a man couldn't growl, not with whisky to be had and beaver still to be caught if he went careful, and the sky over him and the country clear to him any way he might want to travel.

Over his can of whisky Boone saw a little bunch of Crow girls coming on parade, dressed in bighorn skin white as milk and fancy with porcupine quills. Some of them would catch themselves a white man, and their pappies would get gifts of blankets or whiskey or maybe a light fusee and powder and ball, and they would be glad to have a white brother in the family, and the white man would ride away from rendezvous with his squaw and keep her while she pleased him and then he would up and leave her, and she would be plumb crazy for a while, taking on like kin had died, but after a while, like as not, she would find another mountaineer, or anyway an Indian, and so get all right again. Sometimes squaws got sure-enough dangerous when their men left them, especially if they left one to take up with another.

Boone saw that Jim's sharp eye had picked up the girls. "Them Crows are slick sometimes. They are, now," Jim said. He added, "And mighty obligin'."

"You ought to know," Summers said and smiled, looking at Jim as if he could see through him, looking at him with a little cloud in his eyes as if he wished he could go back to Jim's age. "Reckon maybe you should take one away with you, and not buzz yourself around like a bee in clover. They ain't after one-night rumpuses so much. Steady is what tickles 'em."

"Jim hankers for the whole damn tribe."

"You ain't so bad yourself, Boone, or didn't used to be. Can't figure you out. Bet you ain't had two women this spree. A body'd think you was still feared of catchin' a cold in your pants."

Some of the Crow girls were smart-looking, all right, and some of the Bannocks and Snakes and Flatheads, too, as far as that went. A man didn't get to see so many Blackfoot girls, but there was one of them, if she kept coming along and grew up to her eyes, would make these other squaws look measly.

Boone said, "Must be there's a right smart more goat in you. I had enough colds so's not to be afraid."

The three of them sat for a while without speaking, watching Russell come lazing over from the store, smoking a pipe.

"How, Russell."

"Hello," said Russell, and stopped and drew on his pipe while his eyes went over Poordevil. Poordevil didn't have anything on but a crotch cloth that came up under his belt and folded over and ended in red tassels. The sun lay on his brown body, catching flecks of old skin and making them shine. Russell put out his toe and poked Poordevil with it to see if he could rouse him. To Boone Russell said, "He isn't worth fighting about, he or any of the rest."

"I reckon I'll make up my own mind."

"As you please."

Russell was a proper man, and educated, but a good hunter, so they said, and cool in a fix. "Too bad you arrived late," he said to Summers. "We had some excitement."

"I been hearin'."

"Such impudence! Those Bannock rascals coming in to trade but still refusing to give up the horses they had stolen!"

"Injuns think different from whites."

"You mean they don't think."

"Stealin's their way of fun," Summers explained.

"They'll have to learn better, even if the learning comes hard. We gave the Bannocks a lesson. Killed thirteen of them right here and chased after the rest and destroyed their village and shot some more during the three days we fought them. In the end they promised to be good Indians. Bloody business, but necessary."

"Maybe so."

"The only way to settle disputes with hostile Indians is with a rifle. It writes a treaty they won't forget."

"Maybe," Summers answered again.

"They'll sing small in a few years. A wave of settlers will wash over them. The country won't be held back by a handful of savages."

Boone said, "What 'ud settlers do out here?"

Russell gave him a look but didn't answer.

"Where you aim to fall-hunt?" Summers asked.

"Upper Yellowstone again, I guess. Fontanelle and Bridger are taking a hundred and ten men to Blackfoot country."

Boone asked, "Far as the Three Forks, or north of there?"

"I wouldn't think so. They're enough Blackfeet on the Gallatin and Madison and Jefferson without going further."

Russell strolled off, still sucking on his pipe.

Boone drank again and then let himself back on his elbows, looking west, yonder to where the sun was about to roll behind the mountains. A current of air whispered by his ear, making a little singing sound. When it died down, the other noises came to him again—the hand players calling out and beating with their sticks, the Indian dogs growling over bones, the horses sneezing while they cropped the grass, and sometimes the Indian children yelling. The sun shed a kind of gentle shine, so that everything seemed soft and warm-colored–the river flowing, the butte hazy in the distance, the squaws with their bright blankets, the red and black and spotted horses stepping with their noses to the grass, the hills sharp against the sky and the sky blue, the lodges painted and pointed neat and the fire smoke rising slow, and high overhead a big hawk gliding.

It was funny, the way Jim and Summers had their eye out for him, not wanting him to frolic until he and Streak had had it out. Boone knew how much he could hold and still move quick and straight. He knew how much he could hold and it was a considerable–as much, maybe, as any man at rendezvous. He wasn't going to cut down on his fun–not much, anyway–just so's to be on guard. Besides, Streak hadn't acted up, not to him, or picked on Poordevil, though he had made his brags around, saying he didn't walk small for any man and would get himself a Blackfoot yet, saying he could whip the likes of Caudill day or night, rain or shine, hot or cold or however. Summers allowed that Streak had held in because there wasn't any whisky in camp until yesterday.

Boone rested back on his elbows, feeling large and good, feeling the whisky warming his belly and spreading out, so that his arms and legs and neck all felt strong and pleasured, as if each had a happy little life of its own. This was the way to live, free and easy, with time all a man's own and none to say no to him. A body got so's he felt everything was kin to him, the earth and sky and buffalo and beaver and the yellow moon at night. It was better than being walled in by a house, better than breathing in spoiled air and feeling caged like a varmint, better than running after the law or having the law running after you and looking to rules all the time until you wondered could you even take down your pants without some-body's say-so. Here a man lived natural. Some day, maybe, it would all end, as Summers said it would, but not any ways soon–not so soon a body had to look ahead and figure what to do with the beaver gone and churches and courthouses and such standing where he used to stand all alone. The country was too wild and cold for settlers. Things went up and down and up again. Everything did. Beaver would come back, and fat prices, and the good times that the old men said were going forever.

Poordevil groaned and opened one red eye and closed it quick, as if he wasn't up, yet, to facing things.

"How, Blackfoot."

Poordevil licked his lips. "Sick. God sick damn." He put his hand out, toward the can at Boone's side, and his eyes begged for a drink.

"First time I ever heerd goddam split," Jim said. "Seems on-religious."

"Not yet, you don't," Boone said to Poordevil. "Medicine first. Good medicine." He heaved himself up and went toward the fire and picked up the can he had set by it. It had water in it and a good splash of gall from the cow Summers had shot that morning. "Bitters. That's medicine now." He lifted the can and let his nose sample the rank smell of it. Before he handed it to the Indian he took a drink himself. "Here, Injun. Swaller away."

Poordevil sniffed of the bitters, like a dog at a heap of fresh dung, and brought up his upper lip in a curl that showed the gap between his teeth. He tilted the can and drank fast, his throat bobbing as he gulped. He threw the can from him and belched, and held out his hand for the whiskey. He had a dull, silly, friendly look on his face like a man might expect to find on a no-account dog's if it so happened a dog could smile. Between the red lids his eyes looked misty, as if they didn't bring things to him clear.

Of a sudden Boone felt like doing something. That was the way it was with whisky. It lay in the stomach comfortable and peaceful for a time, and then it made a body get up and do. All around, the fires were beginning to show red, now that dark was starting to close in. Boone could see men moving around them, or sitting, and sometimes a camp kicker jerking a buffalo ham high from the fire to get off the ashes. There were talk and shouts and laughter and the chant and rattle of the hand players. It was a time when men let go of themselves, feeling full and big in the chest. It was a time to talk high, to make jokes and laugh and drink and fight, a time to see who had the fastest horse and the truest eye and the plumb-center rifle, a time to see who was the best man.

"I aim to move around," Boone said, and picked up his empty can.

"Last night you wasn't up to so much, Boone." It was Jim talking. "Me and Dick, we kep' our nose out of the strong water, just in case."

"Goddam it! You going to be dry all rendezvous? I ain't skeered."

Jim didn't answer, but Summers looked up with his little smile and said, "Not the whole livin' time, Boone. Just long enough, is all."

"Best get it over with right now, then."

Summers lifted himself and felt of the knife in his belt and took his rifle in his hand. "This nigger wouldn't say so, son. It's poor doin's, makin' up to trouble. Put out; we'll foller."

"Git up, Poordevil." Boone toed the Indian's ribs. "Whiskey. Heap whiskey."

Poordevil hoisted his tail in the air, like a cow getting up, and came to his feet staggering a little. "Love whisky, me. Love white brother."

"White brother love Poordevil," Jim said with his eyes on Boone. "Love Poordevil heap. He's bound to, ain't he, Dick, with whisky four dollars a pint? Nigh a plew a pint."

Poordevil put on a ragged cotton shirt that Boone had given him earlier.

"What's beaver for?" Boone asked, leading off toward the counter. "Just to spend, ain't it? For drinks and rifles and fixin's? You thinkin' to line your grave with it?"

All Jim answered was, "That Injun can drink a sight of whisky."

From the store they went to a fire that a dozen free trappers were sitting around, telling stories and drinking and cutting slices of meat from sides of ribs banked around the flames.

"Make way for an honest-to-God man," Summers ordered.

Boone put in, "Make way for three of 'em."

From the far side of the fire a voice said, "Summers' talk is just foolin', but that Caudill, now, he sounds like he sure enough believes it."

Boone squinted across and saw that the speaker was Foley, a long, strong, bony man with a lip that stuck out as if for a fight.

A little silence came on everybody. Boone stood motionless. "I ain't one to take low and go down, Foley. Make what you want out'n it."

There was the little silence again, and then Foley saying, "Plank your ass down, Caudill. You git r'iled too easy."

Summers lowered himself and put his can of whisky between his knees. "How," the others said now. "Move in and set."

Foley started the talk again. "Allen was sayin' as how he had a tool once would shoot around a corner."

"I did that. Right or left or up or down it would, and sharp or gentle, just accordin'. Hang me, I would have it yet, only one time I got 'er set wrong, and the ball made a plumb circle and came back to the bar'l like a chicken to roost. Knocked things all to hell."

"This child shot a kind of corner onc't," said Summers, "and I swear it saved my hair."

"So?"

Summers fired his pipe. "It was ten years ago, or nigh to it, and the Pawnees was bad. They ketched me out alone, on the Platte, and there was a passel of 'em whoopin' and comin' at me. First arrow made wolf's meat of my horse, and there this nigger was, facin' up to a party as could take a fort."

Allen said, "I heerd you was kilt away back then, Dick. Sometimes be damned if you ain't like a dead one."

"Ain't near so dead as some, I'm thinkin'. It was lucky I had Patsy Plumb here with me." Summers patted the butt of his old rifle. "This here piece now, it don't know itself how far it can shoot. It scares me, sometimes, dogged if it don't, thinkin' how the ball goes on and on and maybe hits a friend in Californy, or maybe the governor of Indiana State. It took me a spell to get on to it, but after while I l'arn't I could kill a goat far as I could see him, only if he was humpin' I might have to face half-around to lead him enough. Yes, ma'am, I've fired at critters an' had time to load up ag'in afore ball and critter come together."

"Keeps you wore out, I'm thinkin', travelin' for your meat."

"That's a smart guess now. Well, here this child was, and the Pawnees comin', and just then I see a buffler about to make over a hill. He was that far away he didn't look no bigger'n a bug. I made the peace sign, quick and positive, and then I p'inted away yonder at the buffler, and the Injuns stopped and looked while I up with Patsy. I knowed'er inside out then, and I waited until the critter's tail switch out of sight over the hill, and then, allowin' for a breeze and a mite of dust in the air, I pulled trigger."

Summers had them all listening. It was as if his voice was a spell, as if his lined face with its topping of gray hair held their eyes and stilled their tongues. He puffed on his pipe, letting them wait, and took the pipe from his mouth and drank just a sip from his can of whisky.

"The Pawnees begun to holler again and prance around, but I helt 'em back with the peace sign and led 'em on, plumb over the hill. Took most of the day to git there. But just like this nigger knowed, there was Mr. Buffler, lyin' where the ball had dropped down on him. I tell you niggers, the Pawnees got a heap respectful. One after the other, they asked could they have meat and horns and hair, figgerin' it was big medicine for 'em, till there wasn't anything left of that bull except a spot on the ground, and dogged if some of the Pawnees didn't eat that!" Summers let a little silence come in before he spoke again. "I ain't never tried any long shots since."

"No?"

"I figger I ain't up to it. I swear I aimed to get that old bull through the heart, and there he was, plain gut-shot. Made me feel ashamed."

They laughed, and some clapped others on the back, and they dipped their noses into whisky, and their voices rang in the night while the dark gathered close around, making the fire like a little sun. In the light of it the men looked flat, as if they had only one side to them. The faces were like Indian faces, dark and weathered and red-lit now, and clean-shaved so as to look free of hair. Boone drank from his can and pushed closer to the fire, feeling the warmth of it wave out at him. Poordevil squatted behind him, seeming comfortable enough in his crotch cloth and cotton shirt. Around them were the keen night and the campfires blazing and the cries of men, good-sounding and cozy, but lost, too in the great dark like a wolf howl rising and dying out to nothing.

"I reckon you two ain't the only ones ever shot a corner," Jim said.

"Sharp or curve?"

"Sharp as could be. A plumb turnabout."

"It's Company firewater makes a man think things," Allen said. "He gets so he don't know going' from comin'."

"In Bayou Salade it was, and we was forted up for the winter." Jim was getting to be a smart liar—as good as Summers, almost. "I took a look out one morning, and there not an arrer shot away was the biggest by-God painter a man ever see. 'Painter meat!' I says and grabbed up my rifle and leveled. The painter had got itself all stretched out and lyin' so's only his head made a target. I aimed for the mouth, I did, and let 'er go, only I didn't take into account how quick that painter was."

Jim looked around the circle of faces. "He was almighty quick. The ball went in his mouth fair, and then that critter swapped ends, faster'n scat. I ain't hankered to look a painter in the tail since." Jim fingered his cheek gently. "That bullet grazed my face, comin' back."

The laughing and the lying went on, but of a sudden Boone found himself tired of it, tired of sitting and chewing and doing nothing. He felt a squirming inside himself, felt the whisky pushing him on. It was as if he had to shoot or run or fight, or else boil over like a pot. He saw Summers lift his can again and take the barest sip. Jim's whisky was untouched beside him. Goddam them, did they think they had to mammy him! Now was a good time, as good as any. The idea rose up in him, hard and sharp, like something a man had set his mind to before everything else. He downed his whisky and stood up. Summers looked around at him, his face asking a question.

"I'm movin' on."

Poordevil had straightened up behind him. Summers poked Jim and made a little motion with his head, and they both came to their feet.

Away from the fire Boone turned on them. "Christ Almighty! You nee'n to trail me. I aim to fix it so's you two dast take a few drams. Come on, Poordevil."

He turned on his heel and went on, knowing that Poordevil was at his back and Jim and Summers coming farther behind, talking so low he couldn't hear. He looked ahead, trying to make out Streak, and pretty soon he saw him, saw the white hair glinting in the firelight. The players chanted and beat on their poles, trying to mix up the other side, and the side in hand passed the cache back and forth, their hands moving this way and that and opening and closing until a man could only guess where the cache was.

The singing and the beating stopped after the guess was made, and winnings were pulled in and new bets laid while the plum-stone cache changed sides.

Boone spoke above the whooping and the swearing. "This here's a Blackfoot Injun, name of Poordevil, and he's a friend of mine."

Some of the players looked up, holding up the bet making. Streak dragged his winnings in.

An older man, with a mouth like a bullet hole and an eye that seemed to have grown up squinting along a barrel, said, "Set, Caudill. Who gives a damn? Me, I had a pet skunk onc't, and it wasn't hardly ever he'd piss on a friend of mine, and when he did the friend like as not didn't stink no worse, but only fresher."

Lanter said, "Let's get on with the game."

"What happened to your skunk friend?" Jim asked.

"It was goin' on the second winter that I had him, and I was holed up with two old hunters, like o' Lanter here, and one night old No-Pee just up and left without givin' no reason at all."

"Likely his pride finally got the best of him," Lanter said.

" 'Twer'nt that. I figgered it out all right. Livin' close up with two hard cases like you, Lanter, his pore nose got so it just couldn't stand it no more."

Boone waited until the voices had quieted down. "I ain't aimin' to let no one pester Poordevil. Anyone's got such an idee, sing out!"

In front of him a man said, "Jesus Christ! My beaver's nigh drunk up already."

Streak's eyes lifted. His face was dark and his mouth tight and straight. A man couldn't tell whether he was going to fight or not. Boone met his gaze and held it, and a silence closed around them with eyes in it and faces waiting.

Streak got up, making out to move lazily. "The damn Blackfoot don't look so purty," he said to the man at his side. His glance rose to Boone. "How'll you have it?"

"Any way."

Streak left his rifle resting against a bush and moved out and came around the players. Boone handed his gun to Jim. Summers had stepped back, his rifle in the crook of his arm. Over at the side Poordevil grunted something in Blackfoot that Boone didn't understand.

Streak was a big man, bigger than he looked at first, and he moved soft and quick like a prime animal, his face closed up and set as if nothing less than a killing would be enough for him.

Boone waited, feeling the blood rise in him hot and ready, feeling something fierce and glad swell in his chest.

Streak bent over and came in fast and swung and missed and caught his balance and swung again before Boone could close with him. His fist struck like a club head, high on Boone's cheek. Boone grabbed for him and the heavy fist struck again and again, and he kept driving into it, feeling the hurt of it like something good and satisfying, while his hands reached out and a dark light went to flashing in his head. He caught an arm and slipped and went down with Streak on top of him. A hand clamped on his throat and another clinched behind, and the two squeezed as if to pinch his head off. The fire circled around him, the fire and the players and Summers standing back with his rifle and Jim with his mouth open and his eyes squinched like he was hurting and Poordevil crouching as if about to dive in. They swung around him, mixed and cloudy, like something only half in the mind, while he threshed against the weight on him. He heard Streak's breath in his ear and his own wind squeaking in and out. He caught Streak's head in his hands and brought it down and ripped an ear with his teeth. Streak jerked the ear free, but in that instant Boone got a gulp of air, and the dizzy world steadied.

He had hold of Streak's wrists. He felt his own muscles swelling along his forearms as he called on his strength. It was as if his hands were something to order the power into. It came a little at a time, but steady and sure—a little and then a wait and then a little more, the hold on his throat barely slipping each time and then loosening more until he held Streak's straining hands away. He called on all his strength and forced Streak's left arm straight, and then he dropped his grip to the other and whipped his free arm across and clamped it above Streak's elbow, straining the forearm back while he bore on the joint.

The arm cracked, going out of place, and Streak cried out and wrenched himself away and lunged to his feet, his face black and twisted and his left arm hanging crooked. As he came in again, his good arm raised, Boone caught the dark flicker of a knife and heard Jim's quick cry of warning.

He hadn't time to get out his own blade. As he twisted away, the knife came down and cut through his shirt, and the bite of it along his arm was like the bite of fire. He snatched at the wrist and caught it. Above the whistle of their lungs Summers' voice came: "By God, he asked for it!"

His hands fought the wrist, the knuckles, the clutched fingers, and caught a thumb and bent it back. He jerked the hand around under his chest and saw it weakening, one finger and another letting up like something dying and the handle coming into sight. The knife slipped out and fell in the grass. Boone snatched it up, holding to Streak with his other hand. A word stuttered on the man's lips, and the campfire showed a sudden look of fear in his face, a look of such fear that a man felt dirtied seeing it. The eyes flicked wide, flicked and fluttered and came wide again and closed slow as Boone wrenched the knife free and drove it in again.

Boone pushed with his hand. Streak fell over backwards, making a soft thump as he hit, and lay on his back, twitching, with the knife upthrust from his chest.

Poordevil let out a whoop and began to caper around, and Jim joined in, dancing with his knees high and yelling, "Hi-ya!"

Summers' rifle still was in the crook of his arm. "I'm thinking the trouble's over," he said, and nobody answered until Lanter spoke up with "Let's git on with the game. The parade's done passed. Any of you niggers want to take Streak's place?" Boone heard him add under his breath, "That damn Caudill's strong as any bull."

Boone turned to Summers. "Maybe you're ready to wet your dry now?"

"'Pears like a time for it, after we doctor you."

"It ain't no more'n a scratch. To hell with it! Let's have some fun."

Summers looked at the long cut on Boone's arm. "Reckon it won't kill ye, at that."

The men went back to playing hand, leaving Streak's body lying. Closed out from the firelight by the rank of players, it was a dark lump on the ground, like a sleeper. A man had to look sharp to see the knife sticking from it.

Boone passed it again, near daylight, after he had drunk he didn't recollect how much whisky and had had himself a woman and won some beaver. There was the taste of alcohol in his mouth, and the gummy taste of Snake tobacco. He held his arm still at his side, now that the wound had started to stiffen. He felt fagged out and peaceful, with every hunger fed except that one hankering to point north. With day coming on the land, the world was like a pond clearing. From far off on a butte came the yipping of coyotes. Suddenly a squaw began to cry out, keening for a dead Bannock probably, her voice rising lonely and thin in the half-night. A man could just see the nearest lodges, standing dark and dead. There was dew on the grass, and a kind of dark mist around Streak's carcass, which lay just as it had before, except that some Indian had lifted the hair, thinking that that plume of white would make a fancy prize.

•   •   •

SUMMERS TOOK ONE LAST LOOK from the little rise on which he and Boone and Jim stood.

The camp had begun to stir now that morning was flooding over the sky. Squaws were laying fires and fixing meat to cook, and so were the white hunters and company *engagés* who didn't have a woman to do the squaw's work. He and Boone and Jim hadn't taken up with the squaws so much as the others, except for a time or two. As far as Summers knew, they hadn't fathered a child either, not anywhere, though like as not they had. Already one Indian was at the counter, probably asking for whisky.

Summers saw a squaw come poking out of a lodge after her two half-breed children, whom the French called brulés on account of their burned look. He wondered whether even the squaw knew who their pappy was. Farther off, horses were running bucking and kicking up and nipping at one another in the early chill. The sun touched the tops of the hills, but lower down the dark lay yet. Against the morning sky the mountains were still dead, waiting for day to get farther along before they came to life.

"Me," said Jim, "I'd wait and go east with the furs."

Summers didn't answer, but it went through his mind again that he didn't want to go back with anybody. He wanted to be by himself, to go along alone with the emptiness that was in him, to look and listen and see and smell, to say goodbye a thousand times and, saying it, maybe to find that the hurt was gone. He wanted to hear water and night and the wind in the trees, to take the mountains and the brown plains sharp and lasting into his mind, to kill a buffalo and cook the *boudins* by his own small fire, feeling the night press in around him, seeing the stars wink and the dipper steady, and everything saying goodbye, goodbye.

Goodbye, Dick Summers. Goodbye, you old nigger, you. We mind the time you came to us, young and green and full of sap. We watched you grow into a proper mountain man. We saw you learning, trapping and fighting and finding trails, and going around then proud-breasted like a young rooster, ready for a frolic or a fracas, your arm strong and your wind sound and the squaws proud to have you under a robe. But new times are a-coming now, and new people, a heap of them, and wheels rolling over the passes, carrying greenhorns and women and maybe children, too, and plows. The old days are gone and beaver's through. We'll see a sight of change, but not you, Dick Summers. The years have fixed you. Time to go now. Time to give up. Time to sit back and remember. Time for a chair and a bed. Time to wait to die. Goodbye, Dick. Goodbye, Old Man Summers.

"We didn't do so bad," Boone said, "what with beaver so trapped out and the price what it was."

Summers wondered whether he had done bad or good. He had saved his hair, where better men had lost theirs. He had seen things a body never would forget and done things that would stay in the mind as long as time. He had lived a man's life, and now it was at an end, and what had he to show for it? Two horses and a few fixin's and a letter of credit for three hundred and forty-three dollars. That was all, unless you counted the way he had felt about living and the fun he had had while time ran along unnoticed. It had been rich doings, except that he wondered at the last, seeing everything behind him and nothing ahead. It was strange about time; it slipped under a man like quiet water, soft and unheeded but taking a part of him with every drop—a little quickness of the muscles, a little sharpness of the eye, a little of his youngness, until by and by he found it had taken the best of him almost unbeknownst. He wanted to fight it then, to hold it back, to catch what had been borne away. It wasn't that he minded going under, it wasn't he was afraid to die and rot and forget and be forgotten; it was that things were lost to him more and more—the happy feeling, the strong doing, the fresh taste for things like drink and women and danger, the friends he had fought and funned with, the notion that each new day would be better than the last, good as the last one was. A man's later life was all a long losing, of friends and fun and hope, until at last time took the mite that was left of him and so closed the score.

"Wisht you'd change your mind," Boone said. "It'll be fat doin's up north, Dick."

Fat doings! Jim and Boone wouldn't understand until they got old. They wouldn't know that a man didn't give up the life but that it was the other way about. What if the doings were fat? What if beaver grew plenty again and the price high? He had seen times right here on the Seeds-kee-dee when beaver were so thick a hunter shot them from the bank, and so dear that a good pack fetched nigh a thousand dollars. Such doings wouldn't put spring in a man's legs or take the stiffness from his joints. They wouldn't make him a proper mountain man again.

The sun was coming up over Sweetwater way. The first red half of it lay lazy on the skyline, making the dew sparkle on the grass. To the west the mountains stood out clean, the last of the night gone from the slopes.

Summers looked east and west and north and south, hating to say goodbye.

"Fair weather for you," Jim said.

"Purty."

Boone's eyes came to his and drifted off.

These were Summers' friends, the best he had in the world, now that the bones of older ones lay scattered from Spanish territory north to British holdings. There was Dave Jackson, who started for California and never was heard from again, and old Hugh Glass, put under by the Rees on the Yellowstone, and Jed Smith, who prayed to God and trusted to his rifle but died young for all of that, and Henry Vanderburgh, a sure-enough man if green, who lost his hair to the Blackfeet, and Andrew Henry, the stout old-timer, who had died in his bed back in Washington County; there were these and more, and they were all gone now, dead or vanished from sight, and sometimes Summers felt that, along with some like old Etienne Provot, he belonged to another time.

And yet it had all been so short that looking back he would say it was only yesterday he had put out for the new land and the new life. A man felt cheated and done in, as if he had just got a taste of things before they were taken away. He no more than got some sense in his head, no more than hit upon the trick of enjoying himself slow and easy, savoring pleasures in his mind as well as his body, than his body began to fail him. The pleasures drew off, farther and farther, like a point on a fair shore, until he could only look back and remember and wish.

These were his best friends, he thought again, while for no good reason he took another look at the pack and saddle and cinches on his two horses. They were his best friends—this Boone Caudill, who acted first and thought afterwards, but acted stout and honest just the same; this Jim Deakins, who saw fun in things and made fun and had God and women on his mind.

"This nigger oughtn't to be takin' your Blackie horse," he said to Boone.

"Might be you'll need him, goin' alone."

"I ain't forgettin'."

"It ain't nothin'."

"Not many gives away their buffler horse."

"Ain't nothin'."

"Wisht I had him to give," Jim said.

Summers turned away from them. It was sure enough time for a mountain man to give up when his guts wrenched and water came to his eyes.

"Whar'll you camp tonight?"

What did it matter? It was all known country to him, the Seeds-kee-dee Agie and the Sandy and the Sweetwater. There was hardly a hill he didn't know, from whatever direction, or a stream he hadn't camped along. He could say goodbye to one as well as another. Leaving, a man didn't set himself a spot to make by night. There wasn't anything waiting for him at the end, except a patch of ground and a mule and a plow. He would take it slow, looking and hearing and remembering, while one by one the old places faded away from him and by and by he came on the settlements, where men let time run their lives—a time to get up, a time to eat, a time to work, a time to be abed so's to meet time again in the morning, a time to plow and sow and harvest. A man didn't live off the land there. He worked it like he would work a nigger, making it put out corn and pigs and garden trash. He didn't go out when he got hungry and kill himself a fat cow. He didn't see his living all around him, free for the shooting of it. He had to nurse things along, to wait and figure and save.

Things pressed him all around. He had to have money in his pocket, had to dicker for this and that and pay out every turn. Without money he

wasn't anything. Without it he couldn't live or hold his head up. Men in the settlements gave a heap of time just to trading money back and forth, each one hoping he had got the best of it and counting his coins and feeling good at having them, as if they were beaver or rifles.

"You bound to go north?" he asked, knowing they were.

"Boone is," Jim said.

"We'll get us aplenty of beaver on the Teton and Marias and along there," Boone explained.

"If the Blackfeet'll let you. If the Piegans ain't trapped it out for Fort McKenzie."

"We'll get it."

"Teal Eye would be how old now?"

Jim said, "Old enough to have a man, and young'uns, too. Eh, Dick?"

"We'll get us beaver," Boone said.

The campfires sent up a thin blue smoke, so many campfires that a man wouldn't want to count them. The smoke rose straight, growing thinner while it climbed, until you couldn't see it at all, but only the clear empty sky it had lost itself in.

"Reckon Poordevil will stick by you?"

"Sure."

"Boone's larn't a right smart of Blackfoot talk."

"I taken notice."

"It'll come in handy. You'll see."

He wouldn't hear these sounds again, Summers told himself, or see these sights, or smell the smoke smell of quaking asp. He could hear the sharp voices of the squaws and the throaty talk of their men and the cries of children. The tones of the hunters came to him, too, and the knock of axes. He looked at the lodges standing in the glistening grass, standing clean against the blue distance. He looked at the dogs and children trotting about the lodges, at the horses done with their playing now and moving purposefully out to good pasture, at the river flowing steady

between its fringe of trees, winding forever to the south to strange land he had never seen. It all was a regular town, of a kind, and it all made a smell and a sound and a picture. Could he get it again in his ear and eye and nose, once he was back in Missouri with time nudging him and his hand always feeling for money?

His eyes went to Jim and Boone. More than ever, the feeling of being father to them rose in him now that he had to leave. It was as if he was casting his young'uns loose to shift for themselves and feeling uneasy at what might happen to them.

"Well," he said, "time to put out. It is, now." He held out his hand. "This nigger can't make talk all day."

He got on his horse and reined it around, toward the rising sun, toward the east from which young Dick Summers had come a long, long time ago.

Glossary

MOUNTAIN MAN WORDS *and* EXPRESSIONS

bells—hawking bells, prized as trading goods, along with beads, blankets, powder and ball, and knives.

boudins—buffalo intestines, a favorite delicacy of mountain men.

Bourgeois—the leader, the boss, of a brigade or band of trappers. Man in charge of a fort.

brigade—a large band of trappers, organized out of necessity to work and travel in dangerous Indian country, especially deep in the lands of the dreaded Blackfeet.

bull-boat—a primitively built craft made of buffalo skins, barely manageable afloat, but able to ferry large loads of furs downriver.

cache—a place to hide or store goods until they were needed. Mountain men usually dug a deep hole and wrapped the supplies or furs for protection, carefully concealing the hiding place.

"The Company"—usually a scowling reference to the much-despised American Fur Company, formed by New Yorker John Jacob Astor. Ruthless in its attempts to break the backs of other companies, the

AFC fought off the Hudson Bay Company, the North West Company, and the Rocky Mountain Fur Company set up by Jim Bridger, Tom Fitzpatrick, Milton Sublette, Jean Gervais and Henry Fraeb.

"coon"—common mountain man self-reference. "This coon . . . " Along with "This child . . . " "This hoss . . . " "This nigger . . . "

Diggers—lowest order of the Ute Indian nation, living miserably in the desert regions of what today are Utah and Nevada.

Divide—the Continental Divide, the backbone of the Rocky Mountains.

doings—any form of happenings, or events. "Poor doings . . . " Or "fat doings . . . "

fat—the best, like "fat" meat, or "fat doings."

fleece—highly prized buffalo meat, the flesh between the spine and the ribs.

fort up—to build a mini-fortress out of whatever materials the forest provided, usually to make a winter encampment.

free trapper—a trapper on his own, not associated with a company or brigade. A very dangerous occupation.

gone under—killed, by Indians or wilderness hardships. [It is interesting today how the expression has been embraced to describe businesses failing.]

Green River knife—really just a generic butcher knife, long wide blade, capable of many tasks.

Hawken—the prize firearm of the mountain man's time. The creation of Jake and Samuel Hawken of St. Louis.

hobble—to tie up horses by linking their two front feet with a short piece of leather so the animals could not wander far from a campsite at night.

hump-rib, or **hump-meat**—prime meat of the buffalo, like tenderloin.

"Hump it!"—expletive: to hurry up, to carry the load, get it done.

Jackson's Hole—famed location below the three Tetons, at the Snake River.

jerky—smoked meat, dried and preserved. Much favored as quick food for the trail.

lodge—an Indian hut or encampment.

lodgepole—the lodgepole pine, very straight and common throughout the west. Useful in building shelters and travois.

medicine—substance made from beaver glands to make the trap irresistible to the animals. Also used as expression by Indians of spiritual powers.

painter—panther. Cougar or mountain lion.

parfleche—leather carrying pouch capable of holding many possessions. Often made by squaws.

pemmican—a higher, tastier form of smoked dried meat like jerky. With fat and gristle removed, pressed into a more cake-like form.

Pierre's Hole—now Teton Basin, near the three Tetons and the Snake River.

plews—prime beaver skins.

possibles—belongings. The bag carrying such items was often called a "possibles bag."

rendezvous—The place where trappers exchanged their skins for money to buy the goods they needed to continue another year in the mountains. There was plenty of whiskey, Indian women, and even games of contest. (See Chapter 17 for a look at A. B. Guthrie Jr.'s fictionalized portrait of the 1837 Green River Rendevous, from his novel *The Big Sky*.)

rubbed out—Killed. Usually by Indians.

Seeds-kee-dee—the Green River today.

shine—to stand out. To achieve.

sign–clues for tracking and locating game, or the presence of Indians. Tracks, broken branches, etc.

stick–attached by a line to a beaver trap, then anchored in the bank or mud to keep the trap from being pulled away. If pulled loose from the ground, the stick would float, showing the trapper the beaver's location.

Three Forks–where the Jefferson, Madison and Gallatin Rivers meet to form the Missouri.

topknot–Hair and skin of your head. "Watch your topknot!" means "Don't get scalped!"

to winter–to stay in an encampment of lodges, or a fort, for the winter, when the mountain passes were closed and serious travel difficult.

travois–Indian contraption built by laying a platform over two long parallel lodge poles. For carrying supplies or even useful for hauling the injured. The poles were pulled dragging over the ground. Wheels were never invented.

"Wagh"–The mountain man's favorite expletive, meaning, "Why . . . ." Not the question *Why?* but as in, "Why . . . it's all obvious. Wait until you hear this!"

Credits